Craig Lesley
WINTERKILL

"THERE ARE MORE THAN A FEW TOUCHES OF MAGIC."
—*The New York Times Book Review*

"A fine old-fashioned yarn, simple, straightforward and full of action. . . . The growth of trust and love between father and son keeps one engrossed in this highly readable first novel."
—*Publishers Weekly*

"Profoundly lyrical, Lesley's story of heritage and kinship that bind a destitute people to each other and to their land does for Native American culture what Toni Morrison did for Southern blacks in *Song of Solomon* . . . Lesley has a rare gift for evoking a timeless quality in a setting littered with modern icons. . . . The honky-tonk glitter of the rodeo gives way to the mystical, sometimes brutal beauty of the wilderness." —*The Plain Dealer* (Cleveland)

"What strikes me first about Craig Lesley's book is the astonishing compassion he extends to the characters who people this very moving novel." —Raymond Carver

"Danny Kachiah remains a figure of complexity, struggling toward salvation . . . an everyman who could stand in for any one of us."
—*Los Angeles Times*

Also by Craig Lesley

RIVER SONG

WINTER-KILL

CRAIG LESLEY

A Laurel Trade Paperback
Published by
Dell Publishing
a division of
Bantam Doubleday Dell Publishing Group, Inc.
666 Fifth Avenue
New York, New York 10103

ISBN: 0-440-50314-0

Reprinted by arrangement with Houghton Mifflin Company

Printed in the United States of America
Published simultaneously in Canada

One Previous Laurel Edition
New Laurel Trade Edition

June 1990

10 9 8 7 6 5 4 3 2

For Katheryn Ann Stavrakis

❖ 1 ❖

Danny Kachiah pulled his hat tight, kicked his left foot free of the stirrup, and hunched forward in the saddle. "Now," he said, and the gateman swung open the doors to both chutes. The roan gelding shot out of its chute after the spurting steer. Shifting his weight so he leaned far to the right, Danny could have touched the bolting steer's black rump. "Faster," he urged the horse, the seconds ticking off in his mind.

The gelding overtook the steer, and for a moment Danny was alongside the dark, shaggy head. His eyes matched the wild, flat-black eyes of the steer. Then he concentrated on the horns, yellowed with brown tips, and lunged. As he dove free of the horse, his hands seemed to float toward the steer's horns, but the brown tips bobbed away from his fingers. For a giddy instant, Danny thought he had missed.

His chest slammed against the steer's front shoulder, jolting him with pain. His left hand grasped one horn and his right clung to the thick hair along the muscled neck. Danny dug his bootheels into the ground and tried to twist the matted head, but the steer's bulging neck refused to yield. Off-balance, Danny was carried along by the steer's momentum and driving legs.

He needed leverage on both horns to dog the steer. As he made a desperate move with his right hand to grab the other horn, the steer thrust its head forward and shrugged its big shoulders. Danny's left hand slipped off the horn and his hat flew away. For a crazy instant, he was running with the steer, flailing its shoulders and back with his right hand. Then he tumbled forward onto the gouged dirt of the rodeo grounds.

Frothing from exertion, the steer shook his head and trotted to the far end of the arena, where a couple of pick-up riders shooed him through the exit gates.

NO TIME FOR DANNY KACHIAH, THE INDIAN RIDER FROM PENDLETON, OREGON, the announcer blared. Danny stood slowly and dusted off his pants. HOW ABOUT A HAND FOR HIM ANYWAY, FOLKS? As he bent to pick up his hat, Danny heard scattered applause. He waved toward the bright blobs of color in the grandstand. NEXT TIME USE BOTH HANDS, DANNY. One of the pick-up riders handed him the gelding's reins. NO MONEY FOR THAT COWBOY . . . DOGGONE.

As he led the horse through the working gates, a moon-faced cowboy sitting on the fence said, "Better go back to the reservation, Chief. You're getting too old to wrestle stock." He smiled but his blue eyes were hard. The cowboy wore a big tag with "12" on it in block print. Danny knew he was a hometown boy who had a good chance of winning the rodeo's All-Around Cowboy purse.

When he got to the area behind the chutes where the rodeo participants kept their pickups and trailers, Danny saw Henry Nine Pipes sitting on the tailgate of his pickup drinking a beer. Danny tied the gelding to the doorhandle of Henry's pickup on the passenger side. "Nice horse you got," Danny said. "He worked that steer just right."

Henry nodded. "I broke him in." He moved over on the tailgate so Danny could sit down.

"Guess my timing was off," Danny said. "Damn near missed the steer." He took a drink of Henry's beer and wiped his forehead. "He sure skittered, but maybe I'd have gotten him with Ring-Eye." Danny had left his horse on the reservation because his pickup had broken down and he had no way of getting him to The Dalles.

"Ring-Eye wouldn't have helped," Henry said. "The hazer didn't keep him close enough. Those hazers don't work as hard for us as for the white boys."

"Damn it, Henry. You could have hazed for me if I wasn't already using your horse." He didn't know if Henry was right or not. Maybe the steer could have been boxed tighter. "Anyway, I sure missed him." He took off his tag with the "42" on it and tossed it away. "So long, bad-luck number." A gust of wind carried it against a strand of barbed wire, where it caught and fluttered.

"Sure has been a long spell out of the money," Henry said.

"For me too," Danny said.

"Let's try a little wild-cow milking," Henry said. "You can mug and I'll rope."

Danny shook his head. "Hell, I can't even mug a steer much less a full-grown cow." He figured he had looked foolish enough for one day. "I'm beat."

Henry got off the tailgate. "I better go scout up someone else, then."

"Thanks for loaning me Cayenne."

"Sure," Henry said. "You thinking about riding in the Round-Up?"

"Not this year, I guess," Danny said. "Don't think I could make entry fees." He felt sorry about it because it had been three years since he'd ridden in a big rodeo. "I got to see about my pickup. And my uncle Billy Que sold some of our cows, so I better head back to get my share before he drinks all the money up."

Henry laughed. "You better run fast. Next year then, for the Round-Up?"

"You bet. Next year."

After Henry left, Danny took the Hamley's sack with his new boots, brown polish, and a change of clothes from behind the front seat of Henry's pickup. The driver's door was broken so it didn't close, and Henry had a piece of rope that he used to tie it shut when he was driving. No one had bothered the stuff in the sack.

He thought about sticking around The Dalles, but he hadn't placed in saddle bronc either and he didn't feel like rubbing shoulders with the winners at the Pastime or Recreation bars. And there was his share of the cattle money. He had been selling frybread the night before to make pocket money when he had seen Pudge Whitecloud, who'd told him about the cows. The way she told it, Billy Que was already cutting a wide swath.

Danny was sorry Pudge had seen him working the frybread stands with the old men and big women. Pudge was his ex-wife Loxie's sister, and he didn't want to give Loxie the satisfaction of knowing he was down on his luck. He knew Loxie couldn't wait to tell his son Jack about it. He had hoped to win in The Dalles and go back to the reservation cashy with rodeo money.

Danny started walking east on I-84, holding the Hamley's sack under his right arm and sticking out his left thumb as the cars sped by. He wished he had his truck and wondered how much Milo would skin him to get it back. Because Danny didn't expect any of the tourists to give him a ride, he figured he might have to hoof it as far as Biggs Junction to get a lift from a trucker. On the outskirts of The Dalles, he stopped under the big billboard that read:

PENDLETON WOOLEN PRODUCTS AT
HAMLEY'S
ONLY 125 MILES
WORLD FAMOUS WESTERN STORE

He put down the sack and waved at the passing cars, hoping someone might figure out where he was headed. When no one stopped, he sat down by the freeway's edge and studied The Dalles Dam.

The spillways were open and the waters from Celilo Lake rushed down the concrete channels into the old Columbia riverbed. Power lines carrying high voltage over the hills on both sides of the river hummed and crackled in the dry afternoon heat. After an hour's wait, Danny felt thirsty. He picked up his sack and stood, then scuffed some loose gravel with the sides of his boots. He started walking again, muttering to himself, "Damn long time between rides."

It was almost dark by the time Danny reached Celilo Village. Both the sky above the gorge and the flat water of Celilo Lake had taken on a slate-gray color. The old village with its salmon-drying shacks and Wy-Am longhouse was gone now that the dam's backwaters had covered Celilo Falls and ended the fishing. Tommy Thompson's home was gone too. The old chief had painted his east door a bright salmon color to catch the sun's first rays each morning.

Yellow corrugated plastic sealed the east end of the new cedar-shake longhouse, and the same plastic covered the peak of its roof, although it had been nailed on earlier and had become faded with passing time. Danny didn't know why the one end had remained unfinished for so long, but he understood the Celilo factions had bickered over the completion of the longhouse. Beside the longhouse, a utility pole had a lead wire strung to a bright blue-and-white Pepsi machine.

Danny was thirsty from walking. As he crossed the railroad

tracks that separated the village from I-84, he toyed with the change in his pocket, making certain he had enough for a cold drink. He passed several gutted houses with caved-in roofs. Two reservation dogs, lean as coyotes, sniffed at Danny. One growled, and when Danny lifted his hand as if to hit it, the dogs slunk away into the shadows of the gutted buildings.

Smoke rose from a cluster of small houses at the west end of the village. Danny figured the Celilos must be cooking, since it was too hot for heating. A couple of small boys shot baskets at a bent rim. A few trailers with blankets covering their windows were scattered behind the longhouse. Each trailer had a fringe of junked cars. One wheelless brown Pontiac boasted a bright green car-lot sign on its windshield: TODAY'S SPECIAL.

Danny checked the selections in the machine. Some of the pop-tops had been pulled and the contents drunk with a straw, but he found an undamaged Pepsi and worked the machine. Carrying his soda, he walked over to the two yellow trailers used for tribal offices. A hanging wooden sign read:

CELILO—WY-AM TRIBAL OFFICES
ADMINISTRATION
PLANNING
EDUCATION
MAINTENANCE
INDIAN HEALTH SERVICES

Danny tried the trailer doors but they were locked. The veneer on all the doors was broken at the bottom where someone had tried to kick his way in.

Danny followed the secondary road under the freeway to the little park the Army Corps of Engineers had put in after they had built the dam and flooded Celilo Falls. Across the river, a long green train, almost black in the dusk, snaked its way upriver at the base of the dry, brown Klickitats. Wishram's lights twinkled in the gathering darkness, their reflections mirrored in the dark, flat lake. Danny closed his eyes and imagined he could still hear the roaring of the falls.

He shivered with the night wind that came off the lake. Across the water, the Wishram lights seemed cold and distant. He turned and began walking back to the nearly deserted village. He was sorry that his son Jack would never get to see the falls.

That night, Danny carried his sack into the longhouse and slept in a corner, out of the wind. He put on his denim jacket and used the new boots for a pillow.

Sitting beside an irrigation pump salesman in an air-conditioned Ford, Danny wondered if Billy Que would already be drinking at one of the Pendleton bars.

"The competition is maddening," the salesman was saying. "Everybody's in the water business now. My outfit Wade Rain was the pioneer, of course, but too many others have crowded into the field since they built the dams. The average Joe can't make a living selling pumps anymore."

"Is that right?"

"What business you say you're in?"

"Livestock, you might say."

The salesman nodded. "Good line. People got to eat. Nothing beats a good steak. I like those bumper stickers the cattlemen put out: 'Beef, Damn it, Beef! Buy it! Eat it!' Say, I could use a cup of coffee. You look a little ragged too." He took the Biggs exit and they passed the Nu-Vu Motel overlooking the green bridge that spanned the Columbia River. "How do you take yours?" the salesman asked, pulling into the parking lot.

"Lots of cream and sugar," Danny said, because he hadn't eaten for a while.

Dinty's Café was topped by a blue neon eagle with a pulsing red eye. A hanging wooden sign offered banquet facilities, although Danny couldn't imagine who would hold a banquet there, since they did mostly a trucker trade.

After a few minutes, the salesman returned with two large Styrofoam cups. He handed one to Danny. "You could plow this."

"Thanks," Danny said.

The salesman drove fast, using one hand for the wheel and the other to hold his coffee. "You gave me a bit of a surprise this morning. I didn't think any Celilos would be up this early."

"I'm not Celilo. Just slept in their longhouse after the rodeo. I sort of missed my ride out of The Dalles last night."

"How was the rodeo?"

Danny shook his head. "I made some others look pretty good."

"I thought you seemed a little tall for a Celilo. Going to Pendleton? You must be Umatilla then. Indians are sort of a hobby with me."

Danny nodded. "Nez Perce, mostly," he said.

"Say, that Chief Joseph was a crafty fellow. Ran the U.S. cavalry all over hell and gone before he surrendered, didn't he? You see that movie? My kids loved it."

Danny shook his head. He had seen it, but he didn't feel like talking about it. They had a Mexican playing Joseph. He put his head back and pretended to sleep.

"Which exit do you want?"

Danny opened his eyes and saw they had reached Pendleton. "This one's fine," he said. "I got to see about my pickup."

The salesman pulled over to let Danny out. Beside the exit sign was a large blue billboard that said:

HOME OF TAYLOR WEBB—PRCA BULL RIDING CHAMPION

Danny was a little surprised at Taylor's success, because when they had been in high school together everyone thought Danny was the better athlete. Now he saw Taylor on TV advertising beer and four-wheel drives. Danny had heard Taylor would be back for the Round-Up, and he was looking forward to seeing him.

"Don't forget your bag," the salesman said.

"You kidding? I got new boots in there." Danny took his sack. "Hey, thanks for the lift."

"Don't mention it. Glad I could help you out a little. Wish I could hang around Pendleton, but I've got to make eastern Idaho tonight. Mormon country." The salesman made a face. "Well, hang in there." He gave Danny a half-wave and pulled back onto the interstate.

Milo's Pioneer Auto was a two-story, pumice-block building painted green with orange trim. Danny's battered turquoise-blue pickup sat in the vacant lot beside Milo's. Milo kept a couple of other pickups there to cannibalize for parts. Although Milo had made a number of improvements recently, including paving the old scraped-dirt parking area, he always complained about the lack of business since he was located on the old highway, some distance from the interstate exits.

No one was in the garage, and Danny figured Milo must be upstairs in the living quarters above the station. He stepped on the bellcord a couple of times so it sounded like a car was pulling up to the pumps. Then he strolled over to the Coke machine and waited.

Milo wasn't such a hot mechanic, but Danny was fascinated by his story. He had been just another drifter working the Pendleton Grain Growers wheat harvest when the dust exploded in a grain elevator. Milo survived and received a nice settlement, but according to him the blast had ruined his nerves, causing his health to decline rapidly. Lately, the trouble had settled in his teeth.

Milo hurried down the outside stairs, buttoning his pants. "I got a customer," he yelled to someone inside. "When he saw no one was at the pumps except Danny, he said, "Son of a bitch."

"Guy was in a hurry to make Boise," Danny said. "Went right back out to the interstate."

Milo sat on a short stack of tires. "Interstate will be our ruin. Whole town's drying up. And those Jap cars can run from Portland to Boise without a fuel stop."

"You fix the pickup?"

"Sure. Between trips to the dentist. There it sits—all fixed. But if you want to know, I've been suffering—"

"I been off my feed lately, too," Danny said. "What's the damage?" He didn't want Milo to get started about his teeth.

"Let me take a squint at the bill. It needed a new timing chain, just like I told you. After that, I tuned it. Cleaned the carb, too. Figured you'd want it running sweet."

Milo might have been testing him, but Danny couldn't tell because Milo had the strangest eyes. The eyeballs were pink and the irises light green, perhaps tinged by the green plastic visor he wore summer and winter. Milo said the explosion had weakened his eyes by bursting the tiny vessels. His thin hair was white, but he wasn't an albino. Milo swore he had thick, jet-black hair before the explosion.

"The bill's right here someplace." Milo dug around on the counter and found a slip of paper under an old copy of *Swank*. "Real Classy Chassis," he said, jerking his thumb at the girl on the cover. "Forty." He started to add. "Then there was the new tire—fifty-five—and the alignment. Front end was really bad. Would have ruined that new tire."

Danny stopped looking at the girl on the cover. "I bought those tires four months ago—right here."

"Good tires, too. Best I sell. But that one had a big gash. You know these reservation roads. Just eat up tires." He didn't offer to show Danny the tire with the gash. "Wouldn't want you to have blowout and wreck. I take responsibility for my customers."

Danny remembered that Milo's first wife had died when her car left the road and struck a telephone pole. The next issue of the local paper had featured a grainy, nighttime photo of the wreck. Milo made some improvements with the insurance.

"Comes to about four hundred and twenty-seven dollars, Danny."

"You'll need a gun to get that much money."

Milo flashed a smile, mostly gold fillings. "That's good. I like your sense of humor. You know, I never even charged you for the tow because you're a preferred customer."

"How's my credit—as a preferred customer?"

Milo shook his head. "Ordinarily, no problem. But right now, there's a cash-flow problem. Oral surgery is an expensive nightmare. They take the tops off my teeth and run needles into the root canals. It's agony. Be thankful you're blessed with sound teeth."

Danny took his checkbook out of his back pocket. "Let me see that pen." If he could find Billy Que right away and get his share of the cattle money, he might beat the check to the bank.

Milo quit smiling. He pointed to the sign above the tire rack. "The bank doesn't fix cars," he said.

"I wrote them here before."

"Took in a new partner. That's the station policy."

"Yeah," Danny said. "I heard you got married again." Milo's new wife had waitressed at the Husky truckstop just out of town. She had slept with so many truckers they called her Freeway, and some of the Indians claimed she had a white line down her back.

"It's tough breaking them in," Milo said, lowering his voice. "This one's crazy for me. I got a business to run, but I need to make her happy too. Teeth and women—can't live with them, can't live without them."

Danny picked up his sack. "I'll come back for the truck. Maybe tomorrow."

"Fine," Milo said. "Remember, cash makes no enemies." He started back up the steps to the living quarters. "Don't wait too long. This isn't a storage lot."

Danny took his new boots out of the Hamley's sack and tugged them on. He was sorry he hadn't won any money at the rodeo to buy a cowboy hat and fancy shirt to go with them. It was almost eleven, and hot. He was sweating freely by the time he had walked from Milo's to downtown Pendleton.

Wilson Windyboy stood outside Terry's Drugstore watching the young girls inside drinking Cokes at the fountain. He wasn't wearing a shirt and his brown belly hung over his belt. When Danny got closer, he could see Wilson didn't have any socks on either, but his ankles were so dirty they looked like socks. Wilson had been the janitor when Danny was in high school, and there had been lots of stories about Wilson taking girls to the janitor's closet.

Across the street from Terry's, on the sidewalk in front of the Stockman's Bank, several Indian loafers were passing around a bottle of wine. Danny waved to Sam CutHorse. Later, he planned to talk with Sam about getting a job rounding up some cattle. But now he wanted to find Billy Que and get his money. After he got his pickup back, he would shop around for a hat and shirt to go with the boots. That way, if he ran into any women, he'd look as though he'd done okay at the rodeo.

Danny tried the Buckhorn first. G. D. Whitney, the halfbreed with the walleye, clucked when he saw Danny come in with the Hamley's sack. "Nice suitcase."

Danny took a stool and put the sack on the bar. No one else was in the place. "Blitz," he said.

G.D. opened two bottles and pushed one across at Danny. He took a drink from the other one and winked with his good eye. "So how was The Dalles? You show those Columbia River cowboys how it's done?"

"I did all right," Danny said and took a drink so he wouldn't have to look at G.D.

"That's funny," G.D. scoffed. "Pudge was by and said you were selling frybread and curios with the old women. Figured you to be broke."

Damn that Pudge, Danny thought. She had a loose mouth. "Hell," he said, "I was just helping a guy out for one night. Henry's bringing my rodeo checks up later."

"Sure," G.D. said. "Around here, everyone's got money coming in. Rodeo money, lease money, wheat money . . . But nobody's got any to put on the counter. Say, you didn't pay for that beer yet."

Danny put some change on the counter. "I hear Billy Que sold some cows," he said, as if it didn't concern him. "You seen him?"

"Spending money like a whore with a credit card. He's busted now. Come by first of the week and tried to bum drinks off the people he bought for earlier. I tossed him out."

"How many cows did he sell?" Danny said. They had only seven.

"I heard two, maybe three. I guess that's all he could find."

Danny nodded. This time of the year, the unfenced stock might range as far as Wildhorse, kegging up in the cool of the high timber and sticking close to water. He finished his beer. "Well, I'm not in the cattle business today. You want to cash a check? Save me a trip to the bank."

"No credit, no checks. That's what the boss says. But if you're short, I'll buy that buckle off you for twenty dollars."

Danny pushed himself away from the bar and felt the silver buckle belt. Fourteen years ago, he had taken first in saddlebronc at the Klamath Falls All-Indian Stampede and Powwow. He could still remember the cheering crowd. Now he gave G.D. a hard look. "The bank's just across the street."

"Suit yourself," G.D. said. "You being a big winner and all, why not take a bottle to them boys in front of the bank? It's a hot day and they'd be obliged."

Danny knew G.D. was curious to see just how much money he had. But it might be a good idea to buy Sam a drink before he asked him about a job. He unsnapped the flap pocket on his cowboy shirt and took out seventeen dollars. He put six on the counter. "I'll take a bottle of Twister and one of rosé."

G.D. got the bottles from the cooler and wrapped them in paper sacks, twisting the ends. He scooped up the six dollars. "Just right, including tip." He seemed disappointed to see that Danny had some money.

The loafers in front of the bank stirred a little when Danny approached them carrying the bottles. "Who's that?" asked Perry Winishite, the old Cayuse.

"Man's best friend," Sam CutHorse told him.

Danny took the Twister out of the sack and handed it to Perry. "Try this, old-timer." Perry nodded his thanks.

"How'd the rodeo go?" Sam asked. "Say, I like them boots."

"Thanks." Danny handed him the rosé. "Not worth a damn. Sure is hot."

"So hot the sheep are lining up for crewcuts." Sam grinned and wiped the wine driblets from his mouth. "I used to ride at The Dalles," he said. "But those damn promoters rig it."

"I don't know," Danny said. "First, I had a bad horse that wouldn't buck. On the reride, I got a good horse, but the judges said I fouled."

"Sounds like The Dalles," Sam said.

"Then I borrowed Henry's horse and tried bulldogging. Damned near missed the steer."

"What do you plan to do now?"

"Punch cows, I guess. You need any help for the fall roundup?"

"Always room for a good rider," Sam said. "In about three weeks. The cattle are spread all over the reservation. It'll take a month to find all of them and check the brands."

"Thanks, Sam. I can use the money." The Twister bottle came round to him and he took a long drink of the peppermint-flavored apple wine. "Beats brushing your teeth," he said. "Anybody seen Billy Que?"

Sam said, "I heard he's up in the county drunk tank. Should be about sobered up by now. He was on a three-day toot with his cattle money. He had a snootful here and caught a ride to Milton-Freewater. The Pea Festival was on and he kept going after the Princesses, so they jugged him."

Danny spit in the dirt. "Half of that money was mine."

Sam shook his head. "If Que didn't blow it all, the cops probably stole it. Well, maybe you can sell some more cows, but you got to find them first, and that won't be until after the roundup now."

"Good thing I got Ring-Eye," Danny said.

Sam laughed. "That's a funny thing. Billy Que tried to sell him too, but no one would buy him since they knew Ring-Eye was your horse. Made him hopping mad. Tried to shoot the horse. But he was too drunk to hit it."

Danny said, "That horse is worth more than Billy Que."

Both bottles were empty so someone suggested taking up a collection. Sam claimed he was broke and no one else offered anything. Danny didn't mention the eleven dollars. He took out his caseknife and began to carve a whistle from a green willow. A couple of white wheat farmers who leased reservation land went into the bank. Danny nodded at one he knew, but he didn't nod back.

He spent the afternoon with the loafers on the sidewalk. It had been almost a day since he had eaten, and the wine and hot sun made his head buzz. Thirty-four, he thought. Too damned old for rodeos.

* * *

Danny dozed most of the afternoon. About sundown, he was awakened by wild honking. Startled, he sat up as a metallic-green Buick with a chrome grill and silver trim came weaving up the street, churning clouds of dust from the back tires. The car slowed as it neared the bank, then raced past the loafers to the end of the block, where it slid around in a wide U-turn. As the driver pointed the car at the men and accelerated, Danny leaped for the protection of the bank. At the last possible second, the car braked and skidded to a halt, its chrome bumper jutting halfway across the sidewalk. The driver, obscured by the dust, laid on the horn.

"Son of a bitch!" Danny yelled as he ran to the side of the Buick and threw open the door. He grabbed the driver's shoulder and twisted him around. Danny recognized Henry's smile.

"Damn," he said, letting go of the shoulder and stepping back.

Henry got out slowly and faced the loafers with a steady smile. He was wearing a cream-colored Western suit, a bright green satin shirt with silver stitching, and a silver belt buckle with a large turquoise thunderbird. His white hat had a silver conch band and a small green-and-red feather. "How does old Henry look?" he said.

"Like you stepped out of *Arizona Highways*," Sam said.

"A dude," Danny said. "A walking bankroll. You tip over a gas station?"

"No," Henry said, then paused a moment. "I won the wild-cow milking contest. Then I met a lonely lady with money. This here's her car. You should have stuck around."

Danny couldn't believe his luck.

"I just drove over to see my thirsty friends and buy them a drink. Let's go to the Buckhorn!"

"Henry's buying!" Danny said.

Henry led the loafers across the dusty street, but paused to bow and wave his hat at the young girls who had stepped out of Terry's Drugstore to see what the noise was about. "Big winner, ladies," he said. "Sorry you missed the action. But look old Henry up in a few years."

G.D.'s good eye bulged when he saw Henry's outfit. "Yes sir, Mr. Nine Pipes."

Henry took a hand-tooled leather wallet from the pocket of his cream-colored suitcoat and thumbed a thick wad of bills. Laying a fifty on the counter, he said, "President Grant wants to buy us Indians some drinks. Whatever these boys want. I'll take a whole bottle of your best Scotch."

G.D. took the fifty and held it up to the light. "Say, this is okay, isn't it?"

"Henry won the cow-milking contest," Danny said. "Now fix the drinks."

G.D. smiled and looked snappy fixing drinks for everyone. He even used the stainless steel cocktail shaker from behind the bar.

They all sat in a booth and Henry told them about meeting the woman after the rodeo. "This Helga, she's got an old Wasco County wheat farmer who works all the time and gets so tired he can't get it up nights. So she comes to Fort Dalles Days looking for action. Likes the rodeo guys for her pleasure. Last night, she called me her Buckskin Buckaroo."

"Let her buck!" Sam whooped, and lifted his glass.

Pretty soon, everyone was feeling good. Henry put another fifty on the table and smiled broadly, but his smile froze when Pudge walked in.

She was tipsy. A pink, rat-tailed comb jutted from the pocket of her taut pedal pushers. Her fat jiggled when she moved, and her feet had gotten so big that she didn't wear laces in her tennis shoes.

Pudge saw the fifty and came over to the table. "Buy me a drink, Cuz," she said, trying to sit in Henry's lap. "I haven't had one since the rodeo."

Henry patted her buttocks. "Two hogs fighting under a sheet," he said, and they all laughed except Pudge. "I never saw you at the rodeo, and you'd be hard to miss."

"I saw *you*," she said. She sat beside Henry and looked at him with bleary eyes. "You didn't look so fancy-assed yesterday, running behind a cow's rump with a milk bottle."

Henry kept smiling. "That's past history."

"Some rodeo," she said. "Danny can't dog a steer and you can't catch a cow. A bunch of gimps and clowns. I'm going to write Loxie all about it."

"Don't get sore, Pudge," Danny said. "Henry's buying with the money he got from the cow milking."

"What money?" Pudge asked.

"Damn! Pudge, it sure is good to see you again," Henry said, and put his arm around her. "Sorry I missed you at the rodeo. Take a look at this buckle I bought. Navajo turquoise, the man said. Cost over a hundred dollars. Hey, G.D., where the hell is her drink? Can't a lady get any service around here? Doubles for these boys while you're at it."

Everybody started laughing and talking again and G.D. brought the drinks. After a while, Sam and the other loafers went into the back room and started playing pool. Pudge said she wanted to dance and got up to put some money in the juke box.

"Let's go," Henry said to Danny, tugging at his sleeve.

"What?"

"Come on. Let's go find some action."

"What's wrong with this?"

Henry jerked his thumb toward Pudge, who was having trouble getting the quarters into the juke box. "Who needs it?"

Danny picked up the sack with his working boots and clothes in it. Henry handed G.D. a ten and took another bottle of Scotch.

"Got to get it down the road," Henry said.

"Congratulations again," G.D. said, sticking the ten in his pocket. "Don't be a stranger."

As they headed for the door, Danny said, "Don't you want to tell Sam goodbye?"

"I'll catch him later."

"You in some kind of a hurry?" Danny asked as they left.

They crossed the street in silence and climbed into the Buick. Henry faced the bank wall and took a long drink of the Scotch. "I got to take care of this car," he said finally. "You want to go?"

After taking a drink, Danny wiped his mouth and said, "Why not? Maybe Helga's got a friend."

"Now you're talking," Henry said, throwing the Buick into reverse and backing it away from the sidewalk. He jammed the accelerator and the car shot down the dusty street. "Lots of horsepower," he said, flashing a grin at Danny. At the west end of town, instead of pulling onto the interstate he took the old river road that paralleled the Umatilla.

"Hey," Danny said. "Aren't you taking the interstate?"

They passed the John Deere farm implement company with the large green-and-yellow sign that read NOTHING RUNS LIKE A DEERE.

Henry switched the lights to bright and shook his head. "It's like this," he said. "The car is sort of overdue. Along I-84, the cops might be looking for it."

Danny whistled softly. "You didn't steal it?"

"Hell no. Helga and I shacked in the motel, just like I said. Whooped it up all night. She was still asleep this morning when I went out to check on my horse at the rodeo grounds. I left her a note saying I borrowed the car."

Danny didn't believe him. It wasn't like Henry to leave a note. "She probably reported it stolen by now."

"Maybe," Henry said. "But I can straighten it out when I take the car back."

"Stop here," Danny said. "I got to take a leak." He wanted

to think things over for a minute. His head hurt from drinking and his tongue felt thick. He leaned against a black-and-yellow sign that said RANGE CATTLE and took a long piss in the barrow pit. Maybe he should just walk back to town. He didn't want to get mixed up with any stolen car business.

"Hey, Buddy, you okay?"

Danny hesitated a moment then got back in. "Fine," he said.

They drove in silence for a few more miles, passing Black Pot, where the old diesel engines had refueled. Eventually, Henry took a dirt road to the left and they crossed the Umatilla River, then bumped across the railroad tracks. Danny didn't know where they were anymore, but he knew they weren't going to The Dalles.

"You took a wrong turn," Danny said.

Henry pressed the accelerator and the Buick picked up speed.

"You stole it, right?"

Henry nodded.

Danny squeezed his eyes shut. "Why take me along?"

"Thought you'd be good company. I'm going to ditch it around Mud Springs. It's about fifteen miles back."

Danny didn't say anything.

"It'll be fine," Henry said. "You know how it is when cops come on the reservation. No one tells them anything."

"Where did you get the money?" Danny asked. He realized why Henry's smile had frozen when he saw Pudge.

"Not from milking cows," Henry said. "That's the best part. You remember that blond, hometown cowboy?"

"Moon-face?"

Henry nodded. "He won All-Around Cowboy and the wad of cash that goes with it. But that night he got to drinking hard in the Pastime. I just followed him into the john and sort of helped him lighten his load."

"That's crazy," Danny said.

"I'm just taking my share. You know that whole rodeo was rigged. The Indians got lousy stock, and you never fouled, but they said you did, so it kept you out of the money. Then the hazer let that steer skitter."

Danny thought maybe Henry was right. "Anybody know you in that bar?"

"We all look the same to them. I bought the clothes later."

"Anyway, you better lie low for a while."

"I'll head up to Spokane and spend this cash. No one will care by the time I get back." He turned the car onto an old gravel road heading south. "Almost there."

"I want to get my working boots on," Danny said. "It's a long walk back and I'm not wearing these new boots." He took his old boots out of the sack and put them on the seat. Wrestling with the new boot on his right foot, he tried to slip the heel. When it came off, he wiggled his toes. They poked through the end of his sock. He worked the left boot off. "This one's easier," he said. Then he tugged his working boots on. "That's better."

"Cows!"

Danny raised his head above the dash and saw the tightly bunched herd in the road. They were Black Angus and blended with the night shadows until the car lights caught their eyes.

Henry gripped the wheel, his knuckles white. He pumped the brakes but couldn't stop the Buick.

Danny dove to the floor as the car plowed into the herd. Metal crunched bone as the front end smashed a cow. The Buick lurched, then slid sideways and shuddered as it hit another cow. Danny's head banged the underside of the dash when the car left the road, turned over, and landed rightside-up in the barrow pit.

He tried to get out, but his door was jammed against the side of the pit. He crawled over Henry and struggled with

the door on the driver's side. It was sprung, but he shouldered it open and tumbled onto the ground.

Feeling as though he had been beat up, he rested on his
hands and knees for a few moments, gulping the night air to
clear the pain. He heard cows bawling on the road. Then he
smelled burning paint. Staggering to his feet, Danny saw
small flames licking the car's hood.

He grabbed Henry's shoulders and tried to pull him free of
the car, but his right leg was caught in the twisted steering
column. "Wake up!" Danny said, slapping Henry's face.

Choking on the acrid fumes of the burning paint, Danny
crawled back over Henry and tugged at the leg until it was
free. Under the cream-colored pants the leg had an odd
warp, and Danny figured it was broken. He dragged Henry
out of the car, pulling him over the rocks and cheatgrass of
the barrow pit until they were a safe distance from the burning wreck.

Henry's eyes opened. When he tried to speak, the words
came out funny because his lips were split and he was missing
his front teeth. "Feels like a bull stepped on my leg," he said,
"and my face."

"Busted, all right," Danny said. "You swallowed some
teeth, too. Hurt much?"

Henry poked at his gums, and spit some blood into the dirt.
"Tough for the women," he said. "I'm okay, if I don't move.
How about them cows?"

Danny listened to them bawling on the road. He crawled
out of the barrow pit on all fours and stood when he reached
the road's gravel surface. In the eerie light of the burning car
the cattle milled about, their eyes wide with fear and confusion. Like a large black sack, one lay dead on the side of the
road. Another was on its back, flailing its hooves and rolling
from side to side. Its ribs were caved in where the bumper
had crushed them, and frothy blood streamed from its
mouth. Danny couldn't make out the brand on its flanks.

Taking the caseknife from his pocket, he opened it and cautiously approached the wounded cow's head, so its hooves couldn't strike him. The cow seemed enormous. "Easy," he said. "Easy now." He grabbed the horns and twisted the dark head quickly to the side, kneeling on the shaggy neck. He didn't want to look at the cow's eye.

Danny plunged the caseknife into the jugular, making a quick slash through the hide and flesh. Blood sprayed from the matted throat and Danny sprang back. The cow kicked weakly a few times, then stopped. Steaming blood trickled from its neck, forming a black pool in the dusty road.

The other cow was easier. Both of them bled good, so he figured somebody might be able to use part of the meat.

Danny wiped the blade on his pants and put the knife back in his pocket. The cows were quiet, but still milling around. He picked up a rock and threw it against the side of the nearest cow. "Scram!" He threw another, and the cows started to run. "Get away!" His voice cracked into a sob. The cows retreated as he chased them waving his arms and yelling. Moving silently like black shadows, they ran until they reached a cheatgrass-covered hillside. Some stopped to watch him. He threw more rocks, but they were out of range.

Exhausted and choking, Danny returned to Henry and sat down. They stared at the burning car. The interior seemed to melt, and Danny thought he saw his new boots burning through the windshield. He waited for the gas tank to explode, but it didn't. Black blisters formed on the sidewalls as the tires started to burn. Spirals of dirty smoke smeared the night sky. One of the tires burst with a loud pop, sending shreds of burning rubber onto the dry ground.

When Danny first heard the sirens, they were still a long way off. The way Henry cocked his head, Danny knew he heard them too.

"Somebody probably saw the fire and called it in," Henry said.

"Maybe we can make it back together," Danny said. "You can lean on me and sort of hop along."

"Fifteen miles?" Henry tapped his broken leg and shook his head. "You go. No sense in both of us going to jail."

Danny knew the cops wouldn't believe he hadn't been in on the stolen car. "All right. I'll come see you in jail. It's not so bad there." He stood.

Henry reached into the pocket of his cream-colored suitcoat and took out his wallet. Handing it to Danny, he said, "I think this burned up in the car."

"No sense in letting the cops spend it," Danny said, putting the wallet in his pocket. "Thanks."

"Bring me some smokes and magazines when you come. And call my brother Nathan. Tell him to get my horse."

"You bet." Danny reached for Henry's hand and they shook lightly, the Indian way.

Danny ran north, toward the river. After half a mile, he stopped near the crest of a knoll to catch his breath. Crouching, he made sure no one could see him against the night skyline. In the distance, near the wreck, he could make out the shapes of the fire truck and a police car, their red lights pulsing in the darkness. The burning Buick illuminated the small figure of Henry huddled in the barrow pit.

Danny took the money out of the wallet and quickly counted it. A little over eleven hundred dollars. He could get his pickup back, buy some new boots and clothes, maybe even pay Billy Que's bail. Suddenly, Danny remembered the turquoise buckle and wished Henry had offered that, but it was too late now. He stuffed the money into his pocket and threw the empty wallet into the brush. Then he turned east and started running toward the reservation.

◈ 2 ◈

Danny awakened at six in the morning. A night breeze had come up and was rustling the plastic curtain of his trailer's bedroom window. Under the sheet and thin army blanket, Danny felt cold and his flesh goosebumped. He wiped his hands across his eyes and tried to clear his head. His legs were stiff and he had blisters on his feet from walking overland back to the reservation. He remembered Henry, dark and huddled in the barrow pit, and it reminded him of his father's death. He and Billy Que had found Red Shirt in February, frozen to death in the front seat of his pickup. He had been drinking and whoring all night in Pendleton and had an accident on a reservation backroad.

After the dressing, Danny had helped Billy Que dig the grave on Reservation Mountain. The ground was frozen, so they had to use an axe and pick to break through. Billy Que had painted Red Shirt's face in the old way and wrapped him in an elk robe. When they returned to the trailer, Billy Que cut Danny's hair short to show his grief.

Danny shivered a moment in the grayness, then got out of

bed and switched on the light. After closing the window, he went into the bathroom and turned on both faucets in the basin, splashing water onto his face. He turned the shower on hot and stepped in, letting the spray strike some of the soreness from his calves and thighs. He stood in the shower a long time, listening to the water and trying to clear his mind of his father's death.

One year, Red Shirt had taken Danny to the All-Indian Rodeo in Tygh Valley, Oregon. Red Shirt was over forty then, but still honking bulls and tough as whang leather. He won first place in bull riding, hanging and rattling on a Brahma called Sugarfoot.

Ass-Out Jones, the Klamath with the crippled hands, and Cecil Funmaker had helped Red Shirt drink up his winnings. After the money was gone, Red Shirt suggested they all go to the Celilo salmon feast because he had promised to take Danny. But Jones said he didn't care much for Fish Indians, so they all agreed to meet at elk camp. Meanwhile, Jones and Cecil planned to tour the powwow circuit, living off friends and commodities.

Danny saw them drive off in a big Checker. They were sitting very straight, pretending to be sober. Both wore tall cowboy hats and brown leather vests. Red Shirt told Danny that Jones had bought the Checker because it had enough room for him to wear his Stetson without crushing the crown.

When Red Shirt actually kept his promise instead of leaving with his friends, Danny figured going to Celilo must be important.

They arrived at midday. The salmon were moving upriver, as they did every spring, and the Celilos were catching them in hooped, long-handled dipnets when they were in the basalt chutes or trying to leap the falls. Danny and Red Shirt watched.

The Celilos stood on shaky wooden platforms extended

over the churning waters, holding the long dipnets steady by bracing the pole handles against their chests and shoulders. They wore rubber boots and raingear to keep from getting soaked by the mists rising above the falls, and they smoked their pipes upside down to prevent the mists from putting out the tobacco. Some wore floppy hats, and all had safety ropes tied to their waists and hooked to support posts on the platforms.

Red Shirt told Danny that if the men fell, they most likely would drown in the churning whitewater before their friends could pull them to safety, but the ropes made them feel better anyway. He added that if a man cheated on his wife, she might cut the rope nearly in half, then cover the cut with grease so it still looked strong. Then he winked and said it was a good thing he wasn't a Celilo.

Danny saw the salmon rise out of the water like silver ribbons as they leaped the tiers of the falls. When the fish bumped against the hoop-shaped nets, the Indians jerked and swung the pole handles down, lifting the fish vertically from the water. With the jerks, metal rings slid down the nets, trapping the salmon inside the twine. After catching fish, the men brought them to the women waiting at the end of the scaffold, who clubbed the salmon as they flopped against the twine webs. The women took the fish from the nets and cleaned them quickly, throwing their entrails into the water before the dogs could eat them and get salmon poisoning. The men joked and relit their pipes, tapping out the damp tobacco. "Huk-toocht," they called to one another as they walked back to the platforms. "Good luck."

Red Shirt sat on a flat rock rolling cigarettes and watching the Celilos fish. Danny tossed rocks into the water, but it was so turbulent he couldn't see the splashes.

"I'll get us a salmon," Red Shirt said.

An old woman in a blue housedress and purple scarf pointed to a good-sized silver salmon and held up five fingers.

Red Shirt shook his head, so the old woman covered the salmon with a wet burlap sack. Red Shirt smoked another cigarette and watched the men fishing. Then he stood. Reaching into his front pocket, he took out four silver dollars and placed them on the rock. Motioning for Danny to follow, he walked away.

In a few minutes, the old woman came up the hill with the salmon flung over her shoulder. She had draped the burlap sack across her shoulder to keep off the slime of the wet fish. She had a difficult time walking over the rocks in her sandals, and once, when she slipped and fell to her knees, Danny saw the notched tail of the salmon hanging below her braid. She put the salmon on the flat rock and picked up the four silver dollars, dropping them into the front pocket of her dress. The sun caught some of the fish scales clinging to the burlap and they glittered like sequins. After the old woman returned to the platform, she relit her pipe, then looked at Red Shirt. Grinning through her toothless gums, she held two fingers in the air and waggled them.

Red Shirt hooked his forefinger into the dark pink gills and lifted the salmon, holding it out from his side. "I paid double for this fish," he said to Danny. "But I don't mind."

"You should have let me bargain for it."

Red Shirt laughed. "You don't know how to pour piss out of a boot yet."

Danny followed his father up the hill, trying to match his stride but sliding on the loose rocks. "Can we eat the fish now?"

"Pretty soon you'll have all the salmon you can eat. We'll add this to Sammy's catch. Look." Red Shirt pointed to a large rock in the river that was separated from the others by two roaring chutes. Seven men stood in a line, dipping side by side.

"Rhythm Rock," his father said. "Only the bravest and the best fish here. No safety ropes."

"Why do they call it Rhythm Rock?"

"They have to work together, in rhythm. Otherwise, they'd foul their nets or knock each other into the chutes."

After a while, one of the men loaded his fish into an overhead cable car and rode it back toward the mainland. Danny shuddered as the car, more like a large wooden fruit crate, wobbled over the whitewater. As the man got closer, Danny could see it was Sammy Colwash.

"Huk-toocht," Sammy greeted them. "You brought the boy."

"I wanted him to see the falls," Red Shirt said. "How's fishing?"

"A little small, maybe. Tommy Thompson and the old men say the Celilos are being punished for letting the white men build the dam. Still, I caught a few Noo-sok today. Help me with these."

They carried eight bright silver salmon to Sammy's drying shack and hung them from the racks. Red Shirt added the salmon he had bought. "We'll feast tonight," Sammy said. "These are fine salmon for silvers. The very best spring salmon were the bluebacks that spawned in Wallowa Lake. By the time they reached Celilo, they had lost their sea lice, and the cold waters of the Columbia made them too firm to pack. The cannery workers threw those bluebacks on the floor overnight to soften up enough to pack the next day."

"I'd like to try eating them," Danny said.

Red Shirt shook his head. "Bluebacks haven't been in the river for years. I remember your grandfather Medicine Bird spearing them from horseback when he got too old to hunt. He dressed up for it, too, brushing his hair into a roll above his forehead like the old Dreamers and putting on his elktooth necklace and beaded apron. Then he rode his Appaloosa out into the river. Since he refused to wear his glasses, he speared about as many logs as fish. Some people smiled at him, but he said it would shame him out if anyone mistook him for a Fish

Indian. By staying on that Appaloosa, he figured everyone would know he was Nez Perce."

Sammy laughed at the story and Danny laughed too, even though he had heard that one many times before.

Red Shirt grew quiet. "The Dreamers lost the Wallowas," he said. "And later, the white man dammed the lower end of Wallowa Lake and destroyed the salmon beds."

"Don't think of the past, right now," Sammy said. "It's time for the feast."

They were Sammy's guests at the celebration, and he made certain they got the best parts of the salmon, the tender a-wiss fillets sliced from the backbone. Sitting cross-legged on tule mats, Danny ate the salmon, venison, roots, and berries until he could hold no more. He turned up his nose at the lok-lok, salmon heads with shriveled eyes floating in black broth, but the men kidded him because Danny had already eaten eel soup without knowing what it was.

Sammy and the other Celilos waited until their guests had finished; then they took their places on the mats to eat. Danny wanted to go outside to play the stick game, but Red Shirt shook his head. "We'll wait for Sammy," he said.

After the feast, in the quiet time before the dancing started, Danny followed Red Shirt and Sammy down to the falls. The platforms were empty.

"No one fishes at night," Sammy told him. "That way enough salmon get upstream to spawn." He turned to Red Shirt. "They tell us the new dam will swallow the falls. How can this happen? The falls are so powerful many Celilos believe the waters will crush the dam when they close the floodgates. We still have our fishing rights, but what good are they if the dam swallows the falls? The fish are more than money."

Red Shirt put his hand on his friend's shoulder. "Come hunt with us in Elkmoon," he said. "You've been around fish so long you're growing scales."

Sammy smiled as he looked across the falls.

Danny followed his gaze. He had never seen anything as powerful as the narrowed river waters roaring down the chutes and crashing over the falls. He didn't believe they could be swallowed either.

"Can you teach a Fish Indian to hunt?" Sammy asked quietly.

Red Shirt grinned. "Probably. If Medicine Bird could fish, you could hunt. Maybe we can chase some elk into your dipnet."

Late in the evening, they ate more salmon. Red Shirt bought Danny two bottles of strawberry pop to drink with the fish. Danny gathered some dry juniper boughs, adding them to the fire and watching the gray smoke rise into the darkening sky. He sat close to the fire with his arms around his knees, listening to his father and Sammy swap stories about elk camp and fishing. Each time Sammy grew quiet about the falls, Red Shirt kidded him by saying he could dipnet elk.

When Danny's head began nodding, Sammy said goodnight and walked down the hill to his shack. Red Shirt took the bedrolls out of the pickup and threw them on the ground. He carefully looped a horsehair rope around them. "That will keep our snaky friends away if they decide to curl up," he said.

Danny climbed into the bedroll, his stomach full of fish and his nostrils keen to the smell of pungent juniper smoke. Red Shirt stared past the fire at the river. Just as Danny fell asleep to the sound of the roaring falls, he thought he heard his father say, "It's over for them."

Red Shirt took Danny back to the falls once after that, the day they closed the floodgates on the dam. Four miles east of Celilo, cars lined both sides of the road. Looking across the river to the Washington side, Danny saw that the cars had stopped there too. Most of the people were dressed up. The men wore light-colored shirts with dark trousers and the women had on Sunday dresses. Some families had spread bright picnic tablecloths and were eating lunches. Nearly everyone had a camera.

Red Shirt stopped the car by Dinty's Café, but he didn't get out. He looked downriver. Danny watched the broad gray water moving swiftly, and he could hear the distant roaring of the falls. "Take a good look," his father said.

Below Dinty's, closer to the river, cement rectangles and bare foundations marked where the railroad houses at Biggs' siding had stood. The Union Pacific had moved them away because they realized the rising waters of Celilo Lake would flood them out.

Red Shirt drove slowly past the spectators and into Celilo Village, where the Indians were clustered in tight groups, smoking their pipes and talking quietly. When Sammy saw them, he nodded and came over.

"I'm glad you're here," Sammy said.

"Huk-toocht," Red Shirt said.

Sammy smiled a little. "Yes. Huk-toocht." He tousled Danny's hair. "Planning on keeping your feet dry?"

"I hope so," Danny said.

Sammy's smile broadened. "We'll see. A lot of people came out expecting something to happen."

They stood for an hour talking of hunting and fishing. Then a man in a brown government car from the Army Corps of Engineers drove into the village and said something to a group of old Celilos. Before long, the word passed: the floodgates had been closed.

Everyone stared downriver at the moving water. For a long time it continued flowing freely, but finally a narrow crescent of flat, quiet water became visible. As they watched, the crescent widened to meet the flowing water.

"It's coming, isn't it?" Danny asked, but no one answered.

It seemed as if everyone held his breath, staring at the widening crescent of smooth water inching toward the falls.

The water turned cold and Danny realized he had been in
the shower a long time. He shut off the faucets and stepped
out of the shower into the steamy bathroom. He wiped the
mirror with a towel and looked at the stubble on his chin.
Usually he would have let it go another day, but now he
shaved because he wanted to look good when he went into
Pendleton.

He found a pair of jeans in the closet that he hadn't worn
much, and a faded denim shirt. The clothes he had worn the
night before were dirty and scorched from the burning car,
so he decided to stuff them into the back of the closet until he
had a chance to take them to the laundromat. He didn't want
to wear them because he thought it was just as well not to
remind anyone that he had been with Henry. Of course, he
had called Nathan like Henry asked him to, but that was all
right because Nathan was Henry's brother.

Danny heated water on the propane stove and made himself a large cup of instant coffee. The milk had spoiled, so he
drank the coffee black. While he sipped it, Danny tried to
think of the places Billy Que might have hidden some of their
cattle money. After finishing the coffee, he put on his boots,
hat, and jacket. Then he took an envelope from the card
table and two fifty-dollar bills out of his wallet. He wrote
"FOR JACK" on a sheet of paper and folded the bills inside so
they couldn't be seen if someone held the envelope to the
light. On the envelope, he scrawled the Nebraska address
where Jack lived with Loxie and her second husband.

He walked to Billy Que's and let himself in the back door.
Then he searched. He checked the chambers of the double-
barrel shotgun, and the black thermos bottle Billy Que carried with him on fishing trips. He examined the hollow
bootheel of the working boots Billy Que kept in the back of

the closet. He even looked in the Gideon's Bible stolen from a Walla Walla motel. Once in the past Billy Que had hidden money there, thinking Danny would never touch the Bible. But this time, even though he shook it vigorously, Danny found nothing. Whatever Billy Que made on those cows he must have already spent, so Danny knew he would have to use some of the money he'd gotten from Henry for the bail.

On the way to Milo's garage, Danny dropped the money for Jack into a corner mailbox. Milo was supposed to be open by eight-thirty, but it was almost nine by the time he came down the steps. He already had his visor on, and when he saw that Danny had the money, he smiled.

After Danny got his truck from Milo, he drove downtown to see Blinky Shakeblanket about getting Billy Que out of jail. It felt good to have his pickup back, and he was also pleased that he had refused to pay the twenty dollars extra Milo had tried to charge him for storage. Milo claimed his insurance company was charging him more to cover vehicles left in the vacant lot.

Danny stopped in front of Darby's Department Store and waited for the green shade on the door to go up. He wanted to buy some new boots and clothes before too many people saw him around town. And he intended to look good when he paid his entry fees for the Heppner Rodeo. Not much seemed to be going on so early. Perry Winishite was asleep in the doorway of the Nugget Lounge, his legs stretched across the sidewalk. Someone had taken his boots, and his toes stuck out from mismatched socks, one blue and the other brown.

The shade went up and the CLOSED sign swung to OPEN. Danny stepped out of the pickup and slapped his hat against his thigh a couple of times to get the dust out. Then he brushed back his hair and replaced the hat.

Inside the store, he recognized Delores Darby counting money at the cash register. At first he was surprised, but then he remembered hearing she was getting a divorce from the rancher she'd married near Walla Walla. When she didn't look up from counting the money, he started browsing through the Western shirts. After a few minutes he found a red one he liked, so he carried it over to the boot section. He studied the boots a while, then picked out a pair of Tony Lama's. "You got any boothooks, Delores?"

"Danny," she said. "Sorry. I was counting this money."

She brought him a pair and he slipped the hooks into the loops and tugged the boots on. He took a couple steps. "Pretty tight."

"Move around a little. They'll limber up. You going to ride at Heppner?"

Danny walked around the boot section, being careful not to step off the carpet. "You bet," he said. "Saddlebronc and bull riding." He could have entered the bulldogging too, but he remembered how it had felt to miss the steer at The Dalles.

"It's going to be like old home week," she said. "I heard Taylor Webb is going to ride too."

Danny sat in a chair and grimaced as he tried to tug off the boots. He had never expected Taylor to ride in such a small rodeo and thought he wouldn't see him until the Round-Up. With Taylor riding, he'd have some tough competition. "Where did you hear that?"

"It's just been going around," she said. "I think it would be kind of good to see him. Say, you ought to have some pants for that new outfit."

"I could use some, all right, as long as they fit over these boots." He took the new pants she offered him, picked up the boots, and stepped inside the changing room. In high school, Delores and Taylor went together for a while, and he wondered if she was still carrying a torch. When the pants were on, he took two fifties from his billfold and put them in the toe of one of his new boots. Then he put the boots on and stepped out of the dressing room.

"Some outfit," she said. "You look great. Of course, I say that to all the handsome guys."

"Still sounds good." Danny grinned. "How much?"

She totaled it on the register. "One sixty-five."

As he started to pay for his clothes and boots, Danny saw a large knuckle ring in the case. It was silver and had a blue-green turquoise stone. "How much you want for that ring?"

"It's fifty," she said. "But I'll knock it down to thirty-five for you. I should tell you it's not real turquoise."

"Looks real to me," Danny said, trying on the ring.

"They make these in Taiwan now. Out of soapstone and some kind of dye. Looks good, though. You almost have to be an expert to tell."

"I'll take it," Danny said, and handed her four fifty-dollar bills.

"Say," she said. "This is rodeo money, all right. Look at how crisp it is."

Danny took four more fifties out of his wallet. "Can you break these for me? It's a little early for the bank."

Delores lifted the cash drawer and took out a bundle of bills. She counted two hundred dollars in wrinkled tens and twenties. "You must have done all right," she said. "But how come you don't flash the big winnings around town?"

Danny folded the money and stuck it in the front pocket of his new pants. "You know how it is. All the losers expect you to buy them drinks."

Danny left the store carrying his old clothes in a Darby's bag. He tossed it on the front seat of the pickup and crossed the street. After looking at himself in the window of Fred's News, he decided it was a pretty sharp outfit. Inside, Danny thumbed through a few of the men's magazines, then bought a pack of Luckies for Billy Que.

* * *

When Danny stepped into the police dispatch room, Blinky Shakeblanket was leaning back in a gray swivel chair with his feet on the desk, reading the latest issue of *Ringside.* "Good to see you, Danny," Blinky said, putting down the magazine and ushering him in with a sweep of his massive arm. "You here on business or you plan to file a complaint?"

It was Blinky's standard line. As far as Danny knew, Blinky had never followed up on a complaint made by someone from the Umatilla Reservation. "I came to get Billy Que out," Danny said, forcing a smile. He tried to look at Blinky's good eye. At one time, Blinky had been a pro wrestler in the Canadian League, but his left eye had been gouged pretty bad, so his eyelid was always fluttering. Blinky was a Cree from around Moosejaw, and he'd been hired on in Pendleton to keep the local Indians in line. Since he was a real trouble-maker, most of them tried to stay clear.

"I'm glad Billy Que's getting out," Blinky said. "We had a swell time, though, just waiting around for you to show up."

"What's bail?"

"Two fifty." Blinky smiled and the bad eye winked. "If that seems a little high, it's because he swung at a cop. But it's written right down here on the judge's sheet. Black and white."

"I'd like to see Billy Que first."

"You carrying anything?"

"Pack of cigarettes."

"Better check anyway. Regulations."

Blinky gave Danny a quick search, then took him to the cell. "Five minutes," Blinky said.

Billy Que got off the cot and shuffled over to the bars. He was tipped at an angle and winced when he moved. "What the hell," Que said. "I wondered when you'd show up."

Danny handed him the Luckies.

Que's hands trembled as he let go of the bars. "No smokes

for three days," he said. He unwrapped the packet and put a cigarette between his lips.

Danny struck a match so Que could get a light. When the match flared, he saw that Que's face was pretty bruised.

Que took a drag from the cigarette, then exhaled. "They got a Mex cooking and I won't touch greaser food. I'm so hungry my stomach thinks my throat's cut. Where you been?"

"The Dalles."

"Do any good?"

"Not much." Danny knew Que wanted to know if he had any money. "How's Blinky been?"

"Meaner than a bootful of barbed wire. You see my face. How much did you make in The Dalles?"

"Not enough to cover bail. Why did you go and swing at a cop?"

Que grinned. "He wasn't a real cop, just part of the Pea Festival parade's mounted sheriff's posse—all gussied up in a tan suit and hat. Anyway, this cute little princess on a palomino winked at me and I swung on behind her. She was so overcome with excitement she started yelling, and this guy rode up alongside and tried to yank me off."

"So you hit him?"

"Not right then. I just grabbed him and pulled him off with me, but the fat bastard landed on top when we hit the road and half sprained my back. *Then* I hit him. Knocked him assbackwards into some of the freshest, greenest road apples you ever saw."

Danny laughed in spite of himself. "Wish I'd been there."

"Well, get me out of here and we'll go take a squint around for that princess."

Danny shook his head. "Not so fast. What about my cows you sold?"

Que glanced away. "Heard a good one over there. You know why they opened a Mexican restaurant in Pendleton?"

When Danny didn't answer, Que finished: "That's where the car broke down. Here's another. You know how to tell the best man at a Mexican wedding? He's the one carrying the jumper cables. Pretty good, huh?"

"What about the money?"

Que flicked the ashes off the cigarette. "I got some cash, but I drank most of it up. I saved a little something for you, though, since we're partners and all."

Danny wanted to believe him, but he didn't. "Those cows ought to bring eight hundred—even now. So I figure there ought to be four hundred around somewhere for me."

"I might have sold a little low."

"Three hundred."

"It wasn't all cash," Que said.

Danny closed his eyes. "You didn't buy another bad horse?"

"Of course not. I got something for you back at the place."

"I looked."

A sly smile came over Que's face. "This time I hid it good."

"All right," Danny said. "Tell me where so I can get you out."

Que's smile disappeared. "Don't you have my bail money with you? You're looking pretty damn good. Even got a fancy dude's ring." It was as though he had noticed the new clothes for the first time.

"Tapped," Danny said. "I had to get my pickup from Milo, and that cleaned me out." When he saw Que was still looking at the new clothes, he added, "I bought these in The Dalles before I heard you got tossed in. Besides, I was sure you saved my share of the money and thought I could get you out with that."

Que didn't say anything for a few minutes. Then he lit another cigarette. "It's not exactly money at the trailer. I bought some certificates, options on a land and mineral deal.

In a few weeks, they'll be worth a bundle. I promise to cut you in for half."

"Damn," Danny said. "I don't even want to hear about it. You might as well have thrown it away at the bar. I have half a notion to leave you in here for being so damn dumb."

Que looked sullen for a few moments. "Maybe you could hock something. My back is killing me and I need a drink. Besides, I told Blinky you'd show up with the money today, and I'd like to get out before he gets downright nasty . . . You can have the rest of the cows, okay?"

"If we ever find them. Oh, to hell with it, Que. I got enough for your bail."

Danny counted out two hundred and fifty dollars in tens and twenties and gave the money to Blinky.

Blinky counted it twice, licking his forefinger before he touched each bill. "That's bail," he said, locking the money inside a cash drawer. "Now I need a hundred for safekeeping."

"The bail wiped me out."

Blinky thought a minute. "Throw in that ring," he said.

"Not the ring," Danny said. "The setting's new, but it's old turquoise. Belonged to my grandfather."

"He got it from a Navajo, I suppose."

"You can't get turquoise like this anymore. Blue-green and flawless."

"Let me try it on," Blinky said.

Danny handed him the ring and Blinky tried it, but his fingers were so large he had to put it on the little one. "Not bad," he said, waggling the finger at Danny. "What do you think?"

"Not bad," Danny said.

"I hear the county boys got that smartface Henry Nine Pipes up to the hospital," Blinky said. "Car theft. Later on, soon as he can travel, they're taking him back to The Dalles."

"What happened to Henry?" Danny asked. He figured Blinky might be up to something, so he was careful not to know too much.

"Busted leg. Like I say, he stole a car, then wrecked it."

"That surprises me," Danny said. "Henry don't need a car."

"I hear you was with Henry last night at the Buckhorn."

Danny sounded natural when he replied. "He bought drinks for everyone with his rodeo winnings. I left him at the bar and hitched a ride back home. Never saw what he was driving."

"A stolen car, that's what. It wouldn't surprise me if your fingerprints was all over that car too," Blinky said.

"Why don't you check it?" Danny looked straight at him.

"It burned up," Blinky said. "The damned car burned up." He seemed disappointed. "Another funny thing. The sheriff from The Dalles called and said Henry beat up a cowboy there and took over a thousand dollars' rodeo winnings."

Danny didn't say anything.

"But he was broke when they found him. Claims the money burned up." Blinky unlocked the cash drawer and looked again at the crumpled bills Danny had given him. "These here don't look like rodeo money."

"I got it out of a bootheel," Danny said. "It was supposed to pay for my fees at Heppner. I wish I'd won some rodeo money, but I never got a good ride."

"Well, maybe it could be like you say," Blinky said. "If I had Henry down here in one of the back rooms, I could find out pretty quick. But those county boys got him outside my jurisdiction. Too bad." Blinky looked at the ring. "How about it? You want to cover the premium? Wouldn't want Billy Que to fall down getting out of here. He's a mite weak from not eating."

Danny could barely believe Blinky had bought the story about the ring. "All right. Call it square."

"My pleasure," Blinky said. "You know, a fellow lost his ear in my jail one time, up in Canada. He was one of them longhair reservation types, a real smartface, and he needed a haircut—sanitary reasons, don't you know. He must have liked that hair, the way he kicked and hollered. But just as the razor come by his ear, he jerked. That ear sliced right off." Blinky spread his large hands. "I believe in safekeeping."

"Why don't you get Que? Then I can worry about him."

Blinky took the keys and opened the steel doors to the back. While he was gone, Danny studied the patch collection they had around the walls. The local police were always going to conventions and trading arm patches with other departments. They had ones from Spearfish, South Dakota; Crazy Woman, Wyoming; Wolf Point, Montana; Bad Axe, Michigan; Secaucus, New Jersey. That last one sounded the funniest to Danny.

When Blinky came out holding onto Billy Que, Danny could see Que was pretty stoved up, and he wished he had come sooner. Blinky reached under the counter and brought out Que's boots, belt, and a paper sack with his personal belongings. He dumped the keys, some change, a wallet, and a blue comb onto the counter. "You got to sign for these," Blinky said.

Que opened the wallet, but it was empty.

"Lots of thirsty friends," Blinky said. "Sign."

"Not that many," Que said as he scrawled his signature. He leaned against Danny while he tugged on his boots.

"Go on outside a minute, Billy Que," Blinky said.

When Que hesitated, Danny nodded. "I'll be right along." Que left.

Blinky stared at Danny. "You better take it real easy."

Danny felt the blood rise in his neck. "I'll try to do that."

"Henry ran into a bunch of cows," Blinky said. "And the county boys said two of them wound up with their throats slit." He studied Danny's hands and the new clothes. "I don't figure Henry climbed out of a barrow pit with a busted leg to slit a cow's throat. And they never done it by themselves. So I'm keeping my eye on you."

"I can see that," Danny said. "But don't count on making detective yet."

Outside, Que was leaning against a parking meter. "I could use a couple of drinks. After that, breakfast."

"Let's get a little distance from this place," Danny said.

"That son of a bitch," Que said. "The best part of him ran down his mother's leg."

"Don't even think about it," Danny said.

"Where in the hell did you get that ring?"

"What difference does it make? It cost me a bundle."

Que chuckled. "I'm glad he's got it. That ring looks like it belongs on a queer."

They had eaten breakfast and were halfway to Billy Que's before Danny said anything else about the money. "I can't believe you sold all those cows and didn't keep some cash. I'm just barely going to be able to scrape up entry fees."

"It didn't turn out quite like I expected," Que said. "I'm sure that wallet had a couple hundred still in it." He looked so glum Danny didn't say anything else.

When they reached the trailer, Que opened the top drawer of his dresser and took out some white slips of paper. "I'll bet you looked right at these, didn't you? If they was snakes, you'd have been bit."

"They don't look like they'll spend."

"Just read it."

Danny squinted at the paper. "Five shares—SUNCO—Northwest Division." He put the certificates down. "Take all these to the bar and I'll bet you can't buy one drink."

Que put the certificates back in the drawer. "Each one is worth a hundred dollars. And there's a deal cooking that will make them worth five, maybe ten, times that much. All we have to do is talk to some people."

"Not me," Danny said. "I've got to drive over to Heppner and pay my fees. You have any cash tucked around here somewhere?"

Que sat on the sofa, leaning back and closing his eyes. "I'm tired. Too long in the pokey. You know, Danny, the trouble you got is thinking small. You need to think big to get ahead. All that land sitting around, and SUNCO wants to pay the tribe money to come develop it. They'll build some nice places, drill a few holes in the ground, like big rabbits, and pay us for the privilege."

"I doubt it," Danny said. "We're not getting something for nothing. Right now, I'd like to cover my entry fees and the loss on those cows."

"I'm just trying to improve things a little," Que said. "No need for you to be so sore."

✦ 3 ✦

When Danny arrived at the Morrow County Fairgrounds in Heppner, he saw Nathan Nine Pipes with Henry's pickup and trailer. Nathan was feeding some oats to Cayenne.

"How's it going?" Danny said.

Nathan grinned. "Going okay."

"I see you got Henry's stuff."

"Thanks for the call," Nathan said. "Henry left it in a good place, but the cops would have found it sooner or later. You want to use Cayenne this afternoon?"

Danny shook his head. "No steers today. Just broncs and bulls. Anyway, I've got Ring-Eye."

"All right," Nathan said. "Let me know if you change your mind."

"You bet," Danny said. "But it's not likely."

He sat on the tailgate of his pickup and tugged off his right boot, then removed the hundred dollars he had saved for entry fees. The saddle bronc was forty and the bull riding fifty, so after he paid his fees to the sandy-haired woman in the booth, Danny tucked the extra ten in his pocket and waited for the draw. Looking around at the cowboys, he saw mostly old-timers and kids. It seemed unlikely Taylor would show for such a small purse.

At noon, the woman closed the booth and came out with the names of the broncs on slips of paper in a straw cowboy hat. One by one, the riders drew out the slips, unfolding them with tobacco-stained fingers, hoping for a good draw. As they drew the broncs, all the cowboys kidded each other, but they grew quiet when they drew for the bulls, because each of them knew a bad bull might end a career. When it was Danny's turn, he reached into the hat and took the third slip of paper he felt. "Cyclops," he said. He didn't know that bull.

An old-timer spit some tobacco flakes from between his lips and muttered, "Better buy some more tape. He'll rattle your ribs."

After all the cowboys had drawn, there was one slip left in the hat. The sandy-haired woman took it out and read it. "Taylor Webb gets Diablo."

"I don't see him," the old-timer said. "He should be here for the draw."

"I've got his letter," she said. "And his manager sent in the money a week ago. It's fair under the new P.R.C.A. laws. If he doesn't show, it's a fee forfeit."

"I liked it better before," the man said.

Danny stood and brushed off his pants. It was almost one, and he thought he'd watch the parade in half an hour. After buying a six-pack of beer at Lem's Market and a Wampus Burger at the Mustang Drive-In, he walked to the little park on Willow Creek. A historical sign there was dedicated to the victims of the Heppner flash flood. Over two hundred and fifty people had been killed in 1903, but since then the control dams upstream had reduced Willow Creek to a trickle he could step across. Danny opened one of the beers and sat on a

park bench, watching a group of kids playing on the merry-
go-round and swings.

Ten years before, Danny had played with Jack at the Pendleton park during the summer. The boy had come to stay with
his aunt Pudge while Loxie took the cure for the first time.
She had worked three years as a chorus girl in Reno and then
married a wheat farmer from Nebraska she met at a feed and
seed conference. After she moved to Nebraska, he made her
take the cure.

When Danny had learned that Jack was coming to visit
Pudge, he'd saved his paychecks from bucking bales. The
three of them went shopping at Darby's the day Jack arrived,
and Danny bought Jack a bright-green cowboy shirt with an
orange yoke, some new Acme boots, and a straw hat. Then
they went to the park. Danny pushed Jack on the horsehead
swings until he went so high the straw hat flew off his head.
He chased Jack, playing tag around the gazebo and among
the poplar trees.

Pudge sat on one of the green park benches eating ice
cream. It was hot and she ate it fast so it wouldn't melt. She
wasn't as big then, but she had already started putting on
weight.

Jack laughed and laughed as Danny pushed him on the
merry-go-round. The boy dragged his feet trying to stop it
and scuffed his new boots, but Danny showed him how to
jump off without losing his balance. "It's like jumping off a
bucking horse," Danny said. Jack threw his head back, showing his straight white teeth and his mother's full mouth.

For almost two weeks, Danny met Pudge and Jack in the
park when he got off work. One day, Pudge drove her old car
out east of Pendleton where Danny was haying for a German
farmer named Bender. Danny followed the tractor, lifting
the bales and stacking them on the trapwagon. Bender gave
Jack a ride on the tractor and let him steer it around the field.

When Bender went into the house for lunch, Pudge brought out some fried chicken and cans of strawberry soda. Jack tried lifting one of the bales, but it wouldn't budge. Danny told him you had to wear a red bandanna to be a hay hauler, and he tied his sweat-stained one around Jack's neck, then helped him lift a bale onto the wagon.

The next day there was a thunderstorm in the early afternoon and Bender didn't want to put the wet bales in the barn, so he let Danny off early. Danny passed the eastbound Greyhound on the way to town. He had a couple of drinks at the Saddleman's, then stopped at Darby's Department Store to buy Jack a red bandanna and a denim jacket.

It started raining again when he came out, so he drove to the park and waited under the cover of the gazebo. Pudge showed up by herself half an hour later. Her hair was wet and sticky and a strand of it trailed across her forehead. She wore a bright-red windbreaker with a large softball emblem and "Bravettes" on the back.

"Where's Jack?"

Pudge shook her head.

"I've got some stuff for him," Danny said, holding out the package.

"Loxie came."

Danny swallowed. Even after four years, his heart ticked when he heard her name. "Where is she?"

Pudge shrugged. "On the bus to Boise. She switches there to Pocatello, Denver, Omaha. She took Jack with her."

"Just like that?"

Pudge nodded.

They went to the Saddleman's and Danny ordered two drinks from the bartender. Danny drank his first one fast and ordered two more.

"Business is good," the bartender said. "It's the rain."

Pudge dug into her purse and pulled out some Polaroid snapshots. The first showed Jack in the shirt and boots Danny had bought for him. He was wearing the stained red bandanna Danny had given him in the field, and pointing a toy pistol at the camera.

In the next picture, Loxie was clowning around wearing some oversized red sunglasses and a blonde wig.

"Hollywood," Danny said.

The third picture was at the bus depot. Loxie had taken off the wig and glasses and her eyes were swollen. Jack stood beside her, a worried look on his face.

"I was hoping she might stick around a few days," Pudge said. "But she didn't want to see anybody."

When they finished their drinks, they bought a bottle of whiskey at the liquor store and drove to Pudge's trailer. Danny filled a couple of tumblers with whiskey while Pudge went into the bedroom to change. After a while, she came out wearing a blue terry-cloth robe and pink slippers with pompoms. She fixed some grilled cheese sandwiches in the kitchen; then they sat together on the couch and watched TV. When the bottle was gone, they went to bed. Pudge took off her glasses and put them on the nightstand beside the clock. Then she pulled Danny to her and pressed his face against her large, soft breasts. He took one of her nipples in his mouth and felt it stiffen. After a while, he became hard and they made love. It took him a long time because of the whiskey.

Danny awoke early, since he was used to being in the field by seven. Pudge was still asleep, so Danny boiled some water and made instant coffee. He drank it in the kitchen, watching the sun come up out the trailer window. When he went back into the bedroom to get his boots, Pudge sat up, revealing her brown shoulders and large breasts. In the morning light, Danny could see the stretch marks radiating from her dark aureolas.

"Why are you up so early?"

"Figured I better get to work," he said.

"Come back to bed a while."

"I don't think so."

"To hell with you, then," she said, and pulled the sheet up to her shoulders.

"Don't be sore, Pudge."

"Get lost."

"Just send the package to Jack, would you?" He put the denim jacket and new bandanna on the table. He took forty dollars out of his wallet and stuffed it into the breast pocket of the jacket. Then he left, quietly closing the trailer door.

Someone slapped Danny on the back and he spilled beer down the front of his shirt. Danny turned around to see Taylor Webb. He was wearing an expensive cream-colored suit and custom-made boots and holding a leather suitcase in his left hand.

"Taylor!" Danny said.

"You old sidewinder," Taylor said, striking Danny's shoulder with his right hand.

"I heard you were going to be in town, but missed you when they drew the bulls."

"Just flew in," Taylor said. "I had some engine trouble with the Cessna and had to put it down in The Dalles for some repairs. Here, have a cold beer." He took out a six-pack and gave Danny a strange-looking bottle with gold foil over the cap. "Imported," Taylor said.

When Danny took the beer, he saw Taylor's crooked thumb and remembered Taylor had been one of the top calf ropers in the country until he missed his dally on a big Hereford that all but took the thumb off. "You drew Diablo," Danny said.

Taylor grinned, looking as boyish as he had in high school. "That's a Mex bull from El Paso, wild as a rattlesnake with hemorrhoids. He'll shake and rattle for a few points."

"I got Cyclops."

Taylor stopped grinning.

"You know him?"

"A one-eyed bastard with a short horn. I know you hate the bulls, and he won't help."

"I need the money," Danny said. "I'm almost busted after paying the fees."

"It's your neck. But since I'm riding, you'll have to take second place. You got a good glove?"

Danny took a leather riding glove out of his back pocket. "I bought this one a few days ago and I've been working it."

Taylor took the glove. "Still too stiff. I got an extra pigskin you can use."

"Thanks," Danny said. "You know, I thought Heppner was a little beneath your style, after you rode in New York and all."

"Oh, I'm just a hometown boy at heart," Taylor said. "Besides, I have a little business in this neck of the woods."

"I saw you on TV," Danny said. "That ad for chewing tobacco."

"Just a way to pick up pin money," Taylor said. "This deal is a lot bigger. Say, can you rustle us up a couple of horses? I want to get in on that parade."

"I got Ring-Eye," Danny said. "And Henry Nine Pipes is in jail, so I figure he won't mind if you borrow Cayenne, seeing as we all go back a long way."

"I'll never forget the way you and Henry blocked for me in the homecoming game," Taylor said. "You Indian boys played pretty good football in those days."

"As I remember it," Danny said, "you were running like molasses most of the night. We had to double back and goose you a couple of times just to make you cross the line of scrimmage."

Taylor grinned. "No wonder I cherish such fond memories of that game."

"You remember? Those Baker linebackers called themselves the Tooth Fairies because they loosened so many teeth. I thought your mind would still be blank."

"It is," Taylor said. "Why else would I ride bulls?"

After they finished saddling the horses, Taylor said, "There's somebody special here I want you to meet. You got a different shirt? That one's a bit mussed." Taylor opened his suitcase and took out half a dozen new shirts still in their cellophane wrappings.

Danny looked at the labels. "Webb's Western Wear—Approved by the Professional Rodeo Cowboys' Association." "Nice duds," Danny said.

"Try the red one," Taylor said. "On credit. I can't afford to be giving these away. Pay me back with your bull-riding money. Besides, it's good advertising."

Danny took the shirt out of the cellophane and removed the pins, letting it fall open. It had white stitching on the yoke and mother-of-pearl snaps. "Feels good," Danny said as he snapped it up.

"A couple of the Pendleton stores will be carrying my shirts soon," Taylor said. "I'll put Panhandle Slim out of business. Say, give me a hand with these." Taylor pulled some fancy calfskin chaps out of the suitcase. "Champion Bull Rider—Madison Square Garden" was written on them.

"Who's the special person?" Danny said.

"You'll know her," Taylor said as he buckled the chaps. "World Class Stock. I ran into her a few days ago in Portland."

They joined the parade and found a place behind the Milton-Freewater marching band and majorettes. The majorettes wore tight blue blouses and red satin hotpants. Taylor nudged Cayenne until the horse was neck-and-neck with a brunette who had long, shapely legs. When she turned to say something to Taylor, he tipped his hat and told Danny, "Some filly. Legs like a quarterhorse." The majorette blushed and got back into step.

When they reached the reviewing stand that held the announcer and celebrities, Taylor reined his horse. "Look at that," he said.

Danny couldn't believe that Tenley Adams was still so beautiful after fifteen years. Her long auburn hair was cut in a style Danny knew must be expensive, and her tan set off the smile and wide green eyes.

"Prettiest woman to ever graduate from Pendleton High," Taylor said.

He was still carrying a torch, but Danny didn't blame him. All of them had admired her in those days. Danny remembered saving Pendleton's Homecoming game his senior year. He and Henry had blocked for Taylor time and again, but the Baker Bulldogs had a stiff defense and kept the Pendleton Bucks from scoring until the closing minutes. Then the Pendleton quarterback threw a little screen pass to Taylor out in the flat while Danny and Henry set up blocking.

Henry took out the corner linebacker and Danny cross-bodied the safety, allowing Taylor to streak into the end zone for the winning score. Tenley had been on the sideline cheerleading, tossing her mane of auburn hair, and she had thrown her green-and-gold pompoms high when she saw Taylor standing with the ball in the end zone. Danny got off the ground and offered his hand to the Baker safety, but he ignored it, calling Danny a "dumb-fuck Indian." It had seemed to Danny that afternoon as if they were all playing for Tenley's attention, and he gazed after her while she joined the throng carrying Taylor across the field.

That night at the dance, Henry and Danny had stayed at the edge of the crowd, wearing their green-and-gold letterman's sweaters and listening to the rock-and-roll band. Looking very spiffy in a dark maroon blazer, Taylor escorted Tenley to the stage where she was crowned Homecoming Queen.

After putting butch wax in their hair and combing it with small bristle brushes, Henry and Danny huddled in the shadows of the parked cars drinking tokay wine with Russell Teewee.

"That Taylor's some lucky guy," Russell had said. "I wouldn't mind checking her oil with my dipstick." Danny had hit him suddenly, knocking Russell sprawling across the hood of a big Chrysler. He didn't know why, and later he told Russell he was sorry.

The parade announcer was saying, "Well, folks, how about a big Heppner welcome for Taylor Webb, last year's National Bull Riding Champion! Would you look at those chaps! They gave him those back east in Madison Square Garden, New York City. He'll show us a little of that riding style later this afternoon, right Taylor?"

As the spectators clapped and waved, Taylor took off his cream-colored Stetson and bowed, holding the hat at arm's length and blowing a kiss to Tenley. She stood, applauding and smiling at Taylor.

"Whoa, boys. Looks like he's got an eye on that little filly," the announcer said. "And riding with Taylor today is a fine First American rodeo rider from just down the road, Billy Kachiah." Someone on the stand whispered to the announcer and he said, "That's *Danny* Kachiah, folks. You may recall that Danny was runner-up All-Around Cowboy here fifteen years back . . . Folks, we've got some *veterans* here with us today, and both these boys will be riding bulls this afternoon in a real outstanding show. So best of luck, Taylor, and to you too, partner."

Danny stopped Ring-Eye in front of the reviewing stand and pulled back on the reins. "Up!" he said, and Ring-Eye reared back on his hind legs, whinnying and pawing the air with his front legs.

Tenley laughed and waved.

"You trying to beat my time?" Taylor asked.

"Only with the bulls," Danny said.

When the parade finished, they unsaddled the horses in

the warm-up area behind the chutes and Danny gave them some grain. "What does she do now?"

"Hangs out with a crowd from Portland," Taylor said. "Gal Friday to a fellow named Ace Bickman. He's into oil, real estate, land development—a real entrepreneur. They'll be back in Pendleton at the Silver Spur later on and I'll introduce you."

"Sounds like too fast a crowd for me," Danny said.

It was late afternoon before the bull riding started. Danny had been disqualified in the saddlebronc event when his free hand slapped his horse's back. But the first bull riders either didn't stay on for eight seconds or received low scores, so Danny figured he had a good shot at some money. He didn't look at the bull until it was time to go into the chute, and his mouth was like metal.

"That's a rank bull," Taylor said. "Stay back because he'll try to downdraft you, whip you into his horns."

Danny climbed onto Cyclops while the chuteman held the noserope. He tugged the pigskin glove onto his right hand and pulled it taut with his teeth. Beneath him the big bull shuddered, and Danny felt like climbing off.

"He might try to brush you at the gate," Taylor said. "Lean left. When you're out of the box, it's up to you."

One of the clowns placed the cowbells around the bull's neck and the sheepskin pad around his flanks, and Danny tucked his testicles into the riding jock. He put his gloved hand under the riding rope and cinched it as tight as he could. Taylor tugged it tighter while Danny took two extra wraps around his hand with the cinch rope. "Enough," he said.

"Whenever you're ready," the gateman said.

Danny pulled his hat tight with his left hand, then raised it into the air. He didn't want to slap the bull and be disqualified.

"Go!"

The chutegate swung open and Cyclops lunged against the gatepost, trying to rub Danny off, but Danny was leaning far to the left, glad for Taylor's warning. The bull raged into the arena, lunging and twisting as the cowbells clanked and the sheepskin pad tickled its flanks. Danny flew into the air, then slammed his groin against the bull's ridged back. Cyclops planted his front feet and kicked high with his back legs, snapping his head back to hook Danny with his short horns, but Danny hung on, leaning back and clenching his teeth against the pain. His hat sailed off and he waved his free hand until he heard the buzzer over the roaring pain in his head.

Danny tried to climb off, but his gloved hand was caught in the rigging. The bull became frenzied as he lunged time and again, and Danny was afraid he would roll over on his back. Jerking his gloved hand and tugging at the cinchrope with his left one, Danny desperately tried to get free. He saw the clowns running toward the bull rolling a red plastic barrel and yelling for Danny to get off. As he pulled his hand out of the glove, Danny felt the bull lower his head and shudder. Losing his balance, he pitched forward, tumbling over the Brahma's hump and landing on the packed dirt, his wind gone.

The bull was on him in a second, and Danny felt the short horns rake his chest and the broad skull pound his ribs as the bull lowered its shoulder and tried to crush him in the dirt. He heard the clowns screaming and saw them waving bright flags, but the bull raked him again as the pain seared through his chest. Danny grabbed Cyclops's nosering, slick with the bull's snot, and twisted with all his might while he plunged his left thumb into the bull's good eye, gouging and cursing. The bull bellowed and raised his head for an instant, allowing Danny to roll free.

He came to his feet and ran for the fence, sticking the pointed toes of his boots into the slats and climbing beyond

the horns of the bull as it banged into the fence a couple of
times, then chased after one of the red plastic barrels. Danny
waited until the clowns shooed the bull into the chasing
gates.

Danny climbed off the fence but held on to the board. He
wanted to retrieve his hat, but his knees were shaking and he
was afraid to let go of the fence. He closed his eyes, taking
shallow breaths, then a deeper one to see if any ribs were
broken. A clown in a blond wig handed him his hat, and
Danny let go of the fence, then took a few steps into the
arena to wave at the crowd. He knew Tenley was in the
grandstand somewhere.

"Folks, he's all right," the announcer said. "These cowboys
are tough as whang leather and thrive on danger. Danny
Kachiah just earned himself a score of seventy-four for riding
one mean old bundle of beefsteaks. How about a big hand for
our Indian cowboy."

As the crowd applauded, Danny kept waving his hat at the
bright blobs of color in the grandstand.

When Danny reached the area behind the chutes, Taylor
slapped him on the back. "Good ride," he said. "But you got
to improve your technique for getting off."

"Damn," Danny said. "This is no way to make a living."

"And no way to treat a friend's shirt," Taylor said. "You
really messed up the merchandise. If that bastard had longer
horns, you'd be planted on the wrong side of the ground."

The shirt was torn open, revealing Danny's chest where
the skin had split apart in places. He took a red bandanna out
of his pocket and dabbed at some of the oozing blood.

"Might need stitches," Taylor said.

"I want to watch your ride first."

Taylor shook his head. "You better start thinking about
diversification."

"What's that?"

"Getting into different kinds of work. I'm serious. Maybe

we should go fishing on the Umatilla up near Reservation Mountain—talk about it some."

"Fishing sounds good to me," Danny said. "Right now, though, you've got some riding to do. I'll help with your rigging, but you don't have a shot at my score."

"Cream rises," Taylor said. "Still, I hate to put an old buddy in second place."

"Cream rises and shit floats," Danny said. "We'll talk about it after you ride."

Taylor never made a score that afternoon. While he was on Diablo adjusting his glove, the chuteman slacked the lead rope on the Brahma's nosering and the big bull climbed the box. Taylor fell under him, and Diablo broke his leg. Danny quickly kicked the gate open to let the bull out, or Taylor would have been trampled to death. When the ambulance came, Danny helped load Taylor, then rode with him up the hill to the hospital.

"God damn!" Taylor grimaced through the pain. "I can't believe this happened in jerkwater Heppner. Now I'll miss all the big rodeos. Can't ride with a busted leg."

"We'll go fishing like you said. That's reservation water, but I'll tell them you're a breed. Besides, old Orville Hoptowit hasn't given anyone a ticket for about thirty years."

"Most popular man on the reservation," Taylor said.

"Something like that."

"Say hello to Tenley for me. Now that I kept you in first place, you can afford to buy her a drink."

"Ho!" Danny said. "You'd need a gift to beat my score."

"It was a good ride," Taylor said. "But you're a natural athlete. I always wondered why you never went with me to rodeo school in Texas. With some good coaching, you could have made top pro."

Danny thought a minute before he answered. "Red Shirt told me I could just pick it up. Figured he knew."

Taylor shook his head. "It's not like that anymore. Anyway, my love to Tenley."

"I don't think I'll be seeing her," Danny said. "She'll have a lot of guys hanging around."

"You'll see her," Taylor said. "And thanks, buddy, for saving my bacon. When that leg snapped, I thought I was down for the count."

At the hospital, the attendants rushed Taylor off to have his leg set. Danny could hear the cheering from the fairgrounds and see the men and animals coming out of the chutes. From the hospital on the hill, they looked like miniatures.

After a while, a doctor came out the swinging doors leading to the emergency room. "That's a nasty break," the doctor said. "Six weeks to mend. Looks like you could use some stitches."

"All right," Danny said.

The doctor sewed five stitches and put bandages over them to keep the sutures from sticking in the weave of Danny's shirt. "Looks like the bulls are way ahead today," the doctor said.

"They usually are."

"No point in coming around until tomorrow," the doctor said. "I gave him a pretty heavy sedative."

"That's Taylor Webb, you know."

The doctor shrugged. "That's just barely anybody." He walked through the swinging doors muttering, "Bull riding."

By the time Danny got back down the hill to the fairgrounds, the rodeo was over. He went to the pay window to collect his money, and saw that he'd been bumped out of first place by a rider named Buck Coe who had scored 76.

"Second place gets three hundred fifty dollars," the woman at the pay window said. "Put your brand across from where your name's typed."

"It beats third, I guess," Danny said, signing for the money. "Who's Buck Coe?"

The woman shrugged. "Some kid, barely shaves. The rodeo's being taken over by professionals and kids. An honest working cowboy can't make a living."

When he got to his pickup, Danny opened Taylor's suitcase and looked at the shirts. On the way out of Heppner, he stopped and bought a six-pack of beer and drank it during the drive back to Pendleton. That made him feel a little better. He slept a couple of hours in the trailer, then took a shower, being careful to keep the soap away from the stitches. After his hair was combed and dried, Danny shook the dust out of his jeans and put on another of Taylor's shirts—midnight blue with pearly snaps. Not bad, he thought, winking at himself in the mirror.

The Silver Spur was crowded, but Danny found a place at the bar next to Fuzzy Paige, the gimped-up rodeo clown. He bought Fuzzy a beer and said, "Thanks for helping with that bull."

"You don't fall off as good as you used to," Fuzzy said. "How's Taylor?"

"He'll be out of the money for six weeks," Danny said.

Fuzzy shook his head. "I can't help them if they don't clear the chute."

Tenley walked in about eight. She was wearing a powder-blue Western suit and a dark blue lady's Stetson. Her cream-colored blouse was unbuttoned enough to show where the tan ended. A tall man was with her. He wore a bolo tie with an oversized chunk of turquoise and a mesquite-colored rancher's hat. A couple of cowboys got up and offered them a table next to the dance floor.

"That's quite a woman," Fuzzy said when he caught Danny staring. "She used to do some trick riding at Cheyenne and Calgary, the big shows. If I was a little younger, I wouldn't mind swapping places with her horse."

"What about the dude?"

"He'd be Ace Bickman, some kind of mucky-muck from Portland," Fuzzy said. "That chunk of turquoise looks like a genuine blue dog turd."

Danny chuckled. "Real Navajo stuff. Old pawn."

As the band played, some of the young cowboys asked Tenley to dance, but she just smiled and shook her head. After a while, Bickman left their table and sat down with some Pendleton bankers near the back. Danny kept looking at Tenley—and the vacant chair.

". . . so she says, 'Well, Doc, my breasts ain't growed any bigger since I come here last time, but my boyfriend got twenty-five percent less cavities.' " Fuzzy laughed at his own joke. "She rubbed that Crest on them, don't you see?"

"What?" Danny asked.

"Hell, you missed my best story," Fuzzy complained. "Go on over there if you want. Stop mooning around."

"Sorry, Fuzzy."

Fuzzy shrugged. "She can't be as mean as Cyclops. But you better take a deep seat and pull your hat down mighty tight. She's a high kicker."

"Maybe I'll just say hello," Danny said. "Taylor wanted me to." He ordered two more beers, and when the band played "Pass Me By if You're Only Passing Through," he carried his over to her table.

"Hello, Tenley," Danny said. "I don't know if you remember me—Danny Kachiah. Taylor asked me to say hello."

"How you been keeping, Danny?" She smiled one of those smiles that seemed just for him.

"Getting by."

"Glad to hear it. Take a load off." She nodded at the chair, and he sat down.

"It's a real shame about Taylor," she said. "Ace and I stopped by the hospital, but he was still under."

"Old Taylor will be back," Danny said. "He's tougher than a stale plug of tobacco."

"When I think of Taylor and that bull in the chute . . ." Tenley shuddered.

"That's where the bad ones usually happen."

"For you cowboys, maybe. Trick riders break their necks in the arena, right in front of the grandstands, so all the crowd can take pictures." She shook her head, then took a sip of her drink. "Anyway, Taylor owes you. You're practically a hero."

Danny shrugged, but he was glad to have her praise. "We all watch out for each other back there," he said.

"Hey, let's not get gloomy. No more talk about accidents," Tenley said. "I thought you might ask a lady to dance."

"All right by me, if you're willing to take a chance on my footwork."

"I'm plenty willing," she said. "They're playing a slow one now, so I think I've got a chance."

Tenley was a little taller than Danny had thought, and her perfume reminded him of desert flowers after a rain. She had a trick rider's strong, straight back and shoulders wide enough to make her waist seem even slimmer. As they danced, Danny tried to imagine what it would have been like to go with her in high school.

They sat back down after dancing a couple fast ones, and Danny ordered more drinks. Tenley was drinking Godfathers. "They'll make me fat, but I love that Amaretto. Besides, after a few of these, I make deals they can't refuse." She laughed.

Danny was glad she was having a good time. He glanced over at the table of bankers. Ace had left. When he saw Tenley was watching him, he cocked an eyebrow.

She smiled. "Nothing heavy. Ace and I are just business associates. That reminds me, did Taylor get a chance to go over the business proposal with you?"

"No," Danny said. "Mostly, we talked rodeo and stock."

"I'm sure you mean *live*stock. That's Taylor. Cowboy first. Business last."

"What's it about?" Danny asked. He wondered how Tenley was mixed up with a sharp like Ace. And what Taylor had to do with it.

"Pleasure before business," she said. "They're playing Johnny Paycheck, and I can't keep my feet still. Besides, you win the night's most improved dancer award."

"Okay," Danny said. "I'm starting to get the hang of it."

Two hours later, the band played "The Girls All Get Prettier at Closing Time," but Danny figured that didn't count for Tenley.

"Let's go," she said. "You know what I'd like to do?"

"No."

"Find the Ladies' Auxiliary food stand and have one of those hamburgers smothered in fried onions. That stand still around?"

"Sure," Danny said. "Open all night. They get the hungry drunks after the bars close."

Outside the Silver Spur, Tenley took Danny's arm, and it felt good to walk down the street with her. Wilson Windyboy was standing outside the Buckhorn. As they passed, he said, "You sure are looking good, Danny." But he was watching Tenley.

They found the stand and Danny ordered a couple burgers. When the woman served them, the fried onions spilled onto the brown butcher paper. Danny carried them to the picnic table where Tenley was sitting.

"As good as I remember," Tenley said after she had eaten some of her burger.

They walked to the park at the edge of town, and Danny saw the moonlight winking off the horsehead swings.

Tenley climbed the steps of the gazebo and said, "When I was in high school, I used to come here and think of all the places I'd go, all the things I'd do. And now I'm back at this gazebo. Some things never change."

"Most do," he said.

Tenley came down the steps and took both his hands. "What about you, Danny? You don't seem much different. I've been married, lived in big cities, traveled to Europe once."

Danny tried to think of those places but couldn't. Maybe they were right for Tenley, went with part of her, anyway, because she seemed out of place with him in the park. Whenever he thought of being there with someone, it was Loxie. "I've been married," he said.

"Loxie. I remember. Miss her?"

Danny paused before he answered. "Now, I mostly miss Jack."

Tenley released his hands and moved against his chest, putting her arms around him and tilting her head to look into his face. "Let's go to my room," she said. "I can offer you a drink."

"All right." He put his arm around her waist, and they walked together—a little awkwardly at first, until he matched her stride. He knew she was offering more than a drink, but he wasn't sure why.

Tenley was staying at the Thunderbird, the best motel in Pendleton. Danny had been in the bar a few times when he felt cashy, but he had never seen the rooms. Hers had deep red carpeting and a gold bedspread.

"I don't need another drink," he said. "Might take the edge off."

"Neither do I." She pressed against him, slipping her hand inside the dark blue shirt and unsnapping it. She ran her lean fingers across his chest, pausing by the sutures. "You hurt?"

"Yes."

She led him to the bed and slipped his shirt off, then gave him a deep kiss. "I must taste like vanilla," she said, pulling away.

"And almonds. You taste good." He sat on the bed and took
off his cowboy boots, socks, and jeans.

She watched him undress, then smiled.

"What's funny?" he asked.

"Back in school, I wondered what you'd be like. But you
never tried to get to know me."

Danny didn't know if it was true, but he liked her saying it.

"Are you still shy?"

"Not much."

She folded her clothes, laying her dark blue underwear on
the dresser like ribbons. She had a good tan, except for her
breasts and pelvis. Her muscular shoulders and thighs made
her seem almost too strong.

Tenley shut off the light, then moved toward him. In the
darkened room, the crescents of her breasts and the V of her
pelvis glowed white. He matched her strength for a while,
amazed by her supple power, and when he could not hold
back, she drew away the hurt.

In the morning they made love again. Then Danny showered, noticing how white the motel towel seemed against his
dark skin. On his chest, the bruises Cyclops had made were a
dark yellow. He hoped Tenley would stay around a while, but
then he wondered what Taylor would think of the setup.
Well, it was just Taylor's hard luck.

While Tenley showered, Danny dressed and made himself
a cup of coffee from the little machine on the wall. He tried to
figure out why the hotplate didn't heat up unless the pot was
filled with water. Sipping coffee from the white styrofoam
cup, Danny watched the sun coming up over the row of
poplar trees in the park. If Tenley invited him to visit her in
Portland, he thought he'd go.

Tenley came out of the bathroom and started combing her
wet hair in front of the mirror. She was wearing another set
of underwear, red this time. When she saw him watching her

in the mirror, she smiled. "Usually, I don't say very much about making love, but it was great with you. I mean really. I hope we can see a lot more of each other."

"Yes," Danny said. "I'd like that."

"I'm supposed to go down and meet Ace for breakfast," she said. "A little business. After that I'm free. Why don't you join us?"

Danny remembered Tenley had mentioned business the night before. "What's the deal?" he asked.

Tenley shifted her eyes away from his and started putting on her lipstick. "Ace is acquiring some land on the Umatilla, up near Reservation Mountain. You know the place?"

Danny looked away from her reflection in the mirror. He remembered fishing that stretch of river with Red Shirt and helping his grandfather Medicine Bird build a sweathouse there from mud and willows. In the winter, after they were through trapping, his grandfather had come naked out of the sweathouse and plunged into the icy water to get the demons out. And now Red Shirt was buried there, but Danny didn't want to tell her. Finally he said, "That's tribal land. You can't buy it."

"Ace can buy the mineral rights and get long-term leases for a development," she said. "He organizes things for SUNCO, so he's been talking to some bankers here and some tribal council members. Now that I've got my broker's license, I'm sort of a junior partner. Taylor put up some money and thought you should come in, since you know most of the Indians on the council, even the old-timers."

Danny knew she had strung him out. When he was ten, he and Red Shirt had been riding horses by the river, and Danny's sorrel mare had shied when a rattlesnake struck at her. As the mare ran through the brakes, Danny was knocked off by a branch, and she dragged him in the stirrups until he was senseless. When Red Shirt found them, he threw the mare down and half-hitched her legs together, then covered her

with a blanket to teach her not to drag a rider. Now, Danny
wished it could be that simple with people. "No," he said. "I
don't think so."

She turned away from the mirror and looked directly at
him. "Someone else will do it if you don't."

"Maybe," he said. But he knew she was right.

"We could see more of each other," she said. "You could be
in on it."

"It won't work," he said.

"You're foolish. It's big money for the tribe, and there's a
nice cut for you. Ace is working on his third million; I'm
doing okay; Taylor's into all sorts of things. But you're still
trying to beat eight seconds without getting bucked off and
kicked to death."

"I'd better get going," Danny said. He set the empty cup
on the veneer nightstand and picked up his hat.

"What are you going to be when you grow up?"

"Older," Danny said. He stepped into the hall and tried to
remember the way out.

As he passed the motel dining room, Danny saw Ace
spreading a white linen napkin on his lap. A young Indian
waitress was pouring his coffee. Ace waved and smiled, but
Danny pulled on his hat and walked into the street. He
wished Taylor hadn't broken his leg, because he wanted to
punch him. That wouldn't square things, but it might make
him feel better. He planned to buy a shirt as soon as the stores
opened; later on, he would go to the hospital and give Taylor's back. He thought he'd better check on the horses, then
drive out and look at the Umatilla near Reservation Mountain.

# 4

The Umatilla was low for August and tufts of grass stuck out of the water. Danny tilted the seat of the pickup and took out a collapsible flypole from behind it. He knew it was not the best time of the season to fish, but after the business with Tenley he wanted to spend some time along the river.

He found his tennis shoes behind the seat and took off his cowboy boots, then slipped on the canvas shoes. He caught grasshoppers in the dry cheatgrass. These he put in a beer can, stuffing some paper in the top to form a kind of stopper.

Danny waded into the water, finding its coolness refreshing in the hot sunshine. He carefully removed a hopper from the can and held it between his thumb and forefinger. He slipped the hook into the grasshopper just behind its head, and the hopper spit dark brown juice at him. He wiped his fingers on his jeans and softly cast the hopper into a riffle. It floated on the water for a few seconds and then sank in a swirl.

On the next try, Danny cast a little farther upstream. As the hopper sank again in the swirl, Danny felt the bump of a

fish and snapped the pole back to hook it. The tip bobbed and
Danny felt the weight of the fish at the other end. The pole
tip jerked four times and then the line went slack as the fish
leaped into the air, shaking shining drops of water off its tail.
Danny saw it spit the hook, and he reeled in. As he cleaned
the mangled hopper from the hook and put on a fresh one, he
decided to let the fish take it deeper the next time.

He moved downstream for two hours, casting hoppers into
the eddies and riffles, but he never had another bite. When
he went around a bend with high banks, he saw the old
sheepwagon and realized he was at the spot where Red Shirt
and Medicine Bird had built the sweathouse.

The sheepwagon's tires were flat and some of the spokes
were missing from the wheels. A wasp's nest hung over the
broken door, and someone had been inside and thrown the
cast-iron cookstove onto the ground. They had probably
looked for hidden money behind the cookstove.

Sammy Colwash had lived in the sheepwagon after he left
Celilo. The dam waters had swallowed the falls, and Sammy
said it made him sick to look at the new lake, so he'd bought
some sheep and moved up the Umatilla.

Danny realized it had been over twenty years since he and
Red Shirt had first come to visit Sammy at his camp. Danny
had played with Judy, the marble-eyed sheepdog that
Sammy claimed was part Australian, and Sammy had given
Danny wedges of sheepherder's bread he'd baked in coffee
cans. During "docking time" each spring, Danny and his
father spent a week with Sammy.

When they rode out one spring, they learned that Sammy
had taken sick and the sheep were scattered in spite of Judy's
attempts to keep them herded. Red Shirt found Sammy lying
on a dirty mattress inside the wagon, his face twisted. He tied
Sammy onto Danny's horse, letting the boy ride behind him
on the way to the pickup. Danny could still remember the

sweet-sour smell of his father, and the way the denim shirt chafed his face as he held onto Red Shirt's waist.

After they had taken Sammy to the hospital, Red Shirt and Danny built a temporary corral for the sheep by stringing three strands of barbed wire around some junipers. Then they had rounded up the sheep on horseback, with Judy helping them by turning in the strays and nipping at their heels. Once, as Danny tried to cut off a hammerhead ewe that bolted for the river, he fell off his horse into the water, and Red Shirt laughed, calling him a "gumboot cowboy."

After the sheep were in the corral, Red Shirt climbed off his horse and wiped his brow with a red bandanna. "Hot work," he said. "Let's have a swim." He stripped off his clothes and stood naked on the shore. "Well," he said, "let's go."

Danny was reaching manhood, and his cheeks felt hot as he took off his clothes, turning so his back was to his father. "That water's swift," he said.

They waded into the water until it was over their waists, and Red Shirt dove in, swimming for the far shore with smooth strokes. Danny reached the opposite shore several yards behind his father. His legs felt weak. "I don't think I can swim back," he said.

"Hang onto my back then," Red Shirt said, and Danny swam beside him, holding on to his father's big shoulders as though he were a horse.

They came out fifty yards below the sheepwagon, and Red Shirt sat on the shore, his chest rising and falling as he tried to catch his breath. Then, for the first time, Danny saw the gray strands in his father's braids and the few white hairs sprouting from the black growth around his groin.

After they had dried in the sun, Danny left some food for Judy and they went into town. Later, Red Shirt went out with a couple of other sheepherders to drive the sheep two miles up to the road. Then they loaded them on a truck, and sold them in Pendleton, using part of the money to help pay for Sammy's hospital bills. That summer, Red Shirt took Danny out twice a week to feed the dog. She ate the food, but whenever Danny tried to pet her she crawled under the sheepwagon and growled. At the end of summer, Sammy had another stroke and died.

After Sammy's dressing and burial, Red Shirt told Danny they had to go back out to the sheepwagon, and this time Red Shirt took a shovel and his old lever-action .30-30. It had belonged to Medicine Bird and was so used that the bluing had worn off the barrel.

When they arrived at Sammy's sheepwagon, Judy was gone. They waited there an hour and Danny searched the brush and called for her, but there was no sign. Finally, they mounted their horses and rode half a mile away from the river. Then Red Shirt tied the horses to a low juniper, and they made their way through some high silver sage until they reached a little knoll that overlooked the sheep camp.

After the sun was down, Red Shirt tugged at Danny's sleeve and pointed past the camp, upriver. Danny watched for several moments before he saw the movement in the brush. A lank coyote skulked from bush to bush, never showing its full form. It paused warily when it caught their scent from the camp, and then circled the sheepwagon a couple of time before it approached the food. When it stepped into the cleared area near the wagon, Danny was startled at the darkness of its coat and realized it was Judy. Her motions were those of a coyote as she slinked to the food, and she paused to look warily around her as she ate.

Red Shirt pulled the hammer back on the .30-30, and when the metal clicked, Judy raised her head. Danny held his breath and squeezed his eyes shut. With the crack of the rifle, Danny opened them and saw Judy leap into the air and twist. She landed on her side, raising a little puff of dust, and came to her feet, snarling and snapping at her flank. Red Shirt fired again and the dog's head whipped back and her legs went out from under her. He fired again as the dog lay quivering. "That should do it," he said.

Red Shirt handed the shovel and rifle to Danny. "I'll go get the horses while you bury Judy," he said. When he saw the boy fighting back tears, he said, "A sheepdog is a one-man dog. They're no good for any other. And when something happens to that man, they're the worst kind of dog to go mean because they're smart and not afraid of humans. If you ever saw a pack of mean dogs ripping apart a newborn calf while its mother is birthing, you'd understand."

"Did Sammy ask you to do this?" Danny said.

"No," Red Shirt said. "But he would have if he could talk."

Danny took the rifle and shovel and started down the knoll.

"Make sure that dog is dead before you put your hand close," Red Shirt called.

Danny stopped about twenty feet from Judy and turned around to see if Red Shirt was watching him, but if he was, Danny couldn't see him. He picked up a couple of stones and tossed them toward the dog, but she didn't move. Danny took several more steps, and he could see the dark wet holes in the dog's side and another in her neck. He was sure she was dead. Both eyes were shut.

With another step, he could almost prod the dog with the shovel. He took a half step and started to put down the rifle when the dog opened her marble-blue eye. Danny dropped the shovel and stared at the eye that fixed him with its vacant stare. After a few moments, he raised the rifle to his shoulder, pointed at her head, and fired. But he was too close, and the bullet blew up a small crater just beyond the head. Danny adjusted his aim and fired again, blowing away part of the dog's skull. He leaned the rifle against a wheel of the sheep-wagon and rested for a few moments, drawing deep breaths of evening air. Above him the stars were beginning to appear, and he knew Red Shirt would be coming back with the horses.

He grabbed the dog's hind legs and dragged her downriver about a hundred yards. Three bloated ticks clung to her belly. He dug the grave rapidly in the sandy earth, cursing at the loose sand that trickled back into the hole when he stepped too close. After it was deep enough, he put the toe of his boot under Judy's side and tipped her into the hole. Then he covered her well, tamping the earth down.

By the time Danny returned to the wagon, Red Shirt had tied the horses to a wagon wheel and built a fire in the cookstove. As Danny approached, he smelled bacon. Inside, Red Shirt had put the coffee can filled with bacon drippings on the stove. He was gathering up Sammy's few possessions and wrapping them in a blanket.

When the bacon grease had melted, Red Shirt picked up the coffee can with a pair of pliers and said, "Show me where you buried Judy."

Danny led him to the spot, and Red Shirt poured a little of the bacon drippings there. Then he dripped a trail of grease away from the spot and poured out the rest of the drippings about twenty-five yards from the place Judy was buried. He walked back to the grave, took a can of pepper from his pocket, then sprinkled it around the grave. "That ought to keep the coyotes away," he said.

He carried the can back to the sheepherder's wagon and set it on the stove. Then he pointed to another can. "There's something in here for you," he told Danny.

"Old grease?"

"Lift it."

Danny picked up the can and was surprised at how heavy it was. He found a spoon and scooped away some of the congealed grease. Underneath, he found thirty-seven silver dollars.

"Sam's cache," Red Shirt said. "Every old sheepherder has

some money tucked away somewhere—under a fence post, buried, in a gallon of sheepdip. None of them trust the banks. Sammy might have some gold around, too. He prospected a little up in these hills, but no one knows what he found."

Danny wiped the grease off the silver dollars with a piece of towel. He wondered how long it had taken Sammy to save the money.

"It's yours," Red Shirt said. "Sammy would want you to have it for helping with the dog."

"What did he die from?" Danny asked.

Red Shirt shrugged. "He was never the same after moving from Celilo."

Danny placed his fishing pole against the side of the sheep-wagon and set the beer can full of hoppers next to one wheel. Sammy's presence still seemed strong around the old sheep-wagon.

Danny looked at the river, the tangle of brush and debris marking the high-water line. Two springs after they had built the sweathouse, the river had flooded, carrying it away and forming a new channel. Danny tried to picture what the land along the river would look like with SUNCO holding the leases. There would be roads and buildings, maybe natural-gas wells and oil derricks. Danny just couldn't see it.

He took off his cowboy hat and wiped the sweat from his brow. Then he cupped some of the water in his hand and drank. It had a slight alkali taste, a sign the river was low. He climbed the cutbank and looked inside the old sheepwagon. A fly buzzed, its wings beating against the last unbroken pane before it found its way out. Rats and mice had carried off most of the mattress, but there were a few scraps of the stained brown cover left. Danny closed the door and sat down, leaning against the side of the wagon. He tilted his hat to shade his eyes and slept.

When he woke, he thought it was about one by the slant of

the sun. He decided to head back into town and pack his gear for Montana's Crow Fair, the last Indian rodeo and celebration of the season. He planned to fish a little on the way back to his pickup, but just for sport because he thought the fish would spoil in the heat before he could get them back.

The stopper had worked loose in the beer can, and all the grasshoppers had escaped. Danny shook the can a couple of times to be certain, but it was empty. In the heat of the day the grasshoppers were quick, and he had a difficult time trying to catch them. He decided it would be easier to wade into the river and knock them from the grass hummocks into the water. On the first hummock he caught two and fished them deep after adding another splitshot weight. He lost the first on a snag. With the second he hooked a large trout, and when it made its run he had to let out line for fear it would snap the leader. He played the fish for about five minutes, then flipped it onto the sandy shore with the toe of his canvas shoe.

The fish lay breathing on its side, its pink gills opening and closing. Danny wet his hands and held the fish lightly, carefully working the barbed hook out of its jaw. When the fish was freed, he put both hands around it gently and held it in the current, watching its gills work. Then it flicked its tail and disappeared into the murky depths.

Danny wished someone else had been there to see the fish. "Damn that Taylor," he said.

At the next hummock he saw a large grasshopper perched on some sticks in the dry grass. He waded beside the hummock and removed his hat, getting ready to flip the hopper into the water. As he slapped the grasshopper with his hat, his knee jarred the hummock and he heard the high-pitched buzz of a snake.

Danny's saliva turned to metal. He saw the coiled snake just past the sticks, one eye blinded by shedding skin, its pink tongue flicking.

Danny remained motionless, staring at the snake's darting tongue and black, expressionless eye. Then he moved his left foot backward, working it through the loose rocks at the river bottom to find solid footing for a quick pivot. He wished the snake would lower its head and slither off, but the head stayed high. For an instant he thought about trying to club it with the pole butt, but he knew the pole was too flimsy.

Danny tried to swallow the metal taste in his mouth. The sun felt very hot on his bare head, and the sunlight on the water dazzled his eyes. Then, for a moment, time seemed to stop. Three things came into focus: the hot sun, his extended arm holding the hat, and the poised snake. The snake struck, its dark, spade-shaped head closing the distance between them. Danny lunged backward, twisting on his left foot. He lost his balance and fell into the water, his knuckles scraping the slimy rocks on the river bottom as he caught himself. For an instant he thought the snake had missed. But he felt the fangs strike his right calf and the hot pain like a wasp's sting.

Danny splashed in the shallow water, becoming aware of the snake lashing its body against him like a frenzied ribbon. It was stuck to his jeans by its fangs. He struck it wildly with the cork-butt of his flypole, knocking it into the water where it writhed and twisted as the current carried it downstream.

Danny sat on the sandy shore, clenching his teeth against the searing pain. He took the knife from his pocket and slit the leg of his wet jeans until he could see the dark red holes and the angry welt around them. He thought of cutting an X over the holes, but realized he could never reach his calf with his mouth to suck out the venom.

Danny took off his belt and put it around the upper part of his thigh, looping it twice and fastening it about six inches below his groin. It was tight enough to slow the lymph but still allow circulation. He eased into the water until his calf was under, hoping the cool water would slow the movement of the poison. He figured it was over two miles back to the pickup, too far to walk in the heat. He just had to tough it out for a few hours until the sun went down.

He saw a log downstream with some branches sticking out, and he eased his way there. He hooked his arm around one of the branches and rested his head against the warm wood. If he passed out, he didn't want to drown, and if he threw up, he didn't want to choke.

He felt feverish now. The pain came in surges up his leg, and his temples pounded. He took off his shirt and wet it in the river, then tied it around his head. That made him hurt less. But he began to get stomach cramps, and his breathing became labored. He remembered that Red Shirt had told him a snakebite would never kill you if you stayed still, but it sure would make you wish you were dead.

Danny threw up. Then he threw up again. His sides heaved and he tasted the galling fluid in his nose. Danny thought the snake must have had a lot of poison in him. Since he was just finishing shedding, he probably hadn't gotten any of the venom out on a rabbit or a ground squirrel. Danny felt the nausea again and pressed his cheek against the warm wood. He took a small stick and put it between his teeth to bite on when the leg hurt too much. He closed his eyes and tried to concentrate on his ragged breathing.

When he opened his eyes, the sun had twinned and everything seemed hazy. The pain in his leg was duller, and Danny figured the poison had worked its way deep into his system. His face was flushed and he felt feverish, so he drank some water, but he threw it up at once. After that, he just splashed water onto his face and closed his eyes. When he opened them, the trees were casting long, undulating shadows on the water, and familiar objects seemed strange. Across the water on the opposite shore he saw three dark shadows, but there were no trees. Then the shadows became figures and the rise in the shoreline looked like a sweathouse. The figures went into the sweathouse, then reappeared. The sun was behind them, so he could not see their features. Then one of the taller figures poised for an instant at the water's edge and dove. He swam briskly, but the current pulled him far from the figures on the shore. The second figure stood poised, and even with the sun at his back Danny knew it was Red Shirt. He dove into the water and swam and swam, but never came closer to Danny's shore. "Father," Danny said huskily. "Grandfather."

The third figure, smaller than the others, stayed on the opposite shore. Then the shadow raised its hand and waved. Danny lifted his arm and waved very slowly at the small figure. When he lifted his other arm, he tumbled into the water.

The cold water cleared Danny's mind. He crawled onto shore and spit out the water he had swallowed. The setting sun cast rosy hues on the water. Danny looked at the opposite shore, but there was no sweathouse, no shadows. He thought about the third figure. "Jack."

He shivered in the sudden chill. A night wind came up and blew the river to a light chop. Danny stood, and found that the bad leg would bear some weight. It was puffy now, swollen against the slit jeans. Although he hurt all over, the leg was practically numb. He cut a notched limb with his caseknife and broke it off to use as a crutch. He started toward the pickup, moving slowly and stopping frequently to rest. Each step hurt, but he said "I can do fifty more," and then he counted them aloud to himself. After that, he tried for a hundred. By the time he reached the pickup, he had counted over three thousand. The sweat poured from him, and his jaws ached from clenching his teeth.

Danny's right leg was useless in the truck, so he used the left to shift and pressed the accelerator with the stick he had broken off. It took some getting used to, and the pickup lurched a lot at first. By the time he got to the hospital in Pendleton he was nauseated again.

In the emergency room, the doctor cut away the dead flesh around the puncture to prevent gangrene. Then he gave Danny a shot of antivenin. "It's a little late for this to do much good," he said. "What you need is lots of rest for that leg and some good sleep. I'll give you a sedative."

"It's all right," Danny said. "I can sleep at home. Just fix me up so I can make it to Crow Fair."

❖ 5 ❖

That year, the Indian encampment at Crow Fair was one of the largest Danny had ever seen, with Indians gathered from as far away as Warm Springs on the Deschutes and Chinle, Arizona. As Danny walked by the tepees at night, he recognized the emblems of the Osage, the Sauk, the Piute, Blackfeet, Northern Cheyenne, Crow, Arapaho, Gros Ventres, and Sioux. Some of the tepees were dark; others were illuminated with hissing Coleman lanterns, and he could see shadow figures inside dressing for the dances or sitting at tables playing cards. Some tepees had brightly painted crescents, stars, and moons. Others had clan emblems of bear, elk, badger, or owl.

Danny felt good. That afternoon he had won the saddlebronc riding with one of his best scores ever, leaning back and spurring a high-bucking albino called Buttermilk. The prize money came to over a thousand dollars, and he still had most of it left after buying a few rounds at the Range Rider. His leg hurt a little where the snake had bitten him, but it was almost healed. All he could see now were the two black marks where the fangs had struck his calf.

He stood in the center of the encampment watching a group of old men gambling around a fire. Two of the gamblers sang in high, nasal voices and passed four bones from hand to hand or exchanged them with each other. The bones were white, but two had black tips.

As their song changed pitch, the gamblers passed the bones more rapidly, trying to confuse the onlookers so they couldn't follow the movements of the black-tipped bones. When they stopped singing, the gamblers held their hands in front of them, fists clenched to conceal the bones. Throwing down money, the onlookers murmured and pointed to the fists they believed held the black-tipped bones. Some guessed correctly and were paid from the pile of money in front of the gamblers, but most lost, so the gamblers stuck their winnings into buckskin shirt pockets or leather pouches, then started another song.

Danny had seen Red Shirt hold the bones, and he knew pretty well how the gambling worked. His eyes never left the cracked brown hands of the oldest gambler, and he saw him shift the bones when the song changed pitch. He threw a ten-dollar bill into the pile, and when the singing stopped, he pointed at the old man's left hand and cried, "Hiyah— There!"

Someone handed him two ten-dollar bills from the pile and Danny bet again, winning this time too. But on the third bet, the old man's deft movement was too much for Danny, forcing him to guess, and he lost. For the next half-hour he played the game, losing some but winning more. When he was through playing, he left a twenty-dollar win in the pot, for luck. "Buy some tobacco, Grandfather," he said, and the old gambler nodded and smiled.

As Danny turned to leave, he bumped into a man with glasses and an expensive camera and tape recorder. "Hey," the man said. "You were pretty good."

"My father showed me," Danny said. "You have to watch carefully."

"I'm glad I got some pictures and this tape," the man said. "It's becoming a lost art, you know."

"I guess so," Danny said. He hadn't thought very much about it.

"Do you know what the gamblers are singing?"

"Yes," Danny said. Red Shirt had taught him that too, and it came back to him. "The gamblers' song is very old and has two parts. In the first, a witch called the Juggler casts a spell so the Indians can't tell which of his hands the bones are in. They become confused and lose their land to him. The Juggler offers to let them win it back, but they have to bet the Chief's son. Of course, it's a trick and they lose."

"So the Juggler wins?"

"Not quite. Did you notice when the song changed pitch?" The man nodded.

"The best Indian gambler, called the Dreamer, is elected to win back the land and the son. The second part of the song is his—given to him by a shaman. In order to confuse the Juggler and reverse the spell, the Dreamer must sing the song exactly right. If he doesn't, he loses his life to the Juggler."

"How does it turn out?"

"Watch," Danny said. "I'm going to get something to eat."

Danny made his way through the crowd watching the gamblers and stopped in front of the frybread stands. Nancy Quapama from Warm Springs was dropping coils of dough into a big pan filled with hissing fat. She turned the coils deftly with a smooth pine stick, and when they had browned, she put them on paper towels to cool.

Danny bought one and bit into the dark brown crust. It tasted sweet and the warm inside smelled like yeast bread. Then he heard the announcer from the dancing arena. "All you people. Let's get started with Frances Short-Face and the

Rocky Boy Chanters. All of you come join in this Greeting Dance." Danny took another bite of the frybread and headed for the arena.

"Surprise!"

It was Tenley. Danny tried to speak, but his mouth was full of bread. Tenley was wearing red pants and a red-and-white-checked Western blouse. "Hey," she said. "Are you okay? You look like you've seen a ghost."

Danny swallowed the bread. He hadn't expected to see her at Crow Fair and wondered if she had been in the grandstands when he rode that afternoon. "Here," he said, tearing off a piece of the frybread. "Try this."

Tenley took it and put it in her mouth.

Danny felt confused because he was glad to see her. He wanted to be angry at her, but he had ridden well that afternoon and the money in his pocket gave him confidence.

"Delicious," she said. "In Portland, we get things like this at the Saturday Market. They're called Elephant Ears and covered with sugar and cinnamon."

Danny shook his head. "Not like this. Real Indian frybread. Nancy has been making it for years."

"All right," she said. "If you say so. But if you're in Portland sometime, I'll treat you to an Elephant Ear and you can decide."

They walked along a few steps toward the dancing arena.

"You rode pretty well today," she said. "Of course, I could probably show you a few pointers about riding."

"Maybe so," he said. "You were a pretty good trick rider. Why did you give it up, anyway?"

Tenley laughed and shook her auburn hair. "I just kind of outgrew it, I think. Wanted to try something else. After I took a bad spill, I thought I'd see what it was like in the grandstands instead of the arena."

"That makes sense, I guess."

"What are you going to do now?"

"Watch the dancers. I saw some of them getting ready in the encampment and just thought I'd take in the dancing for a while."

"Would you like some company?"

"Where's your partner?"

"If you mean Ace," she said, "I suppose he's out trying to make a deal."

Danny laughed and it felt good. "Yeah, the Crow Reservation is a lot bigger than the Umatilla. More land, more minerals . . ."

"I just want to see the dancing," she said. "How long will it last?"

"Usually all night," Danny said. "Once those Rocky Boy Chanters get fired up, they don't want to quit."

"I left my camera at the motel," she said. "If I run and get it, can I meet you at the arena?"

"All right," Danny said. He watched her walking away, and there was something beautiful about the way she moved. Remembering the night at the Thunderbird, Danny shook his head. She had a way of making him want her, but she was in a different league.

As Danny turned to watch the dancers, he half hoped to see Loxie among them. When she had danced with her red-beaded shawl draped across her shoulders, he had loved to watch, because she was as graceful as an antelope. But the summer after Jack was born, Loxie had started modern dance lessons at the studio above the Starlite Lounge, where Madame Renée encouraged her dreams of becoming a famous dancer. When Danny learned she had used his rodeo money to pay for her lessons, they quarreled so violently that Wilson Windyboy, who lived in the trailer next to theirs, closed his doors and windows in spite of the August heat.

Danny stayed outside the arena among the spectators viewing the figures through a haze of campfire smoke. Their movements shifted with the high-pitched chants and drum throbs. Against the flickering light of campfires, he saw the kaleidoscopic pattern of feathers, bracelets, and beads. The women's nut-brown arms and legs contrasted with their tan doeskin dresses. Some of the men wore harness bells that tinkled with their movements.

Danny listened to the drums and became almost hypnotized as their beating matched his pulse. Then from the midst of dancers in the arena, the figure of a large, cloaked dancer caught Danny's attention. He had dark, almost sepia, arms and legs, and as he moved, thick muscles bulged under his glistening skin. A wolfskin cloak covered his broad shoulders, and a wolf-claw necklace adorned his throat. His features were partially hidden behind a wolf's-head mask, but Danny could see that the indistinct face was painted a dull blue, with crimson streaks along the cheekbones and under the eyes.

When directly in front of Danny, the figure nodded almost imperceptibly, and for the first time since his boyhood Danny heard the song in the drum, a song so old he had almost forgotten it.

Spellbound, he remembered the first time he had danced. His grandfather Medicine Bird had put streaks of blue paint on his face and tied a gray feather in his hair. Red Shirt had given him a pair of beaded elkskin moccasins and a doeskin shirt so soft and light it seemed made of wind. Then he had joined Medicine Bird and Red Shirt in the Circle Dance.

With a ten-year-old's pride and strength, he had danced with the older men until he fell exhausted and they carried him asleep into a tepee with a wolf emblem. In the morning, he had awakened first, lying next to his father on a gray woolen blanket. Watching the opaque light on the tepee wall, he had recalled the dance as if it were a dream, uncertain about his part until he felt the stiffness in his legs and wiped some blue paint from his face with his fingers.

Now, as Danny listened to the old song again, his heart stirred. The song and the wolf-cloaked figure compelled him into the circle of dancers. He saw the broad shoulders of the big dancer on the other side of the arena, but the man's face was obscured by the hazy smoke from the campfires. He spread his cloak and turned, motioning at Danny with an eagle-feather fan as if casting a spell. Then he moved into the clustered dancers at the center of the arena, and Danny caught only glimpses of him. But the song was with Danny, and his feet danced with the drums. Moving without effort, Danny imagined he was that young boy again, where he belonged, in the center of things with his father and grandfather.

The chant reached its highest pitch and trailed off into a ghostly hush. Carried by the echoes, Danny danced on for a moment, then stopped, suddenly conscious that he had no costume. His cowboy boots gouged the soft dirt of the arena. Most of the dancers had joined friends around the circle, and the arena was nearly empty.

Danny strained to see the wolf-cloaked dancer.

"I took your picture," he heard someone say.

Danny expected Tenley, but it was the man with glasses he had talked to after gambling.

"I got some others, too. Magnificent costumes! Wait until my classes see these!"

"Did you see the one with the wolf cloak and mask?" Danny asked. "A big man with his face painted blue?"

"No, I missed him." He seemed disappointed. "Maybe he'll dance again."

"I don't think so," Danny said. He had a strange feeling about the dancer and wished his face hadn't been hidden. He started moving through the spectators and dancers, trying to locate the figure again. When he was halfway around the circle, someone took his arm.

"Danny."

It was Pudge. She looked dressed up, wearing a dark blue

blouse over black stretch pants. But her eyes were red-rimmed and swollen and her mascara had run.

"I need to talk with you." She stood unsteadily on her high heels.

"All right."

"Not here."

They walked away from the arena, past the gamblers and to the dark area where the cars were parked. The footing became uncertain among the ruts, and Pudge took off her high heels. Suddenly she stopped and leaned close to Danny. "Hold me," she said. "Hold me tight."

Danny smelled the sweet liquor on her breath and figured Pudge had been drinking, but he was confused by her actions. Leaning against his chest, she started crying. Then she took out a white handkerchief from her purse and blew her nose. "It's my birthday," she said. "It's my birthday and I'm going to get drunk."

"Happy birthday, then, I guess." Danny was trying to figure out how old Pudge was.

"I came to find you," she said. "I had to tell you about Loxie, and I knew you'd be at Crow Fair."

Danny felt a sudden iciness in his chest. The way Pudge's voice dropped when she said Loxie's name told him the news was bad.

"She's dead," Pudge said. "My sister."

Danny slumped against the side of a car. He felt like he had been kicked in the stomach and was gasping for breath. After so many years, he still cared. Something he had loved was gone. When he caught his breath, he asked, "How?"

"She got drunk and ran head-on into a county gravel truck. Broke her neck."

Danny sat on the ground and put his head in his hands. He thought of how Loxie had looked the first time they made love, on a blanket beside the river, and the soft brown of her eyes when they brought Jack home from the hospital. "I can't believe she's dead," he said. "I even thought she might come to Crow Fair this year."

"I knew you'd be here," Pudge said. "When you weren't at the dressing, I was sure you hadn't heard about it."

"That's right," Danny said. "I'd have come."

"It was a nice dressing," she said. "Loxie was fixed up and looked real good . . . considering everything."

Danny tried to picture Loxie dead and lying in a casket, but he couldn't. He kept seeing Red Shirt lying there in new Levi's, a dark blue shirt, and his best pair of boots. The funeral director had tried to cover the large bruise on his forehead where he had smashed against the windshield.

"I drove all the way here to tell you about it," she said.

"What about Jack?"

Pudge shook her head. "That's the other thing I wanted to tell you. Then I've done my part and I'm going to get drunk, forget things for a while. Hanson treats him bad. Even at the funeral you could tell. And Jack said Hanson was sending him to an Indian boarding school called Timbler."

"That doesn't sound so good."

"Maybe you should do something. Loxie even told me she was going to run out on Hanson, but she didn't know what to do. Well, I told you and I'm leaving now."

"Do you want a ride into town?"

"No, I can still drive. Take care of yourself, Danny."

"Thanks."

Danny stood in the darkness among the parked cars. Over at the arena he could hear the high-pitched chant of the callers. He thought again of the big dancer and started running toward the hills south of the encampment.

Danny was winded by the time he reached the crest of the tallest hill overlooking the flickering campfires at Crow Fair. Behind him was Medicine Tail Coulee, and beyond that, past the hills that stretched away in the pale moonlight, was the

Little Big Horn. The markers from the battle were scattered across the dry hills, standing white and stiff in the buffalo grass.

The morning after he had danced with Red Shirt and Medicine Bird, his father had taken Danny to the place where he now stood. "This is a mystical place," his father had said. "It has power like the Wallowas, home of the Nez Perce."

"But some Nez Perce left the mountains and went to the reservation in Idaho," Danny had said.

"Only Christian Indians with dead hearts. The Dreamers stayed in their mountains. When the government sent blue-coats to make them leave, they followed Young Joseph and took up the rifle. After the fighting became too heavy, the Dreamers tried to reach Canada and the safety of Sitting Bull's camp there, but they were caught in the Bear Paws and had to surrender."

There had been a sadness and pride on his father's face that Danny saw for the first time then. Red Shirt was still wearing streaks of blue paint from the Circle Dance, and Danny imagined him as one of the Dreamer warriors who had fought with Joseph.

Red Shirt turned his broad back to the boy and stared over the battlefield. "There is still power in the land," he said. "Sitting Bull and Joseph dreamed the white man's spell would be broken and the people could return home. Even now, when there is a special need, the Dreamers' ghosts will rise from the land."

The wind winnowed his father's hair. Red Shirt put his large hands on Danny's shoulders and held him at arm's length. Danny looked into his father's eyes and saw his own image reflected in the pupils. Then Red Shirt sang an old Dreamers' song:

> The wind stirs the grasses
> And the people return to their land

I have given you my shirt
Return home in strength.

His father's words seemed to be carried across the hills by
the wind rustling the grass. Danny knew he remembered the
song for a special reason. He thought again about the dancer
at the Fair, the hidden face, and he recalled that Red Shirt
had once worn a cloak like the dancer's.

Standing in the pale moonlight, watching the night wind in
the buffalo grass, Danny shivered. He wiped his hand across
his eyes, and it gleamed wet in the moonlight. He knew the
dark figures he had seen after the snake bit him were a sign.
And so was the dancer. Now Danny realized he must go after
Jack.

❖ 6 ❖

The Wigwam Café and Motel was located just across the street from Timbler Vocational School for Indians. Some of the motel units were concrete and shaped like tepees. These were white and decorated with red fringe. Danny stopped his truck in front of the café and went in for coffee. He wanted to think about what he should say to Jack.

The waitress was pretty chipper, and Danny figured she had just come on shift. Danny ordered pie and coffee, then watched the electric sign machine on top of the stainless steel pie case. The signs were framed by a blue neon bug-killing light, and a different sign flipped over every twenty seconds. Most of the signs were for realtors or women's styling salons, but Danny's favorites said "Dwain Crumbliss Radiators" and "Classy Chassis Body Works." Below the pie case was a wooden plaque that read "Wonder Waitress Award— Wilma Tiblett." Danny noticed his waitress's name was Madge.

When the waitress came back with a coffee refill, he asked, "Where's Wilma?"

"Wilma's on nights," Madge said. "The tips are bigger at suppertime. Anything wrong with my service?"

"It's fine," Danny said. "Coffee's good, too." He smiled and took another gulp as if to prove it.

"Well, good," Madge said. "I'm glad you're not a wise guy."

"Just curious. What do you think of that school across the street?"

"Who wants to know?"

"My boy's over there." When Madge raised her eyebrows, Danny added, "His stepfather enrolled him."

"It's none of my business," she said. "But if I had a kid, which I don't, and if I was Indian, which I'm not, I still wouldn't send him there. Refill?"

"No thanks," Danny said. He finished his pie and put two dollars beside the plate. "I'd like to leave the truck while I check around."

"Whatever." She picked up the tip. "And good luck with the boy."

He walked across the street and under a stone arch with the inscription "Timbler—Established 1873—Knowledge Is Power." The school was typical of the places he'd seen while playing Indian ball for the Magpies. The administration building sat at the center of a small green. The dorms were on one side of the building and the classrooms on the other. Across the lawn were the gym and cafeteria; the machine shops, gardens, and dairy barns were out back.

Maples lined the walkway to the administration building, so the cement was slick with brown-and-yellow leaves. The building was three-story, white frame with green shutters and a black metal fire escape that came out of a second-story window. When Danny passed the porch, he saw a sign made from construction paper: ART SHOW—WORKS BY INDIAN STUDENTS.

He stepped inside the first dorm and called out, "Anybody here?" When no one answered, he called again, louder.

A girl of about sixteen stuck her head out one of the far doorways. Her hair was in curlers and she had on a pink flannel robe. "What do you think you're doing? This is the girls' dorm."

Danny took off his hat and smiled. "Sorry, I'm new around here."

"Go over to the cafeteria," she said. "The art show's over there."

"I'm trying to find my boy and sure could use some help. Came all the way from Oregon."

"Is that so? Just a minute, then." She went back into her room and came out wearing a pair of dark horn-rimmed glasses. "I'm sick this morning, not going to class. At first, I thought you might be checking up." As she walked toward him she pressed her hand against her side, as if she had a hitch.

Danny could see her cheek was swollen, and he guessed her glasses hid black eyes. Her right ear lobe was torn and scabby. Inflamed, it stuck out from the side of her head like a tab. He remembered that Loxie had always taken off her earrings before she went into the school bathroom.

"Yeah," she said. "I'm not winning any beauty contests for a while." She touched her ear lobe with her forefinger. "Sore as hell," she said, "but Waffles Yellow Bear is missing two teeth. The bitch tried to take my guy. Who you looking for?"

"Jack Kachiah," Danny said. "Maybe you know him."

"No," she said. "And I know most of the boys."

"Jack Hanson, then," Danny said. "It's probably Hanson here."

"Oh, sure. I know him. He's good looking, but kind of quiet."

Danny grinned. "The looks he gets from me. I don't know about the quiet."

"You might try the gym. It's after ten and the boys should be in P.E."

"Thanks," Danny said.

"Hey," she said. "His mother just died, didn't she?"

"That's right."

"I'm really sorry. It must be tough losing your wife like that."

Danny lowered his eyes. "I know it's hard on Jack," he said. "She and I split the sheets a long time ago."

"I saw there wasn't a ring on your finger. But then these days a lot of guys take them off, so you have to be kind of careful. Say, my older sister's coming to the art show this afternoon. Maybe you'd like to meet her."

"Thanks," Danny said. "But I might not be sticking around."

"Be a sport. She's fun. She's twenty-six and only been married once. Works as a security guard in Omaha."

"We'll see," Danny said. "Thanks for the help."

As Danny started for the gym, he knew by the way his stomach clenched that Jack was there, and he thought about how easy it had been to find him. Fourteen years before, after Loxie had taken Jack and run away, Danny had spent much of the fall looking for them.

Three weeks after Loxie left, Danny had received a postcard from her. It was a free card from a place called the Deluxe Motel, in Portland. In the picture, the motel was a dirty pink color and slightly out of focus. The card read:

Dear Danny—I miss you now and want to come back. The baby misses you too. We saw the ocean and it was beautiful. There were big rocks on the shore and some people were looking for whales. I hope the rodeo is going well. If you can send some money, the car needs work to be safe.

Take care now, Sweetie,
Loxie

Danny had five hundred dollars in his pocket from the Walla Walla rodeo when the card arrived. He kept two hundred for fees and stuffed six fifties in an envelope, folding a plain piece of paper around the money. After he had sealed it, he wrote "See you soon" on the envelope and sent it to her care of the Deluxe Motel. That night, he got some change and tried calling her from the pay phone at Melody Muffler. They were working on his truck's exhaust so he had trouble hearing, but the clerk said there were no phones in the rooms. He said he would try to get her, and then he was gone a long time. The operator had Danny put in a dollar seventy-five while the clerk was gone. When the clerk got on the line again, he said she was away, so Danny told him to have Loxie call him at that number. He went next door and bought some beer, then hung around the pay phone, watching an occasional car head out toward the freeway. She hadn't called by ten, so he left.

Danny won twelve hundred dollars and a silver belt buckle at the Klamath Stampede, with a first place overall finish among the Indian riders. By the time he was through celebrating, a week had passed since he had sent the money, and there was still no word from Loxie. He decided to look for her. Stoney Suppay, his high school assistant football and basketball coach, tried to discourage him and insisted he should leave for Eastern Oregon College right away.

"You'll be off the team if you miss practice," Stoney said.

"I won't be gone more than a week," Danny replied. "And I'm in great shape. I punished those horses at the Stampede."

"I know Coach Larson. He's a hardhead."

"He wants to win, doesn't he? He'll make a place for me."

"You got a scholarship," Stoney said. "Football and basketball. Don't blow it."

"A week," Danny said. "Tops."

When Danny got to Portland, he found the Deluxe with no trouble, but Loxie had checked out. All the clerk remembered was that she had mentioned the Apache Club, an Indian bar on Burnside. Danny hung out there for two days, looking for Loxie and buying drinks with his rodeo winnings. He told the people there he was going to Eastern Oregon on a full-ride athletic scholarship. For quarter bets, he arm-wrestled all comers and beat most of them. On the third day, he met a Klamath from the V.A. hospital who had lost a leg in Vietnam. The Klamath told him he had seen Loxie dancing at Mary's Topless on Broadway.

At Mary's, a platinum blonde named Chiffon told him Loxie used to work there but had come into a little money a week or so before and taken off for Nevada, where the money for dancing was better. She had a couple of drinks with Danny and introduced him to a Filipino girl named Princess. Princess had sometimes watched Jack in the back room to keep him from fussing while Loxie did her numbers. She was pretty sure Loxie had said Vegas. They encouraged Danny to stay around that evening. Chiffon had a specialty number where she poured lighter fluid over herself and set it on fire. Danny watched the act during both shows, amazed that she didn't get burned.

He spent two weeks in Vegas, but there was no sign of Loxie. In Reno his money ran out and he parked cars for a week, until he thought he had enough money to make it back to the reservation. He managed some good tips by telling people he would be playing basketball for the University of Nevada. Danny made it to Winnemucca, where he sold the spare tire for gas money home. He rested in Pendleton for a week, then borrowed two hundred dollars from Billy Que and went over to see the coach at Eastern Oregon.

They had revoked his scholarship when he didn't show up for football, but the coach agreed to let Danny try out for the team as a walk-on. He was too tired from all the travel, though. His wind was gone and he couldn't keep up on defense. On offense, his timing was bad and he didn't know the plays. After he had practiced for three days, the coach told him it wasn't going to work out, so he went back to the reservation.

Without sports Danny soon grew restless, and there was still no word from Loxie, so he joined the Magpies, an all-Indian basketball team, and went on tour, playing against teams from other reservations, taverns, town clubs, radio stations. Most of the Magpies were older and out of shape, so Danny often starred. In Spokane, a big Irish kid who had once played for Gonzaga undercut Danny on a lay-in and broke his ankle. Danny was still on crutches when he ran into Stoney outside the Buckhorn one day, and his old coach told him he was a "damned fool." After that, whenever Stoney saw Danny on the street, he just looked past him.

The Timbler gym reminded Danny of the places he had played with the Magpies. As he stepped into the locker room, the smell of wet towels, sweat, and analgesic balm made him feel at home. Once in Yakima he had scored thirty-two points in the second half of an Indian tournament game, and he figured that must still be some kind of record there. After the game, he had sat on the rough pine bench with its blistered paint, just staring at his hands and studying the palms and fingertips. He hadn't been able to get them to stop trembling, and he couldn't figure out how so many of his shots had gone in. The Yakima coach came by and told him he should have gone to college.

Now Danny heard the dribble of balls and the squeak of tennis shoes on the court above him. Every few seconds someone thudded to the floor. He climbed the circular metal staircase that wound up to the basketball court. A game of skins and shirts was going on, and after a few moments watching, Danny spotted Jack playing forward for the skins. He wore his hair long, nearly touching his shoulders, and he had a red bandanna around his forehead as a sweatband.

Jack was tall for fifteen, and lean but hard-muscled. He moved well without the ball, confusing his man and cutting to the basket for a pass and lay-up. When the shirts brought the ball downcourt and missed, Jack pulled the rebound off the weak side.

A tall Indian wearing gray sweat clothes and a whistle around his neck came out of a storeroom door on the far side of the gym. He nodded at Danny across the gym floor, then watched the players. The skins brought the ball upcourt and passed to Jack in the corner. He started to drive the lane, but when he was cut off by a chunky kid in hightops, he put up a jump shot that rattled the rim and dropped through. A couple of the shirts pointed in his direction and shook their heads.

The coach blew his whistle. "Ten laps. Then hit the showers."

The boys groaned and the chunky kid put up a shot that got only air. Then the boys ran laps. As Jack passed Danny, he turned his head away and ran harder.

The coach retrieved the ball from where it had rolled and walked over to Danny. "How's it going?"

"All right," Danny said. "You've got some scrappers there."

The coach shook his head. "Tough schedule this year. I wouldn't buy a season ticket yet. You here for the art show?"

"No," Danny said. "I want to see my boy, Jack Kachiah." When the coach looked puzzled, Danny said, "Jack Hanson. He's forward for the skins."

"Good player," he said. "Probably my best, now that Otter Boy is gone." The big Indian dribbled the ball a couple of times. "Kachiah," he said. "You know anything about a Kachiah that played in the Yakima Indian Tournament . . . let's see . . . about 1967?"

Danny nodded. "You're looking at him."

The big Indian grinned and stuck out his hand. "Wilson Wewa."

Danny shook it.

"I was just a kid then, but you played some game against my older brother Francis. Your set shot was uncanny."

"No one shoots that shot anymore," Danny said. "It's a quicker game now. All jump shots."

"I suppose. How many did you score that game? Fifty?"

"Maybe forty," Danny said. "It's been a long time and I don't remember exactly."

"I'll bet Francis knows exactly. He hardly scored a point, and you knocked him on his ass a couple of times blocking his shots. You want to see Jack?"

"I came all the way from Oregon."

"Saturday is usually visiting day," Wilson said. "Ruggs, the vice-principal, has all these rules. But what Jack does after he finishes P.E. isn't my concern. I'll send him up. Here." He tossed Danny the ball. "Try a couple of shots."

"These boots will scratch the floor," Danny said.

"Take them off." Wilson stood under the basket to rebound.

The leather ball felt smooth and good in Danny's hands. He took off his hat and boots. His socks were shiny and matted, and he thought he should stop at a laundromat soon and do a wash. He moved outside the twenty-foot stripe and pushed off a set shot that never reached the backboard. Wilson retrieved the ball for him. Danny moved inside the twenty-foot stripe and put up a few more. Then he got the feel of it and sank three in a row. After two more baskets, Danny moved outside the stripe and potted four out of the next five.

"That's cooking," Wilson said. He walked off the court and stopped at the top of the stairs. "I'll send Jack up." As he disappeared down the steps, he said, "Danny Kachiah. Wait until Francis hears about this."

Danny moved into the corner and tried a couple more set shots. As the ball cut the twine, he remembered the applause at Yakima when he received the tournament trophy. He shot for ten more minutes before he had the feeling that someone was watching him.

Danny put in a shot from twenty feet that spun on the rim and dropped through. The ball rolled away into the corner of the gym. "Still a little of the old touch," Danny said.

"Am I supposed to be impressed?" Jack said.

"I guess not," Danny answered, looking at the boy. "It's been a long time."

"It depends on how you figure it. You missed the funeral by about a week."

"I didn't know about it," Danny said. "Pudge came up to Crow Fair and told me two days ago, and that's the first I heard of it." He sat on the bench and began tugging on one of his boots, hoping that Jack hadn't seen how dirty his socks were. "If I knew, I'd have been there."

"So what are you here for now? The rodeo was over a month ago."

"I came to see how you were getting along," Danny said. "Pudge said things could be going a little better here."

Jack laughed and cut it short. "Since when did you care so much or bother to keep in touch?"

Danny thought about the money he had sent Jack when the rodeoing was good. How much had he sent? Not much, he decided. Maybe a couple hundred dollars in a good summer.

The boy continued, "And what about the way Hanson treated her? Who cared about that?"

"Look," Danny said. "There's a lot of blood under the bridge. Let's not spill more."

"Easy to say," Jack said. "You weren't even at the funeral."

Danny pulled on his other boot and stood. Although Jack was tall, with his boots on Danny was a good deal taller. "I told you about that already." He had known it wasn't going to be easy when he came, but he was determined to stick it through. He thought he understood Jack's bitterness. Now, he waited for the boy's next move.

"So you came to see me," Jack said. "And the coach told me I should come up and talk with you. So long." He turned and went down the steps into the locker room.

Danny retrieved the ball from the corner of the gym and turned off the lights. Then he went down the steps after Jack.

The rest of the boys had showered and were gone. Danny saw Jack's gym clothes on the bench and heard a single shower running. He knew Jack was thinking, and he didn't want to push him too hard. It was like getting to know a horse after wintering—a little at a time.

Wilson Wewa came out of the office that said "Coach" on the door. He was wearing a navy blue windbreaker with "Timbler Tech Tigers" on the back. "I'm going over to get some lunch," he told Danny. "You can eat too if you buy a ticket. Just close the door when you leave."

"Fine," Danny said. "Thanks."

When Jack came out of the shower, he had a towel tied around his waist. He was wiping his face with another towel, and Danny wondered if he had been crying.

"I see you're still here," Jack said.

"I hear there's a pretty good art show this afternoon," Danny said. "Maybe I'll stick around." He pretended to study the trophies on the shelf so Jack could dress unobserved.

"Suit yourself," Jack said. "Most of it is pretty dumb. There'll be at least five bad copies of 'The End of the Trail.' "

"I saw one at the restaurant across the street," Danny said. "What did you put in the show?"

"A bad hand-tooled wallet. I could have done some bead-work. She showed me how. But I wouldn't want these people to have it."

"That makes sense, I guess."

Jack combed his hair in front of the mirror. "Its about time for lunch," he said. "I want to eat."

"We could try some lunch in town. Or the food's not bad across the street."

"We get off every other Saturday," Jack said. "That's the rule. Otherwise, I eat in the cafeteria."

"It seems like this place has lots of rules," Danny said.

"Maybe so," Jack said. "But you get used to it."

They left the gym and Danny checked the door to make sure it was closed. Jack started for the cafeteria but stopped after a few steps when he realized Danny was staying with him. "Aren't you going to eat in town?" Jack asked. "The food here stinks."

"With the show today, it'll be a little better," Danny said. "The judges have to eat too."

Jack stood silently for a moment, visibly confused. "I have to get something in my room," he said.

Danny followed him into the boys' dormitory and up to the empty second floor. "Everyone's at lunch," Jack said.

His room was small, about ten by twelve, with a bunk bed, two desks, and an old four-drawer pine dresser with three missing knobs. Danny noticed that only one of the bunks had bedding.

"You stay by yourself?" He poked at the stained mattress on the upper bunk.

"Yeah. Now that Otter Boy is gone."

"The coach mentioned him," Danny said. "He seemed sorry to lose him. Did he transfer?"

Jack sat on the bottom bed and ran his fingers through his hair. "You could say that. He wasn't too happy here." Jack stood.

"What about you?"

Jack shrugged. "That's another story," he said. He opened his closet door and took out a shiny blue suitcoat and a thin, short-sleeved white shirt. "I forgot we were supposed to dress up today on account of the show," Jack said. He clipped on a red tie the color of a tongue. "Dress dinners on Wednesdays and Sundays and special occasions. How do I look?"

"Pretty silly, if you want the truth," Danny said. "Why don't you put on some clothes you can be comfortable in and we'll have lunch across the street." As Jack started to think it over, Danny added, "I'm buying and they make good desserts."

Jack took off the tie and tossed it on the pine dresser. He stared out the window for a while, and without turning to look at Danny said quietly, "You didn't come all the way here to go to lunch with me."

"No," Danny said. He wanted to tell Jack how he felt, and about the figures he had seen after he had been bitten by the snake. And he wanted to describe Crow Fair, when he had thought of the dancing with Red Shirt and Medicine Bird, and how the large wolf-cloaked figure had beckoned to him. But he didn't think he could tell it right, so he decided to tell Jack later. "No," he said again. "I came to take you back to Pendleton."

When Jack spoke again, his voice cracked. "She's buried not far from here."

"That's not her," Danny said. "That's just something they put in the ground. She's gone from here, and you should be too."

Jack was still at the window and Danny knew he was fighting back tears. He wanted to touch Jack, put his arm on the boy's shoulder, but he didn't want to spook him.

Jack turned from the window and looked at Danny. "So what am I supposed to get out of this?"

The question caught Danny off guard. After a moment, he said, "No special deals." Then he remembered Henry's horse Cayenne. "There's a good horse you can take care of. Belongs

to a friend of mine who's . . . away for a while. Take care of
that horse right and we might see about your own. Of course
your Aunt Pudge is there and she wouldn't mind a visit."

"I don't want to let the team down."

"The coach said it was going to be a bad season anyway,"
Danny said. "Pendleton has good teams. If you practice hard,
you can probably play."

"You used to be pretty good," Jack said. "She showed me
some clippings one time."

"Maybe I can teach you a couple of things," Danny said.
"I'm not too rusty." Then he decided to press Jack just a little.
"You got a suitcase to put your gear in?"

"I guess I wouldn't mind seeing the Round-Up," Jack said.

"If it works out, I can probably get you a job there, tending
stock."

Jack took a battered suitcase from the back of his closet. Its
handle was missing and it had a peeling travel sticker that
said "Reno." "If I leave," he said, "I can't come back."

Danny knew it was true. "You won't want to," he said. "It's
not any good here and it will be better there."

"How can I know that?"

Danny tapped his heart with his fist. "In here," he said.
"The way you feel. Remember too, sometimes you have to
take a chance."

Jack opened his suitcase and put in the suitcoat and tie. He
took off the white shirt and put on a faded blue Western shirt
from his top drawer. Then he dumped the remaining contents of the drawer into the suitcase. He did the same with
the second drawer. Danny noticed a faded red bandanna and
wondered if it was the one he had given Jack the summer
Jack rode the tractor at Bender's farm.

Jack took three pair of jeans out of the closet, and a pair of
good brown pants. Danny counted four shirts. When Jack
had put his good shoes in the suitcase, he took a rope from the

bottom of the closet and looped it around the suitcase.
"That's about it," he said.

"You travel light."

"Hanson's not one to buy me a lot of stuff," Jack said. He
pulled some old cowboy boots out of the closet and put them
in a paper sack.

Danny checked under the bed. "There's some newer boots
here," he said.

"Leave them. They were Otter Boy's."

"They look like good boots," Danny said. "Maybe he'll
come get them." He picked up the suitcase and the sack.
"Get your coat," he said. "It's a long way and we should get
started."

Jack took a Timbler windbreaker out of the closet. "Hanson's place isn't far from here. Maybe three hours. There's
some gear there I'd like to get. A rifle, some fishing stuff,
pictures of Mom, and a buckskin shirt she made for me."

"What about him?" Danny wasn't anxious to see the boy's
stepfather.

"There shouldn't be any trouble," Jack said. "Hanson's usually out burning stubble this time of year. And after he's
cleaned up he stays in town late, drinking."

"All right," Danny said.

They left the room and walked out onto the school
grounds. Danny could see his pickup across the street and it
gave him a good feeling to think they would be on the road
soon.

"Maybe I should stop by the cafeteria a minute," Jack said.
"Say goodbye to the coach and a couple other guys."

"Fine," Danny said. "I'll wait right here." He put the suitcase down. The early September sun felt warm and seemed
to tighten the jacket across his shoulders. He took a deep
breath and thought of Red Shirt. After a few minutes, Jack
came out of the cafeteria and started walking quickly toward
him. Danny smiled and picked up the suitcase.

* * *

The land had been planted in soybeans, corn, and wheat, but now that the harvest was over the land stretched flat and gray to the horizon, where it met the sullen sky. Dry cornstalks littered some of the fields, and others were blackened where the wheat stubble had been burned. They passed one field as two men in striped caps and coveralls were lighting the stubble with a long propane burner on a trapwagon.

Every mile, a straight gravel road intersected the one they were traveling. At these crossroads, gray or brown two-story houses rose out of the stark landscape. Behind the houses were the chicken coops and barns, as well as the metal silos.

"You can measure the wealth by the silos," Jack said. "Three is okay. Four or more is pretty good."

Danny nodded. "The land's all the same," he said. "It seems like we already passed that place."

"We're almost to Hanson's," Jack said. "It'll just take a few minutes. I don't want to lose that buckskin shirt she made for me."

Danny thought of the beaded elkskin moccasins Red Shirt had given him, but figured that she had sold those a long time ago. "Is there a dog?"

"What? No," Jack said. "There was a German shepherd, but he got run over. Hanson probably won't be around. Slow down. There it is."

Danny stopped beside a black mailbox with an American flag and turned up the dirt driveway. The dark gray house sat back from the road. To the right, a cyclone fence separated the weedy yard from the first blackened wheatfield. In back were a barn and three silos. They got out of the truck.

A Case tractor was pulled up on the lawn. Hanson's car sat in front of the house with its hood up. The battery was attached to a Quik-Charg.

"He probably came home drunk and left the lights on," Jack said.

Hanson came to the door wearing only bib overalls and clodhoppers. Bits of singed wheat stubble clung to his overalls and flecked his thin brown hair. Danny was surprised he was so large and rawboned, with wide shoulders and long arms. His thick wrists were sunburned and chafed from being outside, and his hands were crooked and lumpy, the way hands get from working with machinery.

Hanson's flat-gray eyes, expressionless as the landscape, moved from Jack to Danny. The eyes were red-rimmed and puffy, and Danny thought he might have been drinking or crying, but more likely his eyes were red from the burning.

"If you got kicked out of that school, there'll be big trouble," Hanson said. "You belong there, now that harvest is done."

"I just wanted to get my things," Jack said. "Then I'll clear out."

Hanson's lower jaw worked a couple of times and he toed the doorjamb with one of his clodhoppers. "This your old man? Got to be. It figures he'd come around scavenging. She didn't have much. The house, land, machinery—all of it's mine."

"Nobody wants anything," Danny said. "He's just getting his stuff."

Jack slipped under Hanson's arm and disappeared into the house.

Hanson shifted his body, blocking the doorway. "So you finally came? Damn funny people. Waited for the rodeos to end and never bothered with her funeral. Now he wants to go right back to the reservation. That doesn't seem odd to you, I suppose." Hanson's gaze drifted past Danny. "Kind of cloudy. Could be some rain coming, don't you think?"

Danny said nothing but kept his eyes on Hanson. The way he talked made Danny's stomach cramp. He had seen men just as expressionless before they swung a club or pulled a trigger. Buddy Little Moon had been like that the night he suckerpunched G. D. Whitney, slashing his eye with a razor he clenched between his knuckles.

"What was it all for, I wonder?" Hanson said. "Putting up with her kid. Watching her run into town and shake her tail. Of course, she was a looker at first—more like a Hawaiian than an Indian. But then she crawled into the bottle. When I think of those nights I had to lock her in the storeroom, screaming with the crazies." Hanson shuddered.

Danny started to say something but choked on the words. He wanted to think of the good times with Loxie, but Hanson's words clouded his mind.

Jack appeared behind Hanson, his arms loaded. "I got my stuff."

"Let's go, then."

Hanson stepped onto the porch and turned sideways as if to let Jack pass, but as the boy started through the doorway, Hanson twisted suddenly and slapped him across the face with his large right hand, knocking the boy down and scattering his gear.

Danny glanced at Jack, then stiffened as Hanson lunged, and even though he had braced himself, Hanson's raw power knocked him backward off the porch, and he sprawled in the grass.

Hanson leaped down the steps, kicking at Danny's head with his clodhoppers, and Danny rolled away, taking the kicks high in his ribs. He scrambled on all fours, then came to his feet as Hanson lunged again. Danny sidestepped, flicking a quick left jab over Hanson's arms that split his lip.

Hanson wiped his mouth with the back of his hand and looked surprised at the smear of blood on his knuckles. Then he moved toward Danny again, crouched like a wrestler, low and dangerous.

"Let's drop it," Danny said, backing away. "Jack, get in the truck."

When Danny saw the knife flick toward him, his cheeks felt

hot. He thought of the rifle behind the seat of the pickup, but
he didn't have time to get it.

Still expressionless, Hanson shuffled closer, making short
jabs with the knife. Danny gave ground until he felt the
pickup behind him. He thought of rolling under it, but the
keys were in it and Hanson might run over him. He put his
hand on the hood and started moving toward the front of the
truck, hoping to get around it before Hanson trapped him.
Then he felt the radio antenna.

Danny snapped it off, and in a clean motion slashed the
metal antenna against Hanson's face, laying open the white
cheekbone just below Hanson's left eye. Hanson cried in pain
as a crimson line formed over the white, and he lifted his
knife hand to protect his face. Danny whipped the antenna
twice against the thick wrist. When Hanson dropped the
knife, Danny kicked it under the truck. Moving into the
swing, he punched Hanson in the gut, feeling the shock in his
fist and forearm. The man gasped, lowering his arms, and
Danny ducked his shoulder, then gave him a forearm shiver
to the jaw. He heard it snap as Hanson's head went back.
Danny grabbed the straps of Hanson's overalls so he couldn't
fall, then hit him again and again with chopping rights until
he saw Hanson's eyes roll and he felt the big man slump.
Danny saw his own bloody knuckles, and when he tried to
swing again, he couldn't move his arm. Turning his head,
Danny saw that Jack was clutching his arm with both hands,
the boy's fingernails digging into his forearm.

"Enough." Jack choked as he said it.

Danny stared at Jack's bloody nose and the angry welt
across his cheek. He let go of the overall straps and Hanson
sank flabbily to the ground. He breathed raggedly, and with
each breath a little rattle came from his throat.

"Let's go," Danny said and started for the truck, but Jack
held back.

"What about him? We can't leave him here."

"All right, then," Danny said, figuring the boy wouldn't leave until he did something. "Let's take him inside." He grabbed Hanson under the shoulders and dragged him toward the house. He needed Jack's help to get him up the steps and into the front room. Danny propped Hanson against the couch, tilting his head so he wouldn't choke if he vomited. He doubted the big Swede would have done as much for him.

The house smelled like liquor and wet wool and kerosene. Danny looked at the worn furniture and shook his head. Whatever money Hanson made, he must have put back into the farm. Loxie hadn't gotten much, Danny decided. Something seemed missing in the house, too, but he couldn't place it. "Are you ready, then?" he asked Jack.

Danny drove to the nearest town, flinching from the pain in his hand whenever he tried to grip the wheel too tightly. He stopped at a drugstore to buy some salve and an Ace bandage to wrap his ribs. He sent Jack across the street to get hamburgers and drinks at the Tastee Freeze.

At the edge of town there was a little park, so Danny stopped and they ate the hamburgers on a pine picnic table chained to a tree. When they had finished eating, Danny took off his shirt and had Jack help him bandage the ribs. After that, he was able to breathe better.

"I called a neighbor lady," Jack said as Danny was snapping his shirt back on.

"That was dumb," Danny said. "He'll be fine in a couple of days. Of course, that jaw will take a while."

"I owed him that much," Jack said. "He was okay a few times when he took me fishing." Jack dumped the ice from his Coke into a handkerchief and pressed it against the bruise on his face.

"What if she calls the police?"

"She won't. Mom went over there a couple of times after

he beat her up. She had to wear dark glasses and everything. The lady will take care of him but figure he had it coming."

"We better stick to the backroads a while, just in case."

They climbed into the truck and Danny drove in silence to the next town. He was feeling pretty tired so he had Jack go into a restaurant and buy a couple cups of coffee. As they drove out of town, he asked, "What's the name of this place?"

"Surprise," Jack said.

"Funny name for a town, isn't it?"

The boy stared out the window. "They were on our basketball schedule," he said. "They beat us bad last year, but we might have won this year—until Otter Boy left."

"What happened to him?"

"Otter Boy," Jack almost whispered. His face was pressed against the side window and he was breathing so hard he had fogged it up. "He killed himself."

Danny didn't say anything.

"He was too far from his people," Jack said. "And it made him wild. Otter Boy said Ruggs's motto was 'Kill the Indian and save the man.'"

"I'm sorry," Danny said. "Did he hang himself?"

"No, it wasn't like that," Jack said. "He broke into a store and they caught him stealing a case of beer. Ruggs forced him to work evenings and weekends there to make up for it, and the town kids came by and shamed him. Then Ruggs threw him off the team—said it was good discipline—because Otter Boy lived for sports. One night he went crazy in the store and swallowed a whole can of Drāno. He washed it down with beer."

"Jesus Christ!"

"Somehow, he made it back here. When he came into the room, he was all doubled over. He tried to talk, but his lips were half gone and nothing came out but some frothy blood and green flakes. I started screaming and he crawled off to the bathroom to drink water. I went after him, but when I got there he was out cold, with foam and steam coming from his mouth." Jack started sobbing.

Danny pulled the pickup over to the side of the road. Jack opened the door and threw up onto the ground. Danny reached across the seat and put his hand on the boy's shoulder. "It's all right," he said. "Get it out."

Jack heaved again. After a few minutes he quit sobbing. Then he wiped his shirtsleeve across his mouth. "I got it out," he said. He closed the door.

"Maybe you should get some sleep," Danny said. "I'm going to drive a while longer." He reached behind the seat and felt around for the wool coat. After he found it, he handed the coat to Jack. "Cover up with this."

Jack put the coat around his shoulders, but he was still shivering, so Danny turned up the heat. "It wasn't such a hot school," Jack said.

Danny pulled onto the road and tried to take a sip of his coffee, but he couldn't swallow it and spit it back into the cup. He watched the steam rise from the cup for a minute, then rolled down the window and threw it out.

He drove west. It had become dark outside, but for a while there was a thin line of light gray where the land met the sky. Then it was gone. Jack was breathing heavily, and Danny knew he was asleep. Danny thought he could drive a few more hours before he became too tired. He had a lot to think about.

So Otter Boy and Loxie had both died this fall. Danny remembered how Loxie had left in late summer fourteen years before, and suddenly he knew what had been missing at Hanson's. The house didn't smell like Loxie. It had been good with her at first, and she smelled like the flowers along the river in spring, sweet and fresh. He remembered her smell lingering after she had left the trailer where they lived.

He had been out getting firewood and had come back with a pickup load of tamarack and alder. His axe, splitting mall, and chain saw were loaded on top of the wood. At first he wondered why the car was gone, but after he stepped inside he knew. When he looked through the rooms, he saw she had taken everything that mattered to her, anything that might be sold, and Jack. She had left a couple of old wigs and some dirty clothes crumpled on the bathroom floor, behind the door. Her dresser wouldn't fit in the car, but she had dragged it as far as the front room. Her perfume had spilled on it, so it smelled like her.

Danny dragged the dresser outside, took the axe from the back of the pickup, and smashed it time and again against the dresser, breaking the frame, the doors, the back. He threw her wigs and clothes on top of it, then unscrewed the gas cap on the chain saw, emptying the mixture of gas and oil over the broken dresser and clothes. He lit it. After it was burning, he opened all the windows in the trailer and left for town. He sold the wood and went on a drunk. A week later, he came back to the trailer. The curtains were flapping in the stiff wind and the rain had come in. It smelled damp and clean; no trace of her lingered. He threw his bedroll into a corner of the front room and slept.

◆ 7 ◆

After he thought he had driven far enough, Danny pulled the pickup over to the side of the road just past a bridge that crossed a fast-moving stream. He was tired but glad Jack had slept most of the night. In sleep, Jack's face had relaxed and he had cried out only once. When Danny shut off the engine, Jack woke up.

"Where are we?" Jack asked.

"Western Nebraska."

"I don't think I've been here before. Why did you stop?"

"Wash up a little."

Danny got out of the truck and walked carefully down the cutbank to the stream. The water was high and roily with rain from the Black Hills. He crouched down, but the water was too dark and swift for him to see his reflection. He held his hands in front of him for a moment. The right hand was purple and swollen like a rotten plum. Deep cuts slashed the knuckles and something inside grated when he tried to flex it.

He scooped some water with his good hand, the left one,

and splashed it onto his face and the back of his neck. Then he plunged the swollen hand into the water and felt it numb in the cold current. He thought of Red Shirt and the way he had looked—dead in the front seat of the pickup, his hands frozen to the steering wheel. Danny crouched for a long time, letting the water sweep by his numb hand, clearing the pain from his mind.

He heard pebbles clatter down the cutbank and turned to see Jack awkwardly making his way to the stream. He knelt beside Danny and plunged both hands into the cold water, then splashed his face vigorously.

"Damn," Jack said. "The water is sure cold."

Danny nodded and pulled a soiled blue bandanna from his back pocket. He soaked the bandanna in the cold water and carefully made a kind of bandage for the swollen hand. With his good hand he pulled up some plants along the stream bank. He crushed their roots and spread the paste on the cuts across his knuckles. Then he finished wrapping the hand. "Plantain takes the infection away. Red Shirt showed me."

"When she talked about him, she called him Forrest."

"He had two names," Danny said. "Forrest was his child-hood name. But after he came back from the war he was sick and his luck was bad, so the old men performed the name ceremony. They called him Red Shirt because he was a war-rior, and they sent his old clothes down the river in a bun-dle."

"At Timbler, some of the kids made fun of the name cere-mony. Do you think it brings good luck?"

"For some, maybe," Danny said, remembering his father's troubles.

Jack picked up a smooth rock and threw it downstream.

"We should get going," Danny said.

Jack threw another rock, farther than the first. "Last spring I played baseball. You want to try it?"

Danny took a rock, held it in his right hand for a moment,

then tossed it down. It was the wrong shape, and he couldn't
grip it because of the bandage. He didn't want to throw more
than once because the hand hurt like hell. He chose another
rock and threw it hard and high, so it arced to a splash
beyond the boy's second throw. "Center field to home plate
—no bounce. Caught a few runners by surprise back then."

"Big deal."

"Let's go."

They walked up the cutbank to the pickup. Danny started
it, reaching across the steering wheel with his left hand, and
shifted into gear.

"How much farther?"

"I don't know," Danny said. "Still a long way."

The early morning sun bothered Danny's eyes. They stung
and burned from lack of sleep, but he kept the speedometer
steady at fifty. He didn't want to attract attention by going
too fast.

Danny drove west until the sun was well above the truck's
windshield. Ahead, he saw some deserted buildings off the
road. A sign above the gate read HISTORICAL FORT ROBIN-
SON MUSEUM.

Danny stopped the truck so they could read the marker
explaining how the fort had been established to protect the
Black Hills settlers.

"It doesn't tell everything," Danny said. "The bluecoats
took the Sioux and Cheyenne from the Black Hills and jailed
them. Some of the young Indians joined the bluecoats as
scouts and policemen. That made Crazy Horse sick. After
they brought him in, a soldier stabbed him with his bayonet
. . . They said he was trying to escape. He died that night,
only a month before Joseph and the Dreamers surrendered
in the Bear Paws."

"Did they bring the Nez Perce here?"

"No. The government shipped them to Kansas. Before Joseph and the others put down their rifles, General Miles

promised they could return to the Wallowas. He broke his word, but your great-great-grandfather Left Hand and some of the other Dreamers snuck back anyway."

"How do you know so much about it?"

"Red Shirt told me."

He drove slowly through the grounds, looking at the stables, the barracks, the camp commander's house. One of the stables had been converted into a summer theater, and the commander's house served as a museum. The rows of officers' houses were clumped in the distance under a stand of cottonwoods.

"It's spooky, isn't it?" said Jack. "No one around."

"Too late for tourists. Not many people come through after summer."

"I'd like to stretch my legs."

"All right." Danny stopped the pickup in front of the row of officers' houses and they got out. Danny sat down and rested against a large tree. Although his hand throbbed with each pulse, he dozed. When he woke up, Jack was standing over him.

"They've got a basket around back, and I saw an old basketball behind the seat. I'd like to shoot some hoop."

"Go ahead." Danny went over to the truck, flipped the seat forward, and took out the ball. It was shiny and smooth from years of play on hard ground. He dribbled it a couple of times with his left hand, then tossed it to the boy.

Jack examined the ball, running his lean brown fingers over the smooth surface. "Where did you get this old ball?"

"Portland."

"Is this the ball you got at the state tournament when Pendleton played Grant?"

"That's right."

"How many did you score that game?"

"Twenty-six."

"Pretty good. But that was a long time ago. Want to try it now?" Jack's tone seemed flat, but there was a challenge in it.

Danny squinted at him. "Right now?"

"Why not?"

After they walked around the buildings to the back of the officers' houses, Danny saw the basket nailed on a board attached to one of the cottonwoods. "I'm used to a better court," he said. He took the ball, bounced it with his left hand, then rested it on top of his bandaged hand and pushed off a shot. It fell short.

"Weak." Jack laughed. He grabbed at the ball and shot a short jump shot that dropped through the iron. "One-on-one or ten or twenty-one?"

"Your choice."

"To ten," he said. "First outs." He dribbled quickly to his left, hesitated when Danny cut off the driving lane, then popped in a short jump shot. "You're slow," he said. "I can make that jumper all day."

Danny took the ball, dribbled with his left hand, stopped, faked, and pushed off a set shot. It caromed off the backboard and dropped through. He smiled.

"That's your luck for the day," Jack said.

"Don't count on it. The old hoopsnake is just warming up."

Jack took a deep breath, faked left, then drove right for a lay-up, beating Danny by a full step. "No prisoners," Jack said, handing him the ball.

Danny tried the set shot again and missed, but Jack brushed his arm after he released the ball. "Foul."

Jack shook his head. "No harm, no foul." He tried the fake and jump shot, but this time Danny read Jack's eyes and blocked it cleanly with his left hand. "Not too slow, I guess," Danny said.

Jack alternated his jump shot with an occasional driving lay-up, elbowing Danny away on his drives. Danny countered by backing in to put up some soft left-handed hooks, but he was getting tired. Finally, he called time. "Seven to seven, and I'm only using one hand."

"You don't need two hands," Jack said. "The way you keep bumping me around with your butt, I should be camped at the foul line."

"It's hardball," Danny said. "You keep elbowing me and pushing off."

"Tough." Jack cast off a couple long shots, then sat beside Danny and chewed a blade of grass. He tried palming the ball, but it slipped away. "What happened in that Portland game, anyway?"

"We lost—three points short of a state championship."

"Mom said that you guys threw the game, that the white guys paid you off. Hanson always laughed when she said it."

"That wasn't how it was," Danny said. He was angry she had lied to Jack about it. Maybe she had lied a lot more about him. "All of the referees were from Portland. Four of our starters sat on the bench with five fouls in the last quarter. I was the only one still playing."

"That's not how she told it."

"Look," Danny said. "If I threw the game, would I keep the tournament ball all these years?"

Jack didn't answer at once. Finally he said, "Probably not."

"Okay," Danny said. "I'm ready."

Jack quickly scored twice, but then Danny tightened his defense and kept him away from the basket. Jack forced a shot and Danny took the rebound. When Jack tried to slap the ball away, he hacked Danny's forearm. "Who's slow now?" Danny said. His shot was short but he regained possession after the boy dribbled the ball off his foot. Jack cursed under his breath.

Danny was moving toward the basket when he felt someone was watching them. He started to turn to look behind him, but he didn't. Instead, he drove and put in a reverse lay-up as Jack slammed against his side, jarring the bruised ribs. The ball dropped through. "Foul and basket."

"Lucky," Jack said.

When Danny went back on defense, he could see the gray-uniformed policeman standing beside one of the houses, his figure almost obscured by the cottonwoods' shadows.

As Jack dribbled toward him, Danny said quietly, "Don't look behind you, but a policeman is watching us." He saw fear flash across Jack's eyes and sensed him stiffen, as though he were about to bolt. "Just go on playing like he's not around."

Jack reversed his dribble and put up a short shot. Danny grabbed the rebound and brought it back. He dribbled slowly so he could talk. "He's probably just checking for vandals."

"I won't go back," Jack whispered.

"You won't have to," Danny said, and hoped it was true.

"What if he knows something?"

"It's not likely." Danny stopped his dribble and put up a set shot that clattered against the backboard and fell through. "Nine to eight."

Jack was too tense, so Danny eased his guard a little and the boy slipped past him for a lay-up. He looked good twisting through the air and placing the ball softly against the wooden board.

"Nice shot, hoopsnake," Danny said.

Jack slowly smiled.

As Danny walked the ball back, he saw that the policeman was no longer watching them. "One point to go," Danny said. "I'm going to take you to the hoop." He started a hard drive and the boy stepped back, waiting for him to go all the way. Danny stopped short and pushed off an easy set shot that finished the game.

Jack protested. "You said you were going to the hoop."

"An old man has to do something to get a fair advantage," Danny said, handing him the ball.

"Do you think he's still there?"

"Probably," Danny said. "We better see what it's about."

They walked in silence from the court to the front of the officers' houses. The Nebraska state patrolman got out of his tan-and-black cruiser and approached them. Danny saw a thin mustache on his lip.

"You Danny Kachiah?" the policeman asked.

"That's right, and this is my son."

"I saw your name on the registration," the policeman said. "Hope you don't mind my looking."

"Fine," Danny said.

"When I saw the out-of-state plates, I figured I better take a look. It's a little late for tourists."

"We're not tourists," Danny said.

"Ahh . . . I knew you were Indians. Sioux or Cheyenne?"

"Nez Perce."

"Oh. A little far from home, then."

"Passing through."

"Well, enjoy the country." The policeman looked at the boy. "What's your name, son?"

Danny held his breath, but Jack's eyes were steady.

"Jack—Jack Kachiah."

"Well, Jack, I was wondering why you weren't in school."

"Just getting a late start. We've been visiting relatives."

"Nothing like playing hooky, is there? Where you headed?"

"Pendleton," Jack said.

The policeman nodded. "I had a great time at the Round-Up once. Cimiyotti's still in business?"

Jack seemed confused and Danny answered, "Best steaks in town."

The policeman studied him. "How about that hand?"

"Careless. Some engine trouble, and I left it running when

I checked under the hood. Whacked my hand with the fan blade."

"Better be more careful," the policeman said. "How did your face get like that?" he asked Jack.

Jack touched his cheek. "Riding horses yesterday—caught a branch."

"Some bruise. Let's see the ball." When Jack handed it to him, the policeman turned it over and over in his hands, feeling the smooth leather. "Who won?"

"My dad," Jack said. "But he was just lucky."

The policeman smiled. "Well, I saw you make a couple of good moves. You'll beat him yet."

"Sure."

The policeman handed Danny the ball. Then he said, "This is a good one. You can still play a lot of games with this." He looked up and down the empty road. "Everything's okay, then?"

"No trouble here," Danny said.

"Everything's fine," Jack said.

"That's the way I figure it," the policeman said. "But you two might want to head down to I-80 where there's more traffic."

"We'll do that," Danny said.

The policeman climbed into his tan-and-black cruiser and left.

"Some luck," Jack said. "Why did he do that?"

"I don't know." Danny handed him the ball. "Caught a branch, huh? Your mother was a quick thinker."

"She never raised a dummy."

"No, I guess not." Danny smiled and put his good hand on his son's shoulder. "Jack Kachiah."

After they left Fort Robinson, Jack turned on the radio. It buzzed but he couldn't find a station. "Damn thing."

"Radio works good," Danny said. "But it won't pick up anything out here without the antenna."

"The new pickups have an antenna in the windshield so you can't bust them off. Hanson had a pickup like that, but he rolled it."

Danny laughed. "Some driver. How do you roll a pickup in Nebraska, with all that flat land?"

Jack shrugged. "I didn't like having his name—or going to that school. You took a long time coming to get me."

"I should have come sooner," Danny said. He figured things went sour way before Loxie's death, but he'd never gotten around to checking.

Jack stared out the window.

After an hour, Danny stopped for groceries at a little store. Inside was a sign reading GOLD MINE FOR SALE: THIS PLACE. When he carried the groceries back to the truck, Danny said, "Why don't you fix us some sandwiches while I drive? I like my peanut butter with cheese."

"You sure?"

"Red Shirt called them 'elk hunt specials.' "

Jack took the bread, peanut butter, and cheese out of the sack. He put the bread beside him on the seat and spread the thick peanut butter over it with his pocketknife. Then he cut wedges of cheese and folded the bread and peanut butter around them. "You can eat these," he said. "I'm having bologna."

When he had finished his sandwich, Jack turned on the radio but got nothing except static. He switched the radio off, then put his head against the back of the seat and closed his eyes. After Danny thought Jack was asleep, he tried the radio. It would be good to have some music. But he couldn't get a station either so he drove along in silence.

"Tell me about elk camp."

Danny started. "I thought you were asleep."

"Resting my eyes. She showed me some pictures of you and Red Shirt up in the mountains."

"That was a long time back."

"She said you brought bad luck."

Danny stared out the window. He didn't think Loxie should have told Jack about things before he could understand them. "I'll tell you what happened," Danny said. He thought a while before he told the story, because he wanted to get the words right.

"I was fifteen, your age, when Red Shirt took me hunting in the Wallowa Mountains across the Snake River from the Seven Devils. It was bitter weather, and there were wolves, not many, but some, and the night howling made me afraid. I slept between Red Shirt and the fire. One morning when I got up there were tracks around camp. I thought about shooting the wolf—you know, making a wolfskin rug—but Red Shirt warned me to leave him alone."

"Some Nez Perce believe the wolf is sacred," Jack said.

"You're right," Danny said, surprised Jack remembered. "Red Shirt took me out to a high point that overlooked a saddle between two long draws. Both draws had tall firs that thinned out in places where bitterbrush grew. Red Shirt told me to watch for elk moving across the saddle, since he would be walking up the draws. I still remember how cold it was as we stood there. The snow froze in my nostrils and eyelashes."

"I know the next part," Jack said. "Before he drove the elk, Red Shirt built a fire. She said you always build a fire on an elk stand."

"Hey," Danny said, "maybe you should tell the story." But he was pleased Loxie had remembered some of the things he'd told her.

"No. You go ahead."

"Okay, you're right. Red Shirt built a warming fire in a pine stump and told me to keep my eyes open."

"I never understood why the fire doesn't scare away the elk," Jack interrupted.

"I don't know," Danny said. "For some reason, it doesn't bother them. Anyway, I stood there a long time, and when I got hungry, I ate the sandwiches—elk hunt specials, just like these. In the afternoon, it snowed so hard I seemed to be staring through a gray-white curtain. My feet got cold and I hopped around some just to keep the blood flowing. I watched those bitterbrush flats and that saddle until my eyes ached. Finally, I saw four elk moving across, and I trembled with excitement. I thought I might kill two if my aim was good.

"But as I waited for a clear shot, I knew something was watching me. When I turned around, there was the gray wolf, standing so close I could see his tongue and the black hair along his muzzle. I was afraid because I thought he was stalking me. I threw the rifle to my shoulder and fired. After he disappeared into the trees, I was still shaking all over."

"Were you afraid of Hanson?" Jack asked.

"Yes," Danny said. "I was afraid when I saw the knife." Danny tried to shut out the fight. "I'll finish telling you about the elk now. They were almost across the saddle by then, running hard. I fired twice, but the angle was bad and I wounded a young bull. He kept going, trailing behind the others. I found some hair and black blood where they crossed the saddle.

"When Red Shirt showed up and I tried to explain what happened, his face grew dark. He took away my rifle because he blamed me for shooting at the wolf and making the luck go bad. He found the elk the next morning, but the wolves got there first. We broke camp and went back to the reservation. Red Shirt never talked about that hunting trip."

"Was it the bad luck?" Jack asked.

"Maybe," Danny said.

8

After they had driven to the interstate, Danny headed west, so tired he wasn't sleepy but instead felt the heightened awareness that comes from lack of sleep and constant motion. Jack slept, leaning against the door of the pickup, Danny's coat bunched between his cheek and the doorframe. The lights on the dashboard panel glowed faintly and the engine hummed in the night.

They met little traffic through eastern Wyoming, and Danny was surprised to see a neon EAT sign still illuminated in one of the small towns. He pulled the pickup into the gravel parking lot and quietly opened the door, not closing it behind him for fear of waking Jack. The night was warm, almost balmy, and insects hummed in the darkness. A window marked ORDER HERE was propped open with a collapsible screen.

When the man inside saw Danny, he put down his mop and opened the screen. "What's yours?"

"A large cup of coffee with cream and a hamburger."

The man poured the coffee from a half-full pot on the

hotplate and handed Danny the cup and a couple packets of whitener.

"Got any real cream? Milk will do."

"I got some milk," he said. He opened the door of the stainless steel cooler and took out a pint, handing it to Danny. "Can't get real cream here anymore," he said. "Don't that take the cake? There's nothing but cattle all through this country; even got a dairy farm three miles from here and you can't get cream. You can't get a hamburger either. Sorry, but I got the grill off. You can have a hot dog from the warming tray, or pie. This time of night, it's mostly pie for the long-haul truckers that come through here. I was almost ready to close so I turned off the grill."

"Apple, then, if you've got it."

The man took a whole pie out of the case and cut a sixth of it for Danny. He handed it through the window. "That's a buck thirty."

Danny gave him two dollars. "Don't worry about the change."

"Thanks," the man said. "Where you from?"

"West. Oregon."

"Nice country, I hear. My brother-in-law went there once in the summer. Which route you taking?"

Danny shrugged and sipped the coffee. "I don't know exactly."

"Makes it harder to get lost then, don't it? Let me fill that coffee cup for you again. You got a good fifty miles before you hit a motel—that is, if you're planning on spending the night."

"Thanks," Danny said. "I got a thermos in the pickup. Maybe I should have you put some in there."

"I don't mind," the man said. "Saves me from pouring it out. I can't drink the stuff because it gives me diarrhea."

Being careful not to wake Jack, Danny slipped the two-quart stainless steel thermos from behind the seat. Although it had a large dent in the lid, the threads still worked. He moved the rubber plug and handed the thermos to the man.

"That's a hell of an old thermos," the man said. "Looks like you got a replacement plug, though."

Danny nodded. "A couple of them. That thermos belonged to my father."

"They don't make them like this anymore," the man said.

"Thanks again for the coffee."

"Don't mention it," the man said. "Come see us again."

Danny finished eating his apple pie at a little pine picnic table. A glowing purple BUG-OFF light hissed and crackled whenever a moth flew against it. Danny put the plastic fork and plate into a trash can and carried the thermos to the truck. Jack didn't wake up when he started the engine. As he drove through the main part of town, Danny saw a month-old banner advertising the county fair and rodeo. He passed the last lights, a gas station on the left with a sign that said: WHOA THERE PARTNER! YOU DANGED NEAR MISSED US!

He glanced at Jack and remembered all the times he had sat in the front seat of Red Shirt's pickup watching his father drive, and the nights when he had awakened to see the rough-hewn face softened by the faint glow of the panel lights. A jack rabbit jumped into the headlights' beam, its eye red for an instant before it bounded across the road. Danny thought of that last elk hunt with his father. He had told Jack a little about it, but now he wanted to go over it again and remember it clearly. He poured a cup of coffee into the dented lid and took a sip. A deserted farmhouse and windmill appeared on the right, then faded into darkness again as the truck passed. Watching the white line roll under the truck, Danny relaxed and thought back to that first morning in the Wallowas.

Danny sat in the front seat of the truck, between his father and Ass-Out Jones. He watched two figures perched on the granite rim overlooking Crazy Man Canyon. The wind blew up the canyon from the Imnaha River, driving the snow into their faces. Danny heard the snick of the snowflakes hitting the truck. The man in the green jacket clutched the gray sticks of dynamite while the thin man in the red hat lit the orange fuse caps. After they were lit, the man in the green jacket hurled the dynamite sticks into the canyon, baseball style. Several seconds passed before the charges went off, and Danny was puzzled because the explosions sounded so small in the vastness of the canyon. "Why are they doing that?" he asked.

"They're just pissing into the wind," Red Shirt said. "They think those explosions will run the elk out of the canyon, but they're in the bottom, near the river, and those little pops won't even make them lift their heads from browsing."

"It's a damn poor excuse for hunting," Jones said. "And with all the stump blasting by the Forest Service, and the lightning strikes, those little dynamite sticks sure seem puny. You want some coffee?"

After Red Shirt nodded, Jones unscrewed the dented cap on the stainless steel thermos and poured it three-fourths full. Then he pulled a whiskey flask from his coat pocket and splashed in enough to almost reach the rim.

Jones had taken off his gloves to pour the coffee and whiskey, and Danny saw how badly crippled his hands were. Even so, he hadn't spilled a drop.

Jones took a sip, smiled, and passed the cap to Red Shirt.

Red Shirt took a few drinks. "Good stuff. But you've got the proportions back-asswards. Too much coffee."

Danny huddled between the two men, trying to keep warm. He wished his father would offer him some of the whiskeyed coffee, but Red Shirt passed it across the boy and back to Jones. Jones set the cap on the dashboard and the pickup's windshield began to fog from the steam. Danny leaned forward and wiped it clear with his gloved hand. He didn't want to miss anything.

"Well," Jones said. "This boy has a new rifle and an eager look in his eyes. You want to try Black Horse and leave this canyon to those two crazies?"

Red Shirt shook his head. "In a few minutes. Let's watch the show. They got something else going on now."

The thin man in the red cap left the canyon rim and took something from the gunrack above the seat of his pickup.

"Can you see what that is?" Jones asked.

"You better get some glasses," Red Shirt said. "Your eyesight is getting as bad as your cooking."

The thin man held what seemed to be a stick, and when he bent it, Danny could see he was stringing a bow.

"I don't believe it," Jones said. "They're going to shoot those dynamite sticks into the canyon."

"This is getting to be good," Red Shirt said. "I wouldn't want to miss this."

The thin man knelt on the ground. He removed his gloves and blew on his hands, warming his fingers so he could tie the dynamite to an arrow shaft. When he finished, he handed the bow to the man in the green jacket, who notched the arrow.

"It looks like he's only got half a stick there," Red Shirt said.

"That won't matter," Jones said. "They might as well tie on a brick."

The thin man lit the fuse while his partner drew the bowstring, leaning back slightly to aim in a high arc. But when he released the bowstring, the arrow shaft split and the lighted dynamite fell at their feet. The thin man stomped furiously on the fuse, then ran, while the man holding the bow stood frozen, looking down at the burning fuse. At the last moment, he turned and ran a couple of steps.

When the dynamite went off, the man in the green jacket pitched forward, landing on his face in the snow. Pieces of dirt and small rock chips landed on the hood and cab of Red

Shirt's pickup. The man in green rolled over onto his back, pressing his gloved hands against the sides of his head.

"I knew it," Jones said. "I knew that shaft would break. There's a fool born a minute and only one dies a day." He spilled the coffee on his wool pants and yelped, "Hot! Hot!"

Red Shirt opened the door of the truck and wiped some of the dirt off the hood and windshield with his hat. "Hey! You guys okay?" he called.

The man in the green jacket stood slowly, still holding his hands to his ears. He began walking toward them as if in a stupor. Snow covered the front of his jacket and his hat was pushed to one side. His face was gray. "I can't hear you," he said.

The thin man came up alongside his friend and took hold of his elbow, trying to direct him back to their pickup. He was saying something to him.

"Are . . . you . . . all . . . right?" Red Shirt asked.

"I can't hear you."

Red Shirt yelled louder as the thin man tried to force his partner's hands away from his ears.

The man in green turned to the other. "Son of a bitch," he said. "You made me deaf."

"You're all right," the thin man said. "You'll be fine." He managed to turn him toward their pickup and then grabbed the man's gloved hands, pulling them away from his ears. "Now you can hear me just fine, can't you?"

Danny stared at the blood coming from the man's ears and felt he was going to be sick.

The snow stopped that afternoon and the wind came up, sweeping bare patches on the west slopes. They decided to drive one of the canyons breaking off Black Horse Ridge, with Red Shirt and Danny moving through the canyon and Jones blocking from a position on an old logging road.

Jones dropped off Red Shirt and Danny on a high overlook

in the Wallowas near Mahogany Corral. The clouds had broken and the bright autumn sun came out, bathing the ridges in light and casting long shadows into the timbered canyons. Danny was awed by the vastness of the landscape, the ruggedness of the hogbacked ridges and deep canyons. He felt the power of the land, the force of its size and silence, and he began to understand why his father always spoke of the Wallowa country with such feeling.

Under a sky so blue now it burned his eyes, Danny stared into the distance at the jagged peaks sawtoothed against the skyline. Their wind-glazed snowy slopes resembled meringue. He knew those mountains from his father's descriptions, and he spoke aloud, "The Seven Devils."

"Yes," Red Shirt said. "They're in Idaho, across Hell's Canyon. You can't see the Snake River from here, but you could if you stood on that next set of ridges across the Imnaha."

Danny saw the Imnaha River below them twisting like a silver ribbon through the dark green timber and lighter meadowlands.

"This is Black Horse Ridge," Red Shirt said. "The canyons we hunt break off here. Black Horse is the deepest. That next one is Gumboot, then Beaverdam and Little Skookum. Gumboot has the granite ridge, and that saddle where the two canyons come together divides Little Skookum and Beaverdam. Ollokot campground is directly below us."

Danny studied the canyons, memorizing their names and features. The Seven Devils lay to the east, so he could always use them as a point of reference. He didn't want to shame himself by getting lost. The landscape seemed immense to him, and the canyons breaking off Black Horse made only one small part. "Do you always hunt here?" he asked.

"I've been coming here a long time," Red Shirt said. "Twenty-seven years."

"You don't hunt the other canyons?"

"We hunt here," Red Shirt said. "Once the Nez Perce

hunted all of this, as far as you can see in any direction. These mountains belonged to the Nez Perce, and their hearts were here. When the settlers came, Old Joseph tried to keep peace by giving them some land, but they insisted on more land, more water, and Young Joseph fought to get it back. After Young Joseph had surrendered in the Bear Paws, some of the warriors came back here. Your great-grandfather Left Hand returned because he and Ollokot had hunted elk here as boys."

"But Ollokot was killed," Danny said. He knew that much about the story. Young Joseph's brother Ollokot, Poker Joe, even Looking Glass, had all been killed in the Bear Paws before Joseph put down the rifle. Only White Bird had escaped to Canada and the safety of Sitting Bull's camp.

Red Shirt nodded as if he too were remembering the story. "Left Hand was taken prisoner with Joseph and the other Dreamers. The soldiers took them to Kansas, then Oklahoma. Left Hand escaped and slipped back to the Nez Perce Reservation at Lapwai. But the Nez Perce there were soft and listened to the missionaries condemn the Dreamers. Those missionaries didn't want them around stirring up old ceremonies and memories of the Wallowas."

"They couldn't get along, then?"

"No. The people were scattered. It made Left Hand sick, so he left Lapwai and came to live on the Umatilla Reservation with old friends. That way, he was near the Wallowas and didn't have to face the ridicule of the missionary Indians.

"In late fall, after the settlers had taken their cattle from the high country, Left Hand and some of the other Dreamers would rendezvous in the Wallowas to hunt elk and practice the old ceremonies. They had to be careful of the settlers in the valley, who were still angry about the war with the Nez Perce. Some say the settlers even dug up Old Joseph's grave and twisted the head off the body, and then they cut off his hands and feet.

"Left Hand and the other Dreamers hunted anyway, camping in the high timber pockets and building small warming fires after dark."

"And they killed elk?"

"Lots of elk. During the days, when the autumn sun warmed the granite hogbacks, they stalked them with bows and arrows. They used rifles to shoot the elk in the deep loose snow of the timber pockets, where the thick trees muffled the shots. If they hunted near the settlers, they built no fires and buried their stool so the dogs would have no scent.

"They hunted into early winter, moving their camps to the windswept south and west sides of the canyons, where the horses foraged for autumn elk grass. When the snow became too deep, they loaded the quartered elk onto the horses and led them back to the reservation through the high passes in the Blues and Wallowas.

"The meat helped stop the winter hunger for the Umatillas. The agents passed out just enough commodities to keep the Indians from starving, and the missionaries expected them to praise God for those—lard, bread, and strange-tasting meat that came from cans. During the long winters, Left Hand and the other Dreamers provided elk meat and told old stories about the Wallowas.

"The Umatillas all respected Left Hand for his hunting and for his bravery. Some said he had covered White Bird's escape to Canada during the battle in the Bear Paws. He built a cabin in a remote section of the reservation and practiced the old religion. He dreamed of war, but his eyes went bad and he took a Umatilla wife who discouraged him from showing the rifle. Eventually, most of the old Dreamers died off or became too weak to continue the hunt. And one winter, when the deep snows came in November, Left Hand never returned from the hunt. In the spring, your grandfather, Medicine Bird, found where a mountain lion had killed his horse, but he found no trace of Left Hand. The wild animals had scattered his bones through these canyons."

When Red Shirt finished talking, his eyes were glistening. The angle of light had changed, and Danny stared into the deep blue shadows of the timbered canyons. Carried along by his father's words, he believed he saw Left Hand, Medicine Bird, even his father as a young man. Their shadowy figures moved through the deep canyons. Their eyes were bright with the hunt. Danny imagined joining them, killing elk on the ridges with the late autumn sun warm at his back as he bled and skinned them. He pictured killing elk in the loose snow of the deep timber pockets, their hot blood steaming and staining the snow bright red. After the day's hunt, he would join the Dreamers for the stories, both old and new, told around campfires.

"Jones is waiting," Red Shirt said. His tone changed and the mood shifted. "We better move out."

As Danny stood overlooking the canyon, his thrill of hunting was dulled by his fear of becoming lost. "What should I do?" He tried to sound casual, so his father wouldn't know his fear.

As if he had read Danny's mind, Red Shirt said, "Only two directions here matter—up and down. We're going down toward the river, so you can't get confused. Don't cross any ridges and you'll be fine. After you walk a mile, you'll come to a creek. Cross it once, but not again."

Danny nodded, listening carefully to his father's directions: "Stay on the south slope about halfway up. The shadows there will make you harder to spot. I'll be on the north slope. If you can, stay even with me. When I'm in the draws you won't see me, but move slowly and keep your eyes open. In about two hours, you'll hit the old skid road. Wait there and we'll find you. Got it?"

"Yes." Danny started down the hill, working his way through a section of bullpines and alders. His heart pounded as if an elk would leap in front of him at any moment. As he moved further down the canyon, he was surprised at how much he started to sweat. He unbuttoned his jacket and took off his hunting cap in order to cool down. The sideslope was steep and his socks kept bunching up in his boots, rubbing sore places on his feet. Crawling over deadfall, he slipped a couple of times, just managing to break his fall with his free hand.

He moved across a bitterbrush flat, pausing on the far side to watch the north slope for his father. In a few moments he saw his father's yellow crusher hat come into view. Instinctively, Red Shirt turned and motioned Danny further up the hill by jerking his thumb toward the rim.

Danny scrambled another hundred yards up the south slope and looked back to where he had last seen his father, but Red Shirt had gone into the deep timber. Danny hurried ahead. He tried to imagine how the elk would move and whether or not they could hear him in the canyon. He admired his new rifle and wanted to impress the men by killing a big bull. Once, when a large buck ran from a clump of jack pines, Danny threw his rifle to his shoulder and flipped off the safety before he realized it was a deer. *Brown,* he thought. *A deer is gray. An elk will be brown or cream-colored against the snow. Maybe I'll see its yellow rump first.* He stopped, straining to see yellow that was not a split branch of pine.

When he came to the creek, Danny crossed on some large flat stones. He crouched on the other side and dipped some of the sparkling water with his folding cup. When he started moving again, he was startled by three blue grouse exploding from the lower branches of a silver spruce. They spread their wings and glided downhill to the safety of other tall trees.

By the time Danny got to the bottom of the canyon, he was steaming from the hard walk. He put his wool cap back on his head and waited at the skid road. After a while he heard a horn honk and started walking in the direction of the sound.

Then he saw the pickup. Red Shirt and Jones were sitting on the tailgate drinking coffee and eating doughnuts, their backs turned to him. "Your doughnuts are on the hood," Red Shirt said. "It's warm there."

Danny picked up a doughnut and joined them at the back of the truck.

"Did you see any elk?" Jones asked.

Danny shook his head.

"I can hear your shells clinking in your pocket," Jones said. "And so can the elk. Better use one of the cartridge belts tomorrow."

When they arrived back at camp, Danny took off his boots and wiggled his toes. The heavy wool socks had wrinkled, blistering his feet, and he poked at the folded wool, feeling the tender flesh beneath.

"Feet bother you?" Jones asked.

"Yeah. My socks keep bunching up when I'm walking down the sidehills."

"Give them socks here." After Danny handed him the socks, Jones took a candle out of his packsack and rubbed candle wax on the toes and heels of the socks. "This will make them slip easier and not bunch up," Jones said. "Now I got to get to the beans."

Jones took a pot of beans from the back of the woodstove and set it on the hottest part. When the beans started to bubble, he diced some onions into the pot and added dry mustard. He took a pinch of green shreds from a pouch and added that to the beans as well. When he saw Danny had been watching him, he held a finger to his lips and whispered, "Moss. That's what does the trick. But you have to know what kind." He set the pot of beans back on the warm part of the stove to simmer.

Red Shirt cut thick slices of venison steak with his hunting knife and put them into a big frying pan with some bacon fat. "That pan can hold two chickens," he said. "All at once."

When supper was ready, they sat at a folding table and ate. After supper, the men drank cups of coffee and talked about the next day's hunt.

"I sure want to see some elk tomorrow," Danny said.

"Sometimes you smell them first," Jones said.

"What do they smell like?"

"Kind of strong and musty. Maybe like dirty socks."

Red Shirt laughed. "He'll be shooting your feet if you tell him that. You'll be humping over the mountains with no toes."

"That's a danger," Jones said. "You remember the time we were on top of Black Horse Ridge in a blizzard and Cecil Funmaker kept swearing he could smell elk?"

"Sure," Red Shirt said. Turning to Danny, he continued, "You should know about this. We were trying to keep warm until we could see where the hell we were, and we built a blazing fire. Old Cecil kept swearing he could smell elk, even though the wind was blowing like old nob and the snow was coming straight in."

Jones picked up the story. "Cecil glanced away from the fire a moment and yelled, 'There's one!' He grabbed his rifle and nearly shot this poor old horse that was coming to the fire. I think he would have shot the horse if your dad hadn't taken the rifle."

"That horse was nearly frozen," Red Shirt said. "God only knows what he was doing that high up in late November. His hooves and fetlocks were solid square chunks of ice and he had shagged ice in his mane and tail. He was so cold he just pushed Cecil aside trying to get near the fire."

"Do you think somebody lost him?" Danny said.

"They damn sure hadn't found him," Jones said. "He was about starved. We fed him whatever we had a horse can eat—apples, candy bars, some raisins—and when it quit snowing enough we headed out and tried to get him to follow us to lower country. But he wouldn't leave the fire, and we didn't have a rope or bridle to lead him."

"Cecil wanted to shoot him," Red Shirt said. "I don't know if we should have. Maybe that horse got found or maybe the wolves took him later on. When we were heading out, we stopped and asked at a couple of farmhouses, but they weren't missing a horse. He might have gotten away from a pack string. That's most likely the case."

"He sure wouldn't leave that fire," Jones said. He opened the stove door with a pair of pliers and added a couple pieces of the white pine they used for firewood. After a moment he said, "That dynamite you saw today was false fire, made by man, but real fire is in the wood." Jones stared into the fire until the flames had blackened the pieces of pine. Then he turned the damper down and shut the door.

Danny started to say something, but his father shook his head and put his fingers to his lips.

Jones poured his coffee cup half full of Old Forester and drew small circles on the tabletop with his forefinger. Then he passed his hands in front of his face and his voice changed pitch. "The fire is in the wood," he repeated.

"A long time ago, when the Nimipu first came, the people had no fire. They were cold because they had no skins like the bear, the wolf, the elk. Even the beaver had a skin and could swim in cold water.

"The Maker had given fire to the devils, but they locked the fire up inside the mountain, so many fires that the people could see smoke rising from the snowfields. When young men tried to get the fire from the mountain, they never returned.

"Two brothers decided to try. The brave one wanted to fight the devils, but the cunning one had another plan. They made their way up the mountainside carefully, traveling at night and hiding in the snow during the day.

"When they reached the large cave where the devils lived and hid the fire, the cunning brother said, 'You wait and I will steal the fire.' Then he sneaked inside the cave, and after his eyes got used to the dark, he could see the devils huddled around the warm fire. Some of them were so hot they glowed red!

"Keeping close to the dark walls and creeping so the devils wouldn't notice him, the youth got right next to the fire and hid in some of the firewood, covering himself with moss and bark.

"But when one of the devils started to put on more wood, he grabbed the youth by mistake and cried, 'This wood is alive!'

" 'Haaaaaa!' the youth screamed, jumping up and snatching some of the fire. Then he ran for the cave's entrance. As soon as he was outside, he showed the fire to his brother.

" 'Run back to the people!' his brother said. While the youth raced down the hill with the fire, the brave brother rolled a rock over the cave's mouth, to slow the devils. Then he ran too.

"The brothers raced down the mountainside. Behind them was a great roaring and shaking as the devils tried to get out. The whole mountain shook. The devils became so angry they blew the top off the mountain and swarmed out. There were so many they blackened the sun.

"The brave brother stopped running and turned, firing his arrows and slaying devils until his quiver was empty. Then both brothers ran and ran until they came to a river. It was too wide to swim, and they had no boat, so they called out to the Maker for help.

"When the Maker saw what was happening, he became furious with the devils for blocking out the sun and not sharing the fire with the people. He made the sun so hot it burned the wings off the devils, and they fell to earth and stuck there in thick bunches, where they remain today as trees.

"Then the Maker had the fire pour out of the mountain and run all over the land so the devils couldn't hide it anymore. One brother turned into a woodpecker and flew across the river to give fire to the cold people. Even today, that woodpecker goes around tapping at trees, to remind the people the fire is in the wood."

When Jones finished the story, he rose from the table and stepped outside the tent. In a few moments he came back. "Windshift," he said. "Coming up the river now."

"Good," Red Shirt said. "We need some snow for tracking."

"It'll snow, all right," Jones said. "Not tonight, but tomorrow."

"How can you tell?" Danny asked.

"He sticks his thumb up his ass," Red Shirt said. "If it stinks when he pulls it out, that means snow. The more stink, the more snow. That's how the Klamaths tell the weather."

"Hell," Jones said. "If it worked like that, the snow would be deep enough to cover your place all winter."

Danny shivered. He liked being there with his father and Jones. It was a man's world and they were telling men's stories and jokes. After this hunt, after he had killed an elk, he thought, they would know he was a man, too.

"Hey," Jones said. "Don't fall asleep before you do the dishes. We cooked, so you have to clean up. Get some water from the river."

Danny took the waterbucket and a lantern down beside the rushing Imnaha. Although he could see the stars above, and a half-moon, the wind coming up the river seemed moist, as if it carried snow. He found the deep hole beside the snowberry bush and dipped the icy water from the river. He thought he heard a noise on the far side and he imagined a herd of elk over there browsing by moonlight. He picked up his lantern and bucket and returned to the tent.

Inside, Jones and Red Shirt sat at the folding table playing cards, the bottle of Old Forester placed between them.

Danny did the dishes quickly, then slid into his sleeping bag. He wore his long underwear and wool socks to bed and pulled a stocking cap down over his ears. He fell asleep dreaming of the fire and thinking of the big elk he would kill on the hunt.

The next afternoon they made a big drive through Black Horse Canyon, and Danny found the bear paws. The way they had been skinned out, Danny at first mistook them for human hands. A wave of panic swept through him because he thought there had been a murder in the mountains. He almost fired distress-signal shots before he calmed down.

The bear paws were under a large tamarack tree near a granite formation that shouldered out of the hillside. Some of the brown tamarack needles had fallen on the paws, so Danny knew they had been there a while. Perhaps some hunter had shot the bear during deer season. Danny broke a brittle stick from a dead limb and poked at the bear paws, turning them palms-down to examine the muscles and sinews on the back. The flesh was dark bluish purple and smelled rancid in spite of the cold. In shape and size, the paws closely resembled the hands of a small man.

Danny took his plastic sandwich sack and scooped the paws into it with the stick. He twisted the sack a couple of times, then tucked it into his coat pocket. He thought that even if he didn't shoot an elk, he would have a story to tell the men back at camp.

Using the tamarack tree as a center, he began searching the area, moving in widening circles away from the tree. About fifty yards down the hill, he found the place where someone had gutted the bear and skinned her. They had killed the cub, too. Its carcass was about fifty feet from the sow's, but they had not bothered to skin it. The dark pelt was bunched and matted like a dirty towel. He thought maybe the cub had been warned off by the sow at first, and then tried to come back to her while they were skinning. But it was hard to tell exactly what had happened. The sow's wasted meat and the dead cub made Danny angry.

That night after supper, Danny took the bear paws out of his pocket to show his father and Jones. He told them about the wasted bear and the dead cub. "Who would do such a thing?" he asked.

Jones shrugged. "Some jerk-off deer hunter wanted a rug. And they probably took the gall bladder. You can sell those to the Chinks. They grind them up and take the powder as an aphrodisiac." He examined the paws carefully. "Funny, they look just like a man's hands, don't they? Maybe a big boy's."

"I don't like it," Red Shirt said. "You shouldn't bring these into camp. It's better to leave such things where you find them."

His father's words hurt. Danny had been excited at the find.

"The boy didn't mean any harm," Jones said.

"Get rid of them," Red Shirt said. "Take the camp shovel and bury the paws out by the river. Go a couple hundred yards from camp and bury them deep. That way no other animals can get at them."

Danny didn't like leaving the tent and the glowing fire, but he took the two-mantled kerosene lantern with him and headed toward the river. Beyond the circle of light the lantern cast, the woods seemed dark and threatening. The chilly wind off the river carried spits of snow and turned his sweat cold as he hurried to cover the distance his father had directed. At one point he saw a charred stump that looked like a bear standing on its hind legs and he dropped the shovel. When he felt he had gone far enough, he hastily dug the hole, pausing only to glance into the darkness beyond the lantern's light. The ground was frozen on top, but he managed to chip through it with the shovel tip. Under the frozen part, the digging was easier. Danny buried the paws deep and filled in the hole.

As he hurried back to camp, the wind blew stronger upriver, carrying a sound more chilling than the snow. It rose and fell, then trailed off in a long, eerie howl, the kind of frightening sound Danny thought a mournful spirit might make. He ran the remaining distance, the light bobbing at his side.

Red Shirt and Jones stood outside looking like black shadows against the tan background of the illuminated tent. When Danny was close enough to see the red glow of Jones's cigarette, he slowed to a walk. He tossed the shovel by the woodpile, then set the lantern down next to the men. "I buried them deep," he said.

"There it is again," Jones said.

"What? I heard it too, coming back."

"Shh," Red Shirt told Danny. "Be quiet."

Danny listened to the wail again, rising and falling on the night wind. He shivered and thrust his hands deep inside his coat pockets. After the sound trailed off, no one spoke for a few moments. Then Jones flipped his cigarette butt into the snow where it hissed out. "It's been a while since I've heard a wolf around here," he said.

"Well," Red Shirt said. "That was a wolf sure enough. Old Hímiin, the Night Hunter."

Danny was surprised his father used the Nez Perce name for wolf.

"Let's try to get some sleep," Jones said.

They went inside the tent and Jones pegged the canvas flap shut. Danny got ready for bed quickly while the others did the same. He snuggled deep in his sleeping bag, but he could feel the cold air coming from beneath and shivered.

Jones turned off the lantern. It glowed feebly for a while until the cooling mantles turned dust-gray. It was quiet for a few moments. Then they heard the wolf again.

"Sure gets cold fast when you hear one of those, doesn't it?" Jones asked.

"The bottom drops out of the thermometer," Red Shirt said.

Danny awakened to the smell of coffee and dressed quickly, embarrassed that he had overslept. The tent was already warm, so he knew the men had fired up the stove. Seeing he was alone in the tent, Danny feared they had left without him, but when he saw the slab of bacon and nine brown eggs on the table, he knew they were just out. He pulled his boots on and splashed some heated water onto his face from the pan on the stove.

Red Shirt came into the tent, stomping the snow from his boots. Large flakes melted on his shoulders and yellow crusher hat. Danny hoped the windshift had brought fresh tracking snow.

"Hey," Red Shirt said. "Don't you have breakfast ready?"

"No," Danny said. "But I'm ready to go."

Red Shirt laughed. "Don't run off without your breakfast. It'll be dark for another hour. If we get an elk down out there and have to pack it out, it could be a long time between meals."

Jones came in, stomping his feet to clear the snow and slapping his hands together. "It got cold," he said. "The boy better bring an extra sweater and throw on another pair of wool socks."

Red Shirt nodded. "We'll put you on a stand today and drive the elk by close enough to tackle. But the waiting can get cold."

While Danny put on more clothes, Jones heated the skillet and cooked the bacon strips until the ends curled dark brown. He speared them with his hunting knife and put them on paper towels to drain. After pouring off some of the grease, he cracked the eggs into the pan and cooked them until the whites turned brown, then black, and bubbled up at the edges. He put three eggs and six pieces of bacon on each tin plate, then ladled out full servings of beans from the pot. "The hen's fruit won't make you toot, but when the trail gets gritty and the sky turns black, my beans will get you there and back," Jones said.

Danny ate quickly, surprised at how hungry he was. With his belly full, he leaned back, yawning and stretching.

"Give him some coffee," Red Shirt said.

"You want to bust his innards? It's six-shooter."

"Doesn't matter. Cut it with some cream and sugar."

Jones poured the steaming black coffee into a mug and added a drench of cream and a couple teaspoons of sugar, then handed it to Danny.

Danny smelled the strong, almost scorched flavor sweetened over by the sugar. When he drank some, the liquid burned bittersweet all the way down. "That's got a stiff punch," he said.

"You like it?" Jones asked.

"It's good," Danny said, trying not to grimace. "Why do you call it six-shooter?"

"Either because it's thick enough to float a pistol or because there's six tablespoons for a four-cup pot. I can't remember which."

"Jones and I will wash up this morning," Red Shirt said. "Get the lantern. I want you to look at something."

"What?" Danny was afraid an animal had dug up the bear paws; that would make his father angry.

"You'll see. Just go outside and follow our tracks. Leave your rifle here."

Danny put on his coat and took the lantern. He found the men's tracks in four inches of new snow, and it was still coming. The falling snow muffled even the sound of the river, and after he had taken a few steps from the tent, all Danny heard was the soft hissing of the lantern. As he followed the

men's tracks about one hundred yards downriver, he started
worrying about the bear paws again. But the men's tracks
intercepted another set of tracks, then changed directions.
Danny lowered the lantern to get a better look and sucked in
his breath. The tracks were like a dog's only much larger.
Wolf!

He lifted the lantern and swung it around quickly, wishing
he had brought his rifle; but Red Shirt had told him to leave
it. After he was satisfied there were no wolves close by,
Danny examined the tracks more carefully. Some snow had
fallen into them, but they were still fresh, the outlines of pads
and paws distinct. He placed his booted foot alongside one of
the tracks and was amazed. Although shorter, the track was
nearly as wide as his bootprint.

The wolf had been traveling upstream, staying about
twenty feet from the riverbank. Where they had intercepted
the wolf's tracks, the men had turned upstream and followed
them until they stopped on a little rise with a clear view of
the tent. Here the wolf's tracks were deeper, and it seemed
he had stood there for some time watching the tent, perhaps
curious about the men inside.

From the rise, Danny could see their camp clearly, the
shapes of familiar objects taking form in the twilight like a
photograph being developed. Red Shirt and Jones were loading the gear into the pickup only seventy feet from where
Danny stood. After standing there, the wolf had turned to
the river, and Danny lost the tracks in the rocky stretch along
the riverbank. The men's tracks led back to camp.

It frightened him that the wolf had been so close and
watched the camp while they slept. He figured he had seen
what his father wanted, so he returned to camp as well.
Making a brave show, Danny picked up his rifle and pointed
it toward the rise where the wolf had stood. "An easy shot,"
he said. He was thinking that a wolfskin would look good on

his bedroom wall and he could make a necklace from the claws, like the men wore at ceremonial dances.

"No!" Red Shirt said. "Old Hímiin belongs here. The Night Hunter wonders what we are doing here this cold day. You won't see him, but if you do, leave him alone."

Red Shirt put the pickup in four-wheel drive and they climbed the twisting skid road on Little Skookum's back-grade. Jones watched for tracks on the downhill side and Danny kept his eyes on the bank above the road. He saw several tracks made by big-footed snowshoe rabbits, but he was not tricked by these and kept quiet. When they were halfway up the grade, Jones said, "Fresh ones—right there!" He pointed to the bank where the torn dark earth showed through the snow.

"Going up or down?" Red Shirt asked as he stopped the truck.

Jones got out and studied the tracks on both sides of the road. Then he climbed back in the truck. "They came in from Gumboot early this morning," he said. "Three or four of them. I reckon they kegged up in one of the pockets in Little Skookum."

Red Shirt nodded. "You plan to follow them?"

Jones grinned. "That's what we're here for."

"How do you want to work it?"

"Put the boy on the saddle, and you drive the pickup around to the other side of the canyon where that second ridge comes in. You walk it up, just in case they crossed over, and we'll meet at the saddle. Maybe we'll roast elk heart for lunch."

"Sounds good," Red Shirt said. "I knew that snow would help." He studied the dark gray sky and the falling snow. "Still and clear," he said. "Still falling and clear up to your ass before long. How far up did you stick that thumb, anyway?"

"Up to the hilt." Jones chuckled. "It's going to snow a

bunch." He put on his skinning belt that held the hatchet, folding meat saw, hunting and skinning knives, and rope. "See you in a few hours." He started downhill, following the tracks.

Red Shirt drove the skid road to the top of the grade and parked the truck. "It's a couple of hundred yards down to the saddle," he said. "I'll show you where to stand."

Danny took his rucksack and lunch from the pickup and slung his rifle over his shoulder. He followed his father downhill through some tall firs and lodgepole pines until the trees thinned out on a broad saddle where two draws came together.

Red Shirt found a deadfall fir stump and hacked away at it until he located a pitch seam. Then he took two stubby white candlebutts from his plaid coat pocket and lit them with a wooden match. He set these in a cut he had made so that the flametips touched the pitch. Once the pitch started, it ignited the wood, and the fire burned hot within a few minutes. Red Shirt handed Danny the candlebutts and said, "It's good to have these in case the wood's damp, too. They'll dry it out and save you matches."

By this time, the pitch seam and wood were burning fiercely and Danny had to move away from the fire. "Wow, that's hot."

"Almost too hot," Red Shirt said. "If the blaze backs you away, then your feet get cold. Stomp up and down to keep the blood moving in your toes. You need a fire, though. It could be three or four hours before we show up, but this stump will burn that long and keep you warm."

"Won't the fire scare the elk?"

Red Shirt shook his head. "For some reason it doesn't bother them, maybe because they see so many lightning strikes."

"Good," Danny said. "What do I do?"

Red Shirt pointed to the right-hand draw. "Jones will be in

Little Skookum. I'll be driving the other draw, pushing ahead any elk that might have crossed over into Beaverdam. From this saddle, you can see any elk that comes out of the draws. Watch for them as they cross the dark patches of bitterbrush. They'll stay away from the river today because they heard the howling wolf." He put his hand on Danny's shoulder. "Today, with the snow falling, it's a good day for hunting. You will shoot your first elk."

Danny was thrilled but he tried to stay calm before his father. "Tell me again about the aim."

"Don't try for the head, because you might miss. Shoot just behind the shoulder and below the back, under the dark mane. That way you'll hit the heart or lungs."

"All right."

Red Shirt started walking back to the truck. When he reached the edge of the woods, he turned and gave Danny a thumbs-up sign. After his father had disappeared into the woods, Danny moved closer to the warming fire. He was still excited. After he had warmed up, he stood behind a small spruce, watching the right-hand draw in case Jones was pushing the elk far ahead. He watched for fifteen minutes but saw nothing.

Danny moved back to the fire. He could warm everything above his thighs, but his knees and feet were cold. He stomped like Red Shirt had told him. From time to time he brushed the snowflakes off his shoulders because he didn't want to become wet as they melted. After another hour passed, he opened his rucksack and ate a chocolate bar from his lunch. The bar was brittle from being frozen and pieces of it fell away. Danny wished he had a thermos of coffee, but he hadn't thought to ask for one. He imagined what it would feel like to pour hot coffee into his boots and warm his icy toes.

It started snowing harder, big wet flakes, and the heads of both draws were almost obscured, as if a white curtain had been pulled across them. Danny noticed that the tracks he and his father had made were covered, and he wondered if Jones was still following the elk trail. The wind picked up enough to start piling the snow on the north side of the fir trees. A fat grouse flew out of one of the trees and tried to eat the snowberries from a bush off to Danny's left. Some of the white berries fell into the snow, and the grouse hunted for them in vain.

"That dumb bird ought to be under a big bough," Danny said. The grouse looked huge, but he knew it was mostly the ruffled feathers. "It's going to be a long hard winter, bird." At school they had studied the brown bands on woolly-worm caterpillars, and the science teacher had told them that the broad markings meant there would be lots of snow.

Danny checked his rifle. He opened the bolt to make certain he had a cartridge in the chamber, then eased it shut after he had seen the bright brass casing. He checked the barrel. Red Shirt had covered the bore with a piece of gray tape to keep the snow out. Danny knew that when the time came he could shoot right through the tape.

His ears felt numb, and he realized he hadn't pulled down the flaps on his green quilted hunting cap. He moved closer to the fire. He was glad for its warmth and thought about Jones's story of how the people got fire.

Another hour had passed, and Danny decided to eat some of the lunch Jones had packed. He took out a cheese and peanut butter sandwich. It tasted delicious even though the peanut butter was so cold it was hard. In the warmth of Danny's mouth it gummed up, so he took a handful of snow to help wash it down. When he put the snow in his mouth his teeth hurt, and he shut his eyes.

When he opened them again, Danny thought he saw a movement in the bitterbrush. It was so slight it might have been the falling snow or his blinking eyelash. Then he saw movement again, and his chest tightened. When his chest began to ache, Danny realized he had stopped breathing. He exhaled, breathed again, and knelt beside the spruce tree, peering through the lower branches at the bitterbrush patches.

The movement became shapes. Elk were moving stealthily along the south slope of Beaverdam. They were so quiet they seemed like brown ghosts moving against a background of snowy hillside and dark bitterbrush.

Danny swept the snow from one of the low limbs on the spruce and rested his rifle against it. He snapped off the scope covers and looked at the hillside through the cross hairs. His hands trembled, and he was glad he had steadied the rifle against the limb.

The leading elk was a large cow, and she had a yearling calf with her. A young bull followed. Through the scope, it seemed like a spike or perhaps a forked-horn. Danny couldn't tell which. But he knew the horns were longer than the ears so he could shoot it. The fourth elk trailed the others, keeping to the thick brush so Danny couldn't get a clear view of its head. The way it lagged made Danny think it was a large bull.

He rested the rifle on the limb and tried to see the last elk with his naked eye, but it kept to the brush. Then he looked at the elk through the scope again and slipped off the safety.

He put the cross hairs on the young bull, just behind the shoulder as Red Shirt had told him. He could have squeezed off the shot, but he chose to wait a few moments. The elk were coming toward him, cautious but steady. The wind was blowing from behind them, so they had Red Shirt's scent but not his. He knew that the elk would be closest to him where the brush thinned out and they had to cross the saddle. Then he'd be able to tell what the fourth elk was. If it was a big bull, he could drop it with his first shots, and perhaps stop the running spike with the rest. A double kill would win him much admiration. He waited.

Suddenly Danny knew something was watching him, and the hair on his neck rose. Instinctively, he turned slowly until his back was to the elk.

The gray timber wolf stood forty feet beyond the warming fire, just at the edge of the dark woods where he and Red Shirt had first come onto the saddle. The wolf was so close that Danny could see the dark hairs of its mane and muzzle. The narrow yellow eyes, dancing with the reflected flames of the warming fire, held Danny spellbound.

His saliva turned to brass; his arms seemed too weak to hold the rifle. He stared at the wolf. Its pink tongue curled over its black-gummed teeth, and Danny panicked, thinking the wolf intended to attack. He threw the rifle to his shoulder and fired before he realized what he was doing. A piece of bark flew from a tree trunk above the wolf's head, and Danny felt himself pushed back by the rifle's recoil. The wolf turned and melted into the trees. Danny worked the bolt, this time conscious of his actions. He fired at the place the wolf had disappeared, slicing off a green branch. The confusion rose in him.

Danny swung around. The elk had broken out of Beaverdam and were running across the saddle past the head of Little Skookum. The fourth elk was a cow, even though she had the dirty-cream coloring of a bull. Danny felt cheated and foolish that he had tried for too much. He put his scope on the spike and fired, but he didn't lead him enough and the snow spit behind. The elk ran harder, and each second made Danny's angle of fire worse. He lay prone in the snow, resting the rifle on his left arm. He fired again, and this time the bull pitched a little, its shoulders humping forward. He worked the bolt and his last cartridge jammed. The elk were quartering away and Danny cursed as he struggled to free the jam. He ran down the hillside, slipping in the snow, until he reached the flat part of the saddle where the elk had crossed.

After finally working the last cartridge into the chamber, he raised the rifle, but the elk were almost up the far hillside, a quarter mile away. The young bull was trailing.

Danny found their trail in the snow and ran along it until he found some dark hair and blood. A few yards farther, he found more blood and a dark green, frothy liquid congealing in the snow. He stared at the spoor.

Red Shirt came out of the trees on the north slope of Beaverdam and Danny waved at him. Red Shirt cut the elks' trail and followed it, pausing to look at the blood and hair, then hurrying on to where Danny stood. "What happened?"

"I think I hit the bull," Danny said. "First I missed, but then I hit him the next shot."

Red Shirt knelt to examine the green liquid. He walked another twenty yards and found more spots. "This one's a leaker," he said. "You shot him low in the guts and he'll run for miles." He looked at Danny. "I heard four shots. Two and then two more."

Danny tried to speak, but his throat tightened and he looked away from his father. When he was able to talk, his voice seemed small and far away. "The elk were coming up the draw. Then I felt something was watching me. When I turned, the wolf was behind me standing at the edge of the woods. I didn't mean to shoot."

He expected his father to become furious, but instead Red Shirt suddenly looked very old. "You shot at Hímiin," he said. "Now my luck will go bad."

There was fear in his father's tone. Danny wanted to say something else, but he tasted the brassy saliva again and could not speak.

"Hand me the rifle." It was his father's normal voice. Danny gave it to him, and Red Shirt worked the bolt, ejecting the last cartridge. He worked the action several more times to make certain there were no other rounds in the rifle.

"Wait for Jones by the warming fire." Red Shirt slung Danny's rifle over his shoulder and began following the elks' trail.

Danny returned to the warming fire and dug in the snow until he found the craters made by the brass casings. He picked the shells up and stuck them in his pocket. He warmed himself by the fire and then searched for the wolf's tracks at the edge of the woods. They were partially covered by the falling snow but easy enough to follow. The piece of bark chipped off by his first shot lay in the snow not far from the green branch his second shot had sliced. The wolf's tracks led into the woods, running parallel to the skid road they had driven. Danny followed them for a quarter mile before they stopped. He searched the area, thinking the wolf had turned or doubled back and he had missed the sign. But the tracks simply stopped, as if the wolf had vanished.

He followed his trail back to the stand where Jones stood by the warming fire, drinking a cup of coffee. Danny took off his gloves and held his bare hands out to the flames. He stomped his feet to get the circulation going. "I'm cold," he said.

Jones nodded. "My damn hands get cold too, now they're so busted up." He poured Danny a cup of steaming coffee and handed it to him.

"Thanks," Danny said. He wanted to ask Jones about the hands, but he didn't because he was afraid his father would call him nosy.

"After you drink up, we'll head for the truck," Jones said. "The way it's snowing, we don't want to get caught out after dark. What happened with that elk?"

"I shot low," Danny said. He didn't feel like talking about the wolf. "There was some blood and green froth in the snow, and he started tracking them."

"He'll trail them until the light gives out," Jones said. "Then he'll wait on one of the lower roads. We better start moving too."

On the way to the pickup, Danny realized it must have seemed strange to Jones that he wasn't carrying his rifle, but he was glad Jones never asked him about it.

When they were on the way back to camp, Danny felt a little better. Inside the vehicle, the incident seemed less important.

"You don't have to be so quiet," Jones said. "Anyone can shoot low. The very first elk I ever shot was a leaker we didn't find until the next day."

"Really? Maybe we'll find him tomorrow, then, if not tonight."

"I wouldn't doubt it. Your father can think just like an elk."

Danny felt less empty inside and decided to tell Jones about the wolf, although he didn't mention the strangeness in his father's voice. "I didn't mean to shoot. The wolf was just so close, something happened."

"Are you sure you didn't wound it?"

Danny shook his head. "I didn't even come close. Both shots went wild. But my father was pretty mad anyway." He hoped Jones would stick up for him when they met Red Shirt.

"Did you see the wolf again?"

"I followed his tracks for maybe a quarter mile. Then they stopped."

"You mean you lost them, or the snow filled them in?"

"It wasn't like that," Danny said. "They just disappeared. At first I thought they had drifted over, or I'd missed them. But the last tracks were so clear I could see the toenails. And that was it."

"It sounds like the Wéyekin," Jones said.

"What's that?"

"A spirit that takes the form of an animal. Your father believes his Wéyekin comes as a wolf and gives him protection. It's an old idea left over from the Dreamers. Some still believe it; others don't."

Danny looked out the window and the woods seemed to crowd the road. He was silent the rest of the way.

Ten inches of snow covered their camp. Jones got the fire going and heated beans, while Danny knocked the snow off the tent with a broom and swept the woodpile clear. Jones took out three small steaks and fried two, leaving the last for Red Shirt. It was almost dark by the time they finished supper, and Jones told Danny he was going to drive the lower roads and pick up Red Shirt. "He can't follow them anymore tonight," Jones said.

Danny washed the dishes quickly, then made a fast trip to the woodpile to supply the fire. When he was outside, he imagined narrow yellow eyes watching him from the dark woods. He unsnapped his hunting knife and took it out of its sheath, laying it on the table in front of him. Jones had taken his rifle with him, or Danny would have brought it into the tent.

Long after dark, Jones came in alone. He shook his head as he undressed. "Still snowing, but he knows the way back."

Danny could not sleep until his father returned. Eyes open, he lay on his back, listening for Red Shirt's footfalls. Once he thought he heard a wolf howl, far away and muffled by the falling snow. He sat up to listen, but he couldn't hear it again and decided it might have been Jones's breathing.

Sometime after midnight Red Shirt came in and turned up the lantern. The snow formed a white mantle, like ermine, across his shoulders. Danny pretended to sleep, but Jones got up and dressed while Red Shirt fried the last steak. The two men sat at the table talking quietly, and Red Shirt asked Jones for some packages of cigarettes. Danny raised his head slightly. Both men sliced the cigarettes open with their pocketknives and dumped the tobacco onto the table. When there was a good-sized pile, Red Shirt scraped it into a leather pouch.

*   *   *

Danny awakened as Jones shook him.

"Rattle your hocks, boy! Rattle your hocks! It's a big snow—still coming—and we better break camp while the gettin's good."

Red Shirt was gone. He had taken the pickup and left before daylight.

Danny helped Jones break camp and load most of the gear into the trailer. They unfastened the stovepipe and carried the stove outside, using slabs of wood as potholders to keep from getting burned. Jones built an open fire to keep them warm, so the stove could cool enough to load. He put a big pot of coffee on the coals.

Red Shirt was back by noon, and his mood was dark. "I found the elk," he said. "But the wolves had been there first." He turned to Jones. "I scattered the tobacco for the Wéyekin back at yesterday's warming fire."

Jones nodded. "Good," he said. "That should do it."

The men drank coffee while they finished loading the gear. Danny worked hard, trying not to give his father reason to criticize.

Red Shirt made Danny crawl under the truck in the snow to hook up the chains. He had to take off his gloves to make the connections, and his fingers became stiff and useless. Jones knelt beside him to help with the last tire, and by the time Danny climbed into the cab he was wet and cold to the bone.

Jones handed Danny a mug of hot coffee, and when he sipped it, he realized Jones had put in a little whiskey. Huddled between the two men, with whiskey coursing through his blood, Danny finally became warm. But he felt an icy spot by his heart whenever he thought of the wolf and his father's fear.

Later that winter, after returning from the elk hunt, Danny learned that the tobacco his father had spread was a kind of charm used to appease the angry Wéyekin. But when he thought of everything that followed, Danny knew the charm had not worked. And like his father, Danny sometimes blamed himself for making the luck go bad.

◆ 9 ◆

"Southern Idaho is sure godforsaken," Jack said, looking out the window at the sagebrush and scrub trees. "A damn desert."

"We're almost through it anyway," Danny said. "A quick stop for gas and coffee and we can push on to Pendleton. Be there by suppertime."

They passed a black-and-yellow Stinker station advertising discount gas. The sign had a cartoon skunk and read:

FREE SAGEBRUSH
TAKE A TRUNKLOAD HOME FOR YOUR MOTHER-IN-LAW

Danny chuckled. "Pretty good, huh?"

"I hope Pendleton is nothing like this," Jack said.

"It's terrific," Danny said. "As soon as you hit the Oregon border, the air smells good again and you know you're back in God's country."

"That's what they said about Nebraska," Jack said. "God made it; God forgot it; God damn it."

"You'll like Pendleton," Danny said, and hoped it was true. He was starting to worry about his trailer. When he'd left, it was in pretty bad shape, but he had sent a card to Billy Que asking him to have Pudge clean it. Up ahead, Danny saw a place called the Oasis Café. "Let's stop here. Get some pie and coffee."

"That's seven pieces of apple pie in three days. It would have been eight, but the one place was out so you settled for berry."

"Who asked you to count?"

"You want to get fat? Move the seat back? Right now, the way the truck vibrates, your stomach shakes like Jell-O."

"The hell." Danny tightened his stomach muscles and looked down. There was still a little bulge in his shirt, but it didn't look like Jell-O. "Apples are good for you, anyway," Danny said. "Every fall, Red Shirt bought boxes of apples and stored them in the tack shed. The gyppo truckers brought them in from Hood River. When I'd open the door and smell those sweet apples along with the leather, that was something. And I never caught a cold."

"Fresh apples are different. They dump two cups of sugar in a pie. Then there's lard. It all goes right to your gut."

Danny stared straight ahead. "Probably can't buy a good apple in Nebraska."

"You missed the turnoff to the Oasis."

"I was thinking about stopping, but you sort of took the joy out."

Four pink plastic flamingos stood on metal legs in front of Billy Que's trailer. Two of them had their necks bent as if looking for aquatic insects. Beyond the flamingos were a brown plastic deer and two spotted fawns.

"Que's been doing a little decorating," Danny said. "Those flamingos brighten up the cheatgrass." He was looking forward to showing off Jack to Que.

"Even Hanson's place looked better than this."

"You're a long way from there now." Danny hoped Jack wouldn't take the edge off.

The door wasn't locked so they stepped inside. Que was standing at the stove, his back turned, stirring something in a frying pan. He wore an old blue-checked shirt with garters holding up the sleeves. After pouring some whiskey from a tin measuring cup into the pan, he took a sip himself.

"Cook's hitting the bottle," Danny yelled.

Que jumped, tipping over the tin cup so the whiskey ran into the burner with a hiss. "Christ on a crutch! There went my heart medicine."

Que wiped his hands on his pants and pumped Jack's hand. "So this here's your new sidekick. Growed up faster than a spring calf in sweet pasture. Look at him. Just like Red Shirt at that age—same build exactly."

Jack half smiled. "It's been a long time. Most people think I look like my mother."

Que shook his head. "That was a shame, what happened. I'm sure sorry." He squinted at Jack. "Could be you look like her . . . some. Maybe that's better. Red Shirt was a homely cuss, like your father here. Que looked at Danny. "I'm damned if I'll shake your hand. Say, it looks a mite swollen. And the boy's got a nice mouse there. Trouble?"

"Nothing we couldn't handle—now that Jack's riding shotgun." He grinned at the boy, but Jack was silent. Danny waited a moment, then said, "Place looks pretty good, Que."

"Saw the stuff outside, huh? Wanted to spruce up the place for the boy. Milo's rented spaces in his vacant lot to a bunch of California artists. They're making all kinds of stuff for the Round-Up, but this was the best of the lot. Lawn sta-tu-a-ry. They had deer heads too, painted on velvet. No matter where I walked in that lot, their eyes followed me around. Spooky."

"They had paintings like that in Nebraska—along the freeway—only they said they came from Colorado," Jack said.

"Must be a real demand. But you can't eat pictures. You boys must be hollow-bellied after that long drive and plumb tired of road cooking. I'm throwing on some more chow."

"What is that stuff?" Jack asked.

"Shanghai beans. That is, beans and Ramen noodles. It's an Oriental dish so your farts come out slanted." He turned up the burner under a large pot.

Jack looked at Danny and raised his eyebrows, then mouthed, "Shanghai beans?"

"Sit a spell while I boil up another package of noodles. Got plenty of beans already. So how was the trip?"

"Real fine," Danny said.

"Hot and boring," Jack said. He picked up a copy of *True West Tales* and started thumbing through it. No one spoke for a few moments, then Jack asked, "Where's the bathroom? I might be a while."

"Straight back," Que said. "Look in the cabinet if you need extra film for your brownie." After Jack closed the door, Que glanced at Danny. "How you been making out?"

"Ever chew a piece of gristle? Don't know whether to swallow or spit."

"Things have been pretty sour for him. Give it a while. He's like a box-eared colt. Bound to be spooky waiting for the next slap."

"Got to make it work," Danny said. He was glad Que hadn't taken offense. But he was starting to worry about taking Jack to his place. "You get my postcard?"

" 'Ski Nebraska'—with that fellow on skis out in the middle of a cornfield. Pretty good."

"I thought you'd like that. Did you talk to Pudge about cleaning the trailer?"

"She said you had a lot of gall."

"I don't care what she said. Did she do it?"

Que shrugged. "Never looked."

A bell went ding-ding-ding-ding.

"What is that?" Danny asked.

"Coffee's ready. Why don't you fix us a couple of cups? I'm still drinking it black. I like my coffee like my women—hot and dark." Billy Que chuckled.

Danny hadn't noticed the new coffee maker until the brew alarm rang, because of all the clutter on the kitchen counters. In addition to the dirty plates and cooking utensils, they were covered with grease cans, ammunition boxes, mink oil, hunting knives, boxes of assorted screws and bolts, and a couple of well-used Ace bandages. Danny shoved some of these aside to get a better view of the coffee maker. It had a clock on it and as many dials and switches as the dashboard of a new pickup.

"That's some coffee maker," Danny said. "You need a license to run it?"

"Damn near as good as a wife," Billy Que said. "It does everything but kiss you goodbye in the morning."

Danny laughed and wondered if Billy Que thought of that or had heard it from the salesman. He took out the glass pot and poured a couple cups of coffee.

"That's not bad," Billy Que said, taking a sip.

"So what's been going on around here?"

"Nothing much." Billy Que took another sip and set his cup down. "Henry busted out of jail."

"The hell he did!"

"The hell he didn't. They made him a trustee around the jail and he went rabbit on them. No one even missed him until they checked that night at lock-up."

"He still out?" Danny couldn't figure how Henry got away from jail with his leg in a cast.

"I guess so. A letter came for you. I took it out of your mailbox because I didn't want the cops to find it." Billy Que opened a drawer beneath the counter and handed Danny an envelope. Danny saw it had a Canadian stamp that had been canceled in Trail, B.C. The envelope held a half-sheet of paper and a four-photo series from a coin booth. The note read:

Buddy,
 Things were a little cramped so I went over the hill. Check on Cayenne until I get back. This here is Alberta, a Canuck cowgirl I'm honking. No brand on my carcass yet tho. The cast comes off in a week, so watch for me at the Calgary Stampede.

Your pal,
H

In the first photo, Henry was grinning and wearing a cowboy hat. Something about him looked funny, and then Danny remembered his front teeth were missing from the wreck. His nose was pushed over to one side and Danny figured maybe someone in jail had broken it. A girl sat on his lap in the second picture. She was blonde with a broad, blunt face and wide eyes. Not bad at all, Danny thought. They were kissing in the third picture, and in the last she was holding her hat over Henry's face and smiling widely.

Danny looked at the envelope again as if it might tell him what Henry was thinking. Trail. He must have gone north through the Colville Reservation and sneaked across the border on one of the backroads. Henry was darned good at working stock, and Danny knew the ranchers around there asked few questions. "He'll probably make out okay, that crazy bastard."

"They come around here a couple times asking if I'd seen Henry and where you were. I told them Henry owed me a bet so it wasn't likely I'd be seeing him, and I told them you was wandering out in Kansas or someplace pretty much like it, so they said they'd be in touch and to let them know if Henry showed up."

"That'll be a cold day," Danny said.

"About how I figure it. Anyway, you're likely to be busy for a while with a little project."

"How's that?"

"Sam CutHorse called and said he saw some range cattle with a few of ours mixed in—at least he thinks they was ours —way up Squaw Creek. He couldn't tell for sure, because they wouldn't let him get too close, but he saw that black stiff-necked steer right good when it came snorting out of the brush, head lowered, and tore out a chunk of his horse's flank. Gypsy's still pretty sore."

Danny set his coffee cup down. "Damn. I was almost hoping that steer was coyote bait."

"He's mean, all right."

"You were so drunk when you cut his nuts I think you missed one," Danny said.

Que looked hurt. "I wouldn't do that. Anyway, Sam claims there's a dozen or so others running with the stiff-neck, three or four of them ours. He wanted you to try to find them and bring them in. Fifty dollars a head, he said, for any besides ours."

"You planning to ride with me?"

"I'd damn sure like to," Que said, lowering his head. "But my bursitis has flared up fierce and I wouldn't be much help. I been working it with Ben-Gay, but I'm still stoved up. I put on that Ace bandage there most of the time. Too bad Henry's not around—damn good sidehill cowboy."

Danny wondered how bad Que's arm really hurt, but before he could think of a question that might trap him, he heard Jack say, "I'll go."

Danny didn't know how long the boy had been standing in the doorway. "How good can you ride a horse?" he asked. It seemed odd to him he didn't know.

"Like it was born under my butt."

"There you go," Que said. "Partners." He seemed relieved. "Sit down now. Sit down. Grub's ready." Que ladled heaping servings of beans and Ramen noodles onto their plates. "Eat it all up, or we'll have to kill the dogs with it."

Jack stared at the food.

"Spoon works but a fork's better. Dig in. The beans are always steady. I had to mix one chicken noodle with one pork."

Danny tried a couple bites. He'd eaten worse. Maybe more whiskey would have helped.

After trying some of the food, Jack looked at Que and asked, "How come you never got married, since you cook so good?"

"Never found a whore that owned a liquor store."

Jack smiled and Danny relaxed.

After they had finished eating, Danny said, "I'll get Cayenne in the morning. Good thing you can ride."

"With somebody else's horse I might be green at first."

"I'll do most of the work. You just need to wing them. It's a good chance for you to see a little of the country."

"Lots of the country," Que added. "Sam said the cattle were way up on Little Buckaroo Creek, but that they'd been running Light Ridge and Elk Canyon too."

Danny shook his head. "It's so brushy in places, you could hide a stockyard and not find it."

"We might try dirt bikes. Back in Nebraska, they worked pretty good for chasing cattle out of the brush. Hanson said he'd buy me one, but he never got around to it."

"Maybe they eat road apples for trail snacks in Nebraska," Danny said. "But it's different here. A dirt bike in these hills will spook the cattle off a cliff or into a fence line, where they'll hang up until the coyotes find them."

"Forget it, then," Jack said.

Danny scraped back his chair and got another cup of coffee. "I know everything's new to you," he said. He hadn't meant to flare, but the idea of snarling dirt bikes in the canyons rankled him. So did Hanson's name.

Que lifted his arm partway over his head, then winced. "I can't ride a horse or a bike. With this arm, I can barely stay on Arletta out in the back room of the Little Brown Jug. Wildest ride I ever had this side of Nevada."

Jack glanced at Danny and widened his eyes.

"You'll find them," Que said. "Sam went around saying it would take a tough brush-busting outfit to get those cattle back, but I bet him you would—good odds, too."

"Bet him?"

"Well, I had to brag you up a little, didn't I?"

"What was the bet—exactly?"

"Now don't go getting sore on me," Que said. "It's fifty dollars a head for each one you bring out of the bush—that includes calves. But the side bet is one hundred dollars on the stiff-necked steer."

"Hell, I don't even know if I can *find* him, much less get him back."

"Show some confidence. I got faith. Sam bragged how it was easy pickings for him. Claimed the only way to bring that steer back was killed and quartered. He said that when Gypsy got a little better, he might go up there for a slow-elk hunt and shoot it himself. I said you'd bring him back *whole.*"

The bet sounded a little doubtful to Danny. "You put up a hundred dollars of *your* money?"

Que got up to get another cup of coffee, and Danny knew he was working on an answer. "Not exactly. The hundred dollars is from the stock you bring in, but that's only if you don't get the steer. So don't get cranky, because it's not a real hundred dollars, you see. All that counts is Sam is going to have to pay us when you come back with that steer."

"I don't like it," Danny said. "I've got to bust my hump up there and win to keep from losing. You weren't going after the cattle anyway, so why did you make a crazy bet like that for me?"

Que shook his head and threw up his hands. "Heck, I saw it as an opportunity for you to make another hundred. Look, I don't want you to be sore. To show there's no hard feelings, I'm going to let you take the coffee maker. Really. I mean it. Think of waking up to fresh-brewed coffee in the morning."

"We'll be up in the hills," Danny said. "There's no use for it up there."

"Take it for tonight, then. I insist. I'll pick it up at the trailer tomorrow after you're gone. Here's how it works, see. You just set the dial. Stop snatching at it. I'll do it for you this time. How does six sound?"

"Make it seven," Danny said. "I'm not in any hurry to go goosing steers around in the puckerbrush." He looked at Jack. "What are you grinning at?"

"Two old magpies quarreling. We ought to leave before you pick it to death."

"You're right," Danny said. "Company's gone bitter, anyway. A hundred-dollar bet . . ."

As Que walked them to the truck, he slapped Jack's shoulder. "Don't be a stranger. You're welcome anytime. We can take a spin into town and gawk at the artwork."

"Maybe he can't stand your corny jokes," Danny said.

"Well," Que said, "you can choose your friends, but you're stuck with relations."

Jack glanced at them both. "That's a fact."

Que chuckled. "Little Red Shirt. Spitting image."

When Danny opened the door to his trailer and looked around, he was amazed at the cleaning job Pudge had done, but his heart also sank a little, because he wondered where she had stashed all his boxes and gear. He hoped she hadn't charged a U-STOR-IT space in the new building just outside town.

The counters were cleaned and wiped down. So was the kitchen table. The old cans filled with grease and coffee grounds were no longer sitting on the back of the stove, and the little plates under the burners had been scoured. The worn rug showed recent vacuum tracks, and Pudge had thrown a nice blanket over the ripped back of the sofa.

She had dusted Red Shirt's old army footlocker and placed it in front of the sofa as a kind of coffee table. On it was a school picture of Jack, outdated by three or four years. Wearing a light brown cowboy shirt and dark cord pants, he was standing in front of trees with bright autumn foliage. Jack's smile seemed too big, and fine lines wrinkled his forehead, giving him a nervous look. He was squinting at the camera, so you couldn't see his eyes clearly. Ever since Danny had picked up Jack at Timbler, he had tried to match the boy with the figure in the picture, but it never quite worked. At times Jack showed the same tension, but there was something else underneath. Danny couldn't get a handle on it.

Alongside the picture were Red Shirt's Korean War medals, in an imitation velvet case, and a yellowed newspaper clipping telling about Danny at the Klamath Stampede. Danny knew Pudge had taken the picture from her own trailer and had found the medals when she cleaned up. He didn't know where she got the clipping.

"So this is it?" Jack said, looking around. "Not too bad."

"I straightened up a little," Danny said. "No one wants to come home to a mess." He set the coffee maker on the counter, then stepped back to take a look. "Pretty fancy. I'll bet the superintendent at Timbler doesn't have a pot like that."

Jack picked up his school photo and examined it. "Those aren't real trees," he said. "No trees that color in Nebraska. They just put up a painted screen and have you stand in front."

"The hell. I thought there was something funny." Danny

had seen backgrounds at the Round-Up where you poked your head through so it looked like you were in jail, but it didn't seem right to phony up school pictures. He hoped Jack would say something about the clipping, but he didn't.

Danny opened the door to Red Shirt's old bedroom. He had been using it to store boxes of hunting and fishing gear and piles of winter clothes, but now it was spotless. The closet had been cleaned out, and the pine shelf above the clothes rod was covered with bright yellow Con-Tact paper. The same paper covered the dresser top. The single bunk was made up with clean sheets and blankets.

"You can bunk in here. I'm giving you Red Shirt's old room because it's the biggest. Lots of space to stow your gear. How about that Con-Tact paper? Spiffy, huh? Maybe we could get a little throw rug to match."

"The room's fine," Jack said.

Danny waited for him to say something else, but Jack just put his suitcase on the bed and started unpacking. He set a framed picture of Loxie on the dresser.

Danny hadn't seen that picture before, but he guessed it had been taken not too long before she died. Although there were circles under her eyes, dark as bruises, she was a beautiful woman. Still, it made him feel odd he had never seen her with her hair cut that short and slightly curled.

Jack saw Danny staring at the picture. "I took this a few months before the wreck," he said quietly. "We both liked it."

Danny nodded. "Good picture. She always was a fine-looking woman."

"I'd like to be alone while I unpack and settle in," Jack said. "That was a pretty long drive today."

Danny wanted to say something else about Loxie, but he couldn't think what. Finally he said, "I'm tuckered too. There's clean towels if you want to wash up when you're through unpacking."

Jack didn't look up from putting away his clothes. "I took care of that at Billy Que's."

"Sure." Danny paused. "Good night, then." He had hoped the boy would be glad about coming back, or at least that he'd like his room. But maybe it was too soon after Loxie's death. Or maybe he was too tired. Well, Danny figured, he'd just have to wait a while. Like Que said, make do.

Opening the refrigerator, Danny saw that Pudge had cleaned it too. It now contained milk, eggs, cheese, juice, bacon, beer, and an open box of baking soda. Danny took one of the beers. A fresh can of coffee was on the stove. He checked the stainless steel coffeepot. She had scrubbed that too, and he shook his head. Red Shirt claimed you never cleaned out a coffeepot, because it made the coffee taste bad. And he refused to drink out of aluminum coffeepots. According to him, aluminum and coffee poisoned you, making you sterile.

Danny opened the beer and sat at the formica table. He closed his eyes and leaned back. He couldn't remember his mother's death because he had been too young. At times, when he was growing up, he wanted to remember, and he tried to piece together something from the old faded photographs and Red Shirt's stories. But it never really worked, so he quit trying and put all the photos away in a shoebox. He figured you just tried to make do with pictures when you didn't have anything better, and even then, like with Jack's school picture, you never knew what you had. But the loss stayed anyway, right at your very center, like a drowning cramp.

One morning years before, Danny had awakened in the pre-dawn twilight and walked groggily into the kitchen. It was a mess. His father had started to make a cake and had spilled flour all over the counters and floor. Five broken eggs were in the sink. Red Shirt was snoring at the table, his head lying in his folded arms. Flour dusted his hair and shoulders, and his hands were white. Danny made strong coffee, and when it finished brewing he set a cup on the table, then nudged his father awake.

Red Shirt drank half the coffee before he said anything. "You know what day this is?" he asked.

Danny shook his head.

"It would have been your mother's birthday."

"No," Danny said. "That's not until next week."

Red Shirt seemed puzzled. "Maybe so. Anyway, she was a damn fine woman. Your good qualities come from her. Here, fill this up again." He held the cup out, and when Danny took it, Red Shirt slumped back in the chair. "She was the only one for me," he said.

As Danny refilled the cup, he knew his father was about to tell the story again. He gave the coffee to Red Shirt, then sat across the table from him.

Red Shirt stared at the coffee cup a while, turning it around in his hands. "Damn fine woman," he repeated. "With her, I might have turned out better. You were only a year and a half old, so you stayed here with me while she took the bus up to Lapwai to help her sister Marnie. Her sister was about due. I promised we'd drive up there in a week or so to get her. That suited me fine. As you know, her old man and I never lost any love between us. While she was gone, I decided to surprise her with a new phone like she wanted, a lemon-yellow Princess to put right on this table." Red Shirt thumped the table twice to make certain Danny was paying attention.

"Then I bought a new rug at Carpeteria, to match the phone. After I unloaded that carpet at home, you played on it most of the afternoon, climbing the roll and sliding off. I put you to bed at eight and I was sitting over on the sofa watching TV. It was late because wrestling was already over, a grudge match between Gorgeous George and The Mangler. Then I guess I dozed off.

"I awoke when I felt a cold draft. The trailer door was open and an old woman stood in the doorway. She was wearing a dark cape with a cowl, so I couldn't see her features very well. She came into the room and took a couple of steps toward me. 'What is it?' I asked. But she didn't answer. She just stood there and shook her head slowly, back and forth. Then she turned and left, closing the door behind her. I went to the door to call after her, and to my surprise, it was locked. By the time I stepped outside, she was gone."

Danny felt the chills that always came during that part of the story. Red Shirt stood to pour some more coffee, then sat back down at the table.

"Maybe ten minutes went by while I was trying to figure it out. Then I heard a knock at the door. When I opened it, Billy Que was standing there, looking strange. 'I'm damn sorry,' he said. 'She's dead.'

"I hit him hard, just once. His knees buckled and he collapsed on the rug. Then I sank to my knees and buried my face in his coat. We both got to our feet and staggered around the trailer, clutching each other like we were doing some kind of crazy dance. Then we got drunk for real, sitting at this table. I told him about the old woman coming in, so we threw tobacco outside for the spirits."

Red Shirt reached across the table and took Danny's slender hands in his broad ones. He almost never finished the story, but Danny knew how it ended. The pilot light went out in the gas heater of Marnie's trailer, and the gas killed his mother. Marnie and her new baby were still at the hospital. That was the only good thing. After the funeral, his father had called Goodwill and told them to come get the rug.

Danny finished the beer and stood. Taking a deep breath, he approached his bedroom door, then opened it carefully. His bed had been stripped, but Pudge had left the dirty sheets and blankets on the stained mattress cover. His rifle and shotgun were on the mattress too, along with several boxes of shells. The closet was jammed with his clothes and hunting gear, including two dozen duck decoys, their weights and lines now hopelessly tangled. His hipboots, three tackle boxes, and two creels cluttered one corner of the room. The fishing poles were scattered across the floor like jackstraws.

"Damn that Pudge," Danny muttered. After seeing the other rooms of the trailer, he had planned on doing something nice for her, but now . . . At least she hadn't taken his stuff to Goodwill. Once when Jimmy Little Badger had gone off to rodeo without cleaning up, his wife had donated all his gear. By the time Jimmy returned, half of it had been sold, and they made him pay for the rest, even though he swore there had been a mistake.

Danny found a little note taped to the headboard:

D,
   You are a slob. I cleaned up for Jack, but the rest of this rat's nest is yours. You owe me, buster, and I'll send you a bill.
                           Ta ta,
                           P

That smartass Pudge, Danny thought. She'd tell Jack as soon as she saw him, too; then he'd know that she, not Danny, had fixed the place up.

Danny took the army blankets and tried to arrange them on the couch, but it was too short to provide much comfort, and he had to sleep on his side with his knees bent. Whenever he moved, the blankets slipped on the slick Naugahyde. He stayed a little angry at Pudge, because he had looked forward to a good night's sleep after the long drive.

He gave up just after midnight. With the blankets draped around him, Danny got up and limped stiff-legged around the room. He opened the door to Jack's bedroom and listened a moment to the boy's steady breathing; he closed the door softly. As he passed the formica table, he said half aloud, "Well, Old Man, I got him this far." Then he walked into his own bedroom. With half-closed eyes, Danny pushed everything off the far side of the bed and onto the floor. "Straighten it out later," he said, tumbling onto the bed.

Danny awakened in the morning to the ding-ding-ding of the alarm and the smell of freshly brewed coffee. The trailer's windows were covered with tinfoil to reflect some of the summer's intense heat, so Danny couldn't tell by the light how early it was. He poured himself a cup of coffee. It was hot and tasted as good as the coffee from the old pot, but he wasn't certain he liked being awakened by a coffeepot. Even so, he blew the pot a little kiss. "Just like a wife," he said.

Jack had slept through the alarm and Danny decided to let him rest a while longer. He dressed quickly, then took his coffee outside. The morning was clear and cold, with a trace of frost on the ground. Danny picked up a couple of windfall apples and whistled for Ring-Eye. The Appaloosa came to the fence and Danny stroked its head and muzzle. He cut the apples into sections and fed them to the horse. "We've got some work cut out," he said.

Danny went over and opened the Sears Port-A-Shed that served as a tack and storage room. He took the saddles, chaps, ropes, and denim jackets he thought they would need and loaded them into the truck. Since Billy Que was small, Danny figured Jack could wear his clothes, even if they fit him loosely. He found the tents and bedrolls and put them in the back of the truck too. The mice had gotten into the blankets a little, but they hadn't done too much damage. When he hitched up the horse trailer, he discovered the back lights didn't work, but it didn't matter since they would be staying mostly on the reservation.

When he went back inside the trailer, the clock on the

coffeepot said eight. The stores would be open in another hour, so he could drive to Pendleton and get supplies.

Jack came out of the bedroom rubbing his eyes. "I guess I overslept. Must be time to pack the gear."

"Just yours," Danny said. "I put most of it in the truck already." Then seeing that Jack was a little embarrassed at oversleeping, he added, "Don't worry. There wasn't much to it."

While Jack dressed, Danny took out the guns and shells. He decided to leave the .30-06 because it was too early to hunt deer, but he took the shotgun in case they wanted to shoot a few birds for camp. He also took the Ruger single-six .22 pistol. It was good to have it, along with some snakeloads, just in case.

They headed into town and bought supplies at the Safeway store, and Danny got some ice blocks for the plastic Igloo coolers. Que had given them some packages of Ramen noodles and several cans of beans, but Danny had left those at the trailer. He filled one ice chest with meat, milk, butter, and some fruit. He put cold Oly tallboys and some Cokes in the other.

They stopped at Mission and got Cayenne from Henry's brother Nathan. Nathan said that ordinarily he wouldn't mind riding along, but he had a job bucking bales for a late cutting. Danny asked him if he knew about Henry going rabbit, and Nathan just grinned.

They drove east on the reservation road, through Minthorn, Cayuse, Thornhollow. Danny pulled the pickup over where the road crossed Little Buckaroo Creek. As dry as it had been, there was still a trickle coming through, and Danny knew the cattle might be kegged up high in the pines.

"Any idea where they'll be?" Jack asked.

"We'll just have to scare them up," Danny said. "There's plenty of good grazing along Little Squaw Creek and Light Ridge. We should set up camp here and scout the area. If that doesn't work out, we'll check Saddle Hollow and Rattlesnake Gulch. We better pitch the tent first. It doesn't look like rain now, but storms come in fast over the Blues."

After they set camp, Danny and Jack saddled the horses. "Try on Que's chaps," Danny said. "We'll wear the denim jackets if the brush gets high."

"Seems pretty hot for all this gear."

"It's better than getting cut up by junipers and stick-erweeds. Don't ride the horses into serviceberries. They've got thorns an inch long."

"Don't worry. I'm not green enough to go ripping up a horse, especially one you borrowed from a friend."

They rode south along Little Buckaroo Creek, one man riding each side of the creek to look for tracks. When they came to the large brushy areas, they hollered and threw rocks. "Keep an eye out for the red ones," Danny said. "They're the easiest to spot. But if they come out boiling, be careful." He didn't want Cayenne to get horned like Gypsy had. "Give Cayenne the rein. He'll cut them off as well as anything."

By one o'clock Danny's arm was tired from throwing rocks into the serviceberry bushes and buckbrush. He peered hard into the thickets of red willows but had no luck.

They sat in the shade of a large juniper and ate lunch. Danny unwrapped the bologna and sliced it along with a couple of tomatoes. "Red Shirt always called this horsecock," Danny said. "Sort of makes it taste different, doesn't it?"

Jack swallowed hard. "So this is range cooking?"

"Tonight we'll fix better grub," Danny said. "At least we won't have to eat Que's Shanghai beans."

Jack opened a brown paper sack and took out something that looked like a pear, then started peeling it. "What is that?" Danny asked.

"Avocado. I picked up a few while you were getting the beer."

"I never heard of a puckerbrush cowboy eating avocados for lunch," Danny said.

"Some women mash these up and put them on their faces for beauty treatments," Jack said. "Lots of vitamins."

"It sounds like fruitcake guacamole," Danny said. "You must think this is a California salad bar. I hope the way you punch cows makes better sense than the way you eat."

After lunch, they rested in the shade for a couple hours. "Can't drive cattle in the heat of the day anyway," Danny said. "Even if we were lucky enough to find them." He enjoyed looking at the scenery. Autumn was his favorite season, and the vine maples were already a deep scarlet. A large hawk circled above them and Danny could see the blue of the sky through its fringed wingtips.

They finished Little Buckaroo Creek that afternoon and checked a little of Stage Gulch, but there were no fresh tracks. They arrived back at camp just before dark.

Jack seemed pretty stiff when he swung off Cayenne.

"Don't worry," Danny said. "I've got some wintergreen liniment."

"I'm not an old geezer," Jack said. "But toss the bottle here anyway, before you go using it all. Damn horse has a funny way of moving across these sidehills. Twists more than a dying snake."

"One nice thing," Danny said. "You don't crab as much as Billy Que."

They built a fire from juniper and locust. Danny chopped carrots, potatoes, and onions, then mixed them with ground beef and wrapped equal portions in tinfoil packets. When the coals were glowing, he tucked the packets in along the edge. "Sheepherder's stew," he said.

The sun set behind Reservation Mountain, and the trees along the ridge turned dark green, then gray in the fading light. An evening breeze stirred and Jack put on his denim jacket.

After half an hour, Danny dragged the darkened tinfoil packets out of the coal bank with a forked stick, then opened them carefully to avoid tearing the crisp foil. The juices from the meat and vegetables had blended together to make a delicious stew.

"Smells great," Jack said. "Where did you learn this?"

"Sammy Colwash. He was an old Celilo sheepherder that used to have a camp on the Umatilla near Shaplish Canyon. Sometimes Red Shirt took me up there. Sammy was always glad for company and used to be mighty free with the grub, especially if you happened to bring him a bottle, which Red Shirt did most of the time."

"He must have been a good cook," Jack said, eating heartily.

"Most sheepherders are," Danny said. "It's a lonely life and good food is one consolation. Sammy was always fun, though. He had in mind that there was lots of gold not far from his camp, but he never told anyone where, not even Red Shirt, and they were good friends. Lots of times, Red Shirt would open a bottle and try to loosen Sammy up with the whiskey, but no matter how drunk or silly he got, Sammy never said much about that gold.

"One spring, I remember, Sammy tricked Red Shirt into helping him dock the sheep. I was sleepy after a big supper of stew, beans, and sheepherder's bread baked in a coffee can. Sammy and Red Shirt started bragging about who had done the most things. Red Shirt was a little ahead because Sammy had never been in the war. Then Sammy told Red Shirt he didn't know anything about sheep because he'd never docked them. Red Shirt claimed he had lots of times, even though he hadn't.

"Sammy said the only way to dock sheep was after a shot of whiskey, so he gave Red Shirt one and he had one too. One led to another. After a while, they were feeling pretty chipper, so Sammy took Red Shirt out to where he kept the new lambs. Sammy picked up one of the males and spread its legs, then bit off the testicles. He spit them on the ground, wiped his mouth, and had a shot of the whiskey. 'Dock whiskey,' he said. 'It tastes better.'

"Red Shirt said he'd try it, so he did exactly like Sammy had done. After he drank the whiskey, he allowed maybe it did taste better after docking sheep. Anyway, Sammy got him to help dock all those lambs, and they finished that bottle and part of another. The next morning, Red Shirt woke up with a bad hangover and blood in his chin. As soon as he was able to move around, he went down to the river and soaked his head. He passed on breakfast, and barely stirred his appetite by lunchtime. For about a year, you couldn't get him to eat lamb. Sammy laughed and told Red Shirt that since he liked Dock whiskey so much, he should come back to drink it every spring."

Jack laughed at that. "I'll remember not to drink Dock whiskey if anybody offers some."

It turned colder and they let the fire die. Fog formed above the river and obscured some of the far hills. "Ghost breath," Danny said. He snapped a couple of small sticks and put them on the coals, where they blazed for a few minutes. The moon loomed large as it rose above Reservation Mountain, then grew pale and colder as it climbed into the black sky. "Time to bed in," Danny said.

"I don't want to dream about docking sheep," Jack said.

Danny smiled. "I've heard of counting them," he said. "Let's sleep outside tonight. It's clear."

Jack crawled inside the tent and threw out the bedrolls and groundcover. Then he took off his clothes and got into his bedroll. "Dock whiskey," he said.

Danny stirred the fire and watched the sparks rise into the night sky. He remembered how his father had looked docking the sheep with Sammy. Away from the campfire, both men had seemed like dark shadows. They had stood in the

wire enclosure with the sheep, lifting the white forms sky-
ward, one by one, their voices coarse and strong. Danny
missed them.

He wiped his shirtsleeve across his face, then pulled off his
pants and boots. Jack's dark head was visible above the bedroll. Asleep, he reminded Danny of Loxie. Danny reached
over and touched the boy's shoulder, as if making sure he was
really there. Then he crawled into his own bedroll and fell
asleep, facing the stars.

❖ 10 ❖

They rode all the next morning without finding the cattle, and by midday high clouds covered much of the sky, although patches of blue showed from time to time. The wind was at their backs and they turned up the collars of their denim jackets to keep it from whistling down their necks. In the late afternoon, the clouds grew scarcer and dappled the landscape with their shadows. They found a field of high wheat stubble at the top of Red Elk Canyon, and Danny suggested they hunt birds for dinner.

He took the Model 12 Winchester out of its sheepskin case and loaded it with waxy, green-ribbed shotgun shells. He checked to make certain he had #6 shot. "Some like #4s," he said to Jack, "but Red Shirt always claimed these patterned better and sifted through the feathers. How's your shooting eye?"

"I used to hunt pheasants around Hanson's place," Jack said. "I was pretty good at it."

"We'll get into some pheasants," Danny said. "But watch

for Huns and chukars, too. You can find a mixed bag around here."

Danny walked about forty yards into the stubble, and Jack remained in the uncultivated land between the field and the canyon's edge. The birds Danny roused would fly for the brushy cover of the canyon, giving Jack a wingshot as they passed. Danny felt good to be off the horse, but he wished he had a pair of walking boots because the field's large clods tripped him. Patches of bearded wheat stood where the combine had cut uneven rows in the rough ground. Danny guessed a hired man, rather than the farmer, had carelessly cut this back acreage.

Danny started at the cackle of a pheasant. The heavy bird's wings beat furiously as it cleared the ground, then stopped as they angled to catch the wind. The sun caught the copper of its feathers, the rainy green of its neck above the white band. Jack fired twice, the second shot as the bird sailed by him. With wings still set, it glided into the bottom of the canyon, where it landed untouched and scooted out of sight into some tall sage.

"Shit!" Jack pumped out the second shell and reloaded. He picked up the two waxy green shells from the ground and carried the gun over to Danny. "I can't hit squat with this. Maybe it's the pump. Hanson had a double barrel and I never missed with that." The disappointment showed in his eyes and his voice was angry.

"Any gun takes a little getting used to," Danny said.

"I missed that bastard clean. Didn't touch a feather."

"Do you know what you did wrong?"

Jack shook his head.

"You shot awful quick and didn't lead him enough."

"Maybe you better get supper, if you're such a hotshot."

Danny almost flared but composed himself before he spoke. "There's plenty of time," he said.

They walked in silence for another hundred yards, then

came upon a drywash where somebody had been dumping garbage. The wash was nearly filled with old auto bodies and tires, discarded household furniture and appliances, rusting cans, and broken bottles.

"This is some mess," Jack said. "Who dumped all this stuff here?"

"A rancher, more than likely. He was probably too cheap to pay county dumping fees."

"But it's on the reservation, right?"

"Yeah," Danny said. "He's probably got a long-term lease."

Jack scrambled over the edge of the wash and started poking at things with a stick. "The dumps were pretty big entertainment back in Nebraska. Some of the older guys drove us out there at night to hunt rats with .22s. We'd wait in the dark, using the fenders for rests, and once those rats started scurrying through the garbage, we'd pop on the high beams and waste them. Those stupid rats froze in the headlights, and if we used hollowpoints they just seemed to explode."

"Some fun," Danny said. "That was probably considered a real hot date back in Nebraska. How'd those rats taste with corn on the cob?"

"Beats me," Jack said, shaking his head. "Sounds like an Oregon recipe."

"Got me on that one," Danny said. He made his way down the drywash bank and joined Jack in the dump. "You know, people throw away a lot of good stuff. Here's some lawn chairs that look okay, even if the webbing's out."

"And look at this pile of bottles," Jack said.

"Tell you what," Danny said. "Why don't you practice a little with that shotgun? I'll toss some bottles and you try to hit them."

"Like clay pigeons," Jack said. "Hanson let me shoot some of those one time. He took a hand trap from the club, and a few dozen clay pigeons; then he threw them for me out in the corn stubble."

"Yeah," Danny said. "Kind of like that." He didn't want to think about Hanson with Jack. He took a stick and dug through the piles of broken glass until he found a few unbroken bottles. He drained the water out of them, then knocked off the loose dirt and tossed them up the bank.

"Where should I stand?" Jack asked.

"Get back from the wash about twenty yards. I'll just find a few more here. Somebody's been drinking a lot of Colonel Lee. Maybe I'll have to try that one."

Jack climbed up the bank and disappeared from Danny's view. Danny threw a brown Wesson oil bottle out, and it broke when it hit one of the others. "Nuts," he said.

"Come on," Jack said. "I'm ready."

"Relax. We don't want any accidents." When Danny picked up another bottle and started to drain it, he smelled the stinking water and saw the drowned mouse floating in the amber liquid. Danny flung the bottle away and pressed his forearm against his nose to keep from gagging.

"What's going on?" Jack yelled.

"Just about ready," Danny said. He had started up the bank when he heard Jack snap off the safety. All of a sudden, Danny had a wave of sick-sweet feeling, like he'd taken his eye off someone just before getting suckerpunched.

Then he remembered Buddy Swett, the retired railroad worker, who took in a troubled boy from Portland. The boy shot Buddy while they were bird hunting along the brakes of the Umatilla. The blast blew a hole through the front and back of Buddy's canvas hunting jacket, and he bled to death in the field. The boy claimed it was an accident, that the shotgun discharged while he was climbing through a fence. Some sided with him, including his school counselor, but Danny had seen the glint in the boy's eye and knew he had done it on purpose.

And he had once shot Red Shirt when he was eight and his father had brought home a BB air rifle as a birthday present.

Danny had been anxious to shoot it and cocked the rifle while his father was setting up the Daisy targets that came with it. One wavered in the breeze, and Danny fired just as his father reached out to straighten it. The BB lodged in the back of Red Shirt's hand, underneath the skin, forming a round purple lump with a copper top where the BB remained half-exposed. As his father came toward him, his trembling hand raised, Danny ran from his dark size and scrambled underneath the trailer just ahead of the pointed boot. Later, Danny realized that he hadn't meant to shoot him, but he couldn't say it was entirely an accident either.

"Hey! Did you fall asleep?" Jack yelled. "Those birds will die of old age before I get another crack at them."

Danny cautiously poked his head over the edge of the drywash and saw Jack standing fifty feet away holding the shotgun with one hand. Its butt was planted in the dirt and the barrel was pointed at the sky.

Danny shook his head to clear away the dark thoughts. Too many of those near him had died early. He climbed out of the wash and picked up a green wine bottle. "Like they say in the navy, 'Fire at will,' " he said.

"Which one's he?" Jack asked.

Danny threw the bottle hard and high over the drywash, watching it turn end over end. He heard the blast behind him and counted a full second until the bottle reached the top of its arc, the green shape hanging for an instant against the pale blue sky, then exploding into hundreds of green shards that caught the light as they fell.

The first pheasant they flushed after the target practice was small and dark coppery gray. It climbed quickly, set its wings, and sailed in front of Jack. He raised the gun but lowered it again without shooting. "Hen," Jack cried.

Danny moved ahead without answering. He knew it was a young rooster, but he didn't want to confuse the boy. There were lots of birds, and plenty of time before dusk obscured their markings. Two brown hens rose together and Danny threw a clod after them. He walked right by the next rooster, but it became scared when he paused and flew out behind him, cackling.

Jack whirled and raised the gun.

Wait, Danny thought. Wait.

The bird climbed toward the sun and Danny counted . . . one . . . two . . . almost too long. He heard the shot and then saw a small puff of feathers separate from the bird. The pheasant shifted course slightly, then lurched crazily sideways and tumbled earthward, landing with a thud. Danny and Jack ran quickly toward the bird in case it got up and tried to run for cover, but it was dead. A few feathers drifted lazily downward.

"I waited," Jack said, grinning.

"Good shooting," Danny said. "Just right." The boy's grin became larger. Danny picked up the bird and turned it over. There was a drop of red blood on the yellow horny beak, and the dusty gray eyelids were closed. A couple of other bright wet spots showed along the bird's green neck feathers. "Put it under your belt," Danny said. "That way both hands are still free to shoot."

Jack flushed several chukars but they refused to fly. Instead, they scooted ahead of him on bright orange legs. Their black eyebands made them look like burglars. "Darned chukars," he said. "I should have sluiced them."

Danny looked up and saw a large hawk circling. "The birds see the hawk's shadow," he said. "They'll stay in thick cover rather than fly and take a chance with that hawk."

Jack pointed his gun in the hawk's direction. "It's a long shot, but maybe I can get him."

"No," Danny said. "He's hunting too. There are enough birds for all of us."

The next covey of chukars flew, winging low and gray over

the sagebrush. Jack fired and one of the birds crumpled into the brush.

"Mark it," Danny yelled.

Jack fired again and the trailing bird's wing broke, but as soon as it hit the ground it was running, the wing dangling. Danny went after the bird. He ran slowly in the plowed field, but picked up speed when he reached its edge. Thirty yards ahead, the chukar crossed a little gulch and raced down the side of the canyon. Danny jumped the gulch and saw the bird slip through some low sagebrush.

When he reached the line of sagebrush, Danny tried to leap over them, but tripped on an old length of fencewire and fell headlong into a patch of Russian thistles and sticker-brush. He lay still for a moment, trying to catch his wind and figure out how badly he was scratched.

Jack came up grinning. "One minute you were setting the record for the hundred-yard dash; the next you disappeared. What a wipeout!"

"Taking a break," Danny grumbled, sitting up and carefully pulling some stickers from his hands. "You get that bird?"

Jack shook his head. "Coyote snack."

"We've got enough for supper," Danny said.

After they had ridden back to camp, Danny twisted the heads off the birds and checked their craws. Both were full of wheat kernels. Using his jackknife, he slit the birds along their bellies, then pulled out the steaming innards and tossed them into the brush for the magpies. He built a fire and waited until he had a good coal bank, then broke off a green willow from the creek and ran it through the birds' necks and anuses, securing the flesh to the stick with twisted baling wire. Then he suspended the birds on slotted sticks about twelve inches above the coals.

While the birds roasted, Danny painted his scratches with iodine. "I got scratched good today," he said.

They split the pheasant and chukar in halves and ate the delicious meat to the bone. "Which did you like better?" Danny asked.

"Can't tell," Jack said. "Whichever one I was eating at the time."

For the second night in a row, the rising fog hid the lower part of Reservation Mountain and its top seemed suspended from the sky. The moon rose over the mountain and hung there like a pale orange wafer.

They stared at the mountain in the moonlight, and Jack asked quietly, "Why are you against leasing that land to SUNCO?"

Danny was surprised by the question. "Who have you been talking to?"

"Pudge said something about it when she was at the funeral."

"Well, your aunt Pudge and Billy Que don't see that deal the same way I do."

Danny didn't know what else to say. Then as he watched the rising fog, he remembered the mists hovering above Celilo Falls before the government built the dam and ended the fishing. When he recalled going there with Red Shirt to see Sammy, he knew how to tell Jack the story.

"You don't know about the Celilos," Danny said. "They lived at Celilo Falls, just east of The Dalles. Different Indians lived there, but they called themselves Celilos or Wy-ams, people of the roaring water. Most of them have gone now because the government destroyed their fishing before you were born. But Red Shirt took me there to see the falls, and we went to the spring salmon feast with Sammy Colwash.

"Every year the salmon came up the Columbia, big silvers and Chinooks, and the Celilos caught them in hooped dipnets as they were trying to leap the falls or swim up the basalt chutes.

"Each man had his fishing place, usually handed down

from grandfather to father to son. No one knows how far back it went—a long time. They ate many salmon, kept some for trade, and sold the rest to the canneries."

"You couldn't make much money selling fish," Jack said. "The cannery people might, but not the fishermen."

Danny nodded. "You've got a point. Maybe no one got rich off the fish, but they got by. And the fishing brought the people together. During the big runs, everyone came to Celilo to fish, eat, and visit friends."

"How many came?" Jack asked.

"Lots," Danny said. "Sometimes thousands. They came from Yakima, Warm Springs, Pendleton. Even the Nez Perce from Lapwai showed up. The Celilos called these visitors comers and treated them like guests.

"There was a treaty that said the Indians could always fish the falls. But the government wanted to build a dam to generate electricity for the cities and store water for the farmers. They offered the Indians money for their fishing rights. It seemed like a lot. Compared to the fish money, it probably was.

"Some wanted to sell, especially the younger ones or those from the reservations who just visited Celilo. But others said no. Old Tommy Thompson, the Celilo chief, begged them not to sell their rights. The Indians argued among themselves so long that the government finally just gave them all checks and went ahead and built the dam."

"So they had the money," Jack said. "And if it was a fair price, they should have been okay."

"Maybe some were," Danny said. "But money gets spent up. It was the same way for the Klamaths when their reservation was sold off for timber. Every car dealer and sharp salesman came around to sign the people up for the good life. Double-wide trailers, new pickups and cars, rifles, TVs, fancy clothes. A lot of the young Indians bought like crazy."

Jack whistled softly. "I'd get a pickup and trailer and a darned good horse—make a living at the rodeos."

Danny shook his head. "No, you couldn't. That's the point. Cars get wrecked up, trailers burn, TVs go out. And the money's gone.

"After the dam, there were no more fish. Before that, no matter what happened, the people always had the fish. For the Celilos, fishing was a way of life. When they caught the first salmon each spring, they laid it on the rocks with its head upstream to make sure more salmon would follow. But after the dam . . ."

Danny shook his head. "Some of the old people like Tommy Thompson never even cashed their checks. They thought maybe if they didn't take any money, things would be okay. They kept their hair long and braided to show the Maker they had been faithful."

"They were really out of it," Jack said. "You need lawyers. Of course, they built the dam anyway."

"That's right," Danny said. "Even then some of the old people refused to believe it could destroy the falls. The river seemed so powerful, and the falls had been there longer than anyone knew.

"Red Shirt took me back to Celilo the day they closed the floodgates on the dam. For a few hours, it didn't seem to make much difference. The whitewater came rushing down the chutes, roaring and crashing over the falls. But down below you could see it hit the dam and start rolling back against itself, like wild horses driven into a blind canyon cutting back on their trail. By the middle of the afternoon, you could tell the water was rising. A large pool of it stretched all across the river and started eddying back toward the falls. But the falls kept on roaring as if nothing could stop them.

"Red Shirt pointed to some sticks floating toward us, and

when I saw they weren't sticks but logs, I knew that rising lake was a lot bigger than I had imagined.

"Finally, the lake reached the base of the first falls, so the engineers in their hardhats and ties, and the politicians, lined up for pictures—the last pictures of the falls.

"Then I heard a high wail. It was even louder than the roar of the falls. All the old Celilos had turned their backs to the rising water and were lined up facing the canyon wall. Their arms were crossed and they were chanting the falls' death chant.

"The lake rose against the falls. The water kept pouring over the falls, but the more it crashed into the lake, the higher the lake rose, choking it back. I closed my eyes, praying it would stop. Then I opened them and stared. One after another, the falls drowned themselves, until the roaring stopped and I couldn't hear anything but the sucking of the dark, eddying lake as it grew larger and larger, filling up the canyon.

"As the noise from the falls died, the wailing grew louder, like a shriek. One of the reservation chiefs, who had been standing with the engineers and photographers, walked away from them and joined the old men and women with their backs turned to the dark water. He was crying when he passed us, and he said, 'We sold our mother, and now they have drowned her.'

"It grew dark and some people built fires. The chanting Celilos cast long shadows against the canyon walls. Some of the young people started up their new cars and pickups. The headlights shone over the smooth black lake as they drove down the hill and into The Dalles to go drinking or to the movies.

"The old Celilos stood like statues, still facing the canyon wall and refusing to look at the lake that drowned the falls. They had stopped wailing by then, but the silence was even worse. We left.

"I remember Red Shirt stayed very quiet all the way back to Pendleton. Later, he told me that Tommy Thompson was in a nursing home the day they flooded the falls. All the Celilos said he could feel the cold water rising, and he kept crying out for more blankets."

When Danny finished talking, Jack didn't say anything. He just looked over toward Reservation Mountain.

"It was very bad for the Celilos," Danny said. "Most left the village and moved into town or back to the reservations. Some catch a few salmon at Cook's Landing or Shearer's Bridge on the Deschutes. After years of quarreling, they've managed to finish the village longhouse. But there are no more big feasts, and if you look into the old people's eyes, you can tell they are still dreaming of the falls and the salmon."

Jack broke a couple of sticks and threw them on the fire. "Was it something like that for the Nez Perce too?" he asked.

"Maybe in a way," Danny said. He had always thought the Nez Perce were better off than the Celilos. "At first, the Nez Perce shared the Wallowas with the gold prospectors and cattle ranchers. Old Joseph didn't want any trouble and tried to work things out. But the newcomers kept taking more, and the government kept shrinking the land it had promised the Nez Perce. Finally, when the government tried to send the Nez Perce away, Young Joseph and the Dreamers took up the rifle."

"But they lost it anyway," Jack said. "Just like the Celilos."

"It doesn't seem that way to me," Danny said. "Some like Left Hand returned to the Wallowas to hunt and practice the old ceremonies. The Dreamers believed those mountains still belonged to them and if they worked the ceremonies right, the white men would leave."

"Come on," Jack said. "No wonder they called them Dreamers. That craziness went out with Ghost Dancing. Exactly how many white people have left?"

Danny shook his head. "Maybe we better turn in. Tomorrow, we'll find the cows."

They found the cattle the next morning near the top of Squaw Creek Canyon, about a mile inside the reservation boundary. They were bunched on the south slope, warming themselves in the morning sun and grazing on clumps of elk grass. Danny and Jack stopped fifty yards short of the cattle to keep from spooking them. There were ten in the bunch, but the black stiff-necked steer and the ginger-colored cow were missing.

Danny left Jack to keep an eye on the cattle and rode the top of the ridge looking for the strays. After about an hour, he found the stiff-necked steer in a thicket of jack pine. When the steer saw Danny approaching on Ring-Eye, he stood and looked around wild-eyed, then trotted down the hill toward the others. Danny wondered where the ginger-colored cow was. He knew she should have a calf with her.

He followed the ridge until he hit the reservation line, then turned and started working back down. When he came out of the timber and into a sagebrush flat, he saw the dark markers in the sky. Beneath the circling vultures Danny found the carcass of the ginger cow in a patch of bitterbrush. She had gotten her leg caught in some old fencewire and the coyotes had found her. They had torn out her belly and eaten about half the carcass, leaving the rest for the vultures and magpies. The magpies flew off as Danny approached, but the vultures stayed with the carcass, tearing away strings of flesh and fixing Danny with their hard black eyes. He took the .22 Ruger from its holster and pointed at the vultures, then put it back in the holster without firing. His grudge was against the coyotes. He could get them later, after he delivered the cattle to Sam.

"Scram!" he yelled. "Bonepickers! Get the hell out!"

The vultures flapped away, shreds of meat still hanging from their curved beaks.

Danny found the dead calf about fifty yards down the hill. Its throat was torn out but little of it had been eaten. He figured the coyotes killed it for blood sport when it came to nurse. He vowed he would return for his payback.

Jack was waiting about one hundred yards from the cattle when Danny rode in from the ridge. "Any luck?" Jack asked.

Danny shook his head. "Coyotes got the cow and her calf."

"That's a tough break," Jack said. He took a deep breath. "Well, how do you want to drive this bunch?"

"We'll take them out along the trail at the bottom of the canyon. That way they'll be close to water. I'll push them along the trail. You stay even with them, but about fifty yards up the slope. In case any of them head for the top, you can cut them off."

They approached the cattle slowly, and when they got close, the cows walked toward the brushy bottom of the canyon along Squaw Creek. Once there, Danny rode behind and the cattle moved ahead down the game trail. "We'll take it nice and easy," he yelled at Jack. "We won't push."

For two hours, the cattle drove easily. Danny started thinking about the money and grinned. He squinted at the sun and guessed it was about two. He took off his denim jacket because it was hot toward the canyon bottom. When he looked ahead, he noticed that the cattle had quit moving. The stiff-necked steer was tossing his head from side to side and trying to turn back, but he was blocked by the rest of the herd. Suddenly he bawled and lunged ahead. A couple of the cows bolted up the hill and two more crashed into the brush. Danny spurred Ring-Eye ahead, but reined in when he saw the hornet's nest on a serviceberry limb overhanging the trail. He felt a burning sting on his wrist and slapped at the hornet. The remaining cows milled for a moment, wide-eyed with confusion, then broke up the hillside or into the brush.

Danny urged Ring-Eye up the hill. Jack had blocked the first two cows, and he waved his hat and yelled to turn them. Ring-Eye overtook the others, and Danny hollered, "Whoa, you bastards, whoa!" Jack came over to help out, and they forced the cattle into the bottom of the canyon, but there they ran into thickets of smokeweed and serviceberry. Danny heard the popping and snapping of limbs as the cattle plunged toward the water.

"It was going so well," Jack said. "What happened?"

"Damn hornet's nest right over the trail," Danny said. He looked at the angry red welt on his wrist where the hornet had found skin above the glove and below the shirt. "Now those cattle will be plenty spooky."

"At least none got up the ridge."

"That's right," Danny said. The boy had shown savvy in turning them back and Danny was pleased. "You did good work."

Jack smiled. "Thanks. Should we try to drive them out of the brush?"

"No," Danny said. "Not until it cools off. They'll stay in the brush until evening, and if we tried to take the horses into the serviceberry, the thorns would rip them up."

Danny sat against a shady juniper a few yards above the trail and decided to take a nap. Jack picked some elderberries by the creek. Holding out his stained hands he offered some to Danny, but Danny said they were too bitter. He dozed for a few moments, and when he awakened, Jack was sitting in the creek trying to cool off. He had hung his clothes on a serviceberry branch and left his boots on some flat stones nearby.

"Come on in!" he yelled when he saw Danny watching him.

"Too shallow," Danny said.

"It's maybe two feet at the deepest part."

Suddenly there was a thrashing in the brush below Jack,

and he stood, then took a step toward his clothes. The stiff-necked steer came out of the elderberry and smokeweed thicket. When he saw Jack, he lowered his head and charged. For a moment Jack stood paralyzed, his mouth open, watching the steer charge. He had one hand half raised, as if already reaching for his clothes.

"Run!" Danny yelled. He leaped to his feet and vaulted onto Ring-Eye. "Run, damn it!"

Jack took a step toward the far side of the creek and slipped, falling into the water on his hands and knees. Then he was up, scrambling across the creek and running down the trail. The steer splashed after him.

"Go!" Danny urged the horse. "Go!" He slapped Ring-Eye's flank. The horse ran after the charging steer, and Danny swung far to his right, grabbing Jack's denim jacket from the serviceberry limb as he galloped by. The horse was across the creek, running hard.

Jack's arms and legs were pumping as he ran down the trail, but the steer had gained on him. "Faster," Danny urged Ring-Eye, and the horse laid back his ears and shot ahead until his head was even with the steer's black rump.

It seemed to Danny they were all moving in slow motion, Jack leading the steer by inches and Ring-Eye so close he was almost on top of the stiff-neck. The trail widened slightly where the creek turned, and Danny yelled, "Jump!"

Jack leaped from the trail into a patch of smokeweed just as Ring-Eye galloped even with the steer, brushing against his left side. Danny leaned right and flung Jack's denim jacket into the steer's face so the flapping sleeves tangled in the steer's horns, blindfolding him. Unable to see, the steer shuddered to a halt. As he tossed his head and snorted, the jacket waved in the air. The steer's hooves caught a sleeve, and the jacket ripped away from the horns. The steer pawed at the grounded jacket a couple of times, then hooked it and tossed it to the side of the trail. He bawled once, then dove into the dense serviceberry thicket.

Danny rode Ring-Eye back to Jack. The boy stood trembling in the smokeweed. His shoulders were scratched from the dive into the brush, but other than that he seemed unharmed. Danny got off the horse and put his arm around Jack. Jack turned his head, but not before Danny saw the terror in his eyes. Then he buried his face in Danny's shoulder and shuddered. Danny held his son close to him. "It's all right," Danny said. "It's okay now."

Jack shook his head and stiffened his back. "I'm not going to cry," he said. "But I'm scared as hell. I ran until I didn't have anything left."

Danny held the boy by his shoulders. "Anybody would be scared," he said. "Lots of times in the chutes I've been so scared I wanted to crawl off."

They walked back to retrieve the jacket. One of the arms had been ripped away, and the steer's horn had made an L-shaped tear in the back. Danny handed it to Jack. "Souvenir."

Jack looked at the torn sleeve and the gash. "He thought he had me, didn't he?"

Danny nodded. "Maybe Pudge can sew it up and you can wear it. A rank steer like that will come at you sometimes, if he thinks you're not keeping a close watch. Remember, they're unpredictable."

Jack's feet were cut up slightly from the running, so Danny had him ride Ring-Eye back to the place he had been swimming. Jack got dressed quietly. Before he put his socks and boots on, Danny painted his cut feet with iodine. The boy bit his lip but did not cry out. After Jack had put his boots and hat on, he said, "I want to teach that bastard a lesson."

"We'll have to wait until evening," Danny said. "When he comes out of the brush, we'll try to get a rope on him." He thought of the coyotes again, and the way they had killed the ginger-colored cow and her calf. He wished they'd gotten the steer. If so, he probably wouldn't have felt so strongly about going after them.

"By the way," Jack said. "Thanks a lot. I thought he was going to bury that horn in my back."

Danny took an apple out of his saddlebag and handed it to Jack. "Cut this up and give it to Ring-Eye. He earned his keep today."

After they rested awhile, Danny showed Jack how to throw a rope for the hind legs. "It's a little like team roping," he said. "I'll try to get my rope around his head before he can get back to the brush; then you come in and rope his back legs. Throw your loop in front of the back feet so he can step into it. Once we've got him, I'll jump off the horse and mug him down."

"What happens if you miss?"

"I guess Sam wins the bet. What worries me more is catching him on the fly and missing the saddlehorn—with him racing like mad for the boonies. Might lose some fingers."

"There was a guy like that in Nebraska," Jack said. "Claw Henderson."

Danny squinted at him. "Bullshit."

They waited on the horses until the big steer came out of the brush. While his head was lowered in the creek, Danny brought Ring-Eye close to him. As the steer headed for the brush, Danny threw the loop, catching the steer by the horns so he wouldn't choke and fight the rope harder. Danny took a couple quick turns on the dally to secure the rope, and when the steer reached the rope's limit, his head snapped back. He fell to his knees, and Danny urged Ring-Eye backward, hoping to keep him on the ground, but he regained his feet. "Damn!" Danny said. "Get him!" he told Jack.

While the steer kept his eye on Danny and Ring-Eye, Jack moved in with Cayenne and threw his loop for the steer's hind legs. He missed but recoiled his rope and got him on the second try, tightening the loop around one rear foot.

"Keep him there," Danny said. Danny got off the horse and approached the big steer carefully. "Steady now, Jack. Don't let him slip that hoof." Ring-Eye was keeping the pressure on and so was Jack; the steer couldn't go either way. It snorted at Danny, blowing a string of snot.

Danny grabbed the horns and twisted, digging his bootheels into the ground and putting his shoulder into the steer's neck. "Slack off a little," he told Jack. Danny grunted and twisted harder, until he felt the blood pound in his temples. The steer's neck came around so far Danny thought it would break. "Now jerk," he said. As Jack tugged on the rope, the steer lost his balance and toppled. Danny jumped away from the flailing hooves. The steer's head started to come up, but Ring-Eye stepped back, taking up the slack, so the steer stayed down.

Danny took the hogging string and wrapped it around both of the front legs, then pulled the free back leg forward and tied it to the others with a hooey hitch. The big steer grunted but could not get up. Danny released Jack's rope and watched the steer struggle for a moment until he was satisfied his hitch would hold.

After walking back to Ring-Eye, Danny took the rope from the saddlehorn and snubbed the steer to a stout juniper. He left enough slack so the steer could struggle and wear itself out. Time and again it tried to get to its feet, then lost balance and rolled over, bawling and kicking.

"Let's eat supper," Danny said. "That ugly fellow will fight the rope most of the night, and by morning maybe he'll be cooled down a bit."

"Listening to him bawl, I almost feel sorry," Jack said.

"Think of the horn he was trying to put in your gut."

By morning the steer had worn itself down and was quiet when Danny and Jack approached. They still had several trail miles to go before they hit the road, and Danny tried to figure out the best way to make the steer move without bolting. He could trim its hooves, paring them back until they were tender, but it would be difficult to determine exactly how much to cut back. Too little and the steer might run; too much and he might be too lame to drive.

Danny looked toward the creek and saw some red willows there. He remembered something Red Shirt had told him a long time ago. "I've got an idea," he said. "I don't know if it will work, but we can give it a try before we start trimming hooves."

He went down to the creek and cut some red willows into short sticks about the length of his thumb, sharpening them at both ends.

Then Danny and Jack pulled the steer closer to the juniper, taking out the slack in the rope. Danny tied the steer's head securely, looping another rope around its neck and horns so it couldn't twist or toss its head and hook him.

He opened the shortest, sharpest blade on his knife. Pulling the upper and lower eyelids away from one of the steer's rolling eyeballs, Danny cut small slits in both lids. As he worked, he gritted his teeth and tried not to listen to the steer's frenzied bawling or look at its eyes, which were white with terror. Then he did the same with the steer's other eye. A few bright drops of blood clung to the stainless steel blade, and Danny wiped them off on his pants before he snapped the blade closed and put the knife back in his pocket.

When Jack saw what Danny was doing, he turned and looked at the creek.

Danny took the red willow sticks and inserted them into the slits, forcing the lids apart so the steer could not blink or close its eyes. Then he stood, rubbing the back of his neck to ease the tension. His own eyes watered and smarted, and he wiped them with the back of his hand.

"Watch him now," Danny said. "Stand clear."

He released the hooey hitch and unwrapped the hogging string from the steer's legs, then removed one rope from its neck and horns, freeing the steer's head from the juniper trunk. He kept one end of the other rope looped around the tree to prevent the steer from charging, just in case the sticks didn't work.

The steer stood stiffly and shook its head a few times. When it tried to walk to the creek, Danny gave it enough slack to reach the water. After the steer had drunk, it looked at the brush but didn't try to run toward it.

"I think he'll follow the trail now," Danny said. "I'll keep a rope on him a while just to be sure. You ride drag and keep the stragglers moving."

"Won't he come at you?"

"I don't think so," Danny said. He felt pleased that he had outwitted the steer. Red Shirt had told him about that trick of slitting the eyelids. He had learned the trick from Fuzzy Paige, the rodeo bullfighter clown, who said a bull always closed his eyes before he tried to horn something, even a man. It made sense, Danny thought. *He* wouldn't run into the brush with his eyes wide open and unprotected either.

By four that afternoon they had reached the road, and Danny drove the cattle toward Thornhollow until he came to the Silverheels' ranch. He offered Lila Silverheels ten dollars to use the old juniper corral until they could get a truck to load the cattle. After they had the cattle in the corral, Lila brought them cold drinks and let Danny use her phone to call Sam CutHorse about a truck. Sam told Danny he could be there in an hour. When Danny told him they were short two head Sam chuckled a little, and Danny knew Sam thought the stiff-necked steer was still on the range.

When he had finished his call, Danny roped the steer and snubbed it against a juniper post, then removed the willow sticks. The steer's eyes were dull and dry looking, and if the day had been hotter, it might have gone blind. When the sticks were out and Danny had untied the steer, it blinked its eyes and wandered around looking a little dazed. Danny didn't think Sam would check close enough to notice the slits in the eyelids.

Sam was grinning when he showed up with the truck, but his lips tightened when he saw the steer and knew he owed Danny an extra hundred dollars. "When you said you were two short, I damn sure thought he'd be one of them," Sam complained.

"Nope," Danny said. "Coyotes got a cow and a calf."

"That ginger-colored cow?" Sam asked.

Danny nodded. "She was my favorite," he said. "And she calved every spring. Twins once."

Sam shook his head, but Danny figured he was probably cheered somewhat by the bad luck. "You going after those coyotes?" Sam asked. "Get some payback?"

"Yes," Danny said. "But that grudge will have to wait until after the Round-Up. I promised the boy here we could go."

They loaded the cattle into the back of the truck, and Sam seemed surprised that the steer didn't even balk going up the ramp. "You didn't have any trouble with that one?" he asked.

"No," Danny said. "He came like flies to honey."

Sam looked over at Jack, but the boy kept a poker face. Then Sam looked at the steer's feet. "I'll bet you snubbed him and trimmed those hooves until they were good and sore."

"Take a good look," Danny said. "They're not trimmed at all. We just sweet-talked him down the trail."

Sam shook his head. "You must be a real spellbinder, then. I'm still doctoring the gash he took out of Gypsy."

"I got a good partner," Danny said, nodding at Jack. "Well, there are the cattle. Must be payday."

Sam counted out five hundred and fifty dollars. "Eleven head. That's a good piece of work," he said. "I still owe you a hundred, but I'm tapped right now. You can collect at the

Round-Up. I just never thought you'd bring in that stiff-necked bastard."

"I know you're good for it," Danny said, putting the money in his pocket. He shook hands with Sam. "It's a pleasure as always." Then he turned to Jack and winked. "Let's go into town for a store-bought steak, partner."

◆ 11 ◆

Danny leaned against a telephone pole to watch the Westward Ho Parade. In the vacant lot to his left, some spectators were sitting on their pickups' tailgates, sharing beers and soft drinks from plastic coolers. To his right, several people put folding lawn chairs in the street, snugging the aluminum back legs against the curb. One man had a difficult time unfolding his chair because his arm was in a sling.

A railroad bull gang was pretending to work on a section of track just across the street, in front of four large grain elevators. Danny knew they had chosen that track section for the day so they could loaf and watch the parade. The railroad gang wore yellow coveralls and orange hardhats. They were the only group of spectators not wearing cowboy hats.

"Look at those loafers," the man with the sling said to his wife. "It's no wonder it costs so much to ship grain."

"Everything's going up, all right," his wife said. She reached into the cooler at her feet and handed the man a beer. "Fred likes to have a drink when he's complaining about somebody else not working," she said to the man on her other side.

The man laughed at that and took a beer himself. He was wearing brown polyester pants and a dark green shirt with pens sticking out the pocket. A green feather in his hatband matched the shirt, and his silver-framed glasses were tinted dark enough to hide his eyes. His hands were soft and white, not the working hands of a rancher, so Danny thought maybe he sold real estate.

At a few minutes past eleven, six musicians shuffled down the street playing off key and stumbling into one another. Their wrinkled black ties matched their shabby suits, and a couple of them took flasks from their pockets and passed them around. One carried a drum that read "Happy Canyon Marching and Drinking Band." He had a plastic red nose and oversized spectacles. When they were pretty close to Danny they started playing for real, and everyone applauded because they were good. Danny figured they were from the college. The band finished the number and the drummer set off a buzz bomb and shouted, "Folks, there's a parade a-comin'!"

Danny settled back to watch. He had wanted Jack to see the parade too, but the boy had gone to the rodeo grounds early for a job tagging steers or cleaning pens, and Danny planned to meet him there afterward. From where he was standing, two blocks away, Danny could see the raised platform for the parade celebrities. The announcer had his back to Danny, and the loudspeakers were turned the other way, so Danny didn't have to listen to him gushing about the colorful Indian people in their ceremonial dress.

The parade had lots of good high school marching bands, but Danny liked the fife and drum corps from Athena best. They wore plaid kilts, even the men, and the leader had a small dagger on his belt. Queens and princesses from every festival around came by, mounted on horseback and waving slowly, as if they were washing windows. The queens from the Big Four rodeos—Ellensburg, Walla Walla, Lewiston, and Pendleton—had bouquets of roses adorning their horses. Danny tried to decide which women were the prettiest, but he couldn't make up his mind. It was hard to believe they were just a couple years older than Jack.

The man in the dark glasses kept yelling, "Throw me a kiss, sweetheart. I'll give it to my friend here to make him well." Danny became annoyed by his shouting.

The governor of Oregon rode by in a white Cadillac convertible with Brahma bull horns on the hood and pearly six-shooters for door handles. The dashboard was myrtlewood inlaid with silver dollars. The governor sat on the top of the back seat, smiling and waving both hands at the crowd. He wore a light brown suit—Western cut—and a cream-colored rancher's Stetson. Danny thought he looked sharp.

Someone shouted, "Hey, Governor! Don't let that mount buck you off!" A lot of people laughed, and someone else yelled, "If the governor's in Pendleton, this must be an election year!"

More people laughed, and some started clapping and cheering. Then an Indian from across the way shouted, "Don't clap unless you have a job." After that, the clapping quieted a little.

Bands of Indian children came walking up both sides of the street. They wore miniature headdresses, rabbit braids, beaded shirts, doeskin dresses, and colorful hand-sewn moccasins. Some of the people along the parade route started throwing handfuls of money at them, and the children scattered to retrieve the coins. After they had picked up the money, they put it in beaded fringed bags or hand-tooled coin purses.

"Getting these young ones ready for the dole," the man with the sling said. He was dipping pennies out of a half-

gallon milk carton and flinging them backhanded with his
good arm.

"Hey, Fred. You better pay them now or they'll get a
sharpie lawyer and claim all of Pendleton is theirs," the man
in dark glasses said.

Danny glared at the man, but he didn't seem to notice.

Caravans of covered wagons, prairie schooners, two-
wheelers, and ox carts swept by Danny. Some of these had
"Oregon or Bust" printed on the sides. There were Mormon
carts, too, pulled by dark-suited men with the funny beards
the early Mormons had worn. Two women in calico dresses
followed the carts, carrying a sign that said FREEDOM OF
WORSHIP. Next came marching missionaries holding Bibles
and pretending to preach to the "Indians" who walked beside them. One man was dressed like Marcus Whitman, and
he led a horse carrying a woman riding sidesaddle who pretended to be Narcissa. Their sign read GOD COMES TO ORE-
GON. Danny shook his head as he thought of all the missionaries and settlers that had invaded the Oregon country.

He heard scattered applause and saw a lanky man accom-
panied by an immense woman in a tentlike prairie dress. The
man was leading an ox and the woman carried an American
flag in one hand and a basket full of Bibles in the other.
Apparently the ox was trained, because it stopped and
kneeled whenever the woman held out a Bible and shook it
in the ox's face. Two dour children lagged behind carrying a
homemade sign that said THE ANIMALS KNEEL BEFORE HIM.

"Isn't that just darling?" Fred's wife said. "Honey, we've
got to get us a good camera."

A tractor pulling a mobile home came alongside advertising the Rancho Estate Trailer Park. Danny knew the owner,
and some said he'd made a million selling "Mobile Homes on
the Range."

The SUNCO float featured a giant rotating sun made from
foil. Models in gold lamé costumes posed under the sun,

pointing to a large display banner that read: SUNCO PRO-
GRESS BRIGHTENS YOUR ENERGY FUTURE. Danny shook his
head because the float looked really professional and he
knew it had cost a lot to decorate.

Behind this float came the Umatilla Sage Riders, a volun-
teer mounted posse riding palomino horses and wearing
white suits, hats, and red silk scarves.

A small Indian boy trailed the Sage Riders. He wore a red
shirt with bead trim and rabbit leggings. He looked as if he
wanted to catch up with the other children but was hanging
back because he was afraid of getting too close to the horses.
As he walked, his rabbit leggings slipped down, causing him
to trip. Tears streaked his face.

"There's a cute one," the woman said. "Throw him some
pennies, Fred. He's been crying."

Fred tossed out some pennies with his awkward backhand
motion, but they rolled under the horses.

"Give that here," said the man in the dark glasses. After
taking the carton from Fred, he reached into it and tossed out
a few more. "There's your first handout, little buck," he said.

The boy picked up some of the pennies from the street and
dug out those that had fallen in a crack between the pave-
ment and the railroad ties. When the horses moved, some
coins glittered where they had been standing, but the boy
held back, not wanting to drag his rabbit leggings through
the green horse turds.

"Throw him some more," Danny said, suddenly moving
toward the man in dark glasses.

"What?"

"I said throw him some more." For a moment Danny
wanted to grab the milk carton and dump the pennies into
the street.

"We have to save some for the others." Fred's wife was
talking. "They all expect something for getting dressed up
and marching in the parade."

Danny saw her mouth working like a fish's. He walked into the street and knelt on one knee beside the boy. "Look, big fellow," he said. "You don't want to get those fine leggings dirty. Let's see if we can catch up to your friends." He lifted the boy onto his shoulders and started walking along the street, hurrying to pass the horses and the pioneer wagons. Behind him he heard the man with the glasses say, "That crazy Cayuse must be hitting the firewater."

"I like your rabbit leggings," Danny said. "Did you make those? Hey, quit crying now. It's okay." He walked a little faster.

"My sister made them."

"Which one's your sister?" He could see the children up ahead.

"There in the blue dress."

"Well, tell your sister she does fine work. What's your name?"

"Jimmy Sam."

"Where do you live, Jimmy?"

"Yakima."

"I'll bet you have a big pony."

He could feel the boy nod. "Her name is Betsy."

"Take good care of her, then."

When he had caught up with the group of children, Danny swung the boy from his shoulders and retied the leggings so the boy wouldn't trip. He took four quarters out of his pocket and handed them to the boy. "So long, little rabbit leggings," he said. "Buy some ice cream for your sister."

The walk had taken Danny close to the platform, and he stepped through the crowd behind it because he didn't want to see Taylor, especially if Tenley was with him. As he made his way through the crowd, he heard the announcer:

"Ladies and gentlemen, the *governor* of Oregon and his lovely wife. I hear you're up for reelection, Governor. Best of luck from all your friends in Pendleton. And behind him are

some fine youngsters from the Indian encampment wearing
their traditional native garb. They do look *festive,* don't they?
And I am here to tell you that these fine Indian people are
the most colorful and hospitable folks you'd ever want to
meet. Every day, after the rodeo performance, you're invited to take a look at the traditional tepees and authentic
craft displays they have set up behind the rodeo grounds.
Believe me, these wonderful people from the Umatilla Reservation and their colorful cousins from throughout the
Northwest are delighted with the opportunity to show you
their ways and testify to how a little of the Old West still lives
on today."

Danny couldn't imagine how the announcer could say so
many words without getting confused, and he wondered if
the man practiced for long hours in front of a mirror, all
slickered up in his announcing outfit. "He probably shits just
as smoothly," Danny mumbled.

Danny walked past the section of town where the carnival
rides and games of chance were set up. When he saw the
basketball shoot, he thought of Henry and how they had
managed to win the large stuffed animals even though the
balls were overinflated and the hoops smaller than regulation
size. They had worked the trick a number of times. Henry
would distract the carny worker by spilling his Coke into the
stand while Danny quickly let some of the air out of the
basketball. With the slightly deflated basketball, Danny and
Henry were able to compensate for the small rims and always
carried off the big prizes. Whenever the carny would at-
tempt to switch balls on them between shots, they would
demand their "lucky" one back. The carnies may have
known something was going on, but they usually blamed
their helpers for not putting enough air in the balls.

Danny followed the road toward the Round-Up grounds
and cut through the park to the Indian encampment. By the
looks of it, they had set up over two hundred tepees. He

walked among them until he found Sam CutHorse's blue-striped tepee near the Let-Er-Buck Tavern under the rodeo bleachers. Sam's daughter was sitting on a folding chair in front of the tepee reading a movie magazine. It featured a blonde starlet who had the "look of the decade."

"You seen Sam around?" Danny asked.

She shook her head without looking up from the magazine. "If he's not in the tavern here, he's probably at the Silver Spur. Unless he's watching the parade, which isn't likely. All I know is that he told me to stick around here until they brought the commodities."

"If he shows up, tell him I came by to check on the hundred dollars. He'll know what I mean."

"Will you be at the Let-Er-Buck?"

"No. I'll be around the chutes and pens. Jack got a job there tending stock."

"I heard something about your boy. Is he cute?"

"You bet. Looks just like his old man."

"Aaay!" She rolled her eyes.

"Well, take off a dozen years, maybe."

On the way to the chutes, Danny ran into two old men trying to set up a tepee. They had unstrapped the lodgepoles from the top of their rig, but they were having trouble angling them to form the tepee frame. Danny watched them for a moment as they argued with one another about how it should work.

"You fellows need a hand?"

"He does," the one in the striped T-shirt said. "This old fart never put up a tepee before."

"Bullshit. Then your mother's a virgin."

"He's a Klallam," the first one said. "Klallams live in the ground like gophers."

Danny helped them hold the poles until they had them notched correctly and lashed together with rawhide thongs. When they were finished, the Klallam gave Danny a beer from the back of his truck. "Thanks," the man said. "This one can't even get his bone up."

"You guys were almost there," Danny said. "It's just a little tricky."

"We wanted to get it set up before they brought around the commodities," Striped Shirt said. "Every tepee gets an allotment from the Round-Up Committee. We're soaking them good this year."

"I know how it works," Danny said.

The Klallam set up a couple of folding chairs and the two old men sat down. "We can finish this later," he said.

"They're bringing a truckload of watermelons from Hermiston this afternoon," Striped Shirt said. "Come on by for some."

"I might do that," Danny said. "It'll be hot. But it's going to rain tomorrow."

"Hope not," the Klallam said. "Who the hell wants to be in a soggy tepee in the rain?"

"It beats being drowned in a burrow," the other one said. "As long as we're eating food. Balls and bellies are all that matter. Keep one empty, the other full. Bring on the commodities and the women."

Danny left them still sitting on their folding chairs, and he wondered if they ever planned to put the canvas over their tepee frame. He remembered the Round-Up when Red Shirt had cut some red willows and draped green army blankets over them. When the members of the committee came by with the commodities for each tepee, Red Shirt solemnly told them that this was his official tepee and that he planned on staying there the duration of the Round-Up. The young man parceling out the goods didn't believe the tepee qualified, and Red Shirt angrily informed him it was a replica Nez Perce mini-tepee used for duck hunting in marshy country where no lodgepoles grew. He threatened that unless he got commodities, he would leave and encourage the other Indians to do so as well, pointing out that the tourists would be cheated if they couldn't visit the tepee village the brochures had promised them. The young man finally relented and grudgingly gave Red Shirt his portion of commodities, but he assured Red Shirt he would be by every day to see if he'd kept his word.

Later, Red Shirt told Danny, "I did it for the peanut butter. I know it was dishonest, but the peanut butter made me do it. Nothing tastes as good as U.S. government peanut butter. The Karo is good sweetening too, but their potted meat is the same horsecock we ate in the army."

Danny located Jack in the stock pens under the bleachers, washing down the calves with a green rubber hose and sticking numbered tags in their ears. Heads down, bawling when the water stream hit them, the calves milled around the enclosure. Jack was so intent upon his task he didn't notice Danny leaning against the fence rail. Jack had put on a pair of knee-high, dark-green rubber boots, but the rest of him was soaked. When a dark brown calf blindsided him, Jack fell backward onto the wet cement. He kicked at the calf but missed. "You bastard," he mumbled.

"Don't abuse the stock," Danny said. "Some cowboy might make five thousand dollars this afternoon by getting a quick rope on that little feller."

Jack got up slowly, rubbing his wet back and butt. "This job sucks hind tit," he said.

"You're as wet as a Beaner crossing the Rio Grande by inner tube," Danny said. He knew working stock was a good way to start learning rodeo. It could even provide a grubstake and bunk for an old hand down on his luck.

"Very funny. I'd like to see you wash these calves."

"I thought you might want to go have some lunch."

"Why not? I was about ready to knock off anyway," Jack said. He filled the watering troughs, then turned off the spigot and coiled the hose, hanging it on a post. "Give me a chance to get out of these rubber boots. They're too damn hot."

"You look like a genuine gumshoe cowboy," Danny said.

"That's not anywhere as good as the real thing," Jack said, kicking off the rubber boots and tugging on his leather ones. "I want to win at Pendleton someday."

"Ho! Sounds like you've got big plans," Danny said.

"I'm not kidding around."

"All right. No reason you can't ride here," Danny said. "I'll teach you what I know about broncs and then turn you over to a pro for some private lessons." He remembered what Taylor had said about spending summers in Texas.

"How long do you think it will take?"

"You should know something in four years or so—if you've got any talent."

Jack cocked an eyebrow. "That's a long time," he said. "A guy came by this morning and offered me fifty dollars to ride today."

"What guy?"

"Just some guy. He works at a horse ranch called Diamond Acres somewhere around Portland."

"What event?"

"The Indian Horse Race. Their regular boy got sick."

Danny shook his head. "Forget it. Too damn dangerous."

"I can ride. You said so yourself when we went after the cows."

"This is different. Diamond Acres horses are high-strung thoroughbreds. The stable gets an Indian kid to ride one for a few thousand dollars' worth of free publicity. But it's your neck on the line. You don't know a thing about racing horses, and the other riders are about as green."

"Me and my big mouth. Should have just done it."

"You got lots of time," Danny said. "Before we go to lunch, I want to show you something."

They left the stock pens, Jack trailing a step, his face set in a sullen expression. "How long will it take?" he asked. "I'm hungry."

"Not long," Danny said. "It's just over at the Hall of Fame."

They entered through the doorway under the bleachers. The room was filled with saddles, trophies, tack, and pictures of the Hall of Famers. Danny headed for the far corner of the room.

Jack stopped at one of the exhibits. "Look at this. I never knew women rode at Pendleton."

"There's a lot you don't know yet. Fox Hastings won the women's bulldogging in 1924. She was as good as they come. But now the Round-Up Committee just lets the women barrel race."

"Probably afraid they'd give the men too much competition," Jack said. "She looks like she could spit nails."

"This is the one I wanted to show you," Danny said. He stopped in front of a picture of a lean man with a wrinkled face and straight nose. Dark bangs showed under his flat-brimmed hat, and he wore a pair of Angora chaps.

"Jackson Sundown." Jack read the inscription under the photograph. "Hey. He was Nez Perce."

"The only Indian rider to ever make the Hall of Fame."

"Bronc Riding—1916. That was a long time ago," Jack said.

Danny nodded. "He won here and the *Police Gazette* named him Rodeo Performer of the Year then. How old do you think he was?"

Jack studied the picture a minute. "He looks pretty old. Thirty-four?"

"*I'm* thirty-four."

"Sorry. Thirty-nine?"

"Fifty," Danny said. "Jackson Sundown was fifty in 1916." Jack shook his head. "Hard to believe."

"That inscription doesn't begin to tell the story," Danny said. "His real name was Blanket of the Sun, and he lived through the Nez Perce War, even though most of his family were killed. When Joseph and the other Dreamers surrendered in the Bear Paws, Jackson was only eleven. Although he was wounded, he snuck away from the soldiers and joined White Bird's band in Canada. By the time he came back here and started serious rodeoing, he was in his late forties.

"That day he won at Pendleton, the judges kept giving him rerides—maybe because they didn't want first prize going to an Indian. But each time he rode he got better, until the crowd got behind him and started yelling at the judges to give him the trophy. On his last reride the sun was going down, and everybody in the place was on his feet shouting, 'Sundown! Sundown!' They couldn't keep going after dark, so the judges had to give him the trophy, like it or not. And he took the moniker 'Sundown' and rode under it from then on. He rode until he was almost seventy."

"That's some story," Jack said. "I'm sure you're trying to make a point in your roundabout way—telling me to take it easy."

"You're not as dumb as you look," Danny said. "Don't enter a damn-fool race and get busted up."

"Maybe I'll do it anyway."

"Then plan on sleeping in the tack shed. I said no."

The corners of Jack's mouth turned down, but he didn't say anything.

"Tell you what," Danny said, remembering how eager he had been. "Next spring we'll get in touch with Corky Freeman. He coached rodeo, and if he thinks you've got the stuff, you can try rodeo school next summer. But you have to stay away from the races."

Jack thought it over. "All right. You got a deal."

"Now that you're not riding, maybe you can do some watching. I bought tickets for this afternoon."

"What about work?"

"It's okay," Danny said. "I already told Shorty."

"I'd like to see the finals Saturday."

"God Almighty couldn't get tickets for Saturday."

The Wagon Wheel was crowded with rodeo spectators and drugstore cowboys, but they managed to find a booth in back. After Jack sat down, he studied the crowd. "I know why you picked this place," he said. "The waitresses are more your style—mature."

"There's no substitute for experience."

"I was thinking of overripe."

"Funny."

The waitress put down their water. "The special today's an Okie Drifter. That's an open-faced chicken-fried steak sandwich with mashed potatoes and gravy. Green beans on the side."

"I'll take it," Danny said. "Seen Pudge around?"

"Working nights during Round-Up. You ready?"

"What's the seafood cocktail?" Jack asked.

"Tuna fish and mayonnaise."

Jack closed his menu. "Buckle-Buster Burger and a large Coke."

"Growing boy," Danny said. He leaned back in the booth. He recognized a couple of cowboys from the old days. None of them were still riding. After Danny nodded at Slim Parker, Slim came over. He had put on weight.

"Long time, Slim," Danny said, shaking his hand. "This is my boy, Jack. Jack—Slim Parker. Slim used to ride bulls— mean old bags of bologna, too. You put on a couple pounds. Still going by 'Slim'?"

Slim grinned. "They call me everything but late to dinner."

Danny laughed, even though the joke was old. "What about Pajama Bill Turner?" he asked. "You hear from him anymore?" Danny turned to Jack. "Pajama Bill was some character—always sleeping around. He'd get drunk and holler out, 'As long as whores live, my name will never die.'"

Slim frowned. "A train ran him over outside of Winnemucca, Danny. Kind of surprised you didn't hear."

"The hell." Danny had always figured Pajama Bill would get shot in a motel room.

"I settled down," Slim said. "Decided to let the young fellows have the bulls. Married a great cook and moved to the city. Now I manage a little trailer park and don't ride anything much wilder than the lawnmower."

"What became of that little ranch you had out near Heppner?"

"Sold that spread, Danny. Still got this one, though." He thumped his stomach. "I better get back to the family. Got a couple of kids that want to see the rodeo. The boy, he's a regular hard-tail buckaroo. Already got him in junior rodeo. Jack, it's been a pleasure. Good-looking boy there, Danny. Must favor his mother."

After Slim left, Jack grew quiet, and Danny figured he was brooding about Loxie. Slim hadn't known her and had meant no insult. But he had sure changed. Danny wondered if *he* looked that different.

"Hey, Longface," he said to Jack. "You know how to tell a good restaurant? Just by looking in the window, I mean."

"I don't know. Fat waitresses?"

"That's a fair poke at it, but you're wrong. Try again."

"I'm not going to guess around all day."

"You look at the calendars. The more they got, the better the restaurant." When Jack's expression didn't change, Danny went on. "It makes sense. The calendars all come from local outfits and they don't want their names hanging all over the walls of a lousy place collecting fly tracks. So they just send out calendars to the good ones."

"Who's the genius that figured that out?"

"Red Shirt. It comes from experience. You learn a lot about

restaurants on the rodeo circuit. Take this place. Five calendars—all from good businesses, too. Pendleton Grain Growers, Inland Empire Bank, Wade Rain, Umatilla Livestock Association, and they even have one from the Confederated Tribes."

"They have six," Jack said. "The one behind you says Shady Lane Mortuary."

Danny turned to look at the picture of the ocean dashing against the rocks. Underneath the picture, the caption said, "Vigilant—Eternal." "You can't take a whole lot of stock in funeral-parlor calendars," Danny said. "Those people don't much care where their calendars get stuck up, because when you die they plan on having your business anyway." He was sorry after he'd said it because he was afraid the talk about funerals might cause Jack to think more about Loxie.

Their food came and they ate in silence for a few minutes. Then Jack said, "Mom told me you rode in Pendleton. Do any good?"

"It depends on how you figure it. I took third in saddlebronc during the qualifying events, but finished out of the money in the final go-round. Had a big old horse named Hot Toddy, and by the time he cranked me into the dirt, I felt like I'd had a few.

"I rode his twin at the Klamath Stampede, a roan called Booger Red. I had a deep seat and a good ride that day—spurred him hard and high all the way. They put on a good show at the Stampede. Monty Montana, the Hollywood trick roper, was there, and I saw him rope four running horses at once. He had a loop the size of a truckbed and he whipped it right over them all as they came galloping past. That was a fine time. I won the bronc riding and got this buckle."

"How does it feel to ride in front of all those people?"

"Well," Danny said. "It feels pretty good. You're on that horse or maybe a bull that's trying like hell to get you off, and you're hanging and rattling, trying just as hard not to get dumped. You don't even hear the crowd, until it's over. Then a lot of guys slap you on the back—that feels good. And maybe that night you get lucky and pick up a buckle bunny somewhere . . ."

"A buckle bunny?"

Danny looked at Jack. "You know. She's the kind of woman who likes to hang out with cowboys and show the winners a good time, help them spend the purse, and later on maybe take some soreness out and make that winning feeling last until morning."

"You mean a rooster booster."

Danny shrugged. "Same thing. And after you've won, you feel just fine for a while. You think that out there in the crowd there's a fancy dude with spiffy boots he bought in Denver or Portland—boots that would cost you a month's pay. And you think he might have a big spread with thousands of acres, or maybe he just practices law or medicine and hangs around rodeos to rub elbows with working cowboys. But you know he wouldn't climb on a real bronc or bull for anything because he doesn't have it here." Danny patted his heart. "He may not have it down here, either.

"And he's got his second or third wife along, or maybe his fiancée, and she's so soft and sweet she even puts lotion on her knees and feet. And she's with him, but you think she's watching you because she knows, down inside somewhere, that you have what that dude doesn't. So that night, after he's rolled over and gone to sleep, she's still lying there with her eyes wide open, remembering what it was like to see you ride that afternoon. She sees your hat fly off, and the green shirt you were wearing, and your chaps flying as your legs go back and forth, back and forth. She can't stand it anymore, so you want to believe she'll get dressed and come looking for you because you can make her feel like a real woman."

"That sounds awfully good," Jack said.

Danny smiled because he had tricked the boy. "I said you

think all that and you *want* to believe it. You've got a lot to learn, boy. If any of that is really true, you never know it. What you know about are busted legs, rope burns, long drives with bad coffee and no sleep, lousy draws, worse hangovers, a horse that won't buck, and some hometown boy getting boosted a couple of points so you finish out of the money."

"Why keep doing it, then?"

Danny picked up the check. "Too damn dumb to quit," he said. "Let's go. It's showtime."

Jack and Danny sat in the south bleachers, about halfway up. Danny liked the south bleachers because the sun was over their shoulders and they had a good side view of the bucking chutes and roping pens. From the more expensive grandstand seats, you had a head-on view across the track and grassy arena. It was like trying to watch a football game from the end zone.

At first, Danny enjoyed the events. The horses were as rugged as their names—Blackjack, Skyrocket, Drygulch, Tombstone—and a couple might have stacked up against War Paint, the legendary Round-Up bronc. But later his enthusiasm faded because he wasn't riding, and when he remembered what Taylor had said about not becoming a pro, it stung. Only a few of the cowboys were local. Most of them had come a long way—from Cheyenne, Prescott, Sioux Falls, Amarillo—and Danny was envious of their chances to ride the great horses, not for purse money but for fame. As Jack applauded each rider, Danny wished some of the boy's praise was reserved for him, and he chafed at his missed opportunity.

When Red Shirt had taken Danny to the rodeos, Danny had felt proud to have a place of honor. He sat with the cowboys on the fence near the chutes. As Red Shirt burst out of the gate, his chaps flying, his braid swinging under the straw cowboy hat, Danny whistled and cheered. He had grown a lot older before he realized those rodeos were small and his father's competition second-rate. But even then, he had wanted to believe that with a fair share of good breaks, Red Shirt could have been one of the best. So now Danny watched, cheering on cue with the crowd but thinking about how to make those breaks for Jack.

Clay Morgan's ride on Mr. Ed, a pattern bucker, brought the crowd to its feet. Clay spurred hard coming out of the chute, and his quick reactions matched the horse's moves, so that his rein hand always showed daylight above the mount's neck. Rider and horse moved as one until the buzzer sounded, and after Clay had swung onto the pick-up rider's horse, he tipped his hat to the cheering crowd.

Jack whistled and stomped with the rest of the crowd. "You ever ride like that?" he asked Danny.

"Too busy hanging and rattling to know if it looked pretty."

"You watch. I'll be out there in four years—five, tops. I'm going to get some weights and lift out in the tack shed—build up my arms and shoulders."

Danny smiled. "You might need to strong-arm a dodger or cranker, but usually timing counts more. You have to stick with the horse."

"How can you tell what he's going to do?"

"You feel the horse, his every move, through your boots. Old boots are best because they're worn and flexible and you can feel the curve of the stirrup's metal through the sole. Slick new boots are terrible. A bronc rider would take a beating rather than lose a pair of old boots."

"He made it look easy."

"The best ones always do."

When the Free-For-All Indian Horse Race began, the riders had a difficult time posting the horses. After two false starts, Jack shook his head and said, "Those wimps can't ride. I lost an easy fifty bucks."

On the far turn of the second lap, one of the horses slipped in the soft dirt and rolled on its side, spilling its rider, a young boy wearing a yellow cap. Although the other riders saw the accident, two horses were out of control and collided with the first animal. The crowd groaned as the horses splayed on the ground, their riders scrambling away from the flailing hooves.

Biting his lip, Danny watched the ambulance come onto the track, its red lights pulsing. Two paramedics leaped out to examine the riders. White-coated veterinarians rushed across the green to attend the horses.

The announcer said, "Folks, please stay in your seats. Everything is under control. These Indian riders are used to thrills and spills here at the Round-Up, and we've got highly trained personnel on hand."

When the horses were untangled and led off, none seemed seriously hurt, although a chestnut limped, favoring a foreleg. The young rider was loaded onto a stretcher and taken away in the ambulance. Danny hadn't seen him move.

Halfway through the bullriding, the announcer said they were passing the hat to help cover hospital expenses.

"Aren't you going to say 'I told you so'?" Jack asked.

"No," Danny said. "I just hate to see a kid get hurt."

When the collection hat passed in front of him, Danny was pleased to see that it was filled with five-, ten-, and twenty-dollar bills. He added a twenty and passed it on.

"They're getting ready for the steer roping," Jack said. "Look, they're setting up right below here."

"That's why I like the south bleachers," Danny said. "Let the dudes sit in the grandstand."

"They never had steer roping in Nebraska," Jack said.

"Pendleton is one of the few rodeos that still has it," Danny said. "And it's big money." He had read in the program that the purse was over twenty thousand dollars; but the entry fees were high and there had been lots of contestants.

"You should put Ring-Eye out there," Jack said. "I bet you'd do okay."

Danny shook his head. He figured you had to be a big-time rancher to go in for steer roping, because it required an unusually strong horse and years of training to consistently stop a running steer without hurting the horse. "I never wanted to risk him," he said. "It's bad enough roping steers in the puckerbrush for a little range doctoring." Danny knew that if things went well, the running steer threw himself when he reached the end of the cowboy's rope. But even if the steer went down, the cowboy had to avoid a horn in the gut or a hoof to the head while he was hogtying.

Several people carrying cameras moved into the aisles in Danny's section of the bleachers to photograph the steer roping. One was a woman wearing a powder-blue tank top and khaki shorts. Her auburn hair hung in a braid down her back, and she had long, tan legs. A man in front of Danny took off his green-and-white cap that said "Mallard Seeds" and had a duck flying across the peak. "Wow," the man said, wiping his brow. "She could rope and hogtie this old steer anytime."

The woman stopped at the box seats below Danny and leaned over to say something to one of the men there. Danny grinned, because the man couldn't keep his eyes off her tank top. Then the man nodded and waved her into the box-seat section. As the woman lifted her camera bag from her shoulder, her lean muscles flexed, and Danny recognized the straight back and strong shoulders, trademarks of the trick rider. It was Tenley.

Danny felt a warmth surge through him as she knelt on one knee and started shooting pictures of the steer ropers. A big man on a deep-chested roan nudged his horse over to her and said a few words. Then he backed his horse away and tipped his hat.

Danny couldn't take his eyes off her. It seemed to him that the rodeo had stopped and everyone was watching Tenley.

"Swallow a marble?" Jack asked.

"What?"

"You look like you swallowed a marble and it got stuck in your craw. That's how your jaw's working. Something's on your mind, because you didn't pay any attention to the last three ropers."

"I did too. The last one was a big bay and the cowboy threw a slow rope."

Jack shook his head. "I'm not blind. She's a showstopper, all right. Know her?"

"I know all the pretty ones," Danny said. "Tenley Adams. She used to be a great trick rider. We went to school together —a long time back."

"She seemed partial to that fellow on the roan," Jack said. "You looking to beat his time?"

Danny cocked one eyebrow. Jack didn't miss much. "Why don't you watch the rodeo?"

Jack grinned. "If you're thinking of asking her out, fix me up with her younger sister."

"Not likely."

"Her daughter?"

"Watch the damn rodeo and quit bugging me," Danny said. He leaned forward, resting his chin on his hands, and tried to concentrate, but the rest of the steer roping passed in a blur. When they announced the winner, he was pleased it wasn't the man who had spoken to Tenley. Then the announcer said it was time for the Wild Horse Race, and Danny noticed that Tenley was packing her camera in the bag. He stood and nudged Jack. "Let's start heading out," he said. "Beat the crowd."

"What's your hurry?" Jack said. He didn't move. "I want to

watch this. Those horses will drag the cowboys all over the place."

Danny glanced at Tenley. The camera bag was strapped over her shoulder and she was shaking hands with the people in the box seat. "Will you come on?"

"You're the one who's chasing her," Jack said. "Go on. I can meet you at the truck."

Tenley started to walk away from the box seats, and Danny was on the bleacher steps, taking them two at a time. He heard the crowd roaring with delight at the Wild Horse Race, but he didn't bother looking into the arena. All he saw was Tenley walking toward the exit, the camera slung over her tan shoulder. When he reached the bottom step, she turned toward him and shaded the sun from her eyes with her hand. "Tenley," he said. When he realized she couldn't see his features against the sun, he added, "It's Danny."

Tenley brushed back some wisps of hair and gave Danny a brittle smile. "Well, if it isn't Mr. Long Lost Kachiah. I thought I'd seen the last of you when you gave me the slip at Crow Fair." She adjusted the camera bag and took a step toward the exit. "Come on along, if you want," she said. "It'll be a mob scene and I don't want to get caught."

Danny walked beside her. In the arena, cowboy teams were trying to ride the bridleless horses across a finish line. The crowd had come to its feet.

"You know I was mad at you for a while—until I found out about Loxie. Jesus, what a lousy deal. I'm sorry as hell. Did you make the funeral?"

"Too late for that," Danny said. "But I went back to Nebraska and picked up my boy."

"He's with you now?"

"That's right. We're batching in the old trailer out on the reservation."

She stopped and looked at him a moment. "Huh. So how does it feel to be a father again after all those years?"

Danny shrugged. It was too complicated to explain, so he just said, "My cooking's getting better."

She laughed. "I guess I'm going to have to start working on mine."

"How's that?"

She held out her hand.

He hadn't noticed the ring because she had been using that hand to hold the camera bag. It was a big stone, maybe two carats, set in white gold. He waited a second to make sure his voice would be steady. "Congratulations. Taylor?"

"You're supposed to say 'Best wishes' to the woman. Anyway, it's not Taylor. Good old Taylor." She shook her head. "He tried damn hard, but he's too much rodeo. I need somebody more . . . settled."

"Not Ace?"

She grimaced. "Not even close. We dissolved. Couldn't agree about anything—even the land deal on the reservation. And Sterling hated his guts."

"Sterling?" Danny thought of the steer roper on the deepchested roan. The way Tenley said the name made Danny pull up short.

"Sterling Bradford. You remember Buddy Bradford, Sterling's younger brother who went to school with us."

"I remember Buddy," Danny said. "He didn't go much for ranching."

"You got it. He builds boats now. Hates this country. So Sterling runs the Bradford place all by himself."

"The Bradford place" sounded odd to Danny. The Bradfords owned ten thousand acres of prime wheat land and had a half-million-bushel storage elevator the Pendleton Grain Growers had built just for them.

"I'm parched," Tenley said. "Buy a girl a drink, cowboy?"

"I've got a little time," Danny said. He felt he needed to catch his breath. He stepped inside the fenced enclosure and pushed his way to the counter.

The man working the keg had a rose tattoo on one forearm and "Born to Raise Hell" on the other. "I heard they had a pileup out there," he said to the man standing in front of Danny. "Anybody get hurt?"

"No," the man said. "Just busted up some Indian kid."

As the man turned around with his beer, Danny jostled his arm, and the man spilled some of it down his pants. "God damn," the man said. "Watch it."

"Kind of crowded in here," Danny said.

He ordered two beers and gave the kegman two dollars. As he started to leave, a member of the sheriff's auxiliary at the gate said, "Rules say you drink it inside, Chief."

Danny nodded his head toward Tenley. "Not if she's outside."

The man smiled. "You got a point. Don't keep that one waiting. I never saw those beers walk out."

Danny handed Tenley her beer and she took a drink, flicking her tongue at a trace of foam on her upper lip. "You got a quiet spot picked out to drink these?" she asked.

"Tailgate. Jack should show up there after a while, and I think he'd kind of like to meet you. He wondered if you had a younger sister."

"Ha! That's flattering. At least he didn't say daughter."

They sat down on the tailgate and watched the crowd coming out of the bleachers.

"So we're all settling down," Tenley said. "Here's to fatherhood and family. Cheers!" She raised her beer cup and Danny met it with his.

"I'm ready," she said. "It's time to move into a new phase or whatever you want to call it. Life's like that, I think. One time I was doing the deathdrag in Flagstaff behind a team of horses, and one of the harnesses broke. All of a sudden it wasn't a trick anymore, but an accident. The horses were out of control and I was being dragged along for real. Most likely I'd have broken my neck if one of the pick-up riders hadn't managed to grab their reins damn fast. My gold lamé outfit was ripped to shreds and my back got all scratched up, but I did a quick change and was out finishing the drag five minutes later. That's what they say you're supposed to do. When it was over, I jumped clear, took my applause, and dashed for the dressing room. I shook for over an hour. I never tricked again. It was like someone was telling me it was time to try something different. And that's how I feel now. So what about you? What's it like to have Jack around?"

Danny shrugged. "He's a good kid. Takes some getting used to."

"That's it?" She squinted at him. "I could get more out of a clam."

"You're right," he said. "It's time we settled down." It occurred to him suddenly that his father never had.

She turned her beer cup around in her hands a few times. "You know, Danny, as long as we ran into each other, there's another thing I was thinking about. You want to hear it?"

"Shoot."

"This is a pretty small town, all things considered."

He chuckled. "I used to think it was big." He didn't know what she was driving at.

"That night we spent together. I'd just as soon you didn't tell it around."

She was staring straight at him, and Danny caught a little glint in the corners of her eyes. He suddenly realized that if you scratched that porcelain surface of hers, there was some pretty hard metal underneath, and he guessed life was going to get a lot more complicated for Sterling. Danny felt like laughing at himself for thinking there could have been something between them. "I don't mind," he said evenly. "I'd almost forgotten about it."

She gave him a half-nod, her face as smooth as glass. "You're so gallant," she said, lifting her beer.

"Hey! How about an introduction?" a voice said.

Danny hadn't noticed Jack approaching. "Sure," he said. "Jack, this is Tenley Adams, soon to be Tenley Bradford. And this here is my boy, Jack Kachiah."

Jack saluted by touching two fingers to his hat brim. "I've been hoping you have a younger sister."

"Thanks a lot," she said. "We were just talking about getting older."

Jack looked embarrassed. "I meant it as a compliment."

"I took it as one," she said, giving Jack one of those smiles that seemed to be reserved just for him.

"Dad says you were one of the best trick riders ever."

"I put on some good shows," she said.

"She's being modest," Danny said. "The apes came out of the brush to see her ride."

"You still trick ride?" Jack asked.

"No," she said. "That's all behind me now." She changed the subject. "Jack, how do you like school here?"

"It's okay, I guess."

"Are you going to play basketball like your father did?"

"Sure, only better. He's showing me all his inside moves, but I've got more talent." He grinned.

Tenley laughed and turned to Danny. "He's got some spunk."

"Oh, I guess he'll get there, all right, if he doesn't fall over himself doing it."

She stood and glanced at her watch. "Say now, I've got to meet Sterling. That steer he roped took a terrible dogfall and he was out of the competition just like that. Blew two hundred dollars in fees, so he'll need some consoling. Before I go, though, I'd like to get a picture of you two. Jack, you stand over there beside your father. Put your arms around each other's shoulders. Smile now. Good, Jack. If these turn out, I'll send you copies. Sterling just gave me this camera and I'm not used to it yet." She put the camera over her shoulder, then shook hands with Jack. "It sure was good meeting you."

She stepped over and gave Danny a quick kiss on the cheek. "You've got a good boy there." She started to walk away, then turned. "Hey, maybe I'll see you at the dance after Happy Canyon. You going?"

"Probably," Danny said. "I like Ferlin Husky."

"See you later, then."

They watched her walk away, the camera slung over her wide shoulders, and neither of them spoke until she had disappeared into the crowd of spectators leaving the Round-Up grounds. Jack said, "I'm in love with an older woman." Then he added, "I wouldn't wash that cheek if I were you."

Danny shook his head. "I'll probably spend the rest of my life trying to keep you out of trouble."

"If she's trouble, I'll take a heap."

"That's some rock he gave her, huh?"

"Bradford? You thinking of beating his time?"

"No," Danny said. "I'm not even paying entry fees. She's not my type." He put his arm around Jack's shoulder. "Come on," he said, "I'll buy you a root beer."

As they passed the displays of jewelry and souvenirs, Jack paused and picked up a necklace. "Look at this."

"Don't get scratched, sonny," the man said. "That's genuine bear claw—a bargain for seventy-five dollars. Last a lifetime." He was wearing a brown cowboy hat with a rattlesnake-skin hatband.

"She had a bear-claw necklace," Jack said.

"Let's see." When Jack handed Danny the necklace, Danny examined it for a few moments, then scraped a little of the claw with his thumbnail. "Badger," he said, tossing it back on the display case.

"Montana bear claw," the man insisted. "I get the real stuff from Chief Spotted Wolf."

"Tell it to the tourists," Danny said. As they walked away, he explained, "Some trappers cut off the long digging claws from the badger's front feet. They put on a little dye and varnish and sell them for bear claws."

"Was hers bear or badger?"

"Bear," Danny said. "I gave it to her before we were married. It was Red Shirt's, and he got it from Medicine Bird. If it lasts that long, it's got to be bear. Badger claws kind of fall apart on you after a while."

"She used to wear it a lot," Jack said. "Even when she was married to Hanson."

"He let her wear it?"

"She told him it was her mother's."

Danny smiled. That sounded like Loxie. She had always been a little careless with the truth, but he figured it was okay this time because it made him feel better to know she had worn it. "I didn't see that necklace with your gear."

"It's with her," Jack said. "I thought maybe that's how she'd want it."

"I'm sure of it," Danny said. "You did the right thing."

"It's hard to think she's dead. I like to imagine she's just away somewhere, you know, on a trip. She took off from Hanson's place a few times and he was never sure when she was going to come back. She'd tell me, though. I used to think she was going to look you up, but I guess she never did. Maybe you two could have gotten together again."

Danny didn't say anything. He had missed her for a long time, and used to believe she'd come back. Sometimes when he had answered the phone but gotten no response, he had been sure it was Loxie. A couple of times, after he'd whispered her name, the dial tone came back, and he figured she had just called to make him think about her.

"Why did you split anyway?"

"It's pretty hard to say, now." Danny shook his head, thinking back. But whenever he thought of himself and Loxie, it all just became more confused in his mind. "I'd been on my own a while, and she was pretty headstrong too," he said. "I spent a lot of time rodeoing. In those days, I figured to be as good as Jackson Sundown and wind up in the Round-Up Hall of Fame. With the right coaching and training, who knows? But that was hard to figure out in Pendleton. And I was a good ballplayer, too, although I didn't work at it enough.

"Your mother was pretty, even prettier than Tenley, but in a different sort of way. I was proud to take her any place. She wanted to dance, and maybe she could have, but she started way too late . . ." He suddenly felt sorry for Loxie and thought maybe she'd never had much chance. She had talked of Broadway and practiced dancing for hours in front of the trailer, the dirt caking her soles, the fine hair around her temples kinking from the heat. And he had grown angry when she rushed dinner, tossing meat and vegetables into a pressure cooker, so everything always tasted the same and watery juice ran over his plate. But the only Broadway she ever made was in Portland, dancing topless at Mary's Club. He wondered how much Jack knew about Loxie's "dancing" in the clubs, and if the boy blamed him for giving her a hard deal. "Neither one of us really knew what we were up against," he said finally.

"I miss her; that's all. Not much family left. You and Aunt Pudge . . . crazy old Que."

Danny put his arm around Jack and smoothed his dark hair. He wondered if he should have tried harder to get her back, but he didn't think it would have worked. He held on to the boy.

When Danny took the envelope out of the mailbox, he read "Park Plaza Hotel" in the upper left-hand corner. "New York," he said. "I don't know anyone in New York." He tore open the flap. The picture of Jack and him was inside a folded note. Tenley's handwriting was clear, with the letters slightly tilted but evenly spaced. Although Danny hadn't thought about it before, he realized it was the kind of handwriting she would have.

Dear Danny and Jack,

   Sterling and I married a week after Round-Up. No big service or church announcements. Just his family at the Bradford place. I always wanted to honeymoon in New York, so here we are. Maybe Jack will ride in Madison Square Garden someday. That's one I missed. There aren't many horses here, but the policemen in Central Park are mounted. Thought you'd like this picture. Take care of each other now.

T.A.B.

P.S. See you at the Round-Ups.

Jack took the picture from Danny and studied it a minute. "Pretty good of me," he said. "But you forgot to smile."

❖ 12 ❖

After the Round-Up, Danny decided he wanted his payback for the ginger-colored cow and her calf. While Jack was in school, Danny fished the slow deep holes of the Umatilla for chubs and suckers. He baited the treble hooks with rotting rabbit meat and let the bait lie on the bottom until the fish found it. When he had filled the five-gallon bucket, he drove back to the trailer. Using some baling wire from the shed, he hung the bucket of fish from a juniper limb, high enough so dogs couldn't get it and low enough from the branch so a cat couldn't reach it. He punched holes in the lid of the bucket to let the gases from the rotting fish escape, then tied burlap around the bucket to prevent the blowflies from getting in.

"What the hell is that mess hanging from the tree?" Jack asked when he got off the school bus.

"Fish lure for coyotes. Should stink good in about a week. That'll give us time to get the rest of the gear together and find the scents we need."

"We?"

"Sure. You're my partner, aren't you? You should learn how

to set traps. Mostly we'll go on weekends so you don't miss school."

"Not next weekend. Pudge wants us to come over for dinner—no excuses."

"That means bologna and corn-flake casserole. Anyway, we might be trapping."

"Ha. You're actually serious about this payback stuff? It sounds pretty barbaric. First, you brew the potion. Then we take off our clothes and dance around the tree. Hii-yip. Hii-yip. Hope nobody sees us as they drive by."

"Make fun if you want. They killed the best cow I had. Killed her calf, too." Danny could have told Jack how they killed a cow, but he figured that should wait until Jack was in a different mood.

"I heard the coyote's protected on the reservation," Jack said. "You planning to trap anyway?"

"They move around a lot." Danny knew that some Indians trapped on the reservation and claimed their coyotes came from somewhere else. "I'll find a fresh kill outside the boundaries and set the traps there. Those cattle were just inside the line, anyway. So, you coming?"

Jack shrugged. "Coyotes are pretty cunning. It might be fun to see if you can outsmart them."

When the fish had been in the bucket for about a week and the neighbor's dogs howled at the bucket but refused to go near, Danny added a few drops of anise and some oil of Tonquin. After school one evening, they drove the secondary roads looking for "the secret ingredient." "Every trapper has one," Danny said. "But it's not in any of the books, so you have to learn it from someone who knows, like Red Shirt or maybe Ass-Out Jones."

"What are you looking for?"

"A dead skunk," Danny said. He waited for Jack's reaction.

"The hell! Aren't those rotten fish stinking bad enough?"

Danny grinned. "Not one that's all smashed up. That's why

we're not looking on the interstate, where the tractor trailers would pulverize a critter. Just look for a basic, well-kept dead skunk. Male." After another half-hour's drive, Danny found what he wanted near Pilot Rock. They got out of the pickup and Danny nudged the skunk with the pointed toe of his cowboy boot. "This one's in good condition," he said. "Only one or two days dead, but cool enough so the fleas and ticks have crawled off." He tossed Jack a pair of cotton gloves. "Put these on."

Jack took the gloves but stood back. He held his nose and seemed to be studying the landscape while Danny bent over the skunk.

"The glands are still okay," Danny said. "Come hold the tail."

Jack put on the gloves and took a deep breath, then knelt beside Danny to hold the tail.

Using his pocketknife, Danny made a small slit in the musk gland just to the side of the anus. "There's just one important thing to remember about this operation," he told Jack.

"What's that?"

"Use a different blade to slice the cheese. Otherwise, it tastes funny."

Jack grimaced. "I don't even want to think about it—or your stinking sense of humor. I might as well go live with Que."

"Water seeking its own level," Danny said. He squeezed the bulb of the medicine dropper and inserted the tip into the tiny slit he had made in the gland. When he released the bulb and pulled out the dropper, it contained a few amber drops of the skunk's scent. After Danny had finished with both glands, he carefully screwed the cap onto the medicine bottle. "If we could figure how to make French-whore perfume out of this, we'd be millionaires," he said.

"Witches' brew," Jack muttered.

* * *

They loaded the trapping gear and drove the pickup as close as they could get to the rim of Squaw Creek Canyon, following a backroad out of Emigrant Springs so they wouldn't need the horses. At this elevation, it had been cold enough for the tamarack needles to turn brown and begin dropping off. The vine maples glowed scarlet. Below, a grove of quaking aspen shimmered golden, their leaves drifting down like bright feathers.

"I have to admit, Nebraska was never like this," said Jack.

Danny smiled. "Sometimes in fall, Red Shirt and I brought the horses here. No roads back then. Fall was his favorite time of year. He claimed you could never count on spring."

"I like both, but spring better, since fall means school. In Nebraska, the winters were miserable like the summers. Did you trap here?"

"No. Down closer to the river." Danny remembered how his father had let him use trapping money to buy a rifle, and he planned to do the same for Jack. "The animals will be getting winter fur and the pelts should bring good prices," Danny said. "Not as much as they once did, but if you put it with your Round-Up money, you can buy a new rifle for elk camp."

"What's so great about elk camp? It's no fun to sit around freezing your ass and listening to old geezers make up stories."

"The Wallowas are a special place. And Jones will be there."

"You guys won't weird out up there, will you?"

"What do you mean 'weird out'?"

"Mumbo jumbo. Start dancing around trying to get the whites to disappear. If you're planning any of that, tell me now. I've got my eye on this little blonde cheerleader, and maybe I should go for her right away—before she vanishes or something."

Danny cracked a smile in spite of himself. "Let's figure out where to set these traps."

They found the carcasses of the ginger cow and calf, now only bleached bones and shreds of hide, the ribs scattered by scavengers. There was no sign of a fresh kill around, but Danny knew the coyote pack that had killed the cow and calf would not be content to hunt patiently for gophers, rabbits, and other small game. They would kill deer in the high country, and when the snow drove their prey down near the river, they would go after sheep and weak cattle as well.

Although there was a light haze making the autumn sky pale blue, they could see for miles from Light Ridge, and Jack spotted the circling vultures near Little Squaw Creek. They hiked into the canyon until they found the coyotes' kill, a small doe. The vultures perched on the doe's carcass and stared at the two of them with their snapping black eyes.

"Those are some ugly fellows," Jack said. "They give me the creeps."

"Bonepickers. They'd pick us clean if they had half a chance," Danny said. He pointed the .22 pistol at them and fired, but his aim was halfhearted and he missed. They flapped away and climbed into the sky, hanging in the hazy distance like black razors.

The doe's carcass lay in a patch of bitterbrush, and the coyotes had used one clear trail to feed on her. There was a similar trail, but less used, on the other side of the brush. Danny studied the coyotes' tracks, following them until he found some soft earth that held an imprint. One track was much larger than the others and the pad was rounded at the back instead of having a little pucker, suggesting that the animal was heavy. One foot had an odd twist, as though the ankle had been broken and had healed badly, and two toes were missing. Danny showed the track to Jack. "Look at this one. That rascal looks big enough to carry off an elk. I'll bet he's trap-shy, too, the way that ankle's warped and those toes are missing."

"It looks big enough to be a wolf," Jack said.

"A wolf doesn't run with coyotes. But it's a damn big track." Danny was puzzled by the shape of the imprint but decided it could have been made when another animal stepped on top of it. "Well, if we catch that one, we'll be the talk of the reservation."

"Are you sure you know the boundary? We're not on the reservation?"

Danny shóok his head. "We're beyond it a quarter mile or so."

"Not that it really matters," Jack said.

"What do you mean?"

"You could trap them anywhere. Coyotes move around a lot and don't carry brands. Just say you got them off the reservation."

"I could do that," Danny said. "But I won't. The Umatillas protect the coyote on the reservation."

"Just because it crosses some boundary doesn't make it sacred. That's tired old men's superstition. Even the Umatilla ranchers would be glad to see the coyotes wiped out. They think that old belief is hooey."

"When you get older, you might think more of those old beliefs," Danny said. "There's a right way to trap and a wrong way. Now quit jawing and watch how I do this."

He spread a canvas kneeling cloth beside the well-traveled trail and with his claw hammer dug a shallow trench in the earth that was deep enough to bed the trap. After putting the trap in the hole, he carefully set the trigger. Then he placed a fish-screen mesh trap cover over the trap, making sure a slit in the screen allowed the trigger to fly freely. Using a flour sifter, he concealed the trap cover with dirt, shaking out any large pebbles and sticks that might foul the trigger.

After wiring a metal stake to the trap chain, he drove the

stake solidly into the ground using the flat side of his hatchet head. He used the same trapset on the other side of the trail, then spread some of the fish lure on the ground in front of the traps, turning his head to avoid the scent. After removing the kneeling cloth, he brushed away his footprints with a broom fashioned from sagebrush.

Chewing on a piece of wild timothy, Jack watched intently. "There's some disturbed dirt around the traps," he said.

"Good eye. Very good." Danny was pleased the boy had been paying attention. "This time, it's okay. By using this type of trapset, we get old mister coyote to outwit himself. He expects the disturbed ground because he thinks a skunk or badger buried some of the bait and intends to dig it up later. The coyote loses some of his caution when he thinks they've dug here already."

"Maybe you'll get the big one."

Danny thought a moment before he replied. "I don't think so. Old Two-Toes has been around a long time."

"He's too smart, then."

"Something like that. Got your gloves?"

Jack nodded.

"I want you to set the traps on the other trail leading in— just like this. But don't get the stinkfinger when you handle the lure, or the schoolgirls will avoid you like VD."

Jack didn't put on his gloves. He stood with his hands at his sides. "No," he said. "I can't."

"Don't worry about making a mistake," Danny said. "I'll help you."

"That's not it. I just can't set the traps."

"You're soft," Danny said, becoming angry.

"Maybe. In Nebraska, Hanson made me trap gophers because they were ruining the corn. We poisoned them for a while, but they got wise to it, so we set traps. I remember how they squealed when we picked them up, and sometimes their eyes popped out when we clubbed them. Hanson always brought home a couple of live ones in a gunnysack and tossed them to the dogs. Those squealed the loudest."

Danny put his gloves back on. He wasn't sure if Jack was soft or not. "The way coyotes kill a cow is pretty bad too," he said. "When she lays down to birth, they eat the calf right out of her and keep going. If she's not birthing, they hamstring her so she can't get up and eat her alive, starting with the back hams and working into her belly. It takes a few days. Maybe, if she's lucky, the rancher comes along and shoots her."

Jack swallowed hard. "I know things can get pretty ugly all the way around." He paused. "Look, I don't mind learning the trapsets. And I like to hunt—that's clean. But there's something about a trapped animal . . . Anyway, the coyotes belong out here, as far as I can tell. I'm sorry they killed the cows, but it's your payback, not mine."

Danny didn't say anything while they walked to the other trail, but he remembered how Red Shirt had forced him to trap the beavers. He didn't want to do that to Jack. Danny spread the kneeling cloth on the ground. "All right," he said. "I'll set the traps myself. This time."

The horse had fallen through the rotten spring ice of the beaver pond and drowned. The hole had frozen over again during a cold spell, and they thought the horse had been stolen, until a Chinook wind swept the snow away from the pond and they could see the horse frozen under the ice.

Red Shirt became angry and gathered his beaver traps. "They are killers," he told Danny. "Not like the mountain lion that stalks its prey and leaps. The beavers make a deep pond, and when the ice is thin or rotten, it's a deathtrap for livestock." The horse had been promised to Danny that coming spring, so that made it his business, too, Red Shirt said.

Danny helped Red Shirt prepare the beaver lure. Since they had trapped no beavers that winter, they had to buy beaver castor from Mookie Pretty Mink, and Red Shirt grumbled that Mookie charged them twice as much as it was worth. Red Shirt ground the beaver castor with an elkbone pestle, then added a dozen drops of cinnamon and half that many of anise. He poured in a little sweet oil to make a paste. "That should do it," he said. "When the women leave the room and the dogs scratch and growl, then it's just right."

They loaded the trapping gear into the back of Red Shirt's green Ford pickup and drove along the Umatilla until they came to Squaw Creek. Danny's breath clouded the glass on the side-window and he wiped away the fog with his mittens. He saw several horses bunched in a snowy field, facing downwind, their winter manes long and braided with ice. Red Shirt drove across the old wooden bridge. Many of the timbers were rotten and someone had laid planks to drive on. Red Shirt told Danny that if they dropped a wheel off the planks, they'd have to get pulled out by a tractor.

Red Shirt stopped where the snowplows had quit clearing the road and made a little turnaround. He and Danny took their snowshoes from the bed of the pickup. Danny's were slightly large and he had to walk with an awkward shuffle, his feet too spread apart. Realizing the difficulty he was having, Red Shirt carried the traps and had Danny carry the lunches and lure. "Next trip, when we come out loaded with beaver, you'll have more to carry," Red Shirt said.

They came to a steep, slick place in the riverbank that led to an opening in the ice.

"What's that?" Danny asked.

"An otter slide. Watch."

After a while, Danny saw a black head poke out of the ice hole. Then an otter climbed out and began waddling up the bank. It was about three and a half feet long, much larger than Danny had expected. When the otter reached the top of the bank, it looked around a moment, then slid into the open water, hitting with a loud smack. The head bobbed up briefly, then disappeared under the ice. In a few minutes, the otter reappeared and again crawled up the bank. This time, a smaller female otter was with it. She slid first and the larger otter followed. Danny and Red Shirt watched the otters slide and climb for half an hour. "Time to trap," Red Shirt said.

As they neared the beaver dam, Red Shirt pointed to the fresh alders the beavers had been cutting. Because the snow had drifted deep that winter, some of the trunks had been gnawed off five feet above the ground. "A bright Forest Service boy will come around with a clipboard this summer and write the beavers here are six feet tall," Red Shirt said. He laughed.

Danny laughed too. He was glad his father was in a good mood.

"Six-foot beavers," Red Shirt said. "You remember that one."

Red Shirt took the burlap sack from his back and dumped the traps onto the ground. He put on two pair of gloves—rubber ones to keep his hands dry, and juniper-smoked elk-skin ones to cover any scent. At a place where the beavers had been dragging freshly cut limbs into the water, Red Shirt set the first trap. He placed it in six inches of water and attached the chain to an L-shaped corner brace with two holes drilled in it. Picking up a fifteen-foot length of wire, he looped one end around a tree and slid the other through one hole in the corner brace, then wrapped the loose end around a large rock. After throwing the rock into four feet of water, Red Shirt tightened the looped wire around the tree until it was taut.

"If you trap a beaver on land, he'll twist and twist until he pulls his foot off," Red Shirt said. "This way, as soon as the beaver feels the trap, he'll dive for deep water. The trap will slide down the wire towards the rock anchor, but when the beaver tries to surface for air, the L-brace kinks the wire and he drowns." Red Shirt paused for emphasis. "He drowns like the horse, and I will have my payback."

Danny didn't like to think of the beavers drowning, but he felt his father must know what he was doing. He watched quietly as Red Shirt set another trap a few feet from the first one.

"Give me the lure now," his father said, and after Danny handed him the beaver-castor lure, Red Shirt coated some peeled alder sticks with it, and placed them in front of the traps.

Red Shirt told Danny to set the next trap. At first Danny was reluctant, but when Red Shirt thrust the trap toward him and shook it, Danny tried to follow the method his father had used. His hands quickly numbed in the cold water, and he felt very clumsy trying to twist the wire. At first he didn't get it taut enough, so Red Shirt made him drag the rock back to the bank and throw it out farther a second time. When Danny saw that his father was satisfied, he took off the elkskin gloves and peeled off the rubber gloves he wore underneath. He stuck his hands into his fur-lined mittens, feeling pins and needles as the circulation returned.

After the traps were set, Red Shirt pulled a flask from his pocket and unscrewed the cap. He smelled it and grinned. "Good stuff," he said. "You try it."

Danny took the flask. The liquid smelled like strong peppermint and something else he could not quite recognize. He took a small sip and the minty taste turned warm in his mouth. He tried a larger sip and felt a coal move down his throat. It tasted like mint and charcoal.

"Not like that," Red Shirt said, taking the flask. "Like this." He tilted the flask so the liquid glugged into his mouth. When half of it was gone, he stopped and wiped his mouth with his coatsleeve.

"All right," Danny said. He tilted quickly and could feel

the back of his throat burning. The tears came to his eyes, but when he blinked them away his father was smiling.

"Snowshoe grog," Red Shirt said. "I got the recipe from an old Assiniboin trapper up in Manitoba. It'll get you there and back."

When they returned the next day to check the traps, Red Shirt brought his hipboots so he could wade out and get the drowned beavers. Although Danny had hoped the traps would be empty, they contained two beavers. He stared at their dark shapes underwater. It looked as if they were swimming tipped at an awkward angle. Red Shirt waded in and pulled them dripping from the traps. Their small black eyes were open, their bodies stiff. One was a good-sized cub, about twenty-five pounds, and the other was a big male, nearly sixty.

"This one's a beaut," Red Shirt said. "Super-blanket size. That's even larger than extra-large. And look at the pelt. Perfect. He hasn't been fighting or worn off any fur crawling under the ice. I can get sixty dollars for him easy, maybe seventy."

Danny smiled, trying to share his father's enthusiasm. He didn't look at the beavers' eyes or the yellow teeth exposed by the pulled gums.

Red Shirt reset the traps. "There are at least two more in this pond, maybe three," he said. He put the beavers into two burlap sacks. "You carry the cub out. He was in your trap."

Carrying the heavy sack made walking in the snowshoes even more difficult for Danny. The dead beaver kept bumping against his back, knocking him off balance, and by the time they reached the truck, it felt like a terrible weight.

Two nights later, after the beavers had dried in the tack shed, Red Shirt showed Danny how to case a pelt by cutting the big beaver from the ankle of one rear foot to the anus, then across to the other foot. Once cut in this manner, the pelt pulled easily from the ankles forward. When the pelt was off, Red Shirt stretched it over a board and scraped off the fat and shreds of meat with his fleshing knife. He made Danny help with the cub, showing him how to keep the blade tilted correctly so the flesh could be scraped away without tearing the hide. After they had finished fleshing the pelts, they wiped off the excess grease with clean rags and stretched the pelts over flat plywood frames, leaving them to hang where there was plenty of ventilation.

"You can have the money from the cub, since he was in your trap," Red Shirt said.

"What will it bring?"

"It depends on the trader and how sharp you are. Maybe thirty dollars."

Danny stared at the cub's dark oval pelt hanging on the stretching frame. Outside, some of the reservation dogs had found the beaver carcasses and were ripping them apart. Their low growls and snarls made his skin turn cold. It was hard for him to see what the cub had to do with anything.

As if Red Shirt was reading his mind, he said, "Remember the drowned horse. Life will teach you about payback."

Red Shirt sold the pelts before they were cured and used the money to go on a toot. When Danny learned he had been thrown in jail for two weeks, he drove the pickup to the Umatilla to check the traps. The snow had melted, so he didn't need snowshoes, but the ground was soft and slick with clay that clung to his boots. The ice had broken up and the horse's carcass had washed against the opposite bank, where it lay black against the shore, the legs sticking out from the bloated trunk. Its lips were pulled back, baring the teeth in a hideous grin, and the blowflies were going in and out of the eye sockets.

Danny tried not to look at the horse. He could smell it, so he took shallow breaths as he checked the traps. There were two medium-sized beavers, each weighing about forty pounds, and Danny worked quickly, slipping on his father's hipboots, then wading awkwardly into the stream and bringing up the stiff, drowned beavers.

His eyes stung as he removed the beavers from the traps and stuffed them into the burlap sacks. He couldn't carry them both at once, so he had to make three trips, bringing out the traps and hipboots last. Each step was difficult because the soft clay clung to his boots and he had to stop frequently to kick loose the clots. Exhaustion set in by the time he had driven back to the trailer. He lugged the beavers into the shed, dumping them out of the sacks and onto the dirt floor with a dull thud. After locking the shed door so dogs couldn't get in, Danny went inside the trailer. Too tired to eat supper, he kicked off his boots and pants, then rolled into bed.

Danny left the beavers in the tack shed four days. Once he went out to skin them, but their musky smell made him sick and he went back to the trailer. Sometime after midnight the fourth day, Danny was awakened by rough shaking. He was still groggy when his father yanked off the covers and grabbed him by the ankles, tugging him until he fell to the cold floor.

"Get up, boy. You never skinned them."

His father's breath smelled of whiskey, and Danny got up, putting on his jeans, tennis shoes, and a sweater. He followed his father to the tack shed, where a fire was going.

"If you leave them out of water too long, you'll ruin them," Red Shirt said. "Good thing they let me out early, or you'd have really screwed it up."

Danny started to protest about his father's selling the pelts and going on a drunk, but he bit his lip to keep quiet and began skinning the beavers. Red Shirt didn't offer to help. Danny made the cuts and tried to peel the skins forward, but they stuck in places, tearing away large chunks of rancid meat. "Use the knife," his father said. Danny tried it, but cut holes in the pelts.

"Not like that. Angle it more."

Danny twisted the knife, imagining for a moment that it was buried in his father's gut.

After he had managed to skin the beavers, Danny threw their carcasses to the dogs outside. He held the door open a minute and gulped the night air.

Red Shirt helped him flesh out the pelts and nail them to the plywood stretching frames. "We'll sew up the tears later with catgut," his father said. "They'll be like new."

Red Shirt took Danny to the Hoot Owl for breakfast. The lumbermill workers from Pilot Rock had come off shift and were bunched at the tables, their hair and shoulders covered with sawdust. The place had the sweet smell of fresh lumber.

Red Shirt slapped Danny on the back and introduced him to a couple of the Indians who worked at the mill. "This boy is going to be a gamy old trapper," he said. "Already, he's got the beaver fever."

"Pretty soon he'll be looking for beavers around the girls' locker room," one of the men said, and they all laughed at that, even Danny. They tried to guess what the pelts would bring. One old Indian said that during the depression he had gone around picking wool off the barbed-wire fences to sell at the Pendleton Woolen Mills. "I only got fifty cents a sack for it, but if I worked hard, I picked a sackful every two days. It wasn't much, but I could buy beans and keep my belly full," he said.

Red Shirt ordered Danny a short stack of pancakes, scrambled eggs, and sausage, then ordered a sheepherder's omelet for himself. He paid with a five-dollar bill he had slipped into his bootheel, where the cops hadn't found it when they took him in on the drunk charge.

Danny tried to eat, but he kept smelling the beavers on his hands. He stared at the sausage patties; they reminded him of the dark oval pelts. He managed some of the eggs and half the pancakes, but Red Shirt had to finish his plate.

Back at the trailer, Danny crawled into bed and slept. He dreamed of beavers swimming underwater, and a horse. Then he dreamed he was drowning, and when he woke up, the rain was hitting the tin roof of the trailer.

Danny dressed and wandered out to the kitchen. Red Shirt was seated at the small formica table sharpening his fleshing knives on an Arkansas stone. He was very sober and had half a pot of coffee going on the propane stove. When he saw Danny, he said, "I sold those pelts because I was thirsty, but since they weren't cured yet, he only gave me forty dollars. After these are good and cured, we'll take them over to Heppner. We might get a hundred dollars for them there, and I know a man who sells good rifles out of a back room. You get a rifle and come up to elk camp this season."

Danny stood still for a moment, and when he realized that Red Shirt meant it, he went over to his father and hugged him. Closing his eyes, he imagined elk camp in the mountains, and he almost forgave his father for making him trap the beavers. Red Shirt put his arms around Danny and pulled him close until the boy smelled his coffee breath and felt his father's hand at the back of his head. When Red Shirt pushed him away, he held a lock of Danny's black hair between his thumb and the knifeblade. "Sharp," he said.

✦ 13 ✦

When Pudge opened the door, Danny looked twice to make certain who it was. She wore a dark brown skirt and a peach-colored blouse with ruffled sleeves and collar. Her hair was fixed up and she wasn't wearing glasses. He tried to think of something to say, but nothing came out at first so he thrust the bottle of wine into her hand. Then he said, "Hey, Pudge, you're looking healthy as a new calf."

"Good to see you, Danny." She smiled and took his coat. "Look at this big lunk here." She gave Jack a hug and kiss. While she put their coats in the closet, Danny took a quick glance around the front room. "Got a new sofa, huh?"

"Try it out," Pudge said. "It's comfortable."

Danny slapped the seat of his pants a couple of times. "Looks fancy," he said. "I hope the pickup seat was clean." He sat stiffly for a moment, his back straight, then eased on down into the sofa. "Say, that *is* nice."

"It makes out into a bed, too, in case company comes. Just a second. I'll get you something to drink."

"Want me to unscrew it for you?"

"I've got it under control," she said, walking over to the kitchenette.

Jack sat down beside Danny and picked up a sports magazine from the coffee table. "Hey, I like this couch all right," he said. "Ours is pretty ratty and that Naugahyde gets cold at night."

"I wanted some new furniture when I move into one of those little BIA houses," Pudge said. "It'll seem funny to leave the trailer, though."

Danny wondered how she managed to swing that deal. "You win a lottery?" he asked.

"No, I just put my name in early for subsidy. Besides, we'll all be cashy when the tribe approves the SUNCO leases."

Jack looked at Danny and raised an eyebrow. Danny just shrugged.

"If you don't mind, I could use a couple of strong backs for moving," Pudge said.

"Sure," Jack said. "Glad to help out."

Danny glared at him. He figured that's why Pudge had invited them over for dinner. "I don't mind, if I'm not busy," he said after a moment.

"Thanks," she said. "So what have you boys been doing?"

"Not much," Danny said.

"He tried trapping," Jack said. "Didn't catch anything but a cold."

"You weren't on the reservation?" she asked.

"No. I've never known that fish lure to fail. I never even caught a nosy skunk."

"The great white hunters got them all," Jack said.

"There's a skiff of snow on Light Ridge every morning now," Danny said. "The coyotes are running in the valley. Killed a bunch of sheep."

"That's too bad," she said. "You going after them?"

"I'm going out to Hardman to check with Jones first."

Pudge came out of the kitchenette carrying three glasses

on a tray. Danny looked at the bubbles in the amber liquid. It wasn't the Gallo he'd brought. "Pretty classy," he said. "You buy some Champale or something?"

"Try it?" She handed a glass to Danny and a second one to Jack.

"What the heck," Jack said. "It's almost a holiday."

Danny tested his. "Apple wine, huh? Funny, there's no kick."

"Sparkling apple cider."

"It's not bad," Danny said. "Pour in a little of Dr. Tremblane's Foot Remedy and it'd get right next to you."

"Hardly."

"No booze. You afraid I'd get lit up and come after you?" Danny winked at Jack, but Jack pretended not to notice.

"I put it away. Two weeks now."

"No kidding. Just like that?" Danny snapped his fingers.

"A little harder than that." Pudge smiled. "I'm getting some help from people at the hospital."

"Gave up your glasses too?" Danny said.

"You look good without them," Jack offered. "You've got real pretty eyes."

"Thanks," she said. "I woke up sick drunk one morning and stepped on those damn glasses again. Busted them all up and the rhinestones popped out. So I said, 'That's the last time for me.' I threw the liquor and the glasses in the garbage and got some contacts. I've been working out, too. Lost fifteen pounds already."

"I knew something was different when I saw that skirt," Danny said. "I can't remember when you weren't wearing pants." He wished she had called him before she threw out all the liquor.

"I bought some new outfits for incentive. Makes me feel good, almost sassy. You should have seen Perry Winishite. He was sitting on the sidewalk holding up the wall of the Silver Spur, just as drunk as a priest. He sees me walking by and figures I don't know him, so he tries to bum some money. For toothache medicine, he says.

"I laughed and said, 'Perry, if you got any teeth left it's a miracle, because that would mean you grew another set after they yanked yours at the V.A. Hospital. Go see those government dentists right away, because they'll want to write you up in a book. A Cayuse with three sets of teeth.' That fixed him. He came over and squinted at me, shook his head, and staggered back into the bar. Hope *your* teeth are okay. That turkey's ready."

"Sure smells good, too," Danny said.

"Delicious," Jack said.

"I decided to have Thanksgiving a little early," Pudge said, "since I don't know how long you'll be up at elk camp. I got a big one so you and Jack can freeze some of the leftovers and take them up with you."

"We can live off the land," Jack said.

"And maybe starve," she said. "Take some turkey."

Danny carved while Pudge poured more sparkling cider. She had candles on the table, and a ceramic pilgrim and Indian salt and pepper set. Danny noticed that the napkins were real cloth.

They ate turkey, chestnut dressing, mashed potatoes and gravy, sweet potatoes baked with marshmallow topping, and green beans with little almond slices on them. Pudge also served a fruit salad with shredded coconut. Even though she had a small plateful, Danny and Jack ate seconds, then thirds. Finally Danny could eat no more and shoved himself away from the table. "I've got Dunlop's disease," he said. "My belly done lops over my belt." He remembered how Red Shirt had always said that and he laughed.

Pudge cleared the table and Jack helped her wash the dishes. Danny sat in the front room relaxing on the sofa. He dozed off for a moment but came awake when he smelled coffee.

They had pumpkin and mince pies in the living room. Pudge served them coffee in thin cups with little handles and Danny kept wishing he had a mug.

"These pies are delicious," Pudge said. "But the crusts are a little soggy. You bring me back some leaf lard from an elk, and I'll treat you to the best pie you ever had. Make your tongue hard."

"It sounds good," Danny said. "You got a deal."

"Thinking of leaf lard, I've got something for you." Pudge took two packages out of a drawer and handed one to each of them. They looked identical, with silver foil wrap and green ribbons. "Christmas is coming a little early," she said.

Jack opened his first. It contained two Buck hunting knives, one with a straight blade and one curved for skinning. There was also a small referee's whistle. "Wow," Jack said. "I've always wanted a knife set like this. Terrific! Maybe I'll have a chance to try it out. But what's the whistle for?"

"If your dad gets you so lost you holler yourself hoarse, try blowing on the whistle."

Danny shook his head.

"No kidding," Pudge said. "I read in the *Star* about a man lost for three days in Canada whose friends finally found him when they heard the whistle. He had laryngitis or something by that time."

Danny opened his package. "Thanks, Pudge," he said. "Really. These are beautiful knives. You shouldn't have spent—"

Pudge put her finger to her lips. "My pleasure. I've got something else I want to show you." She went to the closet and returned with a bulky-knit sweater fashioned like a jacket, with a big collar and four antler buttons. "Look at this," she said.

Danny thought it was a beautiful sweater. It had brown ducks on both sides in front, one above each straight pocket. The ducks had green heads and were flying over green cattails with brown tops.

When Pudge turned the sweater around, Danny saw there was a duck on each sleeve the size of the ones in front. Two larger ducks flew across the back.

"What do you think?" Pudge asked.

"You got a limit there," Danny said. "In fact, you might be one over."

"That's a nice sweater, Pudge," Jack offered. "Looks like it'll keep you warm."

"I'm glad you like it," Pudge said. "I'm going to knit one for you. Phyllis, she's a woman I work with, has patterns and sells the yarn and everything. This one's just a demonstration model. Do you want green heads or red heads on the ducks?"

Jack hesitated. "For me? Gee, Pudge, isn't that a lot of work? I don't want you to go and put yourself out."

"I want to make it for you. Besides, it'll make me proud to see you wearing it. Green or red?"

Jack frowned, then turned to Danny. "What do you think?"

"Green heads," Danny said. "There's more mallards around here than canvasbacks." He wished Pudge would offer to make him a sweater like that.

"Sure. Green," Jack said. "This one looks fine." His voice dropped off.

"Good," Pudge said. "That way I don't have to buy four colors of yarn. Of course, you could have red-headed ducks with red cattails, but that might look a little funny." She took a tape measure out of a drawer. "Stand up here."

Pudge measured Jack's waist, shoulders, arms, and chest. "He's pretty stout," she said. "Look at those shoulders. When he fills out a little, he'll be a husky buffalo. Hey, hold out your arms so I can get the sleeves right. I'll make them a little long to allow for growth, and you can have a roll cuff at first."

When she had finished measuring Jack, Pudge said, "It'll take a couple of weeks to get this knitted up. Phyllis helps out with any problems during lunch breaks. I just wish you could have this before you go up to elk camp, because it would be so warm, but I guess you'll have to wait."

"Well, it'll sure be nice whenever he gets it," Danny said. "I'd say he's a pretty lucky fellow."

"Sure," Jack said. "Pretty lucky."

Jack offered to clean up after he had carried the dishes to the sink. Pudge put a Christmas album on the portable record player. "You want to dance?" she asked Danny.

"To Christmas music? It's a little early."

"Don't be backward," she said. "That's why the record was on sale."

"All right then." Danny didn't feel like dancing, but he didn't want to hurt Pudge's feelings. They danced slowly to "Silent Night" and Pudge felt good in Danny's arms. Her shoulders and back were firm, and when he moved his hand lower she pressed closer. Her perfume smelled like apricots, and Danny tried to remember if he had ever danced with Pudge when he wasn't drunk. "Jingle Bell Rock" came on next, and Danny pushed Pudge away to arm's length. "I can't dance to that," he said.

"Sure, just like high school."

He felt a little foolish, but he didn't want to spoil it for Pudge, so he worked at it. When the song was over, she laughed and said, "You dance pretty good."

Danny was embarrassed by the compliment. "Not so bad yourself," he said.

Pudge yawned and covered her mouth. "Sorry. I was up pretty early getting things ready. I don't mean to rush you off, but I've got to show up at work tomorrow—bright and early."

"On Sunday?"

"It's terrible," she said. "But that's how it is at the café. Truckers don't take holidays."

She went to the kitchenette and put most of the leftover turkey, dressing, and sweet potatoes in plastic containers and tucked aluminum foil around the leftover pie. Then she got their coats from the closet. "I hate to rush you, but . . ."

"This ought to last the winter," Danny said. He put on his coat, and she loaded his arms with containers. "Hey, Pudge," he said. "Thanks for everything. It was real nice."

"That's right," Jack said. "Those knives are great. And I'm stuffed. Thanks." He went out.

Danny was trying to balance all the containers. "Catch the door, would you please?"

"Danny, look at this."

He stopped in the doorway and looked up. Pudge was holding mistletoe over his head. Then she put her arms around his neck and kissed him. She closed her eyes a moment, making the kiss last, then opened them and winked. "Gotcha!"

"It's not even Thanksgiving yet," he protested.

"I was just getting a fair advantage. I might not see you before the hunt, and that should bring some luck."

"What kept you?" Jack asked when Danny reached the pickup.

"You writing a book or what? Pudge just wanted to ask about something."

After a pause, Jack said, "You could do worse than Pudge."

"In a pig's eye!"

When they were back at the trailer, Danny shoved the beer cans out of the way and Jack stacked the plastic containers in the refrigerator. "We can eat on this for a week," Jack said. "That Pudge can cook."

Danny glanced at him. "She paying you to brag her up?"

"I just know what I know. You want a turkey sandwich?"

"Not right now."

As Jack fixed his sandwich, he said, "I didn't know what to say about that sweater."

"Green heads look best."

"That's not it," Jack said. "If I wear that sweater around school, the kids will think I'm a geek."

Danny took out his new Buck knife with the straight blade. Then he got some 3-IN-ONE oil out of the cupboard and sat down at the table. "Tell them to shove it," he said. "That's a nice sweater. When Pudge finishes yours, maybe she'll make one for me." He put some drops of oil on the blade and started rubbing it with a piece of cloth.

"You can wear mine. Pudge must think I'm an old geezer."

"Hey," Danny said. "Don't badmouth Pudge. I'll bet that's a lot of work."

"Who's sticking up for her now? She knows how to set you up, all right." Jack took his sandwich into the bedroom and closed the door.

Danny spit on the blade the way Red Shirt used to when he sharpened his knives with the Arkansas stone. After a few minutes he got up and made a sandwich, slicing the turkey thin with the sharp knife but spreading the mayonnaise with a kitchen knife, because Red Shirt always said mayonnaise bitched a game blade. Danny sat at the table eating his sandwich. Pudge could cook. And she looked good, too. Pudge looked good? Danny grinned. *I must be crazy or long overdue for a drink,* he thought. Then he remembered the women Red Shirt had chased, especially the last one. Maybe Jack was right. You could do worse than Pudge.

Verline was a big blonde woman, about thirty, with large wrists and hands that looked like they were used to work. They stuck out of the arms of her bulky white sweater. She had on green stretch pants and white crepe-soled shoes, but she didn't look like a nurse, and Danny guessed maybe she was a cook at the hospital or worked in a laundry.

She had driven up to the Lariat Lanes bar and bowling alley in a powder-blue Falcon station wagon with a rippled tan door on the driver's side and a tailpipe that barely cleared the ground. Whoever had hung that door had done a lousy job. The Falcon had bald tires, too, and it was snowing like hell.

She sat at the bar, took her cigarettes from her purse, and ordered her first drink before she turned and smiled at Red Shirt, who was sitting at the end of the bar. Taking the stool beside her, Red Shirt said something and she tossed back her head and laughed. From where he was sitting, in a booth in the restaurant section, Danny could tell that her smile was her best feature.

Danny figured if the light had been a little better, or if his father hadn't drunk so much already, he might not have paid her much attention. But Danny knew Red Shirt had drunk too much, because his lower lip hung out, making his mouth slack. Red Shirt went over to the jukebox and dropped in some coins. Marty Robbins came on singing "White Sport Coat and a Pink Carnation," and Red Shirt and the blonde started dancing. His father held her close, leaning slightly forward, and she put both arms around his neck as though they were kids at a prom. "I Walk the Line" came on next and they kept dancing.

Eddy Spino came out of the bowling alley and asked Danny if he wanted to bowl a few games. Eddy had thick glasses and a short nose, so they called him "Mole" at school, but Danny figured he needed some way to pass the time, so he bowled with Eddy until after ten. When Danny returned to check out the bar, Red Shirt and the blonde were at a back table holding hands and playing kissy-face over their drinks. Danny ordered French fries and a Coke, then sat at a booth where Red Shirt could see him. He thought if he acted bored enough and a little sullen, the old man might head for home before midnight. When the blonde got up to select a song on the jukebox, Red Shirt flashed the okay sign at Danny.

Figuring it was going to be a long wait, Danny ordered some more fries and stared out the window at the heavy snowfall. After a while, he leaned his head against the back of the booth and dozed.

Two men came in about eleven. One was big and the other about average. The smaller one wore a red-and-white Cenex hat. They stomped the snow off their feet and looked around the restaurant. Cenex looked in the bar and came back. "You seen Verline?" he asked the cook.

The cook jerked his thumb toward the bar and said, "In there."

"Don't be a dope," the big man said. "We just looked."

"Maybe she's in the john," the cook said. "Maybe she left with the Indian."

Danny became wide awake.

The jukebox in the bar started up again and Cenex strode over to the doorway. "By God, she *was* in the john, gussying up for that bastard featherhead," he said. Both men rushed into the bar and Danny jumped from his seat.

Someone kicked the jukebox off, and Danny heard two men's voices, one his father's, rise in anger. Then he heard a sound like a hammer hitting a melon. When he reached the doorway, he saw a chair turned over and Red Shirt sprawled backward on the floor. The big man kicked at him, but Red Shirt rolled away and scrambled to his feet. His left eye was puffy and swelling shut, as if he was winking.

The man in the Cenex hat grabbed Verline by the back of the neck and was trying to shake her, but she was too strong. "Now it's Indians, huh?" he yelled. "Get home, you dumb bitch!"

Distracted by the yelling, the big man lowered his guard, and Red Shirt moved in, jabbing twice with his left hand, then counterpunching with his right. The jabs landed, but the big man ducked away from the right, and Danny knew his father had drunk so much his timing was off.

"Cheap shot!" the big man said. "You'll pay for it."

"Look here!" It was the bartender, and he was pointing a

.357 magnum at the ceiling. "Take it outside. All of you." He brought the gun down until it pointed just over their heads. "I mean it."

Cenex dragged Verline toward the door and the big man followed. "I'll be outside," he said to Red Shirt.

Red Shirt put on his hat. He looked at Danny and shook his head. "You might have to drive back," he said, then stepped out.

The bartender hadn't noticed Danny standing in the door-way. "Take a hike, kid," he said. "This ain't no arcade. And try to keep your old man out of here from now on."

Danny retrieved his jacket from the booth. When he stepped outside, he saw the four figures arguing and waving their arms under the neon LARIAT sign. Then they split into twos and went at it.

Red Shirt and the big man leaped at each other and grappled for a moment before they fell to the ground and rolled over and over in the snow. Danny heard the thump of fists, grunts, and curses of the men as they threshed. Then the big man was on top, clutching Red Shirt's hair with his left hand as he drove his right fist into his face. Verline screamed and kicked the side of the big man's head. Red Shirt hooked the man's ear with his thumb and jerked him over onto the ground. Then both men stood, taking deep breaths to clear the pain, and squared off.

Cenex suddenly grabbed Verline's wrist with both hands and twisted, forcing her to her knees. She cursed and spit at him, swinging wildly with her free hand. He let go and cocked his arm, then punched her, pivoting on his foot so his weight was behind the blow. He hit her full in the face, snapping her head back. That stopped her screaming. She fell forward on her hands and knees, spitting blood into the snow.

Taking quick, short punches, the big man forced Red Shirt back to the door of his truck, pinning him against the metal.

"Now we got him," Cenex cap said, leaving Verline and moving toward the truck.

Danny grabbed a large lava rock from the border of the parking lot. The two men were concentrating on punching his father and didn't notice him until he brought the rock overhand against the big man's neck. He had aimed for the head, just behind the ear, but the man had moved and Danny missed that spot in the confusion.

"Jesus! Shit!" the man yelled. He turned and lunged for Danny, but missed. Danny backpedaled, stumbled over Verline, and fell backward in the snow. The man grabbed his coat collar, jerking him to his feet, then cuffed him twice, open-palmed, like a bear cuffs her cub. Danny felt a roaring in his head. Then the man punched him in the gut, driving out his wind, and he was doubled up on the ground, watching black spots swirl before his eyes and counting the seconds until he could breathe.

"Bert, help me!" Cenex screamed. Red Shirt had knocked him down and was kicking him. When Red Shirt saw Bert turn away from Danny, he kicked Cenex in the nuts, then broke off the fight and jumped into his pickup. He threw it into reverse and backed up twenty feet. He shifted gears and made a run at Bert, but the big man grabbed Danny again and held him like a shield, so Red Shirt swerved.

As Red Shirt was making a U-turn in the parking lot, Bert let go of Danny and grabbed a shotgun from his pickup's rack. "If he comes at me again, he's a dead man," he said.

Red Shirt swung wide and drove the pickup onto the highway, fishtailing as soon as he goosed it on the snow-covered blacktop.

Bert grabbed Cenex, who was still writhing on the ground clutching his crotch. "Come on," Bert said. "Let's get that son of a bitch."

Danny figured his father had a good half-mile head start by the time Bert got Cenex into the truck and reached the highway. He stood and watched the winking taillights of both pickups until they disappeared. His nose felt wet, and when he wiped it with the back of his hand, he saw that the smeared blood looked black in the neon light.

Verline was still on all fours, muttering and wiping her mouth with her white sweater. She groped in the snow, where she had been spitting blood, until she located something. She stood, holding her compact up to the light and squinting at it. The mirror was broken into dozens of silver shards. She probed her mouth a couple of times with her finger and started to cry. "The son of a bitch almost knocked out my tooth," she complained.

Danny watched her a moment, then touched her shoulder. "I'm sorry," he said.

She put her compact back in her sweater pocket and looked at Danny as though she had seen him for the first time. Then she stopped crying and put her hand to her mouth. "Do you need a ride home?" she asked behind her hand.

"I could sure use one," Danny said. "It's snowing like hell."

She nodded. "Do you think you can drive?" she asked. "I'm not up to it just yet. My purse is around here somewhere."

"All right." Danny found her purse lying in the snow and took out the keys. He drove carefully because the snowy roads were slick. When he tried to brake at one intersection, the car slid sideways and stalled. He managed to start it and straighten it out.

Red Shirt wasn't at the trailer. It was cold inside and Danny started the propane heater.

Verline sat down on the couch. She had bled all down the front of her sweater. "I'm going to have to take this to the cleaners," she said. When she talked, she held her hand over her mouth so Danny couldn't see the split lip. "You got a couple aspirin, Hon? Make it four, if you have them."

Danny found some aspirin in the medicine cabinet and shook out six. He took two before leaving the bathroom.

"Thanks," Verline said when he handed them to her. "I could use a drink to wash these down. Got any whiskey?"

Danny found a half-bottle of Old Forester in the cupboard and poured her two-thirds of a glass. He brought out the bottle and put it on the floor beside the couch. He thought Verline would have to take her hand away from her mouth to take the aspirin and whiskey at the same time, but she managed with just one hand. Balancing the glass in her palm, she picked up the aspirin tablets with her forefinger and thumb, one at a time, and chased them with whiskey. She finished the whiskey along with the aspirin and poured herself another. "That's better," she said.

She leaned back and closed her eyes, and for a while Danny thought she had fallen asleep. Then she began to talk, still covering her mouth with her hand. "The one in the cap is Wendell," she said. "God, what a name! We're separated, so he's got no real hold on me. Bert—he's the one that hit you— that's Wendell's brother. He used to be in the marines and it made him crazy or something. But he's loyal to Wendell, that bastard." She laughed, but it sounded more like a sob. "Wendell and Bert, Bert and Wendell—that's my life." She took her hand away from her mouth, showing her split lip.

Danny looked away.

"Not very pretty anymore, am I? Even before this, I mean. Twelve years ago I was something else." She poured the rest of the whiskey into her glass. "Like the saying goes, 'If I knew I was going to live this long, I'd have taken better care of myself.' " She paused. "You don't have to listen to this, you know. You can run on to bed or whatever. It's not your story. I'm just going to wait here a while until my hurt clears up and see if your father shows. That's okay, isn't it?"

"Sure," Danny said. "I'll get you a couple blankets and a pillow." When he came back with the bedding, she was asleep. He put the pillow under her head, trying not to look at her split lip. She had dark circles under her eyes, like bruises. He slipped off her shoes and was surprised that her feet looked so dainty. He tucked one blanket around her feet and legs and covered her shoulders and neck with the second.

Danny climbed into his bed. He listened to the snick of snowflakes against the tin trailer and tried to stay awake until he heard his father's truck coming into the driveway. But he fell asleep while it was still snowing.

When Danny awakened, he thought his father was in bed with him, but when he rolled over, he saw it was Verline wearing one of his father's flannel shirts. Her back was to him, but her warmth felt good, and he lay there a few minutes before moving again. He wondered if his father had come in, and what he would say about Verline being in his bed.

Verline opened her eyes and blinked when she saw Danny. Then she sat up. Her lips were bruised and puffy, but her eyes were clear. She tried to smile. "That hurts," she said, touching her lips with her fingertips. "It was cold in there. I guess I got up and came in here. I hope you don't mind, Hon. Your father never came back, of course. Even if he wanted to, he probably couldn't get through that snow."

"I don't mind," Danny said, relieved that Red Shirt wasn't back.

"You look like him, you know, a little bit. I didn't notice last night."

Danny propped himself up on one elbow. "I look more like my mother, I guess. Maybe half and half."

"I'm going to take a shower. Hope there's lots of hot water. Then I'll fix you some breakfast. Even Wendell thought I was a good cook. Look the other way a minute, would you? I've got nothing on but this shirt." As she sat up, the flannel shirt fell open, revealing the creamy swell of her breasts and one pink nipple.

As if by instinct, Danny reached out and touched her cheek. "You don't have to go," he said. "It's cold."

Something changed in her eyes and her mouth parted slightly.

He moved closer and reached between her legs, but she had put her hand there, blocking him. He tried to move it, but she shook her head. "No," she said. "I've got to draw the line someplace. You're a good kid. I wouldn't feel right about it. Just look the other way, please."

Danny rolled over and stared at the wall. Verline got up and went into the bathroom. He heard her turn on the shower. In a few minutes the bed seemed cold, so he got up. He stood in front of the mirror and looked at his chest, flat stomach, penis and thighs. He looked good. Red Shirt was already getting a beer gut. He dressed quickly, putting on boots to make him a little taller, then went into the kitchen. He wondered where in hell his old man was.

Verline came out of the shower, a towel wrapped around her and her hair plastered back. "I didn't know you were up," she said. Taking her clothes off the couch, she went into Red Shirt's bedroom to change. A varicose vein the size of a small blue marble bulged from one of her calves.

Danny looked out the kitchen window. It had finally stopped snowing, but the sky was dull gray and heavy looking. It was almost black over the Blue Mountains and Danny guessed it was probably still snowing there. A snowplow came down the road, its yellow light flashing as it turned.

Verline emerged from the bedroom, toweling her hair. "There's no school today," she announced. "I heard it on the radio. The buses can't get through, so there's no school."

"Fine," Danny said flatly, without moving from the window.

Verline hadn't missed the tone. "Say, I thought you'd be

happy about missing school. It's a play day. No more school; no more books; no more teachers' dirty looks . . ."

"The way that snowplow threw snow into the driveway, I'll have to dig out behind your back tires so you can get to the road."

She stopped toweling her hair and started running a comb through it. "You don't have to try to make me feel bad," she said. "I can leave just as soon as my hair dries a little, if that's what you want. I don't want to catch pneumonia out there."

He felt the windowpane with his palm. It was cold. "It's all right," he said. "You don't have to rush off or anything. There's bread and some eggs."

She put her comb back in her purse and walked into the kitchen. "How do you like yours?" she asked.

"Over easy."

He sat at the table and watched her cook. She knew her way around a stove, all right, and looked good doing it.

When she saw that he was looking, she kind of laughed. "I was part owner of a restaurant once," she said. "In Portland on Third Avenue. It was called the Third Avenue Café. The waitresses stole us blind." She buttered the toast and sprinkled cinnamon and sugar on it, then served it to him with his eggs.

"How about you?" he asked.

"I'm just drinking coffee until I see about this tooth. It seems loose as hell."

She smoked three cigarettes while she cleaned up the dishes. "Well, I guess I should try to make it back to town," she said. "Maybe I can find a dentist."

Danny put on his coat and got the shovel out of the tool shed. The plow had thrown up a lot of snow, and he was sweating by the time he had dug out the driveway to the road. Verline came out to help him with the snow behind the tires. They took turns shoveling, their breaths coming out in white puffs. It seemed odd to Danny that she was leaving, but he didn't think he wanted her to stay.

When Verline could back the Falcon out, she opened the door and got in. Danny stood beside her holding the shovel.

She took his free hand in hers and said, "Tell your old man he missed a good breakfast." Then she let go.

"Sure," Danny said. "Take care, Verline." He stepped back so she could close the car door.

After Danny had watched her car disappear down the road, he shoveled the rest of the snow from the driveway. Then he leaned the shovel against the trailer and went back inside. He turned on the TV for company and watched the game shows. A woman dressed like a pizza was trying to guess which door had a refrigerator behind it. About noon he called Billy Que to ask if Red Shirt had spent the night there, but Billy hadn't seen him. He told Danny the heat was out at his place and he might be over later on to warm up.

At two, Doney Silverheels called to tell Danny someone had seen a pickup like theirs off a reservation backroad near Thornhollow. The truck was in a ditch and partially covered with snow.

When Billy Que showed, they chained up his truck and drove out to Thornhollow. They found the pickup just like Doney had said. Red Shirt was dead in the front seat. His frozen hands clenched the steering wheel, and pieces of his palms tore off when they pulled him out. His left eye had swollen shut, and there was a prune-sized lump on his temple where he had cracked his head against the windshield. The ice formed little crystal patterns in the corners of the glass.

❖ 14 ❖

Everyone called Hardman a ghost town, although there were fourteen mailboxes in front of the weather-beaten general store. When sheep ranching and gold prospecting had flourished, Hardman had been two towns—Raw Dog and Yellow Dog. No one knew for sure where those names came from, but one story had it that two prospectors had fought their dogs over a land claim and the yellow dog chewed the other one raw. Eventually, as the territory became more civilized, the residents wanted postal service, but the U.S. Post Office wouldn't deliver mail to a town named either Raw Dog or Yellow Dog. As a result, the people grudgingly agreed to call the town Hardman after Dave Hardman, the first postmaster. Still, most old-timers refused to call Hardman anything but Dog Town.

Ass-Out Jones lived in the back of the old general store. The gas pump was still outside and the large orange UNION ball hung above the leaning porch. Danny knocked hard on the door because it was difficult to hear from the back.

Across the way at the grange hall, some bearded young

men in carpenter's overalls were hammering and sawing in an effort to fix the supports for the clapboard porch.

Danny knocked again, harder. He heard someone inside.

"For Christ sakes! Don't knock it down. You're not borrowing any more tools." Jones opened the door. "Danny! Come in, come in. I thought it was one of those fuzz-cheeked bastards from across the way wanting to borrow a plane or miter board. Step in, now; rattle your hocks."

Danny was surprised that Jones looked so thin. His dark skin had taken on a grayish quality and there were dark pockets below his eyes.

"Watch where you step, there," Jones said. "I'm getting my gear together for elk camp. You'll be coming up?"

Danny saw the chain saw, splitting mall, tent, rifle, sleeping bags, cooler, and all the rest of the gear scattered across the floor. Jones also had two venison hindquarters hanging in the cool outer room that had once housed the store merchandise. "I'm bringing up my boy," Danny said.

"Fine," Jones said. "I want to meet him."

They stepped into the small back room where Jones cooked and slept. "I've got a bottle of Old Forester here somewhere," Jones said. "How about a splash for good hunting?"

"Sure thing," Danny said.

Jones took a couple of tumblers from the cupboard with his crippled hands. He filled them nearly to the brim with whiskey, and into his own glass he added a few drops from a brown bottle. Danny's glass was decorated with red-and-green pheasants.

"Bloody hands," Jones toasted, raising his glass.

Danny raised his, then took a sip. "You feeling okay, Jones?"

"Over the hump," Jones said. "I had these stomach pains and was losing weight, so they had me in for one of those damn routine examinations people die from. The doctors at the Heppner hospital told me to quit drinking. I laid off for a week, but got to feeling worse. Then I saw Doc Shank—you know, the old vet—and he told me my system was so used to the red-eye, it went into shock when I cut it off. He give me some DMSO, too, just in case. That was those drops. Now I drink all I want and feel a sight better."

"Well, those doctors don't know everything," Danny said. He didn't think Jones looked very good, but maybe he hadn't been back on the booze long enough yet. "What are those guys doing across the street at the old grange?" Danny asked.

"Fixing it up," Jones said. "Bunch of longhairs came here from California someplace with all kinds of strange ideas. They want to take over the town, starting with the grange. Say they're going to have dances there and sell natural foods. Sell to who, I wonder? Ever since those hippies up at Pine Grove got into the death camas thinking it was wild parsnip, most people have stayed clear of natural-food stores. Wasn't that a mess, though? Four dead and the rest not feeling well."

"Red Shirt said there used to be some big dances at the grange."

"Sure. People came from all over. Heppner, Spray, Monument, Ione, maybe even Kinzua and Fossil. Not like that now, though. You should hear the weird music they got coming out some nights. How about another splash?"

"Just a small one, maybe," Danny said.

"So what brings you way out to Hardman?" Jones asked as he filled Danny's glass.

"I need your advice and some coyote urine."

"Got plenty of both. You trapping now?"

"A pack killed my cow and calf up Squaw Creek. Now, Doney Silverheels says they killed some of his sheep on Wildhorse Mountain. Got his dog, too."

Jones shook his head. "Sheep-killing sons of bitches. Poor Doney did love that dog."

"Busted up while he was telling me. Seems Doney left

Char with the herder because the dog was sheep-smart, and those coyotes lured him away from the trailer. Doney said he fought hard, by the signs of it, before they tore open his throat. Doney threw some poison around, but he asked me to try trapping them."

"Most of Wildhorse is on the reservation."

"I know. That's why I want to take a look first. I won't trap them on the reservation, even though I'm damned sorry about Char. And I'm still steamed about my cows. But there's another reason, kind of curious. Doney claims he saw some big tracks, more like a wolf's, mixed up with the coyotes' tracks. Those big ones had a rounded pad, like the animal was pretty heavy. Thing is, I saw tracks like that up Squaw Creek."

"Couldn't be a wolf," Jones said. "Not running with coyotes. A big dog's making that track—maybe a German shepherd gone bad."

"But those coyotes would kill a dog."

Jones shrugged. "You can't predict coyotes—even what might bring them around. You already try that fish lure me and your dad worked out?"

"No luck," Danny said.

"That lure should work," Jones said. "But for real smart old-timers, you need urine on a scent post. There are other tricks, too. Down by Klamath, I remember, one trap-shy old bastard kept fooling everybody, so they brought in Curry Hebo. He was a trapper's trapper—half Modoc and half jack Mormon, with the meanest streaks of each."

"What did he use?"

"Curry put cyanide in the wool of a spring lamb, still nursing and coated with milk, then set it loose for the coyote to kill. Turned out to be the biggest coyote ever around these parts—damned near sixty pounds. That old long-fang ripped up a good chunk of real estate with his guts ablaze."

"I don't think much of poison."

"Last resort. There was a bonus, though. Two wild dogs had been running with that varmint, and they tried to eat off the lamb's carcass too. Curry found them all yowling and staggering in blind circles. Just walked up close as me to you and shot them with his pistol. Sheep-eating sons of bitches had their last feast." Jones nodded for emphasis. "Come on. The urine's out in the woodshed."

As Danny followed Jones outside, he wondered if a big dog might be running with the coyotes. But he didn't think that settled right this time.

Jones filled a spray bottle with coyote urine he kept in a jar wrapped in gunnysacks. "Douse your post good with this, a couple of times if need be," he said. "But spray some around in the bushes, too. Make it seem natural. Don't just go pouring it all on the post, because those coyotes will sniff around some and be looking for scent on the bushes too."

"I'm obliged," Danny said.

"You taking Jack along?"

"No. I've got to check this out myself, but we'll meet you in elk camp early next week."

"If you don't get them by then, I'll help out after camp, so long as they're off the reservation."

"Thanks," Danny said. "I appreciate it."

Danny drove to Wildhorse Mountain the next morning and spent an hour sweeping the trailer and bringing in firewood. Although Doney had taken the sheep in, he had left his cattle, a mixture of Angus and white-faced Holsteins. Danny found a dozen head down by the river in the locust trees. He remembered how Doney had planted the locusts and thought he'd get rich harvesting them for cooperage, but then all the egg companies and fruit packers started using plastic cartons. Doney was still powerfully glum about the fortune he could have made.

About one, while he was scouting the river, Danny found

the carcass of Char. Doney hadn't buried it deep enough, and the coyotes had dug it up and dragged it around some. Danny went back to the pickup for the shovel, then buried the dog's body good and deep, placing some large rocks and old fence posts over the grave. As a final precaution, he pissed on the dirt, hoping the human scent in this setting would scare off the coyotes.

In the late afternoon, Danny found the place where Doney had spread the poison, and two dead skunks that had eaten some of the bait. He was glad there were no dead coyotes, because Doney had used the poison on the reservation. Danny buried the tainted bait to keep it away from dogs and badgers, even though he knew they could dig it up again if they were determined. At twilight he found a scent post the coyotes used to mark their territory and gave it a good dousing with the coyote urine Jones had given him. He sprayed some around in the bushes, too, in order to make it seem as natural as possible. When he had finished, he swept away his footprints with a sage branch. He set no traps, because the post was clearly inside the reservation boundary, but he scouted a knoll he planned to watch from in the morning. By the time he had hiked back to the trailer, it was dark.

Danny ate early that night since he would be up before dawn and waiting above the scent post at first light. He set up the cot and unrolled his sleeping bag, then fell asleep, using his rolled-up jeans for a pillow.

Sometime after midnight he awakened, chilled by the rising wails of coyotes carried by the night wind from somewhere on the river. From their cries, Danny knew they had a fresh kill, and he hoped it was a deer rather than one of Doney's calves. One edge of the canvas he had tacked up to block the wind had pulled loose and was flapping. Danny weighted it with his boots and took the revolver out of his pack, setting it on the floor beside the cot. He burrowed into the sleeping bag, covering his head with his arms to muffle the night howls.

The second time Danny awoke, he listened for the coyotes but heard nothing. Yet he was certain something had awakened him. Then he felt a slight tremor, as if someone had stepped onto the trailer threshold. He tensed for two breaths while he groped for the pistol beside the cot. Something brushed against the canvas with a dry, scratching sound as Danny's fingers touched the .22. He sat up quickly, pointing the revolver at a white face, the size of a paper plate, thrust in the doorway. "Don't move, you bastard, or you're dead!"

The face hung suspended in the doorway of the trailer, but the intruder said nothing.

Danny kept the pistol pointed at the face while he eased out of the sleeping bag and reached for the light. As he flipped the flashlight on, he felt the hot grassy breath of the white-faced cow that had poked its shoulders and shaggy head through the canvas door, overcome by curiosity. The cow blinked in the bright light and opened its mouth again, emitting the strong grassy odor Danny smelled.

Danny relaxed and eased the hammer down. "Scram, you bag of baloney."

The cow, seeming to oblige, removed first one front leg, then the other, shaking the trailer a little each time. Danny knew the tremors that had awakened him were the jars of the cow's legs as she stepped into the trailer.

He shook his head and put the revolver back on the floor. He felt foolish. What if he had fired in his half-sleep? How could he have explained to Doney a dead cow by the door of the trailer? Restless and fitful, he got out of bed and dressed, knowing that he could not sleep now and did not want to.

Danny ate some cold bread and beans, then left the trailer. He carried the .30-06 with the 4X Redfield scope, as well as the .22 pistol. Using the flashlight to probe the darkness, he walked quickly in the predawn. By the time he reached the

little knoll that overlooked the scent post there were light
gray streaks in the eastern sky, although the morning star still
twinkled. The wind had faded to a slight breeze that came
upriver, and he chose to wait on the knoll, because from
there his scent would not carry. He hunkered in the sage
clumps, resting his weight on his heels and occasionally blowing on his hands. Well before sunrise, the sky lightened, so he
could make out trees and objects on the hillsides. Soon,
enough light broke for him to study the area around the scent
post.

He moved slightly, to ease the ache in his thighs, and listened to the creak of his leather boots as he shifted his
weight. While he waited, he tried to figure out a plan of
action. He was disappointed that the scent post had attracted
nothing so far. After it was good and light, he'd have to find
the fresh kill, if it was a kill the coyotes had been howling
over the night before. Once he'd found it, he could use the
rest of the coyote urine to begin a new scent post near the
carcass. A light frost had moistened the ground, and Danny
thought that if he hurried, he might find the large tracks near
the fresh kill.

The lean gray coyote came out of the chokecherry tangle
near the river and was in the clearing before Danny spotted
it. It stopped as it approached the scent post, then began
circling, keeping its distance from the post. After a few moments it paused to look at the hillside, but Danny remained
well concealed and motionless, so the coyote started circling
again. A second coyote trotted into the clearing and stopped,
seeming to study the ground. Danny was pleased he had
remembered to sweep away his footprints. He wondered
how many more coyotes were waiting in the thick brush by
the riverbank. He studied the light a moment but knew it
was still too dark to sight through the scope.

The first coyote circled to the far side of the clearing, and a
third coyote, smaller than the others, emerged but stayed at

the edge when the second one snapped at it. Danny guessed the first coyote had the superior role and the others would wait until it used the scent post. Danny shook his head and chuckled. Jones was sure right about them coming to the post.

A quick movement in the brush some fifty yards upriver caught Danny's eye. Although he had just a glimpse as the animal veered away from the river and moved quickly up the sagebrush hillside, Danny knew it was much larger than the other coyotes, and lighter gray. The animal didn't move like a dog, either, and that realization sent Danny's blood coursing. He quietly shifted to higher ground in order to get a better look. Glancing back at the clearing, he saw that it was empty; the other coyotes had melted into the brush. Now moving on the hill above, the animal stuck close to the thick sage, and Danny had only snapshot glimpses in the flat morning light.

As the gray shape went over the hill, it paused a moment on the ridge, and Danny put the scope on it, trying for a better view. The sun coming over the Blues filled the glass with an intense glare, and Danny squeezed his eyes closed, seeing the black image against the bright red background of his inner eye. When he opened his eyes again and blinked them clear, the animal was gone.

After hurrying up the hill, Danny found the tracks easily on top of the little ridge that overlooked his knoll. He stared at one print—very clear in the frosty ground—and his mouth went dry. Two toes were missing.

Danny took the cartridge from the chamber of his .30-06 because he didn't want to fire by accident. Then he started following the tracks. Two-Toes moved southwest, down the Umatilla River valley and deeper into the reservation. By noon Danny was across the valley from Plenty-Bears Ridge, so he figured he was somewhere near the center of Reservation Mountain. He sat on a granite outcropping and studied the terrain. Behind him, the Blues rose dark, almost purple, against the turquoise sky. Below, perhaps a mile away, the Umatilla glistened like a silver ribbon winding through the bright yellow aspen. Danny marked the place where the river angled south and realized he was within the boundaries of the land SUNCO planned to develop once it got the leases. By his reckoning, another mile downriver would put him somewhere above Sammy's old sheep camp.

As he began tracking again, Danny discovered that Two-Toes was leaving an even clearer trail, and he wondered why it stayed on open ground rather than in thick brush or along the rocky ridges. Of course, he wouldn't shoot at the animal, so it was safe, but it had no way of knowing that.

Danny crossed another ridge and found himself in a steep, narrow canyon. The near side was thick with juniper, and the far side was forested with stands of yellow pine. Danny paused for a few moments to study the canyon. The trees were dense enough to conceal the animal, but Danny believed it had probably outdistanced him and was at least another ridge away. The tracks went straight toward the bottom of the canyon, and Danny scrambled downhill until he was twenty yards from the bottom. There the trees thinned out and the rich soil gave way to sand and gravel. A few smaller trees had been uprooted, and Danny guessed this narrow canyon had flashflooded in the spring. At the bottom there was a trickle of water and the tracks turned downhill, toward the river.

For a quarter mile, the tracks stayed in the canyon bottom. Suddenly there was more gravel and more washout where a side canyon joined the one Danny was in. In the far distance, across the valley, Danny made out Rattlesnake Ridge a little south of Plenty-Bears. The animal had ranged into the heart of the reservation, and Danny wondered if it would double back to the remote mountains before long.

Surprisingly, the tracks turned up the side canyon. Danny

went another hundred yards and lost them. He couldn't believe it. Even though there was too much gravel for a clear imprint, an animal as heavy as Two-Toes had to leave a trail. Danny went back until he was positive he had Two-Toes' trail, then retraced the disturbed gravel bed until the trail ended. There were three places where the animal's feet had overturned stones, but that was it. Danny shrugged his shoulders and tugged at his ear. He returned to the convergence of the two canyons, to make certain he hadn't missed something, but Two-Toes had clearly turned up the second canyon. Danny wound up in the same spot, staring at the three places with the overturned stones. After that, the track vanished. Recognition burned in the back of Danny's mind, and a dark space seemed to open there, revealing a memory from many years before. And this time he was not afraid.

Danny laid down his rifle in the gravel, then took out his pistol and set it beside the rifle. Moving slowly away from the weapons, Danny turned in a full circle, searching the canyon walls for whatever watched him. The dark shape appeared on the canyon rim. The sun blazed behind it. Using his hands to shield the brightness, Danny gazed at the shape, but he could see no more than an outline, the black silhouette of a large wolf burning against the pulsing sun.

Danny lowered his head, and when he looked again, the image was gone. The sun seemed cool against the azure sky and outlined only the sharp line of the canyon rim. Danny closed his eyes and imagined the black form again, realizing that the trail had not been made by a coyote or a dog. It was the Wéyekin, his protecting spirit.

✦ 15 ✦

Danny and Jack stopped in Enterprise to fill the thermos with hot coffee and gas up the pickup. While the waitress filled the dented thermos, Danny and Jack sat on counter stools eating big pieces of apple pie à la mode. They were the only Indians in the place, but no one seemed to notice. The elk hunters, tired-faced men in plaid shirts and dark wool pants, bent over platefuls of steaks and potatoes. Their camp beards and haggard appearances made them seem old.

"You sure our stuff is all right in the pickup?" Jack asked.

"It's fine," Danny said. "No one will bother it out there."

"I wouldn't want to lose my new rifle," Jack said. "My door doesn't even lock."

"Everyone around here already has a rifle. Now finish that pie. We don't want Jones shooting all the elk before we even get to camp."

"We should have started sooner," Jack said. "I was ready way ahead of you. How come you got to be so slow?"

"Practice," Danny said out the corner of his mouth. "When

you get to be my age, you won't be half as perfect as you are now. Anyway, you forgot half the gear, so it's a good thing I double-checked."

"That going to do it for you fellows?" the waitress asked as she put the dented thermos on the counter. She tapped it with her pencil. "Thermos looks like it came out with Lewis and Clark."

"It's an old one, all right," Danny said. He liked the waitress and another time he might have tried to pick her up, but now he just left her a dollar. "See you next trip," he said as they left.

After driving the seven miles to Joseph, Danny passed through the center of town without taking the turnoff to the Imnaha River and their elk camp above Indian Crossing.

"Hey! Didn't you miss the turn?" Jack asked. "That sign said Imnaha. Want me to drive? Are you sleepy or what?"

"Just hang on to your pants. There's something I want to show you." Danny passed the last lights of Joseph and went over a little rise.

Wallowa Lake stretched before them, its waters black and silver in the moonlight. A low fog bank hovered over the south shore, partially obscuring the timbered shoreline. To the west, the densely wooded foothills seemed to rise out of the lake, and behind them, snow-covered Chief Joseph Mountain towered against the background of black sky. Even with the moonlight softening the definitions of its ridges and canyons, the mountain peaked as sharply as a dragon's back.

A slight knoll rose to their right and sloped to the lake's southern shore. At the top of the rise, a stone monument, twice the height of a man, rose from the rustling grasses. Tall sentinel spruces surrounded the monument.

"Let's take a look from up there," Danny said.

A swinging gate placed between two posts held a sign:

GRAVE OF OLD CHIEF JOSEPH
MAINTAINED BY WALLOWA COUNTY
JUNIOR WOMEN'S CLUB

When they reached the top of the knoll and stood next to the monument, they had an even better view of the lake. A light breeze silvered the little ripples.

"It's incredible," Jack said.

"Nez Perce country," Danny said. "At least it used to be."

Jack tried to read the words on the monument by moonlight. "Old Joseph is buried here, huh?"

"It's a grave," Danny said. "There are probably some bones. A lot of Nez Perce and Walla Wallas are buried on this knoll and by the water."

"This place gives me a strange feeling," Jack said.

Danny smiled. He felt it too, just as he had when Red Shirt brought him to the Wallowas for the first time. "It's the Nez Perce in you coming out."

"There must be dozens of stories about this place."

"Probably hundreds," Danny said. "The explorers and anthropologists came here and collected as many as they could, and the Indians didn't want to disappoint anybody so they just kept making them up."

"That's pretty good," Jack said. "Back at Timbler, some of the kids used to talk about their tribal legends. A lot of them sounded the same, but no one really knows if they're true or not anymore."

"It's hard to tell," Danny said. "Red Shirt told me this story the only time we stood together at Wallowa Lake." Danny half-closed his eyes, gazing at the moonlight dancing on the water and trying to remember the words and tone his father had used to tell the story. Then he began.

"One winter, a large herd of elk, thirty-five or perhaps forty, tried to cross the frozen lake during Elkmoon. Somewhere near the black cliff face, the ice was thin and the herd broke through. No one saw them flailing their hooves and cutting their legs on the shards of ice, but one by one they sank, their hot breath extinguished by the black water. Two days later an old Nez Perce hunter, one of the Dreamers following their trail, came upon the spot where they had fallen through. New ice had formed by then, so their tracks disappeared in the middle of the lake.

"Many stories about that lost elk herd were told around Dreamer campfires in the Wallowas. Some said they had gone into the world below the water. Others said they were ghost elk that had disappeared during Elkmoon. Sometimes, looking over the frozen lake in winter, the hunters thought they saw the elk herd crossing the lake. Their hides were white as ermine, and their eyes glittered like diamonds. The breath from their nostrils came so thick it formed a low fog.

"The old men who first told the stories eventually died, but versions of the story were well known around the lake for many, many years.

"Then one summer a rich doctor from one of the cities lost his motor overboard near the black cliff face, and he offered any diver one hundred dollars to find the motor and pull it out. A young diver searching the area found the water to be deep and cold, but with the aid of an underwater light, he located the motor. When he came up, he told a strange account of seeing the skeletons of elk down there. But everyone around the lodge laughed at him because the elk bones would have been buried by silt or washed apart many years before. Still, he insisted, claiming these skeletons were of the largest elk he had ever seen, standing maybe seven feet tall at the shoulder. The men laughed harder, and some suggested he was crazy, for no elk is that tall.

"A businessman from Portland heard of his discovery and offered him twenty dollars for every elk tooth he could bring up. He planned to have them made into watch fobs, tie tacks, and the like, then sell them as curiosities at the lodge.

"One of the old Nez Perce guides tried to stop the young man from diving after the elk teeth, but he got the help of a friend, and the two took turns diving off the cliff face. All morning, the first diver was perplexed because he could not find the skeletons, for he had marked the place well when he went down after the doctor's motor. They moved the boat out farther into the lake that afternoon, and he dived again. When he didn't come back up in twenty minutes, his friend went after him.

"At the coroner's inquest, the second diver said the water was much deeper than he would have expected, and extremely cold. He went through two thermoplanes before he found the lake bottom. There, the diver claimed, he saw the most unusual sight he ever could imagine—the bare-boned skeletons of the entire herd of elk. The bones were not weathered but gleamed white in the light from his underwater torch. The legs moved slightly in the deep current of the lake.

"He found his friend at one of the larger skeletons. His weight belt had somehow fouled in the antlers of the elk, and in trying to twist free, he had pulled loose his air hose and drowned. The diver was puzzled as to how his friend's belt fouled, for this elk's antlers were tilted at a different angle from the others, and its head was lifted, perhaps from his friend's struggles. He cut the body free and began swimming to the surface. But when he switched off the underwater torch, he swore he saw the elk bones still gleaming in the black water, and a light-red glowing where their eyes should be.

"As the men on the dock helped unload the body, they found two elk teeth in the sack the dead man clutched. Those who saw the teeth claim they were exceptionally large and white and seemed to glow—even in the afternoon sun. But by the time of the inquest, the molars had disappeared. Some think they were stolen and worked into cuff links, but others believe the old Nez Perce guide rowed them out by the cliff face and threw them into the deep water to appease the ghost elk.

"In any case, several other divers tried for the next few weeks to find the skeletons again, but no one could. The coroner ruled death by accidental drowning, and the stories about the ghost elk go on. Those who believe there actually were some elk molars think they must have come from an elk that drowned the winter before in a similar spot. Sometimes at night, though, if someone is brave enough to try fishing near that black cliff face, they say they can see something glowing way down in the depths of the black water. But others just think it's the reflection of the moon dancing on the waves."

When Danny finished the story, he looked across the lake at the hovering fog bank. On the far shore, the lights of cabins glowed like campfires, and he imagined the old Dreamers telling their stories. He wondered how Red Shirt had felt telling the story to him.

"I've never heard a story like that one," Jack said.

"Neither had I, until Red Shirt told me."

"Do you think it really happened?"

"That's the way Red Shirt told it."

Danny wanted to save a little time, so he took the short cut over Sheep Creek Ridge. There wasn't much snow on the high road, and Danny figured he could make it without chaining the pickup. While Jack dozed beside him, he sipped strong coffee from the dented thermos lid. When the road became steeper, sharp granite rocks jutted from the places where four-wheel drives had packed the snow.

Ten miles in, the road forked, but Danny couldn't see a sign. He stopped the pickup and took a three-celled flashlight from behind the seat.

"What's the deal?" asked Jack.

"I'm not sure which fork to take." Danny walked fifty yards down the right fork, the cold air erasing his grogginess. When he shone the light into the woods, the beam illuminated stumps of big trees and piles of charred slash. So the right fork was a new logging road that went nowhere, he figured. On the way back to the pickup, Danny looked in the ditch and saw a broken sign that said "Limited Access Road—Crown Pacific Lumber." It had been broken off at the post, probably by a bumper, and there were four bullet holes in it. "Loggers," Danny said when he got back to the pickup.

"I thought they didn't log here," Jack said.

"Looks like they are now."

They passed Big Sheep Creek campground and Danny started to drive faster. The truck fishtailed on a patch of ice.

"You're going to run off the road," Jack said. "Poky as molasses until the last minute."

"I don't want to miss Jones," Danny said. "He knows these mountains better than anyone. And all the old stories, too."

"Ass-Out's a damn funny name," Jack said.

"His real name is Gilbert Jones," Danny said. "But they called him Ass-Out after the fire."

"You may as well tell me about it. I'm wide awake with your driving."

"Jones is a Klamath, and before their reservation was terminated and their timber sold, he worked as a blackjack dealer around Klamath Falls. He was pretty good, too, until one night he won a bunch of money off a couple drunk ranchers. They came back the next day, mean and sober, then stuck his hands in a drawer and kicked it shut a couple of times."

"He couldn't deal after that," Jack said.

"That's right. He just hung around watching the others. Sometimes he'd play a little, for pin money.

"On New Year's Eve, 1954, there were a lot of people in the Antlers, drinking hard and dancing. Jones was in the back room with the gamblers, watching a Reno dealer called Gypsy Slim, when a fire started in the kitchen—no one knows how. It spread fast. The people in the front and the band got out okay. But the cardplayers got caught in the back room. For some reason, the back door was padlocked on the outside."

"That's a tight spot," Jack said.

Danny nodded. "Jones realized he couldn't get out so he ran to the ice machine in the hallway and stuck his head and shoulders in just as far as he could. Then he jammed the sliding door against his ribs. When the firemen axed through the padlocked door, they found seventeen people dead. They either burned up or breathed the smoke. But Jones was still stuck in the ice machine, with his ass sticking out of his pants and burned pretty good."

Jack chuckled. "So that's how he got the name."

"There's more," Danny said. "After the firemen pulled him out, Jones managed to walk over to the blackjack table and cash in everyone's chips. He took all the money from the pit—about four thousand dollars. And I heard he lifted the wallets of a couple dead ranchers while he was at it. No one said anything. I guess they figured he had it coming, on account of the busted hands."

Jack shook his head. "That money must have been a little scorched. If even half that story's true, I should meet him, all right."

They drove through the Wallowas until they reached the high rim overlooking the Imnaha River Canyon. The light-gray streaks of dawn silhouetted the peaks on the opposite side. Danny put the pickup in low and drove down the five-mile grade into the canyon. He turned upriver and passed a few flickering campfires at Coverdale. When they reached the camp above Indian Crossing, it was fireless and dark.

Danny shut off the pickup's engine and looked around the camp. The meat pole was empty. The only vehicle was

Jones's red Bronco with its little three-wheel trailer. There were no tracks in the snow, so Danny figured the Bronco hadn't been out for a couple of days. The large canvas tent sat under a lodge-pole pine, its back to the Imnaha River. The face cord of wood was about a third of the way used up. Jones's H&H magnum stood just outside the tent, its barrel covered by wax paper and a rubber band to keep it from filling with snow.

"That lazy Jones is still asleep," Danny said. "Why don't you go on in and give Easy Living a couple of shakes?"

"You do it," Jack said. "I'm awful sleepy myself."

"Step out and start unloading the gear. That should wake you up right quick."

"Daylight in the swamp!" Danny yelled as he walked over to the tent. He stepped inside and took the Coleman lantern off the hook, pumped it a couple of times, then lit the mantle. When the lantern stopped hissing and the mantle glowed yellow, Danny turned down the gas and set it on the folding table. "Rattle your hocks, Jones! Rattle your hocks!"

Jones was deep inside a sleeping bag, lying on the cot. Only his orange wool cap was visible. He coughed a couple of times, and without sitting up reached with a crippled hand for a cigarette pack from the apple box beside the cot. "Son of a bitch!" Jones said. "It's only four-thirty." He raised his head and struck a match. His face seemed gaunt in the glare.

Danny said, "I'll fix breakfast. Jack's outside unloading some of the gear." He opened the front of the woodstove with the telephone-pole insulator they used for a handle and put in some pine kindling. When the kindling flared, Danny added a couple lengths of stovewood. He stuck his head outside the tent and yelled to Jack, "If there's any leftover coffee in that thermos, bring it here. Got a corpse that needs reviving."

"I can't drink that Mormon poison until I've had a shot," Jones said. "You bring any whiskey?"

"Sure," Danny said. "But we better have a little breakfast first."

"Most overrated meal of the day," Jones said. "I'm not eating so good these days." He put his feet onto the floor and reached for the liniment bottle, then poured some onto his hands and rubbed it over his knees and the calves of his legs. "Not worth a damn anymore. All stoved up."

"You'll revive when you smell elk," Danny said.

"You find that big coyote on Doney's place?"

Danny shook his head. "Not exactly. That's kind of a long story, so I'll tell you later."

Jack came in carrying the thermos and a big Igloo cooler. "Where do you want this?" he asked.

"Out of the way, maybe under the table. First pour Jones some coffee, then get out the bacon and cut us some fair-sized pieces. Jones, this is my boy, Jack."

"I'm glad to see you don't look like him," Jones said, sticking out his hand. "My pleasure."

"I've heard a lot about you," Jack said. "Good to meet you."

"I can pour my own coffee," Jones said. "I'm not that gimped up. Say, you've still got Red Shirt's old thermos. I doubt there's two that are dented up like that." He poured himself most of a cup and set the empty thermos back on the table. "Dead soldier," he muttered.

"I'll make some more," Danny said. "What about that bacon?"

Jack reached inside the burlap sack and took out a slab of bacon that was wrapped in cheesecloth. He used the Buck knife Pudge had given him to cut off quarter-inch slices, and Danny put them into the heated cast-iron frying pan on top of the cookstove.

"You boys do a pig proud," Jones said. "That's a fancy toad stabber you got there. It's so shiny you could shave in it."

"Thanks," Jack said. "Pudge gave it to me."

Jones lit another cigarette and held it between his lips,

then stuck his thin legs into the heavy wool Northland hunting pants that were folded at the foot of the cot. He had lost so much weight, he was using a rope to cinch the pants around his waist, and he looked like a rodeo clown. "I'm damn glad you made it up," Jones said. "I was tired of talking to myself. Scouted around a couple days, but I haven't been out after that. Need reinforcements, I guess. Just plumb tuckered."

"You still look a little off your feed," Danny said. He turned the bacon, moving it to the side of the pan, and cracked half a dozen eggs into the bubbling grease.

Jack put three tin plates on the table and cut thick slices of bread. "Hurry up, you guys," he said. "It'll be light soon."

Jones grinned. "Just full of piss and vinegar, aren't you? I can remember when your dad was that green."

"Belly up to the table," Danny said, ignoring the remark. He put the bacon and eggs on the plates. "Let's eat, Jones. Get your strength up."

Danny and Jack finished quickly, but Jones picked at his food. Danny poured steaming cups of dark coffee all around. "Six-shooter," he said, winking at Jones.

"It's thick enough to plow," Jack said, stirring his with a spoon.

"Well, Jones, where do you want to hunt?" Danny asked.

Jones shrugged. "It's like ass. Every piece is good, but some's a little better than others."

"Gumboot?"

"We could, but they've been doing some logging in there and have a few gates up now."

"I thought it was all Forest Service."

"They leased out some timber contracts, so that's fouled things up a little."

"Little Skookum Creek?"

Jones shook his head. "Let's show the boy big country."

"Black Horse."

Jones's eyes gleamed. "I've been saving it up until you came. It's got so many draws and side canyons, you need about a dozen guys to hunt it."

Danny finished his coffee and thumped the mug on the table. "Then three Indians ought to be about right."

Jones smiled. "Sounds good," he said. "We'll just send young Piss-and-Vinegar through the bottom and shoot the elk as they boil out the sides."

Jones drove the red Bronco to the rim overlooking Black Horse Canyon. They got out of the rig and stood on a granite outcropping, looking into the gray-green depths of the forested canyon. By squinting, Danny could make out the saddle that traversed Black Horse and Skookum, about five miles below, and he remembered the last hunt there with Red Shirt.

"It's big country," Jones said, breaking the silence. "I'll drive close to that saddle and build a warming fire. It'll take you three or four hours to work your way down. If you push some elk ahead, I'll have a good shot as they break over the saddle."

"All right," Danny said. "Put horns on them."

Jones climbed into the Bronco and left. At a distance, the rig seemed like a red toy in the open country.

"This is sure some canyon," Jack said. "Deep."

"Red Shirt used to say you had to look in relays to see the bottom."

"What are those mountains?"

"The Seven Devils," Danny said. "They're in Idaho, across the Snake. But *this* is where we hunt." Then he told Jack about Left Hand and the other Dreamers coming back to the Wallowas after surrendering in Montana's Bear Paws.

"I can see why they came back," Jack said. "It's fantastic country." He was still staring into the canyon. "Did Red Shirt ever take you to the Bear Paws?"

Danny shook his head. "Tourists might go there, or a few missionary Indians," he said. "But none of the Dreamers, their sons, or grandsons go near it. Red Shirt said it's a bitter place, even now.

"Young Joseph and the Nez Perce were heading for safety at Sitting Bull's camp in Canada. When they were cut off by General Miles in the Bear Paws, the Nez Perce hid in the coulees and dug shallow rifle pits with camas hooks and spoons. The Dreamer warriors were such good shots that each time the cavalry charged, it had to retreat. Finally, General Miles buried his cannons on end in the ground and used them as mortars to fire shrapnel into the coulees. The women covered their children and the old people with elk robes for some protection from the cannons, and the snow that swept down from Canada. During the night, the wails for the dead mingled with the cries of freezing children.

"After five days the losses were too great, and Young Joseph surrendered. His arms showed bullet wounds, and one had creased his forehead.

"One by one, the Dreamers came out of the shallow rifle pits like ghosts rising from the ground. Their long, dark braids were shagged with ice, and their blankets were stiff with frozen snow. Behind them, the women sang the death chant for the warriors—Ollokot, Looking Glass, Poker Joe— the old people, and the children; all the Nez Perce that lay frozen under the elk robes.

"One by one, each Dreamer held his rifle to the weak winter sun glinting like a pale white wafer in the gray sky. Then they put down their rifles and surrendered to the blue-coats.

"No," Danny concluded. "There's no point in going to the Bear Paws. We hunt here." He blinked the tears back from his eyes, turning toward the Seven Devils so Jack couldn't see him crying. But when Danny looked at Jack, the boy was wiping his wet face with his coatsleeve.

Jack chambered a shell into his new .30-06. "Well, if this is where we hunt, let's get started," he said quietly. "What do you want me to do?"

"Don't get lost."

"Come on," Jack said. "Give me a break."

Danny knelt and with his gloved finger drew a map of Black Horse in the snow. "You walk the bottom along the frozen creek," he said. "The bitterbrush is thick there, and the elk will bed down out of the wind. Don't take any side canyons. Stay along the creek and you won't get into trouble. If you get mixed up, you can always follow the creek down to the Imnaha, then walk it back to camp."

Jack nodded. "Don't worry. I'm not about to get lost," he said.

Danny grinned. "Jones is right. Piss and vinegar."

"Where will you be?"

"Above you, on the north slope. The pines and brush are thick in there, so you won't see me. But you'll see the Bronco and Jones's warming fire when you get near the saddle."

"Ten dollars says I shoot the first elk," Jack said.

"Save your money—and your breath. You'll need it for walking."

Danny waited until Jack made his way to the bottom of the canyon. Then he started moving along the north slope, about a third of the way below the rim. He watched the clearings on the south slope where the cover was thin. The manzanita brushed against his soft wool pants but made little noise.

On the north slope there was over a foot of snow, enough to cover the sharp granite rocks and make footing treacherous. Danny knew that Jack would move too quickly through the bottom, pushing the game out, but some of the elk might try to climb out of the bottom and double back. Danny walked below the rim because he knew that elk, unlike deer, were too smart to expose themselves along the skyline.

After two hours, Danny figured he had covered half the

distance to the saddle. He was sweating freely, so he unbuttoned his plaid hunting coat and took off his red flannel hat. His feet hurt from walking the steep sidehill, and he felt the pressure in his calves. He carefully placed his rifle in the fork of a spruce so the barrel wouldn't clog with snow. Then he brushed the snow off a stump and sat down.

Ahead was an alder thicket that ran to the rim of the canyon. On the south slope, a logging road came over the notch and about a third of the way down the hill, but no trees had been taken out. Danny figured the Crown Pacific people must have decided it was too expensive to log the big country, at least for now. He thought of the mills in Enterprise and Joseph, and the contracts for millions of board feet of lumber. If the loggers came into Black Horse, ruining the elk cover and browse, some of the best country would be gone.

Danny took a peanut butter and cheese sandwich from a pocket in his hunting coat and began to eat. He wondered if Jack had some avocados tucked away in the food coolers, and he grinned as he imagined what Jones would say about that.

Then he smelled the elk.

The wind was blowing up the canyon, so Danny knew they were in front of him. Afraid to stand in case he might spook them, he stayed motionless on the stump and searched the alder thicket. His eyes strained to see the elk among the gray trunks of the alders and the grayish white patches of bitterbrush. When he finally saw the dark yellow rumps of the two elk, they were fifty yards above him, in the thickest part of the alders.

Danny figured Jack had probably flushed the elk out of the creek bottom and they were picking their way carefully up the hillside. He didn't want to go into the thick alders where he'd break twigs, so he crouched and moved uphill, keeping parallel with the elks' path while trying to get close enough for a clear view.

After a hundred yards, he stopped to catch his breath. The

elk had moved further uphill, and there was still too much thick brush blocking his view. He had glimpses of yellow rump, but that was all. Once he thought he saw testicles dangling, but by the time he looked through the rifle's scope, he couldn't be certain. He moved uphill faster, trying to overtake the elk before they reached the rim, but his foot caught on a wood-rose vine and he fell into a clump of bitter-brush with a grunt, snapping off several twigs.

The elk snorted and he heard them dislodging rocks as they ran ahead of him. He brushed the snow off a limb and rested his rifle, sighting through the scope at the place where the alders thinned at the top of the ridge. He caught a glimpse of the elk, their hides the dirty cream color bulls usually had, but what he thought was horn might have been a branch, so he did not fire. After the elk disappeared over the ridge, Danny ran to the top.

Leaning against a gnarled yellow pine bent from the wind, he caught his breath. Minutes later, he saw the two large bulls break into a clearing on the far side of Gumboot Canyon, about half a mile away. Their black manes rose in the wind, and the sun glinted from their antlers. Danny admired the way they moved up the canyon, fast yet without effort, their dark hooves striking sparks on the granite and starting little ribbon slides on the talus.

Danny slung his rifle over his shoulder and watched the elk until they crossed the next rim into Little Skookum. Then he picked up their trail and retraced it to the alder thicket. In the snow, he found the two bulls' yellow pissholes, still steaming.

"It would have helped to know the elk chant," Jones said that night in camp. He was frying thick sirloin steaks in the cast-iron skillet.

Danny prepared a special salad dressing Red Shirt had taught him to make. He mixed ketchup and pickles, then added mayonnaise and half a cup of gin. "I don't know," he said. "Those elk were pretty smart."

"Smart don't have nothing to do with it," Jones said. "Not the way Red Shirt worked it. The night before a hunt, he'd wrap an elk hide around himself, then go out in the woods alone and chant. The next day he could walk right up to elk. That made him a great hunter."

"Can you do that?" Jack asked Danny.

Danny shook his head. "Your grandfather never taught me that old ceremony." He knew the Dreamers passed it down from father to son, but Red Shirt had died before teaching him.

"It was something to see, all right," Jones said, then glanced away quickly. "That's what I hear, anyway."

Danny gave him a curious look, but Jones seemed intent on his cooking. "These steaks are about ready," Jones said. "Let's praise the grub and eat." He didn't mention the elk chant again.

After supper, Jones suggested that Jack go down to the river and fill the water bucket. "Go to the deep hole," he told the boy. "You might have to break through a skim of ice. Then set the lantern on the gravel creekbed a few minutes and watch the deep hole."

"What for?"

"Just take a look."

After Jack had left, Danny cocked an eyebrow at Jones. "What's going on?"

"Checking something out," Jones said. "I'm getting to be such a nearsighted and feeble-minded old fart, I think I might be seeing things up in these mountains."

After a little while, Jack rushed inside the tent. "Biggest fish I ever saw! Half again as long as my arm!"

"The hell!" Danny said. He looked at Jones, then at Jack. "I get it. You guys are trying to trick me into a snipe hunt."

"No kidding," Jack said. "He came right up to the light while I was filling the bucket."

"Maybe we should all go have a look," Jones said.

Half-expecting Jones and Jack to start laughing, Danny laced his boots slowly. "Five minutes, maybe. I'm not going to freeze my ass on the riverbank all night watching that hole."

When they reached the river's edge, Jack set the lantern on the gravelbed beside the water. "Just watch now," he told Danny.

"Five minutes tops," Danny said. "I didn't just fall off the turnip truck." In a few moments, Danny saw a dark shadow appear in the deep hole and move to within three feet of the lantern. The fish was so large it looked like a submerged piece of log. "So that's what you've been seeing," he said.

"Every night," Jones said. "Darned big salmon. Hard to tell because of the dark water, but that fish has the shape of those bluebacks that used to spawn in the Wallowas."

Danny picked up the lantern and held it close to the water for a better view. As the salmon turned toward the light, Danny saw the white circle on its side, an eel wound. One of its fins was half missing, perhaps chopped off by a sea lion's bite as the salmon started into the Columbia. "Rough trip," Danny half-whispered. Leaning too far, he stepped into the water, jostling the light as he felt the cold water pour over his boot. Spooked by the sudden movement, the salmon disappeared from the circle of light.

"I can't believe that fish is here," Danny said. "Even if it came up to spawn, it should have died by now."

"That's why I thought I was seeing things," Jones said.

"Wonder how it found its way around the dams?" Danny said. "Maybe there's a crack or a new channel somewhere."

"It beats me," Jones said. "I thought those bluebacks were long gone."

"A couple of times each fall, they'd find salmon in the

Nebraska irrigation ditches," Jack said. "No one knows how they got there. The farmers waded out in their coveralls and tried to pitchfork the fish. Sometimes they'd stab each other in the legs, but they never got those salmon."

"In Nebraska?" Danny shook his head. "Sounds like a fish story to me."

"How do you explain this one?" Jones asked, jerking his thumb at the river.

"I don't," Danny said.

The three of them walked back to the tent. It had started snowing heavily, and the woods were quiet. Even the river's song seemed muffled.

"I made lemonade," Jones said. "Jack, how about some?"

"Too cold. I got chilled standing by the river."

"Damn boot's full of water," Danny said. "Foot feels like a side of beef in a freezer." He took off his sock and wrung it out. Then he wiped the inside of the boot with crumpled newspaper and put some more inside to absorb the moisture.

Jones dipped a tin cup half full of lemonade from the mixture on the stove. He splashed some gin into the cup and handed it to Jack. "Hot lemonade takes the chill right out," he said. Jones fixed two more cups and handed one to Danny. Then he opened the door of the woodstove and filled the firebox with alder. As Jones stared at the flames and sipped the lemonade, it almost seemed as if he was going to sleep. His eyelids drooped and his head started to nod. But then he opened his eyes wide and handed his cup to Jack, motioning for him to put in some more lemonade.

"It's snowing out there pretty good, so we should find some fresh tracks in the morning," Jones said as he began sipping his second cup of gin and lemonade. "The worst snow I ever saw here was in '51. Four of us came to camp that year. Your grandfather, Cecil Funmaker, Wilson Spino, and me. We took two big elk early, but then it dried up. With just three days left in the season, Red Shirt and Wilson left with the elk, but

Cecil and I decided to see it through. So the day after they
went up the old road to Halfway, it started to snow. And I
mean *snow*—that day, all night, the next day and night. Forty
inches, almost four feet. Cecil and I had to shovel a mountain
of snow to uncover the woodpile. We had the old Willys
pickup then, and it was just a hump in the snow."

"I've never seen that much snow," Jack said.

"I never want to again," Jones said. "But anything can
happen in these mountains. Well, at first we weren't worried
because we figured as how the road crews or forest rangers or
somebody would come in after us, but they never did. The
guys in the lower elk camps walked to farmhouses. But we
was just *stuck*. There was wood and a little whiskey, but not
much food. After a week, it got right lean. The whiskey was
gone, and Cecil drank some liniment that made him half
crazy. For three days we ate nothing but Violet Supreme."

"What's that?" Jack asked.

"Violet Supreme? Awfullest stuff ever. White rice and
grape jelly—heated up. I still can't eat grape jelly without
thinking of it. By that time I was too weak to cut wood, and
Cecil just stayed in his sleeping bag and moaned. Finally, it
got so cold in the tent that his false teeth froze in the glass.

"I about give up myself, and just crawled in my sleeping
bag to freeze, figuring they could bury me in it. I closed my
eyes and dreamed I was back on the reservation drinking
whiskey with Red Shirt and Wilson . . .

"Then, all of a sudden, the tent flap goes back and there's
something white there—I figure maybe my angel—but it was
Red Shirt all covered with snow from walking under pine
branches. He had food and whiskey with him, and extra
snowshoes so we could walk as far as the bridge at Indian
Crossing."

"How'd he get there?" Jack asked.

Jones had another cupful of the lemonade and gin, favoring the gin this time. "Three's about right," he said. "He

come by snowplow. Wilson's brother-in-law worked for county roads up around Baker. When Red Shirt and Wilson found out the highway crews wasn't going to plow thirty-five miles of switchback road from Halfway for two froze-ass Indians, they got Wilson's brother-in-law's keys and swiped a snowplow from the county yard. They damn near ruined it, too, learning how she worked, but they plowed the road from Halfway. It took three days. The bridge at Indian Crossing wouldn't hold a plow, so Red Shirt snowshoed the rest of the way.

"When he dumped his pack, he had six of the biggest steaks you ever saw—store-bought—none of your tough reservation beef. Red Shirt built up the fire good and started cooking those steaks. Then he saw the pan that still had some of the Violet Supreme in it. He stuck his finger into the rice and grape jam, tasted it, then smiled and said, 'Well, now. I see while you boys was up here you learned to cook Chinese style.' "

Jack and Danny laughed. It was always a good story, and most of it was true. Red Shirt and Wilson had stolen the plow and saved Jones and Cecil from freezing or starving. When the county found out what had happened, they fired Wilson's brother-in-law and tossed him in jail for six months. Later, some federal agents came onto the reservation with a warrant, looking for Red Shirt. But he and Wilson hid in a trapping cabin up near Reservation Mountain until the agents got tired and left.

"Well, I better go see a man about a dog," Jones said, standing and ducking outside the tent.

Jack yawned, trying to cover his mouth, and his eyes drooped.

"You better bunk in," Danny said. "Tomorrow we might run you through some canyon bottoms again."

"Sounds fine to me," Jack said. "I've got to rest my eyes right now, though. I'm bushed."

Danny put a foam-rubber pad under Jack's sleeping bag. "This will keep the cold air from coming up and freezing you during the night," he said.

Jack undressed except for his socks and long underwear. "Just sleep in these?" he asked.

"Sure," Danny said. "But put a dry pair on in the morning. Otherwise, your sweat freezes and it'll be damn cold."

Jones came in and got ready for bed, lining up his cigarettes, liniment, and alarm clock on the apple-box nightstand. He winked at Danny. "I don't need to set this clock. Young Piss-and-Vinegar there will wake us up before the crack."

"Better wind it anyway," Danny said, grinning. After Jones crawled into his sleeping bag, Danny checked on Jack. "Everything set?" he asked, but the boy was already asleep. Danny took Jack's coat from the wooden peg and tucked it around his son's shoulders, sealing off the sleeping bag to keep the cold air from seeping in.

Danny went outside. It had stopped snowing, and the moon shone through scuttling clouds. Almost full, it was not the warm, hazy moon that rose over harvest fields but the silver-white Elkmoon that made the entire countryside sharp and distinct. Danny marveled at the cold, magical beauty of the Wallowas. Shivering, he watched the steam rising from his piss and his puffs of breath disappearing into the night landscape. When he had the entire scene clear in his mind, he ducked back inside the tent.

After putting two knotty alder chunks in the firebox, Danny turned down the stove's damper. He shut off the gas to the Coleman lantern and crawled into his sleeping bag, watching the mantle turn ash-gray as it cooled, and the familiar objects in the tent gradually blur to dark shadows.

Jones started snoring and Danny smiled. In the night, Jones would have to get up twice to go outside the tent, but Danny was still young and could stay in the warm bag until morning, keeping the picture of the moonlit Wallowa country in his mind. He fell asleep listening to the alder hissing in the woodstove and the wind blowing high in the trees.

They hunted Black Horse again the next morning. It had snowed more during the night and turned colder, with a freezing wind blowing up the canyon from the river.

"We better get out after today," Jones said, studying the dark sky. "When it gets like this and the wind starts blowing from the north, a big storm is likely coming in."

"All right," Danny said. "Let's make it count, then." He buttoned his coat at the throat and turned up the collar. Then he slung his rifle over his shoulder so he wouldn't feel the cold gunmetal through his gloves. "You take the bottom again," he told Jack, figuring the boy could stay more out of the wind there. "And go a little slower today."

"If I go too slow, I'll freeze," Jack said.

"Think of those high school muffins, still warm and toasty in their beds," Jones said. "That should raise your boiler a notch or two."

"He's supposed to be thinking about elk," Danny said. "You dirty-minded old coot."

Jones winked. "Just because there's snow on the roof

doesn't mean the coals aren't hot. I'll see you boys below."
He climbed into the Bronco and left.

"You ready?" Danny asked.

"Let's do it."

They dropped over the rim into Black Horse. On the north
slope, the wind had piled the snow into drifts under the
lodgepoles, and Danny had to buck through them. At times
the drifts reached his thighs, making the going rough. Whenever he paused to rest, his sweat chilled on him, and he had to
start moving again to keep warm. By midmorning, the wind
picked up a little, blowing the snow into Danny's face. He
saw blue grouse huddled in the low branches of trees, their
backs to the wind.

As Jack moved slowly through the canyon bottom, Danny
caught glimpses of his bright hunting coat in spite of the
falling snow. He stayed above the boy and slightly ahead,
carefully watching the canyon bottom and opposite slope.
Even though they hadn't seen any elk, Danny was pleased
they were hunting right, and he suddenly missed his father,
wishing the three of them were hunting the canyon together. Half-closing his eyes, he pictured his father on the far
hillside, his plaid coat turned up at the collar, the grizzled
braid hanging from beneath the yellow felt crusher.

Danny had almost reached the saddle and could see Jones's
Bronco and the warming fire ahead when he cut a set of fresh
elk tracks dropping off the north slope and into the bottom of
Black Horse. From their size and shape, he could tell they
belonged to a bull. Danny took a stand on a little rise because
he didn't want the elk to sneak back up the hill behind him. If
the bull was still in the bottom, Jack should spook him out or
push him ahead to Jones. Danny studied the south slope,
watching for telltale movements in the jack pines and bitterbrush.

Then he heard Jack yell, and in a few moments he saw the
boy running up from the canyon bottom until he reached a

small ridge on the south slope. Jack dropped to one knee, pointed his rifle, and fired—*kapow*. Danny heard the bullet splinter a rock and he knew that Jack had missed. As Danny watched, Jack kept working the bolt of his rifle, but he didn't fire again, so Danny ran toward the saddle, trying to see the elk. He heard the deep booming of Jones's H&H magnum, three bullets sailing over the canyon rim, the fourth hitting flesh with a dull *chuck*.

When Danny reached Jones's warming fire five minutes later, he glanced at the four bright brass casings lying in the snow. Jones stood at the edge of the saddle, staring into Little Skookum and shaking his head. "I hit him once," he said. "Saw him flinch."

Danny nodded. "Any sign?"

Jones pointed, and Danny saw the crimson drops of blood in the snow.

"There's a mile of big timber before you get to the logged-over part where Crown's done some clear-cutting," Jones said. "He's most likely laid up in the big woods."

Jack ran up, breathing heavily. "I missed," he said. "Damn it!"

"That was a long shot across the canyon," Danny said.

"Sure was," Jones agreed. "Even Red Shirt couldn't make that shot."

"I should have fired again," Jack said. He threw open the bolt on his .30-06.

When Jack worked the action of his rifle, Danny realized the chamber and the magazine were empty. He had seen grown men, excited by game, repeatedly work the bolt actions of their rifles without firing a shot, until all their unfired cartridges lay on the ground. He knew Jack had done the same, but he didn't say anything.

"Better load up," Jones said as he slid some H&H cartridges into his clip, and Danny figured Jones knew what had happened too.

Jones sat on a log and lit a cigarette. He took a metal flask out of his faded plaid hunting coat and had a drink. Then he handed the flask to Danny. "Put some blood in your eyes."

"Shouldn't we get going?" Jack asked. "That bull's getting a big head start."

"It's better to wait a while," Jones said. "That gives him a chance to lie down and stiffen up. If that elk hears you coming after him, he'll get pumped and run ten miles, then drop dead. But you'll never find him."

Danny thought of the elk he had wounded on that saddle, and how Red Shirt had found it ruined the next morning. He wanted to get this one. "Somebody better drive the Bronco down and block Skookum at the bottom," he said. "We don't want him crossing the river. I doubt he'll get that far if you hit him, but just in case."

"I *know* I hit him," Jones said. "Heard the smack. I been sitting all morning and don't mind a little walking."

Jack didn't say anything for a few moments, and Danny knew he wanted to walk Skookum too, but a wounded elk could be tricky and hide in places you'd think were too small for concealment. You could pass right by him, especially if you were green.

"Do you think the elk could make it all the way to the river?" Jack asked.

Jones shrugged. "I doubt it, but you can never tell. I busted him pretty good. Just behind the brisket, I think."

Jack stood and brushed the snow from his pants. "I'll drive the Bronco anyway, I guess. You two are better trackers."

"The keys are in it," Jones told him.

Danny walked with Jack to the Bronco. "You can find your way off this saddle easy enough," he said. "Once you get down to the road, it's tricky because of the blind canyons. Watch for a logging road with a yellow gate."

"I remember," Jack said. He opened the door of the Bronco, then looked around. "This is the place, isn't it?"

"What place?"

"You shot at the wolf here."

Danny didn't answer for a moment. Then he said, "That was a long time back."

"There's been a lot of bad blood under the bridge since then," Jack said.

"What do you mean by that?"

"Red Shirt said you brought bad luck."

"Is that what you think?"

"I didn't say it," Jack said.

"Right now, you'd be better off thinking about Jones's elk."

"Whatever you say." Jack climbed into the Bronco. "Well, see you below. Fire some shots if you old guys get into something you can't handle."

Danny stood watching the Bronco until it disappeared. Then he returned to Jones.

"Two cigarettes is about right," Jones said, lighting his second. "Keeps a man from hurrying. Something rankle you?"

"That boy can be just like his mother."

"Maybe more like Red Shirt. He'll be okay. Right now he showed some savvy. Even though he wanted to walk Skookum, he knew we were better trackers. Anyway, you were right not to say anything about emptying his rifle. He won't make that mistake again, and he's still got his pride." Jones stuck the cigarette butt in the snow. "Too much gab. Let's get tracking."

Dropping off the saddle into Skookum, Danny and Jones followed the bloody spoor for about a half-mile into the woods. In a couple of places the elk had stopped to rest, and the snow there was bright with gouts of blood. Then he had quit bleeding.

"Wound must have closed up," Danny said.

"He's bleeding inside, then, I guess," Jones said.

Danny hoped the elk didn't push too far. They followed

the tracks until they hit a rocky talus slope where the wind had swept away the snow. On the other side of the slope, the woods had been clear-cut by Crown Pacific. The sidehills were a tangle of slash and branches. Rotting logs were strewn about like jackstraws. In places where the loggers had been careless, the ground was blackened from slash fires. The wasteful cutting made Danny sick. And they couldn't pick up the trail.

"What do you want to do?" Danny asked.

"Think he might have gone to the bottom?"

"I don't know."

"You stay about this level," Jones said. "I'll move into the gully and try to spook him out. Check behind all the logs you can. He might just lie down and wait for us to walk past him."

Danny rested against a stump while Jones made his way to the bottom. Viewing the clear-cut, Danny realized that even now the sawmills in Enterprise and Joseph were running, the workers automatically pulling boards off the green chain. Then Danny saw Jones wave, so he started moving along the sideslope. The blackberry and wood-rose vines had taken over since the big trees had been cut, and he kept tangling his feet. He wondered how far the wounded elk could get before a vine or an old piece of choker cable tripped him. Danny made his way noisily now, hoping to scare up the elk if it was lying behind one of the rotten logs or in a berry thicket.

Three shots came from the gully; each one hit with a *chunk*. Danny couldn't see Jones, and nothing came out of the gully, so he figured Jones had finished the elk. Then he heard another sound, a low animal gurgling unlike anything he had heard before, and it made his flesh crawl and his saliva turn to bitter metal.

"Jones," he called. "Ass-Out."

The gully was choked with deadfall and slash. Danny carefully made his way around the charred logs and broken branches. When he heard the low animal gurgle again, he slipped off the safety on his rifle. He smelled a putrid stench and pressed the forearm of his wool coat against his nostrils to keep from vomiting.

"Jones," he whispered when he saw the worn plaid coat.

Jones was on his hands and knees in the snow, his hunting knife clutched in one hand and his rifle in the other. His sides trembled and the low gurgle came again from deep in his throat. But he had quit puking. His vomit was dirty yellow in the snow and there was blood in it. For the first time, Danny knew how sick Jones was.

An elk lay against a fallen log. It had been dead a long time, but the way its head and neck were raised made it look alive. Danny figured that a deer hunter or logger had shot it out of season and then couldn't find it. The elk had collapsed behind the log and died with its head up, watching for the hunter. Its shattered jaw rested on top of the log, and its horns were propped by a withered branch. Jones's bullets had ripped through the carcass, allowing the putrid insides to gush out. They lay stinking in the snow, gray-green and curdled.

Danny put the safety on and slipped his rifle over his shoulder. He did the same with Jones's H&H, after gently prying it loose from the old man's fingers. With his sleeve still pressed to his face, Danny took his free hand and helped Jones to his feet. There didn't seem to be any flesh on the arm when he took hold of it.

Neither man spoke while they made their way a hundred yards away from the elk and out of the gully. Jones sat down and leaned against a jack pine. His skin was grayish brown, the color of bad coffee. His eyes had turned bloodshot from the vomiting. Danny removed the flask from Jones's coat and handed it to him. Jones's Adam's apple bobbed three times, and the flask was empty. He closed his eyes for a few minutes and breathed deeply. When he opened them again, they were clearer.

"He seemed to be looking right at me," Jones said. "Lying against that log with his head propped, I thought it was my elk."

"It looked real enough," Danny said. "I wonder why the wolves didn't get that one."

"The logging, maybe," Jones said. "No wolves for twenty miles. They got pushed back into the high country where you have to go in by horse."

"How you feeling now?"

"Still bad," Jones said. "Ten more minutes." He tried to light a cigarette, but his hands were trembling and Danny had to help him.

Jones had nearly finished the cigarette when he said, "That dead elk—with its head up like that—makes me think of the trick Red Shirt and I did one time on Cecil Funmaker. You heard it?"

"No," Danny said. "I don't think so."

"Sometimes those tricks were the best part of the camp," Jones said. "And telling about them made winter a whole lot easier on the reservation."

"Still does."

"Cecil was in such a sweat to shoot an elk that he talked about it in his sleep. Wilson Spino shot a big bull opening day, and he kept telling Cecil he could have some of it if he could have some of Cecil's wife. Cecil was married to that Pima girl then."

"The one that went back to Arizona because she couldn't stand the winters?"

"That's her. Anyway, Cecil swore he'd shoot an elk that would make Wilson's look puny. So Red Shirt and I decided to fix him. Red Shirt got up real early one morning and took the head from Wilson's elk up the road about a mile. Then while Cecil was in the outhouse, I took his rifle into the warm tent and set it next to the stove."

"That made the metal sweat good," Danny said.

"When I stuck it back outside, the action froze up solid. Of course, Cecil never knew it. After that, Cecil and I left to do a little road hunting. I drove.

"When Red Shirt saw us coming, he put the elk head up on a log and wiggled it a little. Sure enough, Cecil saw it. 'God damn!' he yelled. 'There's a big elk!' And he stuck his rifle out the window. But when he tried to work the bolt nothing happened, because it was still frozen. 'It's jammed,' he said. 'Give me your gun.' But I told him I'd left mine in camp.

"Cecil got out his cigarette lighter and tried to unthaw that bolt, but his hands were shaking so much he just set one of his gloves on fire. 'Use your pistol,' I said. Cecil carried a .38 Chief's Special with a two-and-a-half-inch barrel on it. Maybe you could shoot someone across a card table with it, but I doubt it.

"He had the shakes so bad that his bullets never came within ten feet of that elk's head. Cecil was trying to reload the pistol, but by that time Red Shirt was laughing so hard he dropped the head off the log and it rolled into plain sight. 'Damn. You shot his head off, Cecil,' I said.

"Cecil was so mad he grabbed the thermos and tried to club Red Shirt with it, but Red Shirt was too fast. Finally, Cecil threw it at him real hard and it hit some granite. That's how it got the dent."

"I never knew that," said Danny. "And I've drunk a lot of coffee out of that dented lid. Did Cecil ever get an elk?"

"No. But we had a lot of fun telling that story during the winter. Cecil was in jail the next year, and Red Shirt only made it back to camp once." Jones shivered and looked at the gathering clouds. "Your father sure loved this country."

"You had lots of good times here," Danny said. "He always talked about it."

"Red Shirt made things happen, all right. He was a natural-born earthshaker and hell-raiser. But he had another side, too. His Wéyekin was here, so he came for strength and guidance. Whenever he saw old Hímiin, or at least some sign —like tracks—he felt protected."

"Until I shot at the wolf," Danny said.

"You were just a green kid."

"He said I made his luck go bad."

Jones shook his head. "Maybe you shamed him a little, but it didn't change his luck," he said. "Your father was a hard old flint. He thought by chipping little pieces he could get you shaped right."

"Maybe he was hard," Danny said. "I miss him anyway. Up here, I feel closer to him."

"Me too," Jones said. He stared into the depths of Little Skookum, then added quietly, "I've seen him."

Danny didn't say anything for a minute, until he understood what Jones meant. "Here?"

Jones nodded. "Cruising the canyons and high ridges."

"You've seen his face?"

"No. He's always been ahead of me in the woods, or higher on the ridge across a canyon. But it's him, all right. He's wearing that plaid coat, and there's a dusting of snow across his shoulders from passing under fir limbs."

Danny shivered, but he felt better, as if Jones had swept away an old doubt. "He always said his heart was in these mountains."

Jones nodded. "They're all here. I see him because we were the closest."

Danny knelt beside Jones. "Maybe you know some more about the Wéyekin," he said. "I saw the wolf on Reservation Mountain . . ."

After Danny had finished talking, Jones said, "That makes sense. The wolf was your father's Wéyekin, so it could be yours too. The way the tracks disappeared, it sure sounds like it." He put his cigarette into the snow and it hissed out. "Here, help me up. If you can get this old fart moving, we've got an elk to find."

They crossed the rest of the clear-cut without finding the elk. After going through another mile of timber, they reached the place where Skookum divided into two smaller draws.

"These split like this for a couple of miles," Jones said, "then come together again about half a mile from the river. I'll take the one on the right."

"Maybe we should stick together," Danny said. "It's getting late."

"He might be in either one," Jones said. "We double the odds by splitting up. Might push him on through to Jack." Jones studied the head of each draw for a minute. "Too bad your father's not here. He'd know which draw, especially after a chant."

"Do you know how that works?"

"No. But I saw your father chant once."

"I thought the chanter performed alone."

Jones glanced down. "I followed him one time . . . just to see it. Probably shouldn't have." He leaned his rifle against a sapling and took out a cigarette. Then he said, "When the Dreamers first came back, they might have starved during winter if they couldn't kill elk. So they chanted for good luck. A man passed it down to his son."

"He never taught me."

"You weren't old enough yet," Jones said. "Anyway, one year we hunted a week with no luck. When the Elkmoon came, I knew Red Shirt would chant, so that night I pretended to be asleep until he went out carrying an elkhide robe. I followed him into a clearing in the woods, staying off to one side of his trail, since I didn't want him cutting my tracks when he came back.

"I hid behind a jack-pine thicket at the edge of the clearing. By that time, he was out in the middle, the elkhide robe draped across his back and shoulders. He started dancing in a circle, chanting as he moved. After half an hour or so, he threw off the robe and danced naked, going into the circle until he reached its center. He threw his arms over his head and held them toward the moon. Then he spun round and round until he finally collapsed in the snow.

"I felt like I should check on him to make sure he didn't freeze, but in a little while he covered himself with the robe and started crawling, moving faster and faster. It was hard to believe a man could move so fast. Clouds hid the moon then and it was dark, even in the clearing. All I could see was a dark shape circling in the snow, so I shifted ground a little for a better view.

"Then I heard another sound—not chanting but clacking, like elk make with their lips when they signal. The moon came out for just an instant, and he stood up. I knew it was your father, all right, but down below, on his legs, he was shaggy where the robe stopped, and when I glanced at his head, that was shaggy too. The moon disappeared behind the clouds again, and he left the clearing.

"I waited a few minutes not knowing what to do. In a way I wanted to go into that clearing, but I couldn't—not that night. So I hightailed it back to camp and was already in my sleeping bag when he came in. My face was to the wall, but after I heard him get into bed, I looked. He was turned the other way, with the elk robe pulled over his head and shoulders. It smelled like elk in the tent, too—mighty strong.

"The next morning, he was already hunting before I got up. I fixed some coffee and went outside. He had put the elk robe, rolled and neatly tied, back in the truck. When the others got ready to go out, I told them I was feeling puny and planned to stay in camp, maybe split a little wood. I went back to the clearing; it was easy to find. The circle was there, with the snow all tramped down, and it was slick and icy, probably from him going over and over the same ground. But the strange part is this: Even though it was icy, I could see elk tracks in the circle—big ones—and there's no doubt about it."

"That might figure," Danny said. "Some elk followed the circle after you left."

"I thought so too," Jones said. "But I searched. Red Shirt's tracks, both in and out, were on the south side of the clearing, and mine were on the north. That's all. No elk tracks anywhere except right in the circle."

Danny shook his head. "I don't know."

"Well, one thing's for damn sure. Your father killed two elk that morning like he had them tied up. So I guess the chant worked."

"I wish I knew it," Danny said.

"You can ask some of the old-timers," Jones said. "They might remember how to chant for elk. But right now, we've got to find our own. You ready?"

"All right," Danny said. "But it'll be dark in a couple of hours so let's move it along."

Jones started down the right fork. When he was about twenty yards from Danny, he turned and said, "Take it easy on that boy, now. He favors Red Shirt a little, I think."

"You bet," Danny said, grinning. "See you below." It had started snowing again, light flakes but steady, so he moved quickly down the left draw, but there was no sign of the elk. By the time he reached the convergence of the two draws it was snowing hard, and he knew there would be no tracks left. He built a blazing warming fire out of a pitchy pine stump and waited until an hour after dark. When Jones still hadn't shown, he walked the half-mile toward the river until he struck the road.

Danny found the Bronco parked by the yellow gate Crown Pacific had put up. Jack had built a warming fire nearby, but his tracks led down the road, so Danny figured the boy had gone to look for them. He dug around in the Bronco until he found a thermos of coffee and some fig bars. He leaned against the fender of the Bronco and waited.

Jack was grinning when he showed up. His hands and forearms were bloody. "I got him," he said. "A big one—down by the river. You guys pushed him through."

"Good work," Danny said.

"I need some help," Jack said. "I slit his throat and rolled the guts, but after that . . . Where's Jones?"

"Still up Skookum," Danny said. "He should be coming along."

"He better tag that elk," Jack said. "His H&H made a hole in the brisket big enough to stick a fist through."

"Let's have a look," Danny said. He took a couple of flashlights out of the Bronco and grabbed the backpack with the rope, hatchet, and game saw in it.

"What about Jones?"

"He'll see the fire and follow our tracks."

"I had just built that fire when I saw the elk stagger onto the road about a hundred yards away. The way his head was down, I don't think he saw me. But I waited ten minutes anyway, like Jones said, then went in after him."

"That's fine," Danny said.

"He was close to the river, in a thicket of snowberries, and he stood up when he heard me. I shot once and hit him—in the lungs, I guess. There was a *whoosh* of air rushing out, and he turned his head and looked at the hole. Then he took a couple of steps and tumbled down the bank toward the river."

Danny listened to the Imnaha rushing by and knew the wounded elk had been too weak to cross it. He had bedded in the snowberries and would have died there if Jack hadn't found him.

The elk lay halfway down the steep slope of the riverbank, with its head downhill. It was a big four-point bull. A ribbon of blood trailed from its slit throat toward the river. The guts lay by the river, steaming in the snow. Jack had placed the heart and liver apart from the rest, but he didn't know about the leaf lard. Danny would cut that off the intestines for Pudge. He dug the sides of his boots into the steep bank and made his way down to the elk.

"He keeps sliding downhill," Jack said.

"We don't want him in the river." Danny took two pieces of rope from the backpack and tied the elk's hind legs to some dwarf pines on the slope. Then he tied the front legs, so the elk was spread-eagled and secure. "Did you offer the elk spirit thanks?" he asked.

Jack shook his head. "I wasn't sure how."

"It's something like this," Danny said. "Weýuukye. Big Elk. For your meat and hide and strength—thank you." There was more, but he couldn't remember it. "Usually, that comes first."

Straddling the elk's head, with his back toward the river, Danny took the game saw and opened the sternum. Jones had sharpened the saw well and it cut the white bone cleanly. Danny spread apart the rib cage with his hands and pulled out the gray-green lungs and corded windpipe. "Now we've got to get the hide off so the meat can cool. Let's see if these skinning knives Pudge gave us are worth a damn."

They untied the legs on one side of the elk and rolled it over onto its side. Then they tied the freed legs to the same trees the other legs were tied to. Starting with the uppermost hind leg, Danny began skinning the elk by drawing the knife-tip along the thin yellow membrane that separated the meat from the hide. Jack pulled on the hide. The footing was difficult, and Danny had to brace himself to keep from sliding toward the river.

"Some steep hill," Jack said. "Do they always wind up like this?"

"Seems like it," Danny said. "Here, you try this." He handed Jack the knife.

Danny pulled on the hide while Jack skinned. At first Jack worked too far back on the blade, and chunks of meat came off with the hide; but Danny showed him how to hold the blade, angling it away from the hide. "Use the tip more," he said. "Don't hurry. It takes time to do it right. But this elk will last the winter."

When they had skinned as far back as they could, Danny said, "Help me roll him over on the other side." They untied the elk and rolled it over so that the steaming meat on the skinned side was lying against the snow. The snow melted, then refroze against the elk, keeping it from sliding downhill.

"That's a good trick," Jack said.

"There are lots of tricks," Danny said. "The hide and hair are slick, but the warm meat sticks to the snow." He retied one of the elk's hind legs, just to be sure. "Keep working on this," he said. "I'm going to see if Jones is back. I'll take the heart and liver to save a trip."

Danny put the heart and liver in a plastic bag, then cut the leaf lard off the intestine and placed it in a separate bag. He thought of the delicious pies Pudge could make.

He left the lights with Jack and followed their trail through the dark woods toward the Bronco. He smiled when he saw the figure hunched over the fire and guessed Jones must have gotten pretty cold during the drive through Little Skookum. "Hey, Jones," he called. "What took you so long? Jack shot your elk and we're doing all your work down at the river. I've got the heart here, and some leaf lard."

Holding up the plastic bags, Danny walked toward the fire, but he stopped when the figure turned. It wasn't Jones. The fire blazed behind the dark form, and Danny couldn't see the face, but it looked like an old woman wearing a cape. As Danny stood frozen, she shook her head slowly, then moved to the far side of the fire and disappeared into the woods.

After throwing the plastic bags into the Bronco, Danny opened the map compartment and took out a pack of Jones's cigarettes. With trembling hands, he broke several open and sprinkled the tobacco around the fire. There were no tracks other than his and Jack's. He searched the Bronco until he found an extra flashlight, then hurried back through the woods to the riverbank, clutching some cigarettes just in case. His heart thumped against his chest until he saw that Jack was okay.

"Any sign of Jones?" Jack asked. He straightened from the task of skinning the elk. "Maybe you better rest a minute. You look a little sick."

Danny sat on the stump to catch his breath. If Jack was okay, that meant the ghost had come about Jones. For a few moments, he thought maybe they should leave the elk and start looking for Jones right away. Then he realized some things couldn't be changed.

"You take up smoking?" Jack pointed at the cigarettes.

Danny put them inside his coat pocket, then stood. "Let's finish this elk talk now," he said.

He decided to cut the elk into seven pieces. First he sawed off the head and had Jack carry it to the flat ground overlooking the river. Then he sawed the elk into forequarters and hindquarters and two sections of back and ribs. He split the thick hams on the hindquarters to help the meat cool. While Danny sawed, Jack lugged the heavy sections up the bank.

Danny dragged the hide to level ground and began to roll it like a blanket. Its inside was slick from the blood and membrane, and the outside stiff with bristling hairs. After some difficulty, Danny got it into a lumpy roll and tied a couple of leather laces around it. During the winter, they would tan the hide and make a coat for Jack. They would use some of the long hairs on the rump for fly hackle and catch summer trout on the reservation waters.

They tied the elk sections onto their packboards and carried them the quarter mile to the Bronco. Before they made the last trip, for the hide and head, Danny said, "Put your tag on it." When Jack hesitated, he added, "We don't want to get caught with this one untagged."

"All right," Jack said. "Jones can put his tag on it when he shows up."

They had to let down the tailgate on the Bronco to load all the sections. Danny tied them in so they were secure. When Jack looked at his watch, it was almost eleven. He fired three shots with his .30-06, but there was no response.

Danny thought about starting back up Skookum after Jones, but the flashlight batteries were weak, and he was afraid of falling over a ledge in the dark. "Let's get something to eat," he said.

"Shouldn't we wait for Jones?"

Danny shook his head. "If Jones comes out, he'll wait by the fire. If he's not out when I check back, I'll search up Skookum."

They reached the camp at midnight and Danny started a fire in the woodstove. Too tired to cook dinner, they ate cold venison sandwiches, apples, and cookies. When Danny was through eating, he checked outside. The snow was falling thickly, and Danny knew Jones had been right about the storm.

"We should get a couple hours sleep," Danny told Jack. "Then I'll see about Jones. You break camp. Can you manage the tent?"

"If Jones can put it up, I can take it down."

"All right," Danny said. "Get everything. There's an axe in the woodpile and a shovel and bucket by the river. Bring a few chunks of wood, in case we have to block the tires. Leave the rest for summer campers."

"How about the stove? I can't lift it by myself."

"I'll help," Danny said. "We'll load it last. Build your fire outside in the morning. Let the stove cool."

Jack crawled into his sleeping bag, but Danny sat in a chair by the fire. He didn't want to oversleep. He knew that after the fire died, the cold would wake him.

When Danny opened his eyes, it was still dark. A few coals glowed in the woodstove, so Danny built a small fire and made coffee. He filled the dented thermos and put it in his pack along with the hatchet, a sturdy canvas tarp, and some rope. He filled another thermos with coffee and left it for Jack. When he was ready, he gently shook the boy. "I need a lift back to Skookum."

Jack drove the pickup, and Danny watched the wipers clear big gobs of snow from the windshield. "Make some sandwiches," Danny said. "We might need to drive straight through to the reservation."

When they reached Jack's warming fire, it was still burning, but there was no sign of Jones.

Jack shook his head. "Maybe Jones walked out to another road."

"I don't think so," Danny said. "What time you got?"

"Almost four."

"Be here at nine, then," Danny said. "Or as close as you can." He climbed out of the pickup and waited by the glow of the fire until the pickup lights disappeared. He drank a cup of coffee, then put the pack on his back.

He turned the flashlight on and headed up Skookum, moving quickly until he reached the point where the two smaller draws met and he had waited earlier for Jones. Twice he crossed the bottom end of the draw Jones had chosen, looking carefully for tracks that hadn't filled with snow. Then he started up the draw. It was steep and heavily timbered. Danny moved slowly, playing the flashlight's beam into the thickets, watching for Jones's plaid coat. Danny figured if he didn't find Jones while going up the draw in the dark, he'd find him in the morning light as he worked back down.

He had hiked for an hour in the big timber when he came to a meadow. A light flickered on the far side. At first, Danny thought it was Jones's flashlight, and he called out. But when he got closer, he could see that Jones had built a warming fire. The old man was sitting with his back against a small jack pine. He was too far from the fire to keep from freezing. His face was covered with a thin glaze of ice that mirrored the fire's flames.

Danny figured Jones had been dead most of the night. The old man had built the big fire as a beacon, then sat away from it and frozen.

Danny took the canvas tarp from his pack and spread it in the snow. As he moved the body, the seat of Jones's pants ripped on a branch. The body was so light inside the heavy clothes that the limbs seemed like sticks, and Danny wondered if this was another of Jones's tricks. Perhaps the old man had stuffed sticks into his clothes to make it seem like a body. He might now be watching Danny from the dark woods, honing another story to help pass time back on the reservation during the long winter and to tell over drinks around elk-camp fires. Danny listened for a moment and believed he heard Jones's chuckle coming from the woods beyond the circle of light made by the warming fire. Then it was gone. He heard the wind rustling the high branches of the pines, and the even drawing of his own quiet breath.

Danny folded the canvas tarp around the body, which seemed diminished and shrunken, as if ages old, then wove the rope back and forth through the grommets until he had a gray bundle, like a cocoon. After making a loop, he tied the rope around his waist, then took Jones's H&H magnum and slung it over his shoulder.

The bundle pulled easily over the flat meadow. On the steep downhill, it bumped against Danny's calves, and he was glad he hadn't brought the sled. The drag of the tarp on the snow held it back, but a sled might have gotten away from him.

When he was about a hundred yards from the road, Danny left the bundle behind a log, where it couldn't be spotted by a casual hunter driving by. Jack was waiting, asleep in the Bronco, but he awakened when Danny climbed in.

"Where's Jones?"

"I left the body in the woods," Danny said. "Let's get the pickup."

Jack swallowed. "Heart attack?"

"Froze," Danny said. "He built a big fire, but sat away from it."

Jack was quiet for a moment. Then he said, "Jones chose his time, then."

"It looks like it," Danny said. He was pleased with Jack's answer.

Jack had broken camp well. The tent and Jones's gear were packed in the three-wheel trailer. So were the gunnysacks filled with trash. The stove sat in the middle of the area where the tent had been, and Jack had built his morning fire outside. Over an inch of snow already covered the place where they had eaten and slept. Jack backed the Bronco to the trailer and Danny hitched them. Then they loaded the stove. Danny checked around the camp, but it was clean. The sky had darkened, and the snow was falling harder.

"We better move out," Danny said.

"What about the campfire?"

"Just leave it." He wondered how long Jones's last fire up Skookum would burn.

Danny drove the pickup to Skookum, with Jack following in the Bronco. "I'll be back in a few minutes," Danny said. "Honk if anyone comes." He trotted into the woods, still half-expecting Jones to step from behind a tree and laugh at his hoax. But the bundled tarp was as he had left it, the ropes woven through the grommets. He brushed the snow from the top of the bundle.

Danny knew he didn't want to report Jones to the authorities. There would be too many questions and forms, then they would send the body to a government cemetery near Klamath Falls. Danny was sure Jones wouldn't want it like that. He planned to bury the body on Reservation Mountain, close to Red Shirt. He and Jack could do it, even though the ground was frozen and they would have to dig with a pick.

When Danny got the bundle back to the pickup, Jack said, "It looks so small—like he really isn't in there."

Danny placed the bundle between the Igloo cooler and the pickup cab, then tucked sleeping bags and blankets around it. He laid a couple of shovels across the top and covered everything with a tarp. Then he said, "Let's go."

They drove the rigs to the bridge at Indian Crossing, then stopped. The snow on the bridge was still unmarked, so Danny knew no one had been up the steep hill to Halfway that morning. He figured all the wardens were back toward Joseph. The elk hunters usually went out that way, since the liquor store in Halfway had closed some years before. It took him twenty minutes to put chains on the pickup and double-check the four-wheel-drive hubs on the Bronco.

"You want me to drive the Bronco?" Danny asked. "That trailer can be tricky."

"I can handle it," Jack said. "Besides, I'm staying with this elk. You might drive off into the canyon."

"All right, Piss-and-Vinegar," Danny said. "I'll break trail and you follow the tracks." He put the pickup in low and started up the hill. On the switchbacks, he looked over into the deep canyon.

The elk in the Bronco was Jones's last, Danny thought. And part of it belonged to Jack, too. They would share the elk meat with some of the old people on the reservation who depended on government commodities and had bitter times during the long winters. Danny hoped one of them might know something about the elk chant.

Later, he would tell Jack about Red Shirt's chant, and that Jones had seen him cruising the canyons and high ridges. And he would tell the boy about seeing the Wéyekin and the dark figure, too. But he needed to think about the stories first, and make sure he told them right.

Jack honked and Danny checked the rearview mirror. Jack pulled the Bronco over on the last switchback and got out, blocking the wheels with two pieces of wood. Danny stopped too, then rolled down the window. He hoped there wasn't any trouble.

"Just wanted to take one more good look," Jack said. "We probably won't get back here for another year."

Danny got out of the pickup, carrying the dented thermos. After joining Jack on the overlook, he poured some coffee into the lid and handed it to the boy. Across from them, Black Horse, Little Skookum, and Gumboot canyons cut from the rugged Wallowas to the river. Far below, the Imnaha sliced through the dark forests.

After a few moments, Danny felt Jack's hand on his arm. They stood quietly, facing the Wallowas while the falling snow mantled their shoulders. Then Jack's grip tightened, and Danny looked to where the boy was pointing.

A herd of elk strung along the river like dark beads on a silver necklace. Backs turned to the wind and driving snow, the elk were headed upriver, into the high Wallowas. Danny saw the campfire, still visible through the falling snow, and he imagined the Dreamers telling stories around glowing fires, their words rising like sparks. Danny covered his son's hand with his own, knowing they must return next camp.